ISLAND FIRE

"I hate you!"

He stood behind her and ran a warm, gentle hand down the curve of her spine until it rested on her hip. She shivered beneath the caress, but didn't move.

"We both know that's not true, don't we, Espri? Look at me. Tell me to my face that you don't want to make love with me."

Heart pounding, Espri stood motionlessly as he took a step forward and crushed her against his chest. His mouth took hers, trying to force the response he knew her so capable of giving.

Espri fought the excitement that was sweeping over her as he parted her lips. She didn't want to give in to his sensual power, but her body was betraying her.

"Tell me you want me, Espri," he whispered. "Tell me."

"Yes," she whispered. "Yes . . ."

Books by Bobbi Smith

DREAM WARRIOR

PIRATE'S PROMISE

TEXAS SPLENDOR

CAPTURE MY HEART

DESERT HEART

THE GUNFIGHTER

CAPTIVE PRIDE

THE VIKING

ARIZONA CARESS

ISLAND FIRE

Published by Kensington Publishing Corporation

ISLAND FIRE

BOBBI SMITH

ZEBRA BOOKS
KENSINGTON PUBLISHING CORP.
http://www.kensingtonbooks.com

ZEBRA BOOKS are published by

Kensington Publishing Corp.
119 West 40th Street
New York, NY 10018

All Kensington titles, imprints, and distributed lines are available at special quantity discounts for bulk purchases for sales
promotion, premiums, fund-raising, educational, or institu-
tional use.

Special book excerpts or customized printings can also be created to fit specific needs. For details, write or phone the office
of the Kensington Special Sales Manager: Attn. Special Sales
Department. Kensington Publishing Corp., 119 West 40th
Street, New York, NY 10018. Phone: 1-800-221-2647.

Zebra and the Z logo Reg. U.S. Pat. & TM Off.

ISBN-13: 978-1-4201-1443-0
ISBN-10: 1-4201-1443-3

First Printing: September 1986

10 9 8 7 6 5 4 3 2

Printed in the United States of America

This book is for my very bestest TBOC—Donna Lee Poulos Byerlotzer and her husband Jimmy. Thanks, Poullouse! Also, a special note of thanks to Margaret Smith for her invaluable assistance in researching San Francisco, and to Mike and Marilyn Maurer for introducing me to the joys of a hot tub.

Prologue

San Francisco

The casual way in which the two men faced each other across the broad expanse of the desk belied the undercurrent of tension between them.

"No," Mitch Williams declared, meeting his brother's gaze levelly.

"No?" Jonathan surged to his feet, unable to believe that he had been refused.

"I'm sorry, Jon," Mitch added succinctly, his tone implying that the matter was closed.

"Sorry? I won't settle for that. I love Catherine and I mean to marry her!" the younger man exclaimed.

"Marry Catherine if you wish"—his brother shrugged—"but you'll never get a cent of your trust fund if you do." His answer, though blandly stated, hinted at the steel will that governed all of Mitchell Williams's decisions.

"That's blackmail!"

"Call it whatever you want, but until you reach your majority, I'm in complete control of your assets. Rest assured, Jon, that I won't hesitate to cut off your more than generous allowance, should you let yourself be carried away by the 'heat of the moment,'" Mitch told him arrogantly. "Do I make myself clear?"

Jon glared at his brother. "You're an unfeeling bastard—"

"Hardly," Mitch drawled. "Our parentage is well established." His amused smile only served to make the hot-headed Jon more angry.

"Someday you'll regret this!"

"Possibly, but I doubt it. I think, in fact, that someday, little brother, you'll be thanking me."

"For ruining my life?"

"I seriously doubt that my refusal to grant you permission to marry Catherine will ruin your life. After all, Jon, all you have to do is wait until you're twenty-one. Now"—Mitch glanced up questioningly as he gestured toward the papers that cluttered his desktop—"if that's all you wanted to discuss, I do have other business to conduct."

"Damn, but you're callous. Catherine and I are in love."

"If she loves you, then she'll be willing to marry you whether you have your inheritance or not," Mitch pointed out.

"No man wants to marry if he can't support his wife." Jon's shoulders slumped slightly as he fully realized his position. "Haven't you ever loved a woman?"

"I've loved many women, but I've never been 'in love,' thank God," Mitch remarked dryly as he leaned back to regard his brother. "Love somehow manages to make fools of even the wisest men."

Jon bristled. "Well, this is one 'fool' who's glad he's in love! Catherine's a wonderful woman and I mean to marry her."

"The decision is yours to make. Now, if you don't mind, I really am busy."

"By all means, don't let me interfere with your work!" Jon headed for the study door and slammed it as he left the room.

Mitch stared after his brother for a moment before turning his attention to the contracts spread out before him. Diligently, he picked up the top sheaf of papers and began to read, but, unable to concentrate, he threw them down in disgust. Rubbing the back of his neck in a weary motion, he flexed his broad shoulders and rose from his place behind the desk. Stalking to the window, he stared out at the gray dullness of the autumn day.

Catherine Chamberlain . . . At the thought of the calculating blond beauty, Mitch scowled blackly. He knew her well . . . almost too well . . . and he knew the real reason behind her interest in Jon—money. He had been tempted to tell his brother the truth about her, but common sense had prevented him from doing so. Jon was stubborn, and Mitch knew he would deny any and all allegations against Catherine, no matter how they were substantiated.

Mitch only hoped that once Catherine discovered the stipulations regarding Jon's inheritance, she would drop him and search for a more likely candidate for a husband. If her financial situation was as dire as he'd heard, she would probably do just that.

He turned from the window and settled back in at his desk, wishing somehow that he could spare Jon the pain of Catherine's rejection, though he knew this would serve his younger brother well for the rest of his life. Hadn't he himself learned the hard way about women and their avarice? He had been young then, and more than a little idealistic, but he had learned.

Mitch now firmly believed that true love does not exist and that most marriages are not made in heaven. Instead, he saw such conjugal alliances as mergers that served the purposes of both parties. Although some husbands and wives did seem to share a deep affection for one another, he was firmly convinced that they were exceptions to the rule. Positive that his decision not to consent to the marriage was right for Jon, Mitch picked up the contracts from his desktop and got down to business.

* * *

"Well, darling, I've done it." Catherine Chamberlain smiled triumphantly at Roland Stuart as she settled herself on the sofa in the parlor of her fashionable home on Rincon Hill.

Stuart glanced at his beautiful lover inquiringly, one hand poised to pour himself a tumbler of bourbon. "Done what?"

"I've accepted Jonathan Williams's proposal of marriage."

"Wonderful! He's an excellent choice. When's the wedding?"

Catherine frowned slightly. "I'm not sure. He's meeting with his brother Mitch this afternoon to tell him the news, and we're to set the date this evening."

"You look concerned. Is there some kind of problem?" Roland joined her on the sofa, his bourbon in hand.

"No, not that I know of. It just irritates me that Jon has to check with his 'big brother' before we can make definite plans."

"I wouldn't worry about that. From what I understand Jon and Mitch are extremely close; after all, Mitch has been head of the family since their parents died."

"I suppose," she agreed, though she was not convinced. "I just wish the whole ordeal was over."

"Eager for young Williams's money, are you?" Stuart grinned, for he knew Catherine's motivation in consenting to the marriage.

"Desperate, darling. You, of all people, should know that. What do I owe you now? Fifteen thousand? Twenty thousand?"

"It was well over twenty thousand at the last count, but you know I'll never pressure you for it."

"I know that, but you must realize I have an image to maintain. I must marry, and soon, if I'm to prevent word of my debts circulating. Why, I wouldn't be able to face anyone in my circle if it became known that I'd lost all of Papa's fortune at the gaming tables."

Roland set aside his empty glass and pulled her into his arms. "Your secret is safe with me."

"Now it is, but you weren't feeling so generous to me a few months ago." Catherine drew away slightly as she recalled the unorthodox manner in which he'd maneuvered her into his bed. "Would you really have revealed everything to my banker if I hadn't come to you?"

"What do you think?" Roland's expression hardened as he remembered the threats he'd used to force her to sleep with him.

Catherine pondered a moment before answering. "Yes, you would have. You're totally ruthless when you're in pursuit of something—or someone—you want."

"You know me far too well, my love," Roland growled as he pressed a heated kiss to her throat.

"And you wanted me then, didn't you, Roland?" she taunted.

"I've never wanted any woman more," he admitted. "But you wouldn't come to me in the beginning. That's why I extended you so much credit at my casino. I knew I could use your indebtedness to force you into my arms."

"And you did."

He shrugged. "How I did it doesn't matter. You're mine now."

"Completely." Catherine's arms encircled his neck, and she kissed him passionately.

"Are you sorry? Have you ever regretted a moment of our time together?"

"Only the first time . . ." Catherine smiled slightly as she remembered how furious she'd been at Roland's blackmail, how resentful and frightened. But her feelings had changed after their first encounter, for he had introduced her to the wonders of carnal delight.

"You regretted our first time together?" He looked at her, his confusion obvious for he vividly remembered their wild, sexual encounter.

"I regretted," she purred, rubbing against him, "that I'd fought you for so long. I should have come to you sooner."

Roland kissed her deeply. "We're alike, you and I. We know what we want and we go for it, consequences be damned."

"What will happen to us when I've married Jonathan?" Catherine was suddenly apprehensive.

"Nothing will change. We've managed to keep our liaison hidden from Susan, so I don't think we'll have a problem with Jon. We just won't be able to meet in your home any longer, that's all."

"That's true. By the way, how is your wife?"

"Susan is fine, but I don't want to waste our time together talking about her. I want you, Cat, and I mean to have you, now." Standing, he pulled Catherine to her feet and swept her up into his arms.

She clung to him excitedly, knowing that the rest of the afternoon would be spent in amorous bliss. "I love you, Roland," she declared.

Striding into the main hall, he mounted the staircase to her second-floor boudoir, then closed and locked the door behind them.

—

The rowdies in the saloon were boisterous, but Jonathan took little notice of them as he sat at a corner table with his friend Nash McKenna.

"I can't believe Mitch told you no," Nash sympathized as he poured them both another drink from the bottle of whiskey the barkeep had left with them. "He's never denied you anything before. Why do you suppose he'd start now, when you've found the woman you want to marry?"

"I don't know. He didn't give me a reason. He just said if I marry Catherine before I come of age, he'll see to it that I forfeit my trust fund."

Nash grimaced, knowing that Mitch Williams was a man of his word. "And you haven't told Catherine?"

"No, not yet." Jon ran a hand through his dark hair in a

nervous gesture. "Damn it, Nash! Catherine expects to finalize our plans tonight. How in the hell am I going to explain?"

"Listen, Jon," his friend said soothingly, "your brother didn't say you couldn't marry her. All he said was that you had to wait until your birthday. Surely if Catherine loves you, she'll be happy to wait."

"I suppose, but the whole situation seems ridiculous. I'm a man, not a child! I shouldn't need anyone's permission to marry."

"I agree, but there's nothing you can do. Mitch *is* in control of your funds."

"But I'm a Williams, too, you know, and one of these days, very soon, I'm going to have an equal hand in running everything."

"I'll be glad when you do, but until then you have to follow Mitch's orders."

"I realize that," Jon ground out. "But it isn't easy to accept the situation." Draining his tumbler of whiskey, he stood up and tossed several silver dollars to Nash. "This should cover the bill."

"Thanks." Nash pocketed the money. "Are you going to see her now?"

"Not until eight, but I think I'd better get out of here before I drink much more. Catherine wouldn't approve of my showing up on her doorstep drunk, and if I stay here matching you drink for drink that's exactly the shape I'll be in in a few hours." His smile was derisive.

"Very true." Nash rose and clapped him on the back. "But don't worry. It's not going to be as bad as you think. I'm sure Catherine loves you, and you'll figure out a way to get around Mitch."

"Right." Jon frowned at the thought of trying to out-maneuver his brother. "I'll see you later."

"Good luck!" Nash shouted as Jon made his way from the

crowded bar, and his friend lifted a hand in salute as he exited through the swinging doors.

"Yes? What is it?" Catherine called out in a sleepy voice as a knock upon her bedroom door woke her.

"Mr. Williams is here, Miss Catherine. He's just arrived and he's waiting downstairs for you," the maid explained through the closed portal.

"Oh! Is it that late already?" Catherine sat up and glanced quickly around her darkened bedroom.

"Yes, ma'am. It's about a quarter to eight."

"I've overslept, Florence. Please make Mr. Williams comfortable and then come and help me dress."

"I will, ma'am."

Rising from the bed on which she'd passed such pleasurable hours in Roland's arms, Catherine lit the lamp on her nightstand and stretched leisurely, relishing the slight feeling of soreness in her slim body. She smiled wickedly as she thought of her afternoon of frenzied lovemaking, and knew it was no wonder she'd slept so deeply once Roland had departed. Running her hands over the tenderness of her full breasts, she sighed contentedly. Soon she would have Roland's passion *and* Jonathan's money.

Catherine had to force herself to hurry. After bathing quickly, she slipped into her silken undergarments and selected a suitably demure, yet stylish, gown of a deep rose color that would enhance her pale beauty. Laying it out on her bed, she seated herself at the dressing table and began to brush out her tangled, golden hair.

"Come in," she called when Florence knocked at the bedroom door. "Is Mr. Williams settled in?"

"Yes, ma'am. He's in the parlor, having a bourbon."

"Good. Hurry and fix my hair for me. I don't want to keep my future husband waiting too long!"

"Husband, Miss Catherine?" Florence was taken by surprise, for she knew her mistress well and it didn't seem plausible that she would marry the young man downstairs.

"Yes. Mr. Williams has proposed and I've accepted him," Catherine explained abruptly. "Now, finish my hair. I mustn't keep him waiting longer than necessary."

Without another word, the servant set to work. She combed Catherine's shimmering tresses into an attractive, up-swept style that set off the perfection of her features. That accomplished, she helped her mistress don the chic rose gown with the modestly cut bodice. Then Catherine stepped into the matching slippers, fastened a single strand of pearls about her throat, and put on pearl and diamond earbobs.

"I want you to see to it that Mr. Williams and I are not disturbed," she ordered as she touched the stopper of her scent bottle to her pulse points.

"Yes, Miss Catherine."

"Good. I'll ring for you if I need you."

"Yes, ma'am," Florence replied as she watched her mistress leave the room.

Catherine paused at the top of the staircase and took a deep breath before descending to greet Jonathan. Though she had plotted carefully to elicit his proposal, she found herself slightly unnerved now that the time had come to set the date for the wedding. Not that she didn't want to marry Jon—the thought of all that Williams money was enough to make her hurry unfaltering to the altar—but she was not in love with him. He was nice and certainly handsome, but he was not Roland. Resigning herself to her need to marry for money, she unconsciously squared her shoulders and entered the parlor.

Jon had been deep in thought. The bourbon that Florence had served him, though a fine one, had tasted bitter as he'd contemplated the upcoming scene. How would he tell Catherine—the woman he loved—that they would have to postpone their nuptials until he came of age? The prospect was so humiliating that he'd been tempted to leave, but he'd forced himself to remain and face the situation squarely.

"Good evening, Jon." Catherine's voice was suitably breathless as she joined him in the sitting room. "I'm sorry I kept you waiting so long."

Jon set his drink aside and quickly rose to his feet. "You were worth the wait," he informed her gallantly as his dark-eyed gaze swept over her admiringly. As always he was impressed by her stunning good looks and he naïvely considered himself the luckiest man in San Francisco to have Catherine Chamberlain's love. He had been paying court to her for many months now, but, social butterfly that she was, it had been only recently that she'd come to return his affection.

"Why, thank you. Has Florence seen to your needs?" Catherine crossed the room to where Jon stood, tall and masculine.

Lifting the half-empty tumbler of bourbon for her inspection, he nodded. "She made me most comfortable, but there was one need she couldn't take care of."

In an impulsive movement, Jon pulled his love into his arms, not noticing her slight hesitation before she surrendered to his ardor. Pretending a response she certainly didn't feel, Catherine clung to Jon's broad shoulders as his lips found hers, and when they finally broke apart, she feigned breathless excitement as she drew him down onto the sofa beside her.

"Jon," she cooed. "I've missed you so and we've only been apart for a day."

"I've missed you too, Catherine," he declared fervently, totally besotted by her charms and the heady, seductive scent of her perfume.

Leaning toward him to encourage another kiss, Catherine felt victorious when he eagerly responded to her unspoken invitation and embraced her again. Though she had no real desire for Jon, she knew the best way to keep a man enamored of her was to promise more than she was willing to give, and that was just what she intended to do until their wedding. Only after the ceremony would she allow him into her bed. Withdrawing with seeming unwillingness from his passionate embrace, Catherine gave him a tender, adoring smile.

"I want you so, Jonathan, but you know we must wait until after the wedding."

"Of course." He touched her cheek with gentle fingers, then stood and moved away from her. "Catherine . . ." He called forth all the bravado he could muster. "Darling, we need to talk about our plans."

"I'm so excited, Jon. Why, just think! In a matter of months—no, weeks—if we want, we'll be man and wife." She turned her most seductive smile on him.

"I'm afraid, my love, that it's not quite that simple," Jon responded hesitantly.

Catherine frowned at his statement. "Is something wrong?"

"We won't be able to marry until late next summer."

"Next summer?" She experienced a moment of panic at the thought of putting off her creditors for almost a year. "But why?"

"It's Mitch, Catherine," he said lamely.

"Mitch?" For the life of her, Catherine could not make the connection. "What in the world does *he* have to do with us?"

"He's refused to give me permission to marry." *There*, Jon thought dramatically, *it is out.*

"Permission? Why do you need your brother's permission to marry me?" Catherine was confused and more than a little shaken.

"In accordance with our parents' will, Mitch was given complete control of my inheritance until I reach my majority."

"So? What does that have to do with our plans?"

"I'm sorry, Catherine, but Mitch told me he'd revoke my trust if I marry before I'm twenty-one."

"But that's not fair!" she cried, the distress in her voice

very real. Then, to cover her blunder, she went into his arms. "I love you. I want to marry you!"

"And I feel the same way, sweetheart, but I won't tie you to me until I'm certain I can support you in the style that befits you."

Catherine was inwardly seething at the thought of Mitchell Williams's high-handed ways. How dare he! And what was she to do now?

"Jon, darling," she began, knowing with sickening certainty what his response would be before she started, "your money's not important to me. Being together is what matters. Let's run away. We can be married tomorrow; then no one can stand in our way."

Jon tightened his arms about her as he held her close. "Catherine, there's nothing I want more than to have you for my wife, but I refuse to marry until I can take care of you."

Catherine suppressed a sigh of relief; then she protested with just the right amount of urgency. "But, Jon! I have money." The lie flowed smoothly from her. "There's no need for us to wait."

Jon's smile was grim as he gripped her by the shoulders and held her away from him. "You're a wonderful, understanding woman, but I refuse to be a burden to my wife." He paused and then continued, his tone resentful. "No. We'll wait. It'll be best for all concerned. I'll be twenty-one next summer and in full control of my inheritance. We can be married then, and I'll never again have to ask Mitch for anything."

Catherine assumed an expression of tender devotion, but her mind was racing, trying to find a solution to her desperate problem.

Gathering her to him, Jon held her close. "Don't worry, and don't look so sad. It isn't that much of a delay; it isn't as though we can't be together."

"I know." Catherine sighed, silently cursing the arrogant

Mitch Williams. *I'll get even with him one of these days*, she thought. "It's just that I had my heart set on being married to you by Christmas."

"And I, you." He bent to kiss her lightly. "But there's no reason why we can't begin to make our plans. My birthday is July fourteenth. Shall we be married on the fifteenth?"

"Why, that sounds lovely."

The evening passed very slowly for Catherine, yet she struggled to maintain the pleasant, sweet façade Jonathan had come to expect from her although she was grappling with seemingly insurmountable problems. She needed money and she needed it now, not next summer! She knew she could get some help from Roland, but her debts were so extensive, she doubted that he could take care of them all.

As the hours passed, her tension increased, and it was with great relief that she finally said good night to Jon. Mentally exhausted, she mounted the staircase, disheartened, hoping that a good night's sleep would give her a better perspective of her situation, but as the long night dragged on, she knew that she would find no relief in slumber.

It was well after two in the morning when Catherine left her bed and began to dress. She donned dark, nondescript clothing, and she didn't ring for Florence until she was almost ready to leave.

"What is it, Miss Catherine?" Florence asked wearily, for she'd been roused from sleep by her mistress's summons.

"Have Toby bring the carriage around. I'm going out."

The maid's eyes widened at the thought of Miss Chamberlain leaving home at such an ungodly hour, but she held her tongue, knowing that any comment would be dealt with severely. Catherine Chamberlain did not like to have her orders questioned.

Florence hurried to do her mistress's bidding, pondering as she did so the changes that had occurred since Gerald

Chamberlain had died two years before. Catherine had only been seventeen at the time of her father's untimely demise, and having no one to set limits for her, she'd indulged to excess in the divertissements available to a woman of wealth.

Who would have thought that this lovely, young heiress would have turned into such a wanton? Florence clucked disapprovingly to herself as she woke Toby and informed him of the mistress's wishes. Though he grumbled in disgust at the interruption of his rest, Toby, too, knew better than to protest. He quickly pulled on his clothes and went to get the carriage as Florence headed back to the house.

The servants were well aware of Catherine's intimate relationship with Roland Stuart, and since Florence had told them the news that evening, they were now all agog at the prospect of her marrying the young Williams boy. Florence, though, knew the real reason behind Catherine's sudden decision to marry. She knew full well that Gerald Chamberlain's money was gone and that the mistress was in deep trouble if she didn't find a rich husband quickly. It only made sense that, desperate as Catherine was, she would try to find the richest, most easily influenced man around. Obviously Jonathan Williams was the man she'd chosen.

Florence almost felt sorry for him, for she knew Catherine would never be able to end her torrid affair with Roland. But there was little she could do; her loyalties lay with the family she had served for over fifteen years.

Moments later, the faithful servant watched unobserved as Catherine slipped quietly from the house and climbed into the coach. Then, with a rumbling of wheels and a muffled clattering of hooves, she and Toby disappeared into the night.

"Mitch Williams has control of Jon's money?" Roland asked incredulously.

"Every last cent!" Catherine declared vehemently as she stormed about Roland's office at the back of his saloon and casino, the Diamonds.

"What are you going to do?"

"I haven't decided yet."

"Have you broken your engagement to Jon?"

"Heavens, no!" Catherine glanced at him quickly. "I'm not burning any bridges yet! It took too long to get him to propose in the first place."

"I can help you somewhat, but most of my money is tied up." He gestured to his opulent surroundings.

"I know. There's got to be an easier way, a better way, than to wait until next July when he becomes twenty-one."

"What about marrying someone else? I've always thought Jon was too young—" Roland broke off as she turned on him angrily.

"That's exactly why I wanted to marry him. He's someone I can control! Damn Mitch Williams!"

Roland strode quietly across the room to where he kept a bottle of bourbon, and he poured a generous amount of it into a glass.

"Here." He handed her the drink. "This will calm you."

Without hesitation, Catherine drank it down. "Thanks."

"You're welcome." He grinned at her. "Now, sit down, and let's think about this."

"What's there to think about?" she remarked as she sat down on the plush love seat.

"Maybe there is some way we can get around this thing. You say Williams still wants to marry you?" he asked as he paced the office.

"Of course. He just doesn't want to do it until he can support me."

"Admirable, I'm sure." Roland sneered. "But not much help in the short run."

"Mitch is the only problem. He's standing in the way of my marriage."

"Didn't you make a play for him awhile back?"

Catherine flushed, a rare occurrence for her. "Yes, I did, and it was a complete fiasco. But that was when I first decided to start looking for a husband."

"That may be why he's so adamant about Jon's waiting." Roland nodded. "Mitch is one shrewd businessman. He probably knows more about your situation than you realize."

"Do you really think so?"

"It's a possibility," he admitted. "It would certainly explain his refusal."

Catherine frowned at the thought that others might know of her dire financial straits. "In that case, what am I going to do?"

"Why don't you leave it all to me; maybe I can come up with something," Roland offered magnanimously, as a devious plan was already taking shape in his mind.

"Really?"

"Have I ever let you down?"

"No, darling." Catherine rose gracefully and went to him. "Never."

"Trust me," he growled, taking her in his arms.

"I do, Roland—with my life," she vowed as she returned his passionate kiss.

Much later, after Catherine had gone, Roland called two of his men into his office.

"Mr. Stuart? Can we do something for you?" Joe Moran asked as he and Bill Roberts came into the room.

"I have a little job for you."

"Yes, sir," they replied, knowing that their boss paid well for "little jobs."

"Someone must disappear—quietly."

"Right," Joe Moran drawled. "How soon should he 'disappear'?"

"As soon as you can make the arrangements."

"We'll get right on it, boss. Who is it?" Bill Roberts asked.

"His name is Mitchell Williams. He runs Williams Shipping."

"I know who he is," Bill declared.

"Good. I don't want any mistakes. This has got to be a neat, clean job."

"You've seen our work before," Joe commented.

"Yes, you've done well for me. Just make sure this time things go smoothly. Do I make myself clear?"

"Completely."

"Good. Keep me informed, and I'll see that you're amply rewarded when the news of his demise is confirmed."

"We'll get back to you as soon as we take care of it."

"I'll be expecting to hear something soon."

"You will," Moran confirmed, and the two men left the office.

As Roland watched them go, he felt immensely pleased with himself. It was all so simple. The only obstacle to Catherine's happiness was Mitch Williams; by removing him, he'd put an end to her problems. He smiled to himself as he realized the opportunities that would come his way when Jonathan gained complete control of the Williamses' fortune. Why, with Catherine's influence, he was certain that he could make a lucrative arrangement with Williams Shipping to import the necessary "merchandise" he needed for his own business. Satisfied that he'd made the correct decision for all concerned, he turned his attention to his immediate affairs, knowing that he would hear from Joe and Bill as soon as they'd completed their assignment.

* * *

"How long has Williams been in there?" Bill whispered to Joe as they crouched outside an impressive South Park mansion the following evening.

"Over two hours now," his companion answered in hushed tones. "What do you suppose he's doing in there?"

"What do you think, stupid?" Bill responded, leering and jabbing Joe in the ribs for emphasis. "That's Lucinda Blake's house."

"Who?"

"You know. Alex Blake's widow."

"He the one that died a year or so ago and left all those millions?"

"The same. I guess the widow and Williams got a thing goin'." Bill chuckled as a light was lit on the second floor.

"Well, I just hope he hurries," Joe complained. "I want to get this over with. I need the money—bad."

"Who doesn't? But we have to be careful. This ain't no ordinary seaman we're going to roll. This guy's important."

"I know, but that doesn't make waiting here any easier. How we gonna do it? You got some kind of plan?"

"Nope. Nothing yet. We just gotta watch and wait until we can catch him unawares."

"Well, it sure ain't gonna be tonight. He's got his damn carriage and driver waiting for him."

Bill's expression brightened as an inspiration came to him. "I got it!"

"What?"

"We'll get rid of his driver. Then when he comes out . . . he's ours!"

"You sure he won't realize something's wrong?"

"No. You can put on the driver's coat. It's so dark, he won't notice anything. Then I'll be waiting inside the carriage."

"All right," Joe agreed enthusiastically. "He won't even know what hit him and . . ."

"And, what?"

"You got any objection to makin' a little extra on this?"

Bill, always eager for an extra buck, eyed him warily. "How?"

"Easy. We sell him to Shanghai Jack."

"You mean, we don't kill him?" Always one to follow orders, Bill hedged. "You know Stuart wants him dead."

"I know, but how long do you think Williams will survive if we give him over to Jack?"

"I see your point." Bill paused thoughtfully. "I tell you, it'll only work if we can convince the boss that we killed him."

"That's the easy part. All we have to do is go down to the Coast," Joe said carelessly. He knew how often unidentified dead men were found in the dark alleys of the infamous Barbary Coast. "We'll find us a stiff, switch their clothes, and dump the other guy in the bay. By the time they pull him back out, nobody—not even his brother—will be able to identify him."

"You're on," Bill declared, anxious to make any additional money he could. Then they settled in to wait for the right time to assault Mitch's unsuspecting driver.

"Darling," Lucinda Blake drawled as she nestled closer to Mitch in the wide expanse of her bed, "when are you going to propose?"

"Lucinda, you know how I feel about marrying. If you can't enjoy what we have, then we'll just have to part." There was a cutting edge to Mitch's voice.

"I most certainly enjoy what we have," Lucinda told him throatily as she rose up on an elbow to gaze down at him, "but we could have so much more!"

"I don't need anything more than what we already share," Mitch stated arrogantly.

"But, darling, I want you so."

"And you have me, Lucinda, but only if you can accept

things as they are." He pulled her down for a deep, sensual kiss. "Don't try to force me. I don't respond well to coercion."

Lucinda feigned a pout, then relaxed a bit and smiled. "Well, I certainly don't want to risk losing you, but, Mitch, why are you so set against marriage?"

He glanced at her sharply, his eyes darkening at the question. "That, my dear, is none of your business. Just rest assured that I have no intention of being caught in that trap."

"I don't know why you consider it such a 'trap.' Why, Alex and I had a wonderful time together, living life to the fullest."

"I have no objection to living life to the fullest." Mitch chuckled, lightening the mood. "I just don't see why wedlock has to be a part of it."

"Oh, Mitch, I adore you." Lucinda laughed easily and then kissed him with spontaneous delight. "And we do get on well together, but someday you're going to meet a woman who won't succumb to your blandishments. Then, I think, you just might have to change your ways. Why, one of these days you might even fall in love." She looked down at Mitch fondly, caring deeply for him and yet knowing that he would never be completely hers. Kissing him softly, she murmured, "Lucky woman."

In a bold, dominant move, he rolled with her and pinned her beneath him. "Well, I don't think you have to worry overmuch on that account—especially right now."

"Oh, Mitch." Lucinda sighed as she gave herself up to the delicious sensations his practiced caresses always aroused.

Much later, when Mitch left Lucinda's home, he was pensive as he made his way to his carriage. Her earlier remarks about marriage troubled him, and he knew it was time to end their relationship. Sophisticated woman that Lucinda was, he had assumed she'd understood his feelings when he'd told her at the beginning of their liaison that he wanted no commitment, no permanent entanglement. Now, after long months of enjoying each other, she had introduced the possibility of wedlock, and that made him uneasy. She had caught him by surprise when she'd brought it up, but he knew that he couldn't continue to see her if she nourished the hope of getting him to the altar. Mitch felt only a little remorse as he decided to end the affair. He liked Lucinda and he found her sharp wit entertaining, but long ago he had decided not to marry.

Mitch sighed to himself as he remembered that time. Almost ten years had passed, but he could still recall the horror he'd felt when the news had reached him that his best friend, Andrew Holmes, had committed suicide. He'd done it, it turned out, because his wife Janette, whom he'd adored, had announced that she was leaving him for another, more wealthy man. Although that had been unsubstantiated at the time of Andrew's death, Janette's subsequent marriage, less than three months after Andrew's suicide, had reaffirmed what Mitch had suspected, and he'd been hardened ever since to women. To this day, Mitch had not forgotten Janette's treachery and he knew he never would. Andrew had loved his wife, and his love had given her the power to destroy him. Mitch knew he would never allow another person to have that kind of control over him—never.

Dismissing such depressing thoughts from his mind, Mitch glanced up at his driver as he neared his carriage. "Let's go home, Nelson."

The driver nodded in agreement, then waited as Mitch opened the door and climbed inside.

Bill had been waiting in the cramped space the carriage floor provided for what seemed an eternity, and he was more than ready to attack when his intended victim entered the conveyance. Springing forward, he took Mitch completely by surprise as he swung his blackjack with unerring accuracy. As Mitch collapsed heavily across the seat, unconscious, Joe, anxious to help, leaped down from his position atop the vehicle and looked inside.

"How'd you do?"

"No problem. He's out like a light," Bill answered proudly.

"You didn't hit him too hard, did you?"

"He's breathin', if that's what you're worried about."

"Good. I didn't want you to hit him like you did to the driver. He ain't worth nothin' to Jack if he's already dead when we get there."

"Don't worry so much. This worked out better. Since he and the driver are about the same size and coloring, we don't have to go lookin' for a stiff now. All we gotta do now is switch their clothes. You got a rope?"

"Yeah, let's tie Williams up real good just in case he does come to. We don't want him givin' us any trouble."

"He ain't goin' to give us any trouble. Why don't you get us out of here before someone wises up? We can take care of the rest of this down on the waterfront."

Without further hesitation, Joe climbed onto the driver's seat and, taking up the reins, guided the carriage away from Lucinda Blake's at a deceptively casual pace.

"Ya only got the one?" Shanghai Jack asked Bill and Joe a short time later.

"Yeah. You want him?"

"You sure he's alive?" He peered eagerly into the darkened interior of the carriage.

"Yeah."

"Good. I'll take him." Shanghai Jack tossed a small sack of coins to the two cohorts. "Help me get him into my boat."

With some difficulty, the three pulled Mitch's unresisting body from the coach and dumped it unceremoniously into Jack's skiff.

"Good doin' business with you, Jack." Joe smiled as he watched the crimper start to row out into the bay where the ships sat at anchor, awaiting "deliveries" by him and his kind.

"We got rid of the driver and Williams, now all we gotta get rid of is the carriage," Bill said when Jack had disappeared into the darkness.

"Let's just leave it in one of the alleys. Nobody'll figure out what happened to him if they find it down here."

"Let's go, then. This is makin' me a little nervous. I want to get back to Stuart and let him know that we took care of everything."

"You got Williams's wallet?"

"Right here."

"Good. We'll park this thing out of sight somewhere and head back to the saloon. I imagine the boss is going to like what we have to tell him."

The gloomy blackness of night closed in around the pair as they rode off into the bowels of the Barbary Coast.

Chapter 1

"Jonathan"—Roland Stuart stood at the head of his massive dining-room table and raised his champagne glass in salute—"to our first successful joint business venture. May there be many more."

"Here, here."

As the toast was seconded by Stuart's associates, Elliot Whitney and Alan Harris, Jon rose in response to Roland's pledge.

"Indeed."

"And to Catherine, your bride of three months, whose loveliness is matched only by my own dear wife Susan's." Roland's eyes held a wicked gleam as he lifted his glass in Catherine's direction.

"To my wife," Jon agreed, gazing down at Catherine's upturned, becomingly flushed features.

Playing her part to the hilt, she smiled her pleasure at their praise. "Why thank you, gentlemen."

"You're more than welcome, my love." Jon's intimate words were meant as a private caress, but they grated on Catherine's nerves, smothering her moment of pleasure in Roland's duplicity.

After they again seated themselves, the meal began. From

the turtle soup to the sumptuous pastries, each course was cooked to perfection by Roland's superb chef. When, at last, everyone was replete, the gentlemen retired to the study for after-dinner brandies and talk of the shipping world, while the women went to the main parlor to enjoy tea and conversation.

"Jon." Roland clapped him on the shoulder as he handed him a snifter of brandy. "I'm pleased that everything is working out so well for both of us. Why, within a year, the profits from our undertaking should more than double."

"We have done well," Jon concurred as he sipped the liquor.

"It's just a shame Mitch didn't live to see your success, Jon," Elliot Whitney, a longtime friend of the Williams family, commented. "You've become quite the astute businessman. I'm sure he would have been very proud of you."

Even after all these months, the memory of Mitch's brutal murder still hurt Jon, and it was only with supreme effort that he kept a tight rein on his emotions. "I have tried, since assuming control of the company, to base my decisions on what I thought Mitch might do under the same circumstances. I can only hope that someday I will be as successful as he was."

"His death was a terrible tragedy," Roland said sympathetically, as he turned away to refill his glass from the decanter in the liquor cabinet.

"And so mysterious," remarked Alan Harris. "Did they ever find the men who were responsible?"

"No," Jon replied. "All we know is that Mitch and his driver, Nelson, disappeared some time after he left Lucinda Blake's house. We found Mitch's body in the bay several days later, but we were never able to find Nelson."

"Do you suspect him?"

"No. They were very close. We think he must have met with foul play too."

"That must have been very difficult for you, having to

identify Mitch after that many days in the water," Alan remarked.

"It wasn't easy." Jon was grim as he answered their gruesome questions. "The final verification was based on his clothing. There was no way I could recognize him." He suppressed a shudder as he remembered that fateful afternoon almost six months before when he'd gone to the morgue to look at the body that had been pulled from the bay.

"I'm sorry, Jon." Roland interrupted the grisly discussion. "This is hardly the time to bring up those unhappy memories. This is supposed to be a celebration."

"It's all right, Roland," Jon replied. "Mitch's death will never be easy to talk about, but with the passing of time some of the pain has eased." He fell silent for a moment as he recalled the agony he'd gone through when he'd learned that Mitch had disappeared and again when he'd confirmed that it was his brother's body in the morgue. If only he could have seen Mitch one more time to clear the air between them . . . to let him know that he would abide by his decision . . . to tell him that he did love him . . .

"You were lucky to have Catherine help you through it all," Roland observed, dragging Jon back from his tortured thoughts.

Jon relaxed at the mention of the wife he so cherished. "She has been a great comfort to me."

"And she's such a beautiful woman," Elliot declared. "Your wedding was a small one, I take it?"

"Yes," Jon told him. "We kept it small and private. That seemed best in light of Mitch's death."

"I understand and I wish you both much happiness."

"Thank you, Elliot. I'm sure we'll be fine. I love Catherine and she loves me."

At Jon's last comment, Roland lifted his snifter to his lips. He took a deep drink of the potent brandy before turning the topic back to shipping. "Well, gentlemen, shall we get down to business?"

In the parlor, Catherine chatted with the ladies, but she was increasingly restive. How long did these interminable after-dinner sessions go on? These women were driving her crazy with all their talk of charities and good works. No wonder their husbands all had mistresses!

Catherine smothered a laugh as she imagined the scandal she'd cause if she told each of these pompous females exactly what their husbands were up to. Why, according to Roland, Elliot and Alan both frequented a certain house of pleasure, in Chinatown, that catered to "exotic" tastes, and she certainly knew personally what Roland enjoyed.

"Why, Catherine, you do look pleased with yourself." Susan had noted her feline smile. "Tell me, whatever are you thinking about?"

Adept at covering her true thoughts, Catherine smiled brightly at Roland's wife. "I do have some free time on my hands now, and I was wondering if it would be possible to join you in your charity work. I'm sure you accomplish so much."

"Thank you, Catherine. How kind of you to offer." Susan smiled at Chelsea Whitney and Laura Harris. "I've hesitated to invite you to join us because I thought you might be busy adjusting to married life, but now that you've expressed an interest, why, it works out perfectly."

"What do you mean?" Catherine sensed an undercurrent in the conversation.

"Susan has good news, but she hasn't made it public yet," Laura stated.

"Good news?" Catherine arched a delicate brow as she glanced at her lover's wife.

"I'm going to have a baby, probably in about six months." Susan's face was radiant.

Only years of successfully hiding her feelings prevented Catherine from losing control. With a gracious

smile plastered on her face, she extended her best wishes.
"That's wonderful, Susan. I'm sure Roland must be thrilled."

"Oh, yes. He was beside himself with joy when I told him.
We're hoping for a son, of course—an heir to carry on the
family name."

"Naturally."

"Are you and Jonathan planning on having children?"

"We haven't really considered it yet." Catherine shrugged.

"God sends them when the time is right," Laura put in
sagely, and Chelsea nodded in agreement. "I'm sure you and
Jon will make many beautiful babies, just as Roland and
Susan will."

It was all Catherine could do to keep from sneering at her
pronouncements. So, Susan was going to have a child, was
she? Jealousy burned deep within her. How dare Roland!
Though they were together as often as possible, he still made
love to Susan! The thought rankled, and she could hardly wait
to be alone with him, to tell him what she thought of him and
of his precious little "pregnant" wife.

The sound of the men's voices in the wide hall relieved
Catherine immensely. She had had about all she could take of
the ladies' talk of the upcoming birth, and she greeted Jon
much more warmly than usual. Though slightly taken aback
by her extra attentiveness, Jon relished the affection she
showered upon him, and when she whispered of her desire to
leave as soon as possible, he quickly extricated them from the
social gathering. As they left, Catherine noted Roland's puzzled expression. His confusion pleased her, and she looked
forward to their rendezvous the next afternoon at his office.

It was just past one o'clock the following day when Catherine instructed Florence to order the carriage brought around.
Ever sensitive to her mistress's wishes, she did as she was
told, reminding Toby, as she did every time Catherine went
out in the afternoon, of the necessity for discretion.

Although it was broad daylight, few people paid any attention to the carriage as it pulled to a stop at the back door of Roland's establishment. Wearing a heavy veil to conceal her identity from prying eyes, Catherine was quickly admitted to the building by the armed guard who was always posted at the door. She hurriedly climbed the rear staircase, and swept into Roland's office, knowing he would be anxiously awaiting her.

"Darling." Roland came to his feet as she entered. "I've been waiting for you." He started toward Catherine, fully intending to embrace her.

"Don't 'darling' me!" she seethed, removing her veil to glare at him.

"Catherine? What's wrong?" He had sensed that something was troubling her last night when she and Jon had left early, but he had no idea what had upset her. Their plans had come to fruition, and he was aware of no problem between them.

"You're certainly very cool about this, Roland."

"Cool about what?" His tone hardened suspiciously as he reached out to place his hands on her shoulders.

It was then that she lost control and struck out at him, her hand connecting viciously with his cheek.

"How dare you spend day after day making love to me and then go home to bed your mewling wife!"

Without thought, Roland backhanded her, bloodying her lip and knocking her to the floor. "Don't ever hit me, woman," he snarled.

Cowed by his unexpected ferocity, Catherine cradled the side of her face and cringed away from him when he reached for her again.

"Look at me," he ordered imperiously, and Catherine looked up, too shaken to defy him. "Now, tell me. What's happened? Why are you so upset?"

Though his tone was cajoling, she knew the steel will his conciliatory manner concealed and she responded quickly, "Susan told me last night that she was pregnant."

"So?"

"So, how can you leave me and go to her?" she demanded heatedly.

"She is my wife, Catherine, or have you forgotten that?"

"How could I forget? Especially now that she's carrying your child."

"Do you want to have my child?" he asked bluntly. When she hesitated, he smiled ferally. "Face it, Catherine. Since we can't marry, there's only one thing we can share."

Grasping her wrist, he pulled her up to him and kissed her passionately. "Jealousy doesn't become you, sweetheart. Remember that."

"Oh, Roland, I was so angry at the thought of your loving her." She sighed, then kissed him.

"My darling, there is no comparison between what we share and what I do with Susan," he muttered as he frantically worked at loosening her clothing.

"I know. I suffer Jon's lovemaking, but I live only for the time we have together."

"As do I." Roland pressed heated kisses to her throat, then drew back to look at her. "And you won't have to worry long about my sleeping with Susan. Once she begins to grow heavy with the baby, I'll make my excuses and move to the guest room. Believe me, Cat, I have no desire to bed a woman who's swollen and misshapen."

His hands roamed freely over her trim waist and hips, and as he continued to strip her garments from her, Catherine, driven by desire, succumbed to Roland's every demand. He, in turn, was consumed by untamed passion.

South Pacific

Far out to sea the day had become as dark as night. The ocean, in the grip of a tropical storm, pitched the *Seastorm* about as though she were no more than a child's toy. Lashed to the wheel, the helmsman fought to maintain some semblance of control over the ship, but nature, in her fury, overruled his feeble efforts.

At the first sign of bad weather, the crew had taken in the sails and had prepared the vessel for the coming battle with the elements. They now waited below in strained silence, hoping the worst of it would pass, but fate did not intend to grant them a reprieve.

A brilliant flash of lightning illuminated the gray-green sky with electrifying clarity. Jagged in its awful beauty, the vivid bolt rent the roiling clouds and speared its way toward the storm-tossed ship. In a crashing collision, the powerful storm-flame split the mast, hurling it to the deck. The helm and helmsman were crushed beneath the huge timber, and, out of control, the ship was at the mercy of the tempest.

Rolling helplessly in the raging, mountainous swells, the craft began to list, and Captain Warson knew with sickening certainty that the end was near. Struggling across the seaswept deck, he reached the companionway and shouted to the men below to abandon ship.

"Aye, Captain, but what about Williams?" came the answering shout.

"Leave the mutinous bastard!" Warson bellowed. "A watery grave is all the swine deserves!"

Then, as he was turning toward the longboat, a huge wave swept the deck, knocking Warson from his feet and washing him overboard. The crew scrambled up from the depths of the ship and tried to save their captain, but they were too late. They watched helplessly as he disappeared in the briny deep.

Realizing that their craft was doomed, the men battled to reach one of the lifeboats. Only one seaman, a young lad of about seventeen years, remained behind.

"Tommy! Why're ya lingerin'?" a mate bellowed to the youngster.

"It's Williams! I can't just leave him down there to die!" Tommy knew that Mitch Williams, the one man who'd befriended him on this voyage, was in irons in the cargo hold.

"You heard the captain! To hell with Williams! Save yourself. There's no time!"

But the youth turned back. "You go on. I won't be leaving without him."

"You're a fool, lad!" a sailor shouted.

Tommy paid him no heed and with a determination unusual in one so young, he began to make his way across the slippery deck of the canting ship to the hold's hatch.

Chained to the wall of the hold, Mitch Williams was giving serious consideration to his own mortality as the *Seastorm* pitched violently in the stormy ocean. With each successive roll, the wallowing vessel had taken on more and more water until he stood knee-deep in the threatening deluge. Most of the cargo had broken loose from its restraints due to the heavy seas, and he'd had to dodge the tumbling crates.

Alone and growing more concerned by the minute about the *Seastorm*'s seaworthiness, Mitch fought against the shackles that restrained him. He knew from previous efforts that his struggles were useless, but he also knew that he wouldn't give up his life without a fight. He did not want to die trapped in the hold like a rat. With all of his might, he pulled at the single length of chain that attached the manacles on his wrists to an iron ring in the wall, trying to dislodge the ring; but the bolts holding it were secure and his efforts were for naught.

Panting and nearly exhausted by his exertions, he leaned back against the wall, trying to brace himself against the ship's constant rolling, but a sudden lurch threw him forward and he was left hanging by his arms as chilling water sloshed over him. When he regained his feet, he noticed that the water level had risen to midthigh.

Mitch knew that the *Seastorm* couldn't survive much longer with this much water in her, and a strange sense of calm overtook him as he faced the very real possibility of his own death. Prayers, taught to him in his childhood by his mother, came to his mind, and he said them silently, hoping for a miraculous deliverance, yet realizing that he had little cause for hope.

The *Seastorm* shuddered under the sweep of a giant wave, and Mitch suddenly wondered how young Tommy was holding up in the face of the storm. Shanghaied during a trip from his family's farm to San Francisco, Tommy had been ill equipped to deal with life at sea so Mitch had protected the lad and had tried to keep him out of the way of the vicious Captain Warson. But Warson was a brutal man, given to flogging the men for no particular offense, and when Mitch had protested a punishment he'd ordered for Tommy, the captain had turned his wrath on him, allowing Mitch to take the stripes in the young man's place.

Tommy had been mortified that Mitch had suffered in his stead, but there had been little either of them could do about it. Then, just last week, when Warson had ordered that another cabin boy be given fifty lashes for dropping his dinner tray, Mitch had no longer been able to stomach the captain's fiendish cruelty. Not that losing his temper had done any good. He'd only managed to land a few strategic blows on the captain before he'd been overpowered and soundly beaten by the men loyal to the ship's master. At the time, Mitch had thought it lucky that they hadn't killed him. Now, imprisoned as he was on the sinking ship, he almost wished that he'd met his fate in a more expedient fashion.

His head drooped in despairing surrender to what he thought was the inevitable. Then, letting his mind wander, Mitch thought of Jon. He wondered how his brother had dealt with his disappearance. Although they had exchanged words about Jon's plan to marry Catherine, Mitch felt certain that his brother would not rest until he'd been located, and he smiled to himself at the irony that he would never be found if he were at the bottom of the Pacific Ocean. An agonized sigh escaped him as he tugged once more at his bonds. He was near the limits of his endurance when he heard a scraping noise at the hatch and looked up to see someone raising it.

Tommy lifted the heavy trapdoor. To make it to the hatch he had had to use all his strength against the elements. As another angry wave washed across the deck, he hung on for dear life while the wall of water pounded him, then tried to tear him loose. Tommy heard screams and he glanced around in time to see the boat in which the others were making their escape tilt crazily and capsize in the onrushing waters. Unable to help them, he took advantage of a momentary righting of the ship to climb down the ladder into the darkened cargo vault.

"Mitch?" His loud call could barely be heard over the tumult of the storm.

"Here." Mitch felt immense relief upon hearing Tommy's voice.

The lad could barely make out Mitch's reply over the deafening roar of the wind, but he pushed his way through the tumbling cargo, heading in what he thought was the right direction. He was greatly heartened when he spotted his friend chained to the far wall.

"The ship's not going to make it! We've got to get you out of here!"

"I feared as much, but you'll have to get the keys." He held up his arms so the youth could see where his irons were attached to a ring in the wall.

"Where are they?"

"On a nail, by the door." Mitch cast a leery eye toward the open hatch through which water was pouring in with each successive, battering wave.

Searching frantically, Tommy finally located the keys and then hurried back to remove the irons.

"Thanks," Mitch said fervently as the last cuff was unlocked. Then they raced to the ladder.

"What do we do now, Mitch?" Tommy was glad to be following the older man's lead.

"Stay with me no matter what!" Mitch instructed as he led the way out of the cryptlike storage area.

Tommy followed him closely up the ladder, but as they neared the top another wash of seawater rushed through the open trap. Tommy slipped as the force of the water hit him and he almost lost his grip, but Mitch reached down and pulled him back up.

"Hang on!" Mitch called out to him over the rising roar of the tempest. "It's going to be even worse once we're on deck."

As the ship rode the trough of a wave and straightened up for a moment, Mitch pulled himself out of the hold, then turned to help Tommy. Once they were on deck, they grabbed the guide ropes strung before the storm and ventured across the vessel in the hope of finding another lifeboat.

Driven by the ferocious winds, the rain was blinding as it pounded against the two men. Time and again, they lost their footing due to the precarious tilting of the wet deck, and they were more than thankful for the rope that was their lifeline. They had almost made it to the side when the end came suddenly. A mammoth mountain of water towered above the ship, and after what seemed a brief hesitation, it descended in full fury, smashing the ship to pieces and tossing Mitch and Tommy into the vast churning sea.

Chapter 2

*Two days later on the island of Malika
 in the South Pacific*

It was first light. The violent storm that had wracked
Malika with high winds and slanting downpours had finally
blown itself out to sea. The surf was calming now that the bad
weather had dissipated, and once again it was serene and
crystal clear. The low-rolling whitecaps seemed to murmur
an apology for their previous fierceness as they caressed the
island's now-welcoming beach with a gentle, soothing ardor.
Peace and tranquility reigned in this tropical paradise as the
birds, sensing that the tempest had finally ended, took to the
dawn skies in a flurry of vibrant colors, piping their joyous
thanksgiving in a cacophony of melodious calls.

Espri Duchant emerged from the protection of the lush
forest, seeming more a pagan goddess than a living being.
Tall and lithe, and clad only in a sarong of the finest white
cloth, she moved with almost regal grace across the wide
expanse of the deserted beach. Pausing at the water's edge
only long enough to undress, she carefully laid her garment
aside and stepped uninhibitedly into the warm, inviting water.

Bathed in the morning sun's golden glow, Espri was

female perfection personified. Her features were pure, her
eyes dark and intelligent, her mouth soft and given to easy
laughter. The long, black cloud of her hair tumbled in disarray about her shoulders and brushed suggestively over her
full, rounded breasts and curving hips; her legs were long and
shapely. She stood still for a moment, innocently enjoying the
sea's swirling embrace, before diving expertly into the next
oncoming wave. With the strong steady strokes of one accustomed to swimming in the ocean, she swam smoothly
through the clear waters of the lagoon, savoring her closeness
to the elements. Finally, as her strength began to ebb, she
started to turn back, and it was then that she noticed a dark
shape lying in the surf some distance down the shore.

At first glance, Espri dismissed the irregular form, thinking it driftwood driven ashore by the storm. But an inner
voice told her to look again, and when she did, she realized it
was the body of a man. Worried that he might be one of her
friends from the village, she stroked at top speed in his direction. When she could touch bottom, she rose from the depths
like a sleek sea nymph and raced quickly ashore through the
foaming crests.

As she drew near him, Espri realized that the man was a
stranger. Unconcerned with her own nudity, she knelt beside
him and gasped as she saw the bloody, jagged wound on his
forehead. Reaching out with nervous fingers, she touched his
throat, seeking and finding the area that would indicate the
pulse of life. Though faint, his pulse seemed steady enough,
and she breathed a sigh of relief.

Sitting back on her heels, she studied him, fascinated.
Where had he come from, and how had he been injured? she
wondered as her gaze lingered upon him. Had the terrible
storm that had struck the island sunk his ship and left him
the lone survivor? Or, had he been washed overboard by one
of the huge waves that were commonplace in such tempests?
He certainly was a magnificent specimen of a man—tall and

broad shouldered, with hair as black as the night. His face was a study of manly harshness, arresting yet disturbingly handsome. He wore only a pair of loose-fitting trousers, and they were in shreds from the violent battering he'd evidently suffered while in the ocean. Without knowing why she did it, Espri reached out and rested a hand on the wide expanse of his bare, hair-roughened chest. A tingle went through her at the contact, so innocently made, and she derived an odd comfort from the heavy thudding of his heart beneath her palm.

Feeling her light touch, Mitch stirred and opened his eyes. Blinking in disbelief, he stared up at the mystical vision of unclad loveliness that seemed, in his befuddled mind, to be hovering over him. He thought for a moment that he'd died and gone to heaven, but the pain in his body was far too real for that. He wanted to reach out to the woman, to try to touch her, to see if she was a vision or actually there; but his arms felt leaden and he couldn't seem to force himself to move.

"Please . . ." he finally managed to croak in a voice that was hoarse and rasping.

Mitch thought he heard her reply, but he couldn't be sure for he drifted into oblivion as his senses surrendered to the overwhelming pain pounding through him.

Espri was gazing down at the man, wondering at the extent of his injuries, when a splashing surge of the breakers, edging ever higher, reminded her that the tide was coming in. Knowing that it was urgent to get the man to safety farther up the beach, she moved so that she stood above and behind him. Bracing herself as best she could in the warm, loose sand, she grasped him under the arms and pulled with all her might. Though the man was big, her efforts were rewarded and she managed to drag him a short distance so he was out of reach of the tenacious sea.

Panting from the exertion, Espri rested by his side for a moment before rising to go for help. She knew that she would have to go home and enlist her father's aid, for the village was too distant and she did not want to leave the unconscious stranger unattended for a long time. The regular rise and fall of his chest assured Espri that he was still breathing. So, casting one last glance at his compelling countenance, she hurried down the beach. She found her sarong, and after wrapping its soft folds securely about her, she headed for home.

"Papa!" Her voice was breathless, her tone a bit sharp, when she finally reached the clearing where the hut was located. "Papa! I need you! Wake up!" Rushing inside, she threw aside the hanging mat that separated their sleeping areas and roughly shook his shoulder. "Papa! Please, it's important!"

Startled into wakefulness, Jacques Duchant rolled over and opened bleary, bloodshot eyes to stare at his offspring. "What is it, Espri? What's wrong?"

"A man's been washed up on the beach," she said urgently. "He's alive, but unconscious. I need your help to carry him up here."

"A man? On the beach? Who is he?" Jacques asked as he struggled to sit up, the copious amounts of liquor he'd consumed the previous night making the task none too easy.

"I don't know who he is. I found him lying in the surf. Will you help me?"

"Of course, *ma petite*, just give me a moment to get my sea legs." He glanced at Espri and tried to smile reassuringly, but even that effort hurt. He buried his head in his hands, groaning. "One of these days, I've got to stop drinking."

Espri's expression was tinged with exasperation as she straightened up and stepped outside. Many times she'd heard her father promise to give up drink, but invariably he had gone back to the bottle when the memory of his last hangover had faded. As she waited for him to join her, she reflected on his self-destructive ways. He hadn't always been like this—intent on dulling life's reality through drink. Why, she could still remember the happy years of her childhood when her mother, the beautiful Princess Tila, had been alive. Jacques had been a different man then. He had been a wealthy ship's master sailing out of France, and he had given that up to marry Tila and stay on in Malika. But when Espri had been ten, Tila had died, and Jacques had never recovered from the loss. Instead he had sought numbing relief for his grief in liquor.

Now, eight years later, Jacques was still indulging in rum and the even more powerful narcotic drink, kava. He had little real interest in anything and seldom remained sober for more than a day. Espri had pleaded with him to stop, telling him of her love for him; but her entreaties had gone unheeded. Jacques had lost his Tila, and he believed that living without her was unbearable.

Espri had loved her mother dearly and she, too, missed Tila's warmth and wise counsel. But she had dealt with the aching emptiness inside her as best she could; she was now able to go on. However, having watched her father's never-ending battle against the agony of his loneliness, Espri had become wary of the love that often existed between a man and a woman. Was that special emotion so strong and abiding that life held no joy for one lover without the other? Her father's suffering convinced her that there was only one way to protect herself against such a tragedy in her own life—she must never fall in love. Surely living alone, as she did, was preferable to the hell that Jacques had been going through since her mother's death. Espri was determined that she would never allow anyone to become *that* important to her.

Jacques finally emerged from the shelter, rousing her from her thoughts, and she looked up as he approached, his gait unsteady.

"Ready?" he asked, drawing a deep breath in an attempt to clear his head of liquor's clinging cobwebs.

"If you are," she responded, and they started off down the beach.

* * *

"He's still unconscious," Espri told her father when she reached the man and sank to her knees beside him.

"He's better off that way for now," Jacques told her gruffly as he took a quick look at the cut on Mitch's forehead. "Help me get him over my shoulder."

Though Jacques staggered slightly under the injured man's weight, he managed to make the trek back to their home without incident. Espri nervously dogged his footsteps until they reached the clearing; then she ran ahead to prepare a place for the stranger in the hut.

"Bring him here, Papa," Espri called as her father appeared in the doorway.

With relief, Jacques started to lower the man onto the bed his daughter had prepared, but her sudden, startled exclamation halted him.

"What is it?"

"His back!" Espri gasped. She had just seen the sand-encrusted, red welts on this stranger's back.

As carefully as possible, Jacques maneuvered the man so he lay facedown on the mat.

"It looks like he's been flogged," he murmured, frowning as he remembered his days at sea and some of the reasons why seamen were whipped aboard ship. An unease settled over him.

"Why would anyone want to whip him?" Espri asked with the innocence of one protected from the cruelties of the white man's world.

"It's a captain's prerogative to punish his crew as he sees fit," he answered as simply as he could. "This man must have been a troublemaker."

Espri gazed down at the stranger, not wanting to believe her father's conclusion. "You can't know that for sure."

"Espri . . ." Jacques was well aware of the general caliber

of the seamen who merited such punishments, and he did not want such a man in his home, near his daughter.

She cut him off quickly. "Bring me some water, Papa. I must wash him."

Jacques recognized the stubbornness of her tone and dropped his objections for the time being. But, as he left to fetch the water, he vowed to himself that, should the stranger live, he was going to keep a very close eye on him.

With gentle hands, Espri set about caring for the unconscious man, wiping the loose sand from his injured back and cutting away the tattered remnants of his pants. Having lived among uninhibited natives all her life, Espri was not in the least discomfited by the sight of his naked buttocks, but upon her father's return, his exclamation made her jump nervously.

"Espri! For God's sake! Cover the man!" Jacques placed the container of cool, clean water by her side and hastily handed her a length of cloth to use as a blanket.

She stared at the material for a moment before looking up at her father in confusion. "But why?"

"He's not one of the native boys," Jacques explained gruffly. "He's a man—full grown."

"But I've seen—"

"I don't care what you've seen here on the island. This man is not one of us; he's a white man." At her puzzled look, he continued. "Trust me in this and do as I say."

Espri obediently draped the covering over the man's lean hips.

"This cut on his forehead is from the coral," she told her father as she brushed back a dark lock of hair that had fallen across his brow, in order to take a closer look at the deep gash that was dangerously close to his right eye.

"It doesn't look good," Jacques muttered. "Will you need limes and purau leaves?"

"Yes." Espri was instantly efficient. "And salve for his back."

"Is his back infected?"

"There's some swelling, but the welts don't appear to be fresh. I'm more worried about the possibility that he will get the fever from a coral infection," Espri told him worriedly. "I've got to get this cleaned out as quickly as I can. There's no telling how long ago it happened."

"I'll get the limes and leaves," Jacques offered. Then he watched silently for a moment as she ministered to the stranger. Agitated, he finally turned and left the hut to search for the needed remedies.

With patient concern, Espri dipped a soft cloth into the water her father had brought and began to wipe the gore from the ugly head wound. She'd had enough experience with coral injuries to know that they were not to be taken lightly, so she cleansed the gash as thoroughly as possible, her efforts eliciting a low moan from her still-unconscious patient. Espri noted with dismay the hot, dry feel of his skin, and she longed for her father to return quickly with the supplies.

With cooling water, she washed the last remains of the grit from the man's back, wondering all the while at her father's warning that he was not like the men she knew. Outwardly, there seemed little difference. His back, abraded though it was, seemed like any other man's—deeply tanned and broad and powerful. His hips were lean; his legs, long and straight; his arms—she now bathed them with strokes that were beginning to seem more like caresses—were strong with thickly corded muscle.

Pausing in her task, she stared down at this stranger, and she felt a strange stirring in her breast as she took in the masculine line of his bearded jaw, the firmness of his chiseled lips. Intrigued and unable to resist the temptation, she reached out and lightly ran a slim finger over the leanness of his cheek, enjoying the feel of his whiskery growth. Only her father's footsteps caused her to hastily withdraw from that innocent, yet sensuous, contact.

"Did you get the limes?" Espri asked as she hurried toward Jacques.

"I think this should be enough." He handed her half a dozen limes, along with the leaves she'd requested and a pot of salve. "Has he stirred yet?"

"Only once, when I was working on the coral cut; otherwise he's been quiet." Espri turned back to the silent stranger. "I'll need a bandage for his head, something that will help hold the leaves in place."

Jacques nodded and went to search among their belongings for a suitable cloth to use for the wrapping while Espri drew out a knife and quickly cut several of the limes in half. Leaning over the man, she shielded his eyes protectively as she squeezed the fruits' caustic juice into the angry wound, cauterizing it. Then, after covering the injury with the healing purau leaves, she took the strip of material her father offered her and secured it about the wounded man's head.

"You have to cover his eyes?" Jacques asked.

"It is the only way I can be sure that the leaves will stay in place. It should hold until he comes around." As Espri spoke, she began to apply the healing salve to the welts on the stranger's back.

"Any sign of the fever yet?" Jacques knew how vicious and unpredictable the fierce fever from an infected coral wound could be.

"He feels somewhat hot, but not unbearably so."

"You've done a fine job, *ma petite*," her father assured her.

"I just hope I've done enough."

"You've done everything possible. Now it's just a matter of waiting."

"I know." Espri glanced worriedly at the unconscious man.

"Do you need my help with anything else right now?" Jacques asked.

"No, why?"

"I thought I'd go to the village and tell Luatu about this

man you've rescued," he explained, starting out of the hut. "Maybe the villagers have heard something about the ship he was on."

Espri's heart sank, for rum and kava flowed freely in the village. She followed Jacques outside. "Give Grandfather my love," she said.

"I'll tell Luatu that you'll come to see him as soon as you can," he promised.

"Papa?" Espri's tone was hopeful.

"Yes, *chérie?*"

"Will you be back today?"

Jacques avoided meeting her eyes for he knew he would see the questioning/censuring look that always haunted her gaze when she was worrying about his drinking. "I'll be back as soon as I can."

Though his words were reassuring, Espri knew the pattern of his behavior, so as she watched him head in the direction of the main village her heart was filled with sadness and bitterness. Though she was sure that, right now, Jacques was sincere in his intention to try to return that day, she would not count on his doing so. His need for the forgetfulness drink provided was more powerful than his desire to please her.

Shrugging off her concern, Espri turned back to the hut to check on the stranger. When she found that there had been no change in his condition, she left him to prepare herself a light breakfast of plantains and fresh coconut milk in the separate, open-sided cooking hut. Returning to the main dwelling, she ate her meal quietly as she maintained a watchful vigil over the injured man.

Sitting in the comfort of Chief Luatu's unwalled dining house, Jacques spoke in earnest to the old man who was his father-in-law. "Espri is with him now."

"Is he badly injured?" Luatu offered his son-in-law a shell

of fresh coconut milk, but Jacques waved it away. He needed something more powerful to ease the pain that throbbed at his temples. Noting Jacques's distress, the chief ordered his servant to bring rum.

"The stranger has a head wound from the coral. He hasn't yet recovered consciousness," Jacques answered as he gratefully accepted the proffered cup of liquor and took a deep sustaining drink.

"What of the fever? Has it taken him?"

"No, not yet."

"Perhaps this white man will be lucky and it will pass him by."

"I don't know."

"Well, if anyone can help him, it will be Espri. She is gifted in healing, much as my daughter was," Luatu stated proudly.

For just an instant Jacques's eyes darkened at the mention of his beloved Tila. "Yes, she is."

"Yours was not the only man found today," Luatu said.

"There were others?" Jacques was astounded by the news. Such incidents were very rare, indeed.

"Just one," the old chief informed him. "Two children found him on the shore near the village."

"Is he still alive?"

"Yes. Anuitua is caring for him now."

"They must have been from the same vessel," Jacques stated thoughtfully.

"Go to Anuitua and see this man," Luatu suggested. "Maybe he will be able to talk with you."

"I will do that."

"Come, enjoy the food also," the chief urged, gesturing expansively toward the platters spread before them. "Plantains and pudding await you."

"As always, your generosity is boundless."

"You are my family." Luatu dismissed the compliment easily. "How is my granddaughter?"

"She is well and sends her love," Jacques replied.

The older man smiled contentedly as he thought of Espri. "That is good. She is the light of my days."

"As she is of mine."

"Have any of the island boys caught her eye yet?" Luatu inquired.

The answer was slow in coming. "No. She shows little interest. Konga pursues her, but she gives him no encouragement."

The chief frowned as he considered this news. "Konga is a strong warrior and has much wealth. She could do worse."

Jacques shrugged. "Who is to know a female's mind? She seems perfectly content as she is."

"It is only a matter of time," Luatu responded sagely. "She has yet to find the man who can awaken the woman in her. When she does she will love with all her heart, just as her mother did."

"It was a beautiful thing—Tila's love."

"Love freely given is always returned tenfold."

"You are right, my old friend. You are right."

Chapter 3

Espri stood in the sun-dappled shade of a grove of iron-wood trees, staring at the sea. The morning hours had passed slowly as she had remained by the stranger's side, but when there had been no significant change in his condition, she'd felt the need to get outside for a while. Breathing deeply of the sweet, flower-scented island air, she turned back toward the hut, knowing that it wasn't wise to leave the man alone too long. He might waken and not know where he was.

Mitch was hot and thirsty and the pounding in his head was nearly unbearable. Rolling over slowly, he winced slightly as his abused back came in contact with the hard mat. His breathing became strained even from that little exertion, and he wondered vaguely at his own weakness as he struggled to subdue the wracking pain that enveloped him. Gritting his teeth, he levered himself up on his elbows and opened his eyes.

Had Mitch not been feverish, he would have understood that the blackness engulfing him was not real, but his senses were confused. Frightened by the thought that he was blind, he jerked upright and reached up to touch his eyes. He breathed a shaky sigh of relief when he discovered the bandage. Then, angered by his own feeling of helplessness, he tore off the offending wrap.

As the bright sunlight pouring through the hut's open doorway assaulted him, pain, sharp and glaring, forced him to turn quickly away. Squinting, Mitch blinked dazedly as he looked around him, but his eyes refused to focus properly and his surroundings remained an unfamiliar blur. *Where am I?* The question pounded through his disoriented mind as he tried to fathom his situation, but the fever drained all rationality from him. Fantasy melded with reality in his thoughts, leaving him more than a little confused. *How did I get here— wherever "here" is—and where are my clothes?* he wondered. Unable to think clearly, he lay back, groaned, and covered his eyes with one hand.

Espri heard him moan as she crossed the glade to the hut, and her heart caught in her throat. She rushed forward.

"Oh, no, *monsieur.*" She was upset to find that he had torn off the protective, healing wrapping, and she hurried to his side, kneeling down.

Mitch had been so engrossed in his own misery that he hadn't heard her approach, and the unexpected sound of her voice startled him. Despite his torment, he took his hand from his eyes and looked at her; but he could not see her clearly.

"Monsieur?" Mitch frowned. *Where the hell was he? The woman was speaking French to him?* His head was throbbing, his thoughts were jumbled as he tried to identify the girl before him. The last time he'd heard a French accent he had been at Madame Sauvigne's Château of Pleasure . . . Was this Fifi? Of course! And that would explain, too, his current state of undress! Eager for this to be the explanation of his dilemma, he reached out and caressed the softness of the girl's shoulder, the heat of his touch branding her cool, sensitive flesh. "Ah, Fifi, how could I have forgotten that I was with you?"

"Fifi?" Espri frowned, momentarily confused until she realized that his features were flushed and that he was burning up with the fever. "*Monsieur,* you're mistaken. My name is . . ."

But before she could continue, his hand dipped lower, skimming with disconcerting accuracy over the soft swell of a breast covered only by her thin sarong. Never before had a man touched her so intimately and with such expertise. Gasping at the sudden, unexpected sensation that raced through her, Espri was dismayed to feel her nipples tauten invitingly against the warmth of his lingering caress.

At her sudden intake of breath, Mitch smiled confidently and moved to draw her to him. "You were saying, Fifi?"

Nervously, Espri shifted position so she would be just out of his reach. "*Monsieur,*" she began again, stiltedly this time for she was still disturbed by the heated tingle that seemed to glow from her breast to the very center of her womanly being. "You have—"

"Missed you greatly." Having finished the sentence for her, he went on. "And, Fifi, have I ever told you how sexy I find your accent?" His voice was low and seductive, and there was a trace of humor in it.

Mesmerized briefly by his tone, Espri stared at him in mute fascination as he took her hand and lifted it to his lips, kissing the sensitive curve of her palm. She couldn't prevent the shudder that quivered through her at the contact of his mouth on her flesh, and though she tried to pull her hand from his firm, yet gentle, grip, Mitch held her fast.

With a little effort, his failing vision had fit Fifi LaRue's dark, French beauty to this woman's blurred countenance. The peach-tinted skin, the cloud of black hair, the marvelous foreign lilt of her speech . . . yes, he truly believed he was at Madame Sauvigne's and the woman beside him was Fifi. With lazy confidence, Mitch drew the woman he thought to be a courtesan toward him, but when he felt her resistance, he frowned.

"Why are you so skittish, *chérie?* We've known each other far too intimately for you to pretend coyness now." Mitch started to sit up in order to pull her across his lap, but the suddenness of his movement sent a shaft of pain through his head. A groan escaped him, and he quickly lay back on the mat, his free hand pressed tentatively to his fevered brow.

"It must have been the whiskey." He tried to lighten the mood by his quip, but the agony he was experiencing had turned his slight smile to a grimace.

"Whiskey? You weren't drinking whiskey!" Espri told him hurriedly.

"That explains it then," he rationalized. "I never did have a head for any other liquor."

"Monsieur," she began.

"There's no need for you to be so formal, Fifi. Madame Sauvigne is gone and we're quite alone." He released her hand and reached up to caress her cheek. "Call me Mitch."

Nonplused by the tenderness of his touch, Espri could only repeat his name, enjoying the hard, masculine sound of it on her tongue. "Mitch."

"Ah, Fifi," he murmured seductively as the agony in his head lessened. "You are a beauty." Ever so gently, Mitch slipped his hand behind her neck, and with an easy pressure, he slowly guided her down to him.

Espri knew she should resist, knew she should tell him once and for all that she wasn't Fifi, but her resolve disappeared as his lips met hers in a first, innocent exchange. While she had been kissed before, the fumbling, pawing embraces she had experienced with the island boys held none of the magical delight of this sweetly shared moment, and she found herself relaxing against this stranger as his hands molded her to him. A low-glowing heat flamed to life deep within her, and she unconsciously nestled more closely to the hardness of his frame.

Mitch teased her with soft, quick kisses until he felt her

inevitable surrender; then he deepened the embrace, his mouth slanting across hers in sudden, fierce possession as his hands traced knowing paths of excitement over her seemingly willing body.

The passion of his kiss took Espri by surprise, and she drew a quick startled breath when he reached down to cup her firm, rounded buttocks and pull her more tightly against him. A shaft of sheer delight soared through her as she felt for the first time the heat of his need pressed intimately against her thighs. Suddenly frightened by the intensity of the emotions he was arousing, Espri began to struggle in earnest to free herself from his demanding embrace.

Lost in a sensual haze of need, Mitch well remembered the real Fifi's abandoned lovemaking, and he interpreted her actions, now, as excited anticipation. Encouraged by her wriggling movements, his mouth seared hers, his tongue delving deeply between her slightly parted lips to taste more fully of her sweetness.

"Fifi . . ." Mitch intoned her name huskily as his hands grazed over her hips and thighs with knowing precision.

"*Monsieur* . . . Mitch . . . you have a fever," Espri protested firmly. She was not Fifi, and she did not like being mistaken for another woman—especially in a passionate embrace!

"Yes, Fifi. I'm feverish, feverish with desire for you!" Mitch's mouth took hers again, plundering it ruthlessly, as his body demanded more—much more—than intoxicating caresses.

Even through the discomfiture of his injuries, Mitch felt himself responding to the woman in his arms with a fervency he'd never before experienced, and he wanted—no, needed— to lose himself in her body, to sink within those hot, silken depths.

In spite of her desire to be free, a whirlwind of enthralling ecstasy swept through Espri as Mitch continued to caress her, and her outrage at being mistaken for someone else faded. Aware only of the pulsing warmth of his manly arousal fitted tightly against her, Espri knew an instinctive urge to wrap herself around him, to absorb him into the very depths of her body.

Mitch could wait no longer to possess her. His need was strong, and her willingness was now more than obvious for she was moving restlessly, hungrily. The sarong was foreign to him, but he had little trouble stripping it from her lithe form. Then, feeling completely in control, he levered himself up and turned, pinning Espri beneath him in order to enter her.

But dizziness suddenly swept over him as he moved atop her, draining all desire from his body and leaving him shaken and cold. Groaning in sudden misery, he closed his eyes and tried desperately to conquer the vertigo that refused to subside. But relief didn't come, and he was forced to roll onto his back to try to regain his equilibrium.

As reality intruded, the powerful excitement that Mitch had aroused faded and Espri grew alarmed, not only by his obvious distress but by the thought of what had almost happened between them. Angry with herself for having lost control of the situation, she got up and draped her sarong about her before moving back to his side.

"Fifi . . . ?" Mitch spoke gruffly as he lay quite still, his breathing shallow, his color ashen.

Knowing that it was useless to explain her identity to him at this point, Espri reached out and laid a comforting hand on his arm. The dry, feverish heat emanating from him seemed to scorch her hand, and her embarrassed anger gave way to serious concern for his health.

"I'm here, Mitch."

"I'm sorry . . . I don't usually have these problems," Mitch explained. He tried to smile, but the throbbing in his head had become too intense. Frowning at his failure to master the pain, he shook his head as if to clear it. "That must have been *some* liqueur you gave me last night."

"You did have a rough night, *monsieur*," Espri agreed, going along with his ramblings.

Mitch turned to her, studying her hazy visage. Funny, he thought in a brief moment of clarity, he didn't remember Fifi being so agreeable. As he recalled, she had the temper of a shrew and a tongue to match. Shrugging off his feeling of confusion, he made an attempt to sit up. "I'd better be going. If you'll just bring me my clothes . . ."

"Please . . ." Espri leaned over him and pressed him back down on the mat. "Don't try to get up yet. I'll bring you something to drink and then after you rest for a while, you'll feel much better."

Giving up without a struggle, Mitch closed his eyes. "Thanks. I could sure use something; my head is pounding."

"I'll be right back." Espri hurried from the hut to get her father's bottle of kava. After mixing a goodly portion of the potent liquor with cool water, she returned to Mitch's side and, raising his head, urged him to drink the soothing, numbing brew.

He drank obediently, frowning slightly at the unfamiliar taste. "That's not bourbon. What is it?"

"It's called kava," she explained softly. "It will help to ease your pain."

Kava . . . Fifi . . . the heated pain that tormented every part of his body . . . Mitch disliked not being in complete control of himself, and once more he tried to get up—to get away. "I really should go. Have my horse brought around front. I'll be fine once I get home."

There was more strength behind his effort this time, and Espri panicked slightly as he brushed her aside. "Mitch. Listen to me," she pleaded, knowing that he might injure himself further if he got to his feet. "You're not drunk. You've been injured."

"Injured?" He paused in his attempt to leave, his tone hardening at this new information that did not make any sense to him. How could he have been injured at Madame Sauvigne's?

"Your head . . . you have a bad cut on your forehead," she explained, hoping against hope that he was lucid enough to understand.

"Everything *is* blurred," he told her as he lifted a hand to his brow and gingerly touched the wound.

"It will pass. You'll be fine," she assured him. "But you must relax and try to rest."

"I'll try," he agreed, suddenly exhausted.

"I need to bind the cut again. It will heal faster that way," she explained as she lowered him back to the mat.

He nodded, tense now. Espri understood what he was going through, but to stop the fever the poison must be drawn from the wound.

"This may hurt, but it's important that I do it," Espri said as she cut several more of the limes.

"That's all right," Mitch replied. "I'll hold still."

Trembling at the thought that she would be causing him pain, Espri quickly squeezed the fresh, astringent juice directly into the vivid gash. Though his jaw tensed as the bitter fluid seared the wound, Mitch remained stoically passive as she carefully cleansed away the excess and pressed purau leaves to the injury.

"The wrapping will hold the medicine in place," she said softly. "I know it will be difficult for you, not being able to see for a while, but I'll be right here if you need anything." Then, taking the wrapping that he'd discarded earlier, Espri efficiently bound his head and eyes. "Try to sleep now." She touched his arm lightly as she started to move away.

But Mitch's senses had been sharpened by the caustic, biting sting of the lime juice, and in a brief moment of clarity, he wondered why Fifi, of all people, would be nursing him. Hadn't it been years since he'd last visited Madame Sauvigne's? Reaching out quickly, he managed to snare her forearm and pull her back to him.

"Fifi? Where am I? This certainly isn't the Château of Pleasure."

"No, it's not, but you are safe here. I'll explain everything to you later, when you're feeling stronger." Espri felt an odd thrill as she stared at the large, tanned hand resting possessively on her arm.

The softness of her exotically accented voice mesmerized Mitch, and he sighed in resignation as a great weariness stole over him. "All right, but first . . ." With a gentle urging, he drew her closer to him, his lips seeking hers in an infinitely tender caress. "Thank you, Fifi."

A shiver of exhilaration raced through Espri as his mouth found hers, and she was stunned by the force of her response to his kiss.

As she pondered her reaction in silence, Mitch settled back, and giving up the fight to remain awake, he slipped off into the oblivion of sleep, the kava having dulled his embattled senses.

"Be gone, woman," Konga ordered brusquely, trying to extricate himself from Tana's clinging embrace. "I have much work to do."

Tana laughed throatily as she pulled his head down to her for another passionate kiss. "I will go, Konga, if you really want me to." Boldly, she ground her full hips erotically against his, feeling his need for her grow. "Are you certain that your 'work' can't wait?"

Konga submitted to her teasing ways for just a moment longer before rudely pushing her from him. He dismissed the dark-haired beauty curtly. "I have stayed with you too long already."

"But you've enjoyed that time, have you not?" Tana asked archly, as she faced him squarely, hands on her hips, her ample breasts thrust forward in invitation.

"You pride yourself too much, Tana. Any number of women on the island would willingly take what I offer and not demand more of me," Konga told her arrogantly. He was sure of himself for he was the most powerful, unmarried man on the island.

Stung by his rejection, Tana smiled slyly as she returned his barb. "What of Espri? Does she long for your favors?"

Konga scowled, his expression turning thunderous. "You would do well to hold your tongue."

"Why? Because you cannot bear to hear the truth?" she challenged. "I love you, Konga. I want to be the one to give you strong handsome sons. You're a fool to desire Espri."

"Espri has no hold on me!'" he denied heatedly.

"Do you think me stupid, Konga?" Tana sneered. "I see how your eyes follow her whenever she is near. I know how her innocence intrigues you, but I tell you this: I am the woman who will make you happy, not Espri!" Infuriated by his refusal to admit the truth, she turned on her heel and stalked away.

Tana was livid as she stormed back to her home. Espri! Espri! Espri! Ever since she could remember, Espri had been the cause of all her troubles. When they were children, as the granddaughter of Chief Luatu, Espri had always been the favored one whose praises were sung at every opportunity. Tana's envy of her had begun then and had only grown stronger through the years.

Unencumbered by the cultural restraints of white societies, the lifestyle on Malika was open and free. Youthful natives enjoyed one another to the fullest before settling into marriages that were arranged strictly for profit, but Espri did not fit into the normal pattern of this life. On Malika, it was a rare woman who went to her marriage bed untouched, but

Tana had no doubt that Espri fitted into that category. Not one of the men on the island had been able to win her heart. She discouraged all attempts to woo her, yet her aloofness enticed the males all the more. It was that way with Konga. Espri had become an obsession to him. He wanted only her, no matter how Tana tried to convince him that she, herself, was the woman he truly needed.

Though Tana understood Konga's behavior, her awareness did not lessen her hatred for Espri, and as she neared her home, she was disgusted to find that Jacques Duchant was talking with her mother Anuitua. Wanting to avoid him if possible, for she was in no mood to be pleasant to her arch-rival's father, Tana slowed her progress. Only after she'd watched Jacques bid Anuitua good-bye did she join her mother.

"What did Jacques want?" she asked casually enough.

"He was asking about the stranger who was found on the beach."

"Why was he asking?" Being more interested in searching out Konga, Tana had paid little attention to the young white man who'd been brought to their hut, unconscious, earlier that morning.

"It seems that the white man we saved was not the only one rescued from the wrath of Moana," Anuitua answered cryptically.

"What do you mean?"

"Espri found another man on the beach by their home. She is with him now."

"Espri is staying with a white man?" Tana's eyes lit with an inner glow. What would Konga say when he learned that?

Anuitua frowned at her daughter's tone. "I'm sure the man must be injured or Jacques would have brought him to the village."

"What else did he tell you?" she probed, interested in finding out what Espri was doing.

"Nothing."

Irritated, Tana was determined to find out more. She had to convince Konga that Espri did not love him! "I will be back later. I think I will go see this other white man."

Very aware of her daughter's feelings toward Espri, Anu-itua glanced at her sharply. "Do not·create trouble where there is none, Daughter."

Feigning an innocent look, Tana answered, "I will cause no trouble, Mother. I only want to see the man."

"But why? He is just a man, most probably a sailor."

"Maybe so," Tana agreed. "But perhaps there is something in this situation that I can use to win Konga for my own."

Leaving her mother perplexed by her reasoning, Tana hurried off toward Espri's hut.

As the hours passed, Espri sat by Mitch's side, noticing with increasing distress that his fever was worsening. His breathing had grown strained and rapid, and his features, once so pale, were now flushed due to the inner heat that was consuming him.

Knowing that the crisis could come any time, Espri disregarded her father's firm directive and threw off the light covering that lay over Mitch's hips so that she might bathe him with cool water. Over and over, she drew her soft, damp cloth across the planes of his manly body, but her efforts seemed to be having no positive effect.

Mitch felt the coolness of someone's gentle touch and he wanted to thank that person, but he could only manage a low, guttural groan. The sound of a woman's voice, soft and slightly foreign, came to him, calling his name and encouraging him to fight the illness that was draining his strength. Semiconscious, he was vaguely aware of someone, possibly the woman who was speaking, sponging him down, and he groaned again as each soft stroke of the cool, wet cloth brought him blessed relief.

Though Mitch struggled against the fever, his efforts were in vain, for the infection grew more intense, driving his temperature to more threatening heights and robbing him of awareness. His mind raced from the effects of the fever, and his thoughts grew tormented. Twisted visions of his shanghaiing and of the long, grueling months at sea haunted him.

What had been quiet sleep became tortured delirium, as Mitch tossed fitfully on the mat and delivered a continuous litany of incoherent, yet despondent, mumblings. Until this moment, when she watched Mitch worsen before her eyes, Espri had not seriously thought that he might not recover. But now, she realized his death was a very real possibility. Renewing her efforts to somehow lower his body temperature, she wet her cloth again and sponged the broad width of his chest, praying all the while that he would have enough resistance to fight against the fever's debilitating power.

Letting her eyes caress him as she bathed him, Espri sensed that there was something very special about Mitch. Reliving in her mind the embrace they had shared, she felt a sensual heat flood through her. This man, even in his delirium, had the power to arouse her. No other man had had such an effect on her. Color stained her cheeks as she thought of her body's abandoned response to his caresses. She scolded herself. It was ridiculous! Why, he didn't even know who she was! He thought she was someone named Fifi! Espri felt desperation for a moment when she suddenly became aware that Mitch might remember what had occurred between them. Embarrassed by that thought, she silently prayed that he would have no recollection of what had passed between them while he'd been feverish.

A sudden dimming of the light in the hut surprised her, and she glanced up to find Tana standing in the doorway, a knowing smirk on her face.

"Tana?" Her surprise evident in her voice, Espri paused in her ministrations to look questioningly at the other woman.

"Hello, Espri." Tana walked brazenly into the hut.

"What are you doing here?" Espri asked cautiously, for she was well aware of Tana's attitude toward her.

"Your father told us you'd rescued a man. He said you might be needing some help. Is there anything I can do?" Actually Tana was hoping that Espri would turn her down, and she was pleased when the other woman did so.

"No. Not right now. Mitch is very ill." Espri suddenly wished that she'd kept the cover over his lower body, for Tana's bold gaze was sweeping over his rugged, masculine form with avid interest.

"His name is Mitch?"

Espri nodded curtly.

"He certainly is an *upalu kane*." Tana's gaze lingered boldly on Mitch's lower body.

A flare of irritation surged through Espri when Tana praised Mitch's good looks, and she glared up at her.

"There really is no point in your staying. If I need help, I will send for you."

But Tana was not so easily put off. Kneeling down on the opposite side of Mitch, she shamelessly reached out to caress his chest. *"Hemakana ka Moana!"* Her words were thick with sensual meaning as she stared down at him appreciatively.

"He was no gift from the sea, Tana," Espri declared. "He is just a very sick man who may not live through the day."

"It would be a loss to all womankind if he were to die, Espri," Tana taunted. "Though I cannot see all of his face, I am certain that he must be the most handsome man on the island."

"He may be dying and all you can think about is how handsome he is!"

Espri's intense reaction told Tana that she did have feelings for this white man. Thrilled with the power that knowledge gave her, she smiled broadly.

"You mean you have not noticed?" she asked audaciously.

"I have been too busy caring for him to be concerned about such things!"

"Your innocence is amusing." Tana hoped to pique Espri's interest in this man even more. "You don't even know what it is you're missing."

"I don't feel that I'm 'missing' anything, Tana."

"Oh? Well, then, I'll come back later when your Mitch might better appreciate my company." She left no doubt as to her intentions. "By then he might be interested in coming to stay at my home, for, after all, that is where his friend will be staying."

"Friend?"

"You haven't heard?"

"Heard what?"

"Another man was saved from the sea this morning."

"And he's alive?"

"Yes, although he's not yet conscious. But I'm sure by the time Mitch is recovered, the man who's staying with us will be well, too. It might prove interesting"—she purred the word—"to have both of the white men living with me and my family."

Unbidden and surprising anger surged through Espri. While she understood the sexual attitudes of those on the island, the thought of Tana making love with Mitch greatly annoyed her.

"He will be free to do as he pleases," she responded as coolly as she could, averting her eyes from Tana's mocking gaze.

"I know," Tana said throatily. "And I hope he 'pleases' me."

With that, she turned and left, a victorious smile playing about her sensuous lips.

Chapter 4

Konga's expression was ominous as he stalked up the long trail through the island's forest to Espri's home in a sheltered glade that overlooked the sea. The news that a shipwrecked white man was staying with Espri and her father had angered him greatly, and he was now on his way to discover exactly what was going on.

Although she has refused to acknowledge it publicly as yet, Espri is mine, Konga thought with fierce possessiveness. He did not want her to be alone with any other man. As he trudged on through the dense tropical foliage, he made a concerted effort to bring his temper under control, but it was not an easy task. He wanted Espri for his wife, yet she treated him, the bravest, most fearsome of the Malikan warriors, with the same indifference she showed all the other island men who pursued her.

Konga was finding it increasingly difficult to remain unperturbed in the face of Espri's continued aloofness. Lately he'd almost been driven to take her in his arms and force some reaction from her. But, knowing what a spirited woman Espri was, Konga had decided to bide his time and wait for the right opportunity to claim her as his own. *Someday very soon*, he vowed silently to himself, *she is going to be my wife*.

The thought brought a lusty smile to his scowling face and soothed his still-ragged temper.

He stood undetected at the edge of the forest, watching Espri emerge slowly from the shaded seclusion of the hut. Stretching wearily, she savored the warmth of the afternoon sun, and closing her eyes, she lifted her face to the soothing heat of its caress.

Time had passed slowly since Tana's unwelcome visit so it seemed much later to Espri than midafternoon. Mitch had shown no improvement during the long, plodding hours. His fever still raged uncontrollably although she had bathed him constantly. She had tried to get him to drink more of the kava and water, but in his delirium he had refused her attempts. Frustrated, and becoming more worried by the minute, she wondered if anything further could be done to help him.

As Espri arched her body in seeming reverence to the sun, Konga's gaze traveled over her supple curves and he felt the all too familiar stirring in his loins at the mere thought of touching her satin flesh. The knowledge that her father was in the village, that they were alone save for the mysterious white man, sent his desire surging until he gritted his teeth against the power of his passion. It was not an easy victory for him, but he finally managed to bring his craving for Espri under control, and holding his emotions tightly in check, he ventured forth from the concealing protection of the trees.

"Espri!"

Thinking herself alone, Espri was startled by Konga's call. She groaned inwardly when she saw the warrior coming across the clearing toward her. While it was true that Konga was the richest and most powerful of the eligible men on the island, she had no interest in him. Love and marriage were not for her so she had constantly refused his advances during the long months of his avid pursuit. But, despite her rejection, he had not lost heart, and the thought of having to fend off

Konga again left Espri greatly irritated. She returned his greeting coolly.

"It is good to see that you are well," he remarked as he joined her before the hut, his eyes lingering overlong on the thrust of her bosom against the whiteness of her sarong.

She frowned at his statement and, growing uncomfortable under his intense gaze, defensively crossed her arms over her breasts.

"Why would I not be?"

"The storm last night was a vicious one and I worried that you might have been injured." Though it was not his main reason for seeking her out, he had, in truth, been concerned about her safety during the night.

"Your worry was unnecessary. My father and I are fine," Espri answered, her tone dismissing his interest.

"It pleases me to concern myself with you," Konga told her imperiously, "for you will one day be my wife."

Though her temper flared at his overbearing assumption, she managed to respond calmly to his proclamation. "I am not ready to marry. I have told you that often enough. Why don't you believe me?"

"I believe that you do not want to marry now, but there is nothing to say that you won't marry me in the future," Konga declared with the pompous assurance of a man used to getting his own way.

"I don't love you, Konga," Espri stated flatly, wanting him, once and for all, to know the truth. She had expected him to react angrily to her declaration, but he only shrugged.

"Love is not important in marriage," Konga replied seriously. "Only wealth and rank matter when two are joined. Our families are equals, so there is no problem." He swept away her objections with no thought.

"There is a problem, Konga. I do not want to marry you," Espri declared, this time with a haughtiness that pushed him too far.

Anger flared in his obsidian gaze, and all thoughts of the white man vanished as he snatched her into his arms and crushed her against his bare chest.

"You continue to refuse me," he snarled threateningly. "It is not wise for you to treat me with such disdain, sweet one. I am Konga! Not some untried youth!"

"Let me go!" she hissed, struggling futilely against his overpowering strength.

"When *I* am ready, Espri. Not at your command. I do not take orders from a mere woman!" He pressed her intimately to his lower body so she could feel the need he had for her. "Once I have touched you and made you mine, you will understand how foolish you've been to resist me."

Whereas Mitch's obvious need for her had excited Espri, Konga's arousal left her feeling degraded. Infuriated by his boldness, she continued to try to free herself from his embrace. "Release me!"

"Ah, Espri, how I will enjoy taming you." With little finesse, he groped at her bosom, touching, at long last, those delectable silken orbs.

Startled by this unexpected intimacy, she fought all the harder to get away, and when he bent to kiss her, she twisted her head to the side to avoid his seeking mouth.

"No!" she gasped, refusing to surrender.

But Konga, in the grip of his passion, grasped her hair in a hamlike hand and held her immobile while his mouth covered hers in a wet, stifling exchange that left her weak with nausea.

"You see!" he exulted when he noticed her flushed features. "You want me. Why won't you just admit it? There would be no objections to our marriage. It would be a wise mating."

Sensing her chance to break away, Espri furiously wrenched herself free, wiping at her mouth with the back of her hand. "I do not want you! And no matter what you think, I will not marry you!"

Overconfident because of his imagined success, Konga only chuckled at her display of pluck. "Have it your way for now"—his smile was benign but there was a steely determination behind his next words—"but I will not wait too much longer. I am not a forgiving man. Come to me; do not force me to take you, Espri."

Knowing that there were many beautiful women in the village who would come to him without hesitation, Konga refused to believe that Espri truly did not wish to marry him. He was positive that she would soon be his and his alone.

Espri was about to declare that she did not want or need his "forgiveness" when Mitch's delirious call interrupted the tense moment. Giving no thought to Konga, she turned and rushed back inside to find that her patient's fever was raging higher than ever.

Konga was not accustomed to being treated so casually by the opposite sex, and he was enraged that she had dismissed him so easily. Infuriated, he followed her into the shelter.

Glowering at Espri as she hovered over the unconscious man lying naked on a mat, he demanded arrogantly, "What are you doing?"

"That is none of your business, Konga," she snapped, not bothering to look up and wishing only that he would leave her.

"I want him out of here," he ordered, watching in great annoyance as she began to stroke the stranger's body intimately with a cool, wet cloth.

"You have no authority over me. This is my father's home, not yours." Espri's temper flared and she stopped her ministrations to glare up at Konga. "This man is sick—maybe dying. I don't have time to argue with you. I must tend to him. Leave me. Get out."

Konga bristled at her churlish manner, but at the same time he was greatly relieved to find that the white man was incapacitated and obviously posed no threat to his quest for Espri.

"I'll go now, but I will return," Konga told her in a menacing tone so his departure would not look like a retreat. "And when I do, I expect to find you much more willing . . . if you understand my meaning."

Espri didn't bother to reply, but when he stalked from the hut, she breathed a deep sigh of relief before turning back to Mitch.

Nights on Malika were idyllic. Splendid in its silvery enchantment, moonlight bathed the island in a soft luminous glow, its gentle touch pearlizing the white sand of the wide, inviting beaches. The sea, surrendering itself caressingly to the shore, murmured its contentment at having finally reached journey's end. The sweet scent of the tropical flowers wafted delicately across the land, borne by breezes that seemed mere wisps of fancy, and only the dulcet song of night birds broke the Elysian stillness.

Darkness had forced Espri to set out several candlenuts, which she'd placed strategically so they would aid her in her continuing vigil. With each passing hour, Mitch had grown more and more restless. As he tossed about in the grip of the fever, Espri grew worried, for she feared his condition might deteriorate so that she wouldn't be able to keep him from further injuring himself.

Although her water supply was running low, she remained by his side, feeling certain that it would be dangerous to leave him alone while she made the trip to the pool. Anxiously hoping for her father's return, she waited in silence, praying that Jacques would come to help her. At one point, Espri's anxiety was so great that when she thought she heard her father returning, she jumped to her feet and raced outside to welcome him back, leaving Mitch briefly unattended.

Lost in a maelstrom of burning misery, Mitch fought for his life. The debilitating fever held him in its grip, and he moved restively on the mat as his mind assaulted him with visions of past horrors. His parents' death . . . then Andrew's . . . his shanghaiing . . . the captain's brutality . . . the painful memories were jumbled together and drawn into a vortex of terror. Thrashing about, he tried to escape his mental torment, totally oblivious to his surroundings. Mitch did not realize that he accidentally knocked over one of the candlenuts and that the small flame spread and began to lap hungrily at the side of the dwelling.

Espri stood in the middle of the deserted clearing, disheartened. Her imagination had been playing tricks on her. Her father had not returned. She knew now that it was futile to look for Jacques that night; she would have to see Mitch through it by herself.

Her shoulders slumping slightly, Espri was starting back toward the hut when the acrid scent of smoke drove all thoughts save one from her mind—*fire!* Looking up she spotted the low, unholy glow illuminating the hut.

"Oh, God! Mitch!" Giving no thought to her own safety, she raced toward the burning dwelling.

Scooping up handfuls of fine coral sand, she rushed inside and threw them on the small fire that was flaring to ever greater life. Again and again she brought sand until she finally succeeded in smothering the potentially devastating blaze. Nerves stretched taut, hands shaking, she then dropped to her knees beside Mitch, who was still struggling against his imaginary demons.

"Mitch, please . . . you're safe . . . the fire's out . . . there's no need . . ." Espri said comfortingly, but he was beyond the reach of her soothing words.

When she fought to press his wide shoulders back down to the mat, he grasped her wrists in a viselike grip. Terrifying phantasms drove him to escape so he threw her from him with a strength induced by delirium.

"No!" The denial exploded from him before he slumped back.

Espri landed heavily on her side, then lay unmoving as she fought to catch her breath. Realizing the room had become silent, she rolled over to look in Mitch's direction. To her surprise and relief, he lay inert on the mat. He had passed out.

Trembling from the effects of his unexpected assault, Espri struggled to her feet. She was frightened by the prospect of what Mitch might do if he were left unrestrained and suffered another heedless rage, so she hurriedly located four lengths of rope and an equal number of stakes. He had not yet begun to stir when she returned to the hut, and she was exceedingly grateful for that. Immediately she drove the stakes into the ground and set about binding him to them. It was not an easy thing for her to do, but for her own safety, as well as his, drastic measures were necessary. Constantly on guard lest he begin to stir, she pinioned him to the ground, effectively spread-eagling him on the mat.

Through the haze of pain that engulfed him, Mitch was aware that something was very wrong. He tried to roll onto his side and sit up, but he found, to his frustration, that he couldn't move. Unable to see, unable to move, his disorientation complete, he thought himself aboard the *Seastorm* and at the mercy of her barbaric captain. Fighting his unwarranted imprisonment, he strained viciously against his restrictive bonds. His muscles bulged in protest as he struggled, and he swore savagely while he twisted and bucked in his attempts to break free.

"Damn you, Warson!" he shouted. "I'll see that you rot in hell for this!"

Espri watched in agonized silence as Mitch battled fruitlessly to escape his bonds. Finally, wanting only to calm him, she brought him a cup of straight kava and held it to his lips.

"Drink," she urged.

Unable to distinguish between reality and fantasy, Mitch quieted at the soft sound of her voice. *A woman on the* Seastorm? No longer capable of logic, he could only respond when he felt the cup touch his lips. He drank thirstily of the potent brew, its tranquilizing effect almost instantly assuaging his battered senses. Though Mitch did not cease his struggles immediately, his efforts became less and less violent until he finally fell completely under the spell of the opiate.

With the last of her precious water supply, Espri then gently bathed him, and that done, she sat on her own mat. As she gazed down at Mitch's fever-flushed features, she wondered just how much longer he could endure the infection's unrelenting siege. Knowing that she should take advantage of his quiescence, she lay down facing him, and curling on her side, she closed her eyes.

On the beach near the village, the bright light thrown off by burning coconut husks split the darkness. The Malikans, gathered around it to recount the events of the day, cast long shadows. Kohea, husband to Anuitua, told those listening that the white man his wife was tending had regained consciousness and was recovering nicely, while Jacques, though well into his cups, proudly added his account of how Espri had rescued the other man.

Standing silently near the edge of the crowd, Tana grew resentful of the praise being heaped on Espri by the rest of the villagers. *Doesn't that woman ever do anything wrong?* she wondered with more than a trace of bitterness. Glancing at Konga, who was standing with several of his friends, she willed him to look her way, but he was too busy listening to the worshipful comments about Espri to notice her. Casting one last longing look in his direction, she turned from the gathering and started off into the forest, anxious to be away.

Konga, too, had remained on the outskirts of the group. Since returning from a late fishing excursion that had taken him beyond the barrier reef, he'd passed the evening drinking rum and visiting with his male friends until it was time for the nightly meeting. He regarded such assemblies as tiresome, but Jacques's mention of Espri had captured his attention. As he listened to Duchant's comments, the memory of the kiss he'd shared with Espri that afternoon returned full force, stirring his blood.

His gaze hooded, he surveyed the women sitting comfortably around the blazing fire, knowing that a number of them would gladly grace his bed given the chance. But that night, Konga wanted more than just a warm, willing body. He wanted a partner who could ease the ache Espri's delectable body and arousing kiss had created within him earlier that day. Then he spotted Tana disappearing into the forest, and he knew that she was the only one, besides Espri, who could satisfy his need. Unobtrusively, Konga slipped away from the group, and tracing the island woman's steps, he followed her down the path to the sea.

Tana was pensive as she sat on the warm sandy beach, staring out across the moon-kissed sea. She felt frustrated and more than a little angry over her lot in life. Was it always to be this way? Would she always be second to Espri? Her heart was heavy as she pondered her love for Konga and the fruitlessness of her situation.

"The night is going to be long . . . and hot." Konga's deep voice intruded into her thoughts, and she gasped in stunned surprise at finding him so close beside her.

"Konga?"

"I have need of you tonight, Tana," he told her, certain of her eager acceptance of him.

She was of a mind to refuse him, to send him in search of his frigid Espri, but her heart would not permit it.

"And I have need of you," she answered huskily, holding out her hand to him. "Only you . . ."

Tana allowed him to draw her to her feet and into his arms.

His eyes closed, his thoughts on Espri, Konga kissed Tana savagely, his mouth possessing hers. Though Konga did not love Tana as he loved Espri, he found her sexually exciting, and his body reacted eagerly as she offered herself to him.

Loving Konga as she did, Tana knew she would take him on any terms, and she responded enthusiastically to his rough lovemaking. He was the only man she wanted, the only one she would ever truly need, and she was thrilled that he had chosen to be with her that night. Casting her thoughts to the winds, she concentrated only on the moment, on the brief period of time Konga was really hers.

Yet, Konga's mind and his senses were flooded with Espri: the way she'd looked earlier today when he'd watched her stretching sensuously before the hut, the softness of her breasts to his touch, the ripeness of her mouth when he'd kissed her. In a frenzy, he sought to deepen his and Tana's embrace, but she stopped him.

"Wait, Konga," she murmured, her tone sultry and sensuous.

"For what?" he demanded hoarsely, wanting only to lose himself within the welcoming confines of Tana's willing body.

"I want to please you tonight," she told him invitingly.

"You always do," he answered, in the heat of his need wanting her then and there.

"Good. There is nothing more important to me than keeping you happy." Tana moved slightly away from him. "Come with me," she coaxed. "We will go to the pool and enjoy the peace of our night there."

Her erotic invitation readily accepted, they crossed the

silvered beach to the path that led to the deep, fresh-water pool near the center of the island.

The moonlight filtered through the high trees and glittered off the cool, clear waters. Crowding the night-shrouded banks, gardenias and wild orchids bloomed in tropical profusion, their heavenly scent delicately perfuming the air. The multi-hued birds who nested in the surrounding foliage were bedded down for the night, but an occasional soft call blended with the musical rush of the sweet water as it cascaded over the low falls and splashed merrily into the welcoming basin below.

Espri stood silently on the bank enjoying the serenity of the deserted pool. For hours Mitch had not stirred so she had felt it reasonably safe to leave him for the short time it took to fetch more water. But she hadn't reckoned with the delightful sense of abandon the waters inspired. She couldn't resist the temptation to bathe in the refreshing pool.

Filling the bucket she'd brought with her, she set it aside, then quickly unfastened her sarong and let it drop unheeded to the ground. Stepping from the slippery bank into the silken waters, she pushed off gracefully and swam at a leisurely pace out to the waterfall. She climbed nimbly onto the rocky ledge that ran beneath the shimmering cascade, then stood beneath the sparkling fall and closed her eyes, raising her arms to the heavens in an innocent, sensual offering.

Having never been aroused by a man before Mitch, Espri was totally unprepared for the sudden stimulation of the water pouring sensuously over her body. Mitch's intimate touch and kiss had awakened her to a new awareness of herself as a woman, and her heart skipped a beat as she remembered with shocking clarity the erotic hardness of his male body and the passion of his embrace. The pink crests of her breasts tautened in response to that memory and the caress of the water only served to heighten their sensitivity. Not fully understanding why her body was reacting this way, Espri rubbed at her breasts, hoping to erase the heated tinglings that were surging through her, but she found even the touch of her own hands strangely arousing.

Frightened by the burning pulse that had flared to life deep in the core of her, she would have dived back into the pool, but the sound of voices and laughter came to her across the water. She recognized the sound of Konga's voice immediately so she stepped behind the veil of the splashing silvery fall and remained perfectly still as she waited to see if he and his companion would pass on by.

Espri watched in silent frustration as Konga appeared at the opposite side of the pool with Tana. She wondered how she could get away without being noticed. Luckily, she'd left her clothing and the bucket on the other bank, but she wanted to go back to the hut—and Mitch.

Espri realized that any other island girl would just swim out casually and make her presence known, naked or not, but she did not want Konga to see her nude. There was something repulsive about the way he had touched her that afternoon, and she refused to give him the opportunity to view her body. The thought of their encounter made her flesh crawl, so she took great care to stay out of sight, and she prayed that whatever Tana and Konga were going to do would be done quickly.

"The pool looks inviting, does it not?" Tana purred as she unwrapped her sarong and carelessly tossed it aside.

"Not nearly as inviting as you," he answered as he took her in his arms and kissed her.

"Let's swim first," she encouraged.

Konga chuckled knowingly as he untied his pareu and followed Tana to the water's edge, but before she could enter the water, he pulled her back against him and openly fondled her full breasts.

Tana, responding eagerly to his desire, rubbed herself

sinuously against him. "You feel good to me, Konga. Your touch fills me with fire."

Aroused by her words and actions, Konga turned her to face him and kissed her passionately. Tana, as always, was more than receptive to his lovemaking. She clung to him, wrapping her arms about his neck and arching against his hardness.

"I am yours, Konga. Love me . . . please, love me." Her voice was a husky plea as his hands explored the curves of her writhing body.

Lifting her, Konga swung around and laid her upon the lush grass, his lust driving him to take her quickly. His big body covered hers, and they moved together in the soft light of the moon, their bodies intertwined, their heated words echoing through the silence of the night.

Espri did not want to watch, but she was trapped in the haven of the waterfall. The narrow shelf of rock on which she stood did not allow her to turn away. She closed her eyes in an effort to give the couple privacy, but visions of Tana and Konga filled her mind, and the tightening deep in the womanly heart of her disturbed her greatly. She wanted to run and hide, but there was to be no escape. Unless she was willing to make her presence known, she was trapped until the two lovers chose to leave.

The sound of splashing interrupted Espri's troubled thoughts and she looked up to see the pair running playfully into the water. A sudden fear of discovery immobilized her, and she bit her lip to steady herself. Terrified, she waited as Tana and Konga swam out into the pool.

"Come, I'll race you to the waterfall!" Tana laughed delightedly as she started off in Espri's direction.

Espri tried to think of a good explanation for not making her presence known as she nervously watched Tana draw nearer to her position, Konga in hot pursuit. She sighed deeply when Konga reached out and snared Tana's ankle, stopping her progress just before she reached the ledge.

Tana sank beneath the surface and came up sputtering angrily, but Konga was there to hold her and silence her protests with a passionate embrace.

"Do you not want to play in the waterfall?" Tana asked breathlessly as she held onto his broad shoulders, allowing him to support her weight as he treaded water.

"The waterfall holds no attraction for me," he told her as she pressed kisses to his throat and shoulder. Slowly, he began to swim back toward the shallows.

When they had stepped from the pool, Tana led Konga back to the soft bed of grass, and she smiled as she urged him to lie down. Eager to keep Konga in her thrall, she lay beside him and began to caress him, first with her knowing hands and then with her lips. He hardened instantly at the touch of her hot, wet mouth, and she was thrilled to know that she had that much power over him. He climaxed quickly, drained by her expertise; then he pulled her up on top of him to rest. Had Konga thought about it, he would have been surprised to note that at that moment he was not thinking of Espri.

However, Espri was thinking of him. She had had a basic knowledge of what went on between a man and a woman when they made love, but she had never been a witness to the act. She had tried not to watch what Tana had done—she had finally closed her eyes against the sight—but the other woman's sexual manipulations had amazed her. She had had no idea . . .

Espri had often heard the village girls insisting that men were essentially the same, so it occurred to her that Mitch might enjoy Tana's lovemaking just as Konga had. There was no doubt in her mind that Tana would be back to look in on Mitch, and she knew that she would not be able to bear it if Tana approached him sexually. Though she tried to dismiss the distressing prospect of Mitch and Tana sharing heated embraces, the threatening thought lingered on.

Looking across the pool to where Tana and Konga lay motionless and seemingly asleep, Espri wished she could somehow escape before they began to make love again. Her emotions were in turmoil due to what she'd observed, and she knew she needed to get away, to get back to Mitch. When a low, scudding cloud briefly obscured the moon's clear light, she decided to chance leaving. She slipped into the pool, the sound of her entry disguised by the splashing of the waterfall. Then she ducked under the water and swam the entire distance to shore beneath the surface. Quickly, she climbed up the bank, and snatching up her rumpled dress and the bucket of water, she disappeared silently into the forest.

Chapter 5

As quickly and as quietly as she could, Espri rushed back toward her home, pausing only once to dress. The sights and sounds of Tana's and Konga's mating were burned into her mind, and no matter how she fought to put them from her, she would never again be truly innocent.

Breathless, she finally reached the glade. Without hesitation, she went to check on Mitch, and she didn't know whether to be disappointed or happy when she found that he had undergone no change. He was seemingly unconscious, and his fever had not abated. Since his skin still felt hot and dry to her touch, she quickly began to bathe him again, soaking her cloth in the cool, fresh water and drawing it in a constant soothing motion over his heated flesh.

With visions of Konga and Tana still fresh in her mind, she couldn't stop herself from remembering what it had felt like when Mitch had touched her, and she wondered what it would have been like had he not stopped. Would she have cried out in pleasure like Tana? Did it actually feel that good to take a man inside your body?

Espri paused in her ministrations to reach out and caress Mitch's chest, letting her fingers rest just over his heart. Then, suddenly conscious of what she was doing, she withdrew that light contact, and for her own peace of mind, she retrieved the light covering and placed it over his hips. Moving to her own mat just a handbreadth away from Mitch, she lay curled on her side, facing him, and tried to rest. Her thoughts reflective, Espri quietly let the tension of the day drain from her. Soon, despite her efforts to stay awake, sleep overtook her.

Her dreams in those predawn hours were filled with confusing, erotic images of Tana and Mitch and herself. At one moment she was sharing a passionate embrace with Mitch; in the next, Tana was in his arms, kissing him and tasting of his desire. The dream was heart wrenching in its power. It taunted her with visions of Tana working her womanly wiles upon Mitch, drawing him to her body and making him her own.

Abruptly awakening, Espri sat up, her heart pounding from the force of some unknown emotion. Glancing quickly at Mitch, she breathed a deep sigh of relief when she noted that he was resting quietly. Tana's and Mitch's lovemaking had just been a very disturbing illusion.

Bewitched by her fantasy, Espri sat staring at him for long, curious minutes. Never before had any of her dreams been so vivid or so arousing, and she couldn't resist touching him, just to make sure that this was reality. Leaning forward, she let her gaze fall upon his lips, so firmly chiseled yet so beautiful and so capable of giving pleasure. She had never thought of a man's mouth in those terms before, but his kiss had done wondrous things to her. It had awakened her to the world of sensuality.

She trailed her hand across his hair-roughened chest and then down his arm, her fingers lingering in silent sympathy over the rope tied securely to his wrist. She longed to free him, to give him at least that much peace, but common sense warned her against doing so. No matter how much it upset her to see him bound, it was better that he be restrained than allowed to injure himself or her unknowingly.

Without conscious thought, she shifted closer and bent slightly to press her lips softly to his, his name escaping her on an anguished sigh.

"Mitch . . ." When there was no answering response to her touch, Espri drew back, embarrassed by her own bold foolishness.

Deciding to keep busy so her mind would not dwell on her dream, she soaked the cloth in the cool water and began, once again, to bathe him. To her dismay, she discovered that this was no longer a mindless job for her. She was more cognizant of him as a man now, and each stroke of the cloth became a caress. Through the balance of the night she cared for him, ceasing only when exhaustion claimed her shortly after daybreak.

Though his eyes were open, Mitch found that he was surrounded by darkness. He lay still, trying to understand exactly what had happened to him. His head was pounding, his mind reeled, and he felt as if he had just suffered the torment of the damned. He wondered where he was and why every inch of him hurt so badly. He tried to move, to shift his position so he would be more comfortable, and it was then he discovered that he was bound, his limbs stretched tautly away from his body, his position immobile and extremely vulnerable.

His thoughts were muddled as he struggled to comprehend his situation. Forcing himself to relax, he took a few deep breaths and then let his mind roam as he attempted to sort through the jumble of impressions his senses were relaying.

Mitch knew immediately that he was not at sea for there was no rocking motion, no telltale creaking of timbers. He frowned as memories of Tommy and the *Seastorm* and Captain Warson's cruelty came to him. He moved his shoulders tentatively, and the tenderness in his back affirmed that, indeed, the flogging he'd suffered had been real. His restraints, too, convinced him that his run-in with Warson over the captain's excessive brutality had also been real. Those long, dark days and nights, in chains, in the damp, disgusting hold, had happened. But this was certainly not the cargo hold of the *Seastorm*. He was on land, of that he had no doubt; yet he was still shackled. Why? What had happened that he couldn't remember?

The storm! In a flash of blinding brilliance, it came to him. Tommy had rescued him from his bonds just in time to save him from certain death. They had been trying to get off the floundering ship when a towering wave had washed them both overboard. But where was he now?

Overcome by his sense of helplessness, Mitch grew despondent. He couldn't move, he couldn't see. For the past six months, ever since he'd been shanghaied and taken aboard the *Seastorm,* his life had been a living hell. Forced to do the work of two men because the crew had been shorthanded, he had suffered the indignities of the sadistic Warson in silence—at least he had until that fateful day when the captain's cruel mistreatment of a cabin boy had driven him over the edge. It seemed to him that he was caught up in the same set of circumstances. Evidently the captain had survived the wreck, and had seen to it that he'd been put in bondage the moment they'd reached shore.

"Oh, my God," Mitch groaned hoarsely as his despair deepened. Then, in an explosion of frustration, he fought his fate. Raging, violent in his need to be free, he used all of his remaining strength to battle against his unseen bonds. In a frenzy of anger, he strained repeatedly at the ropes, until in one last desperate burst of energy he pulled from the ground the stake that had held his right arm pinioned. Panting, his breath rasping painfully in his throat, he quickly reached up to pull off what he thought was a blindfold.

Espri, asleep when she first heard Mitch's voice, low and troubled, thought she was dreaming. Only when he began to move did she realize she was actually awake. Thinking him in the tortured grasp of the fever again and giving no thought to her own safety, she rushed to his side, pleading with him not to remove the wrapping from his head.

"Wait! Mitch! Don't touch your bandage!"

About to throw off the "blindfold," Mitch was unprepared for the sound of a woman's voice and he stopped suddenly. "Bandage?"

"You're better." Espri sighed gratefully, and she touched his arm as she knelt beside him.

Mitch flinched at the contact so she hastened to reassure him.

"I'm sorry if I startled you," she told him earnestly. "It's just that I was surprised to find you awake. You've been ill with the fever for some time now. Here"—Espri hurriedly disentangled the ropes—"let me finish untying you."

"Fever?" Mitch caught the relief in her voice and wondered at it. "What are you talking about? What fever?"

"You were cut by coral when you were in the sea and the wound became infected. That's why you have the bandage."

"Where am I? And who are you?" he demanded, trying to place this woman's intriguing accent. It seemed vaguely familiar to him—almost as if he had heard her voice before.

Smiling widely in her joy at his recovery, she answered him honestly, "My name is Espri Duchant, and we're on the island of Malika."

Mitch was silent. Malika? He'd never heard of it. He wondered just how far off course the vicious cyclone had blown the *Seastorm.*

"I'm glad that you're finally better," she continued as she struggled with the last knot in the rope that bound his left arm. "I'm sorry I had to do this."

"What do you mean?" Mitch asked, stunned to learn that he hadn't been restrained on the orders of Captain Warson.

"I had to tie you down last night. Your fever was high, and

in your delirium, you knocked over one of the candles and started a small fire." She decided not to tell him of his violence toward her. "It was safer for you this way."

Mitch nodded solemnly. "I'm sorry if I've caused you any trouble." His mood was lightened by knowing the reason for his restraint, but the thought of Warson still gave him pause. He asked cautiously, "Was the captain rescued?"

"I'm not sure," she replied, moving to untie the ropes at his ankles. "I do know that another man was washed ashore, but that was on the other side of the island. He's being cared for in the village. I haven't yet learned his name. Would you like me to find out for you?"

"Please." He idly rubbed his chafed wrists and then touched his forehead carefully. "Will I be able to remove this bandage soon?"

"It would be best if you would leave it on one more day. The cut was deep and you'd complained earlier that your vision was blurred."

"I did?" He sounded incredulous.

"That's how I came to know your name—at least your first name."

"My last name is Williams," he said quickly. "I don't remember talking to you before . . . although your voice does sound familiar."

Flushing guiltily, Espri answered, "You were feverish . . . and you thought I was someone else."

"I did? I don't remember." He was mystified by the news. "Who did I think you were?"

"I believe her name was Fifi," Espri replied, grateful that he did not recall the intimacy they'd shared. It had been one thing to imagine, when he'd been ill, his lovemaking being taken to completion, but it was another thing entirely to face him as a rational, healthy male. She was glad that he couldn't see her face and read the confused embarrassment there.

Fifi? The only woman he'd ever known by that name was

Fifi LaRue and it had been a long time since he'd even thought of that delectably wild Frenchwoman who'd worked for Madame Sauvigne at her infamous house of pleasure. Surely, he couldn't have mistaken this gentle, caring woman for Fifi. A flash of a remembered, sensuous embrace played about the corners of his mind, but he quickly dismissed it as ridiculous. The fever must have affected him more than he realized.

"I'm sorry."

"There's no need for you to apologize," Espri told him, and then, unable to stop herself, she asked as casually as possible, "Is Fifi your wife?"

"No, I'm not married. Fifi was just a friend and she was French. It was probably because of your accent that I mistook you for her. Your accent is French, isn't it?"

"Yes, I suppose it is; my father came from France and the missionary who comes to our island is French."

Tired of lying down, Mitch levered himself onto an elbow in an effort to sit up, but a moment of dizziness stopped his progress. Espri hurried to assist him. Bending near, she slipped an arm around his wide shoulders and helped him to an upright position.

Until that instant, Mitch had had no definite impression of Espri as a woman. In his mind, she had seemed ageless—an exotically voiced creature to whom he was grateful for saving him—but when she touched him, pressing close to aid him in his struggle to rise, all that changed. The feel of her bare arm, the thinly clad swell of her firm bosom against his back, sent shock waves of sensual awareness through him, and the delicate scent of her perfume—a combination of tropical wildflowers and coconut oil—lingered on, sweetly tantalizing him. Mitch was glad when she moved away, but he knew a moment of supreme confusion when she reached across his lap and strategically adjusted the lightweight covering.

"How's that? Are you comfortable?" Though she managed to keep her tone coolly efficient, Espri's feelings were anything but cool. Just touching Mitch had filled her with an unexpected longing to be in his embrace . . . to have those powerful arms pull her close, to feel his thighs hard and demanding against her, his mouth exploring hers once more. She moved hastily from him, flustered by the direction of her thoughts.

"Yes, thank you, Miss Duchant," Mitch answered, struggling to maintain a sense of control despite the unwelcome urging of his body.

"Please, call me Espri," she returned quickly.

"Espri . . ."

His voice was deep and gruff and she was spellbound for a moment by its innate sensuality.

"How are you feeling?" she asked, forcing herself to think of other things.

"I know I'm alive." Mitch grinned fleetingly, but Espri could tell that the smile was strained. "There's no way I couldn't be, not the way my head aches right now."

"Would rum help?" Espri offered.

"It certainly couldn't hurt," he admitted wryly.

"I'll be right back."

Mitch listened to the sand-muffled sound of her footsteps as she left the hut, and he wondered at the power of his reaction to her. Through the years he had had more than his share of women, yet none had disturbed him so with just an innocent touch. Was Espri Duchant that different? He pondered the question only briefly before his more rational side asserted itself, then he smiled at the absurdity of his thoughts. Good Lord, he hadn't even seen the woman. Surely, his reaction to her was instinctive and basically the result of all he'd been through. No doubt in this situation any woman would have had the same effect on him. Shifting uncomfortably on the hardness of the pandanus mat, he arranged the cloth more securely about his waist and then sat back to await Espri's return.

* * *

The sun was edging above the horizon, reaching out gold-and pink-streaked tendrils of light to erase the night's black velvet possession of the land. Songbirds, roused by the dawn, soared gracefully through the air, their warbling calls an accompaniment to the sun's long-awaited reappearance.

In the village, Jacques awoke, his head throbbing from the aftereffects of the liquor he'd consumed the night before. Though the hut he was sleeping in did not look familiar, the bottle at his side did. He tilted it to his lips, groaning in dismay to find that he'd consumed every drop the night before. Cursing, he rose to stagger outside in the hope of discovering where he'd passed the night.

Short in stature, her figure plumply rounded, Laiti, a widow for many years, stood in her cooking hut a short distance away. She smiled to herself as she saw Jacques emerge from her home. For a long time she had been hoping to attract his attentions, and last night had provided the perfect opportunity. Drunk as Jacques had been, she'd had no difficulty encouraging him to spend the night with her. She waved a greeting, then watched him frown in confusion as he tried to sort out what had passed between them the night before.

Her greeting was merry as he strode toward her, her expression welcoming. "Good morning, Jacques."

"Is it?" he asked brusquely, still trying to recall exactly how he'd ended up in Laiti's bed.

"After a night of love, the world is always more beautiful." She smiled shyly at him. Laiti had been in love with the silver-haired Frenchman for many years, but only recently had she decided to take matters into her own hands. She knew Jacques had been devastated by Tila's death, but she felt he'd grieved enough. Though she was aware that she would have to be patient if she wanted to win his total devotion, she felt that the time had come to make him aware of her feelings.

At her words, he looked up, shocked.

"A night of love?" he croaked in disbelief.

"It was a beautiful night, Jacques. Thank you." Laiti's black eyes glowed with warmth.

Jacques shifted uncomfortably as his mind raced through the events of the previous evening. He found that he could barely remember the gathering, let alone what had occurred afterward. Had he really spent the night making love with Laiti? The prospect shook him. Since Tila's death, he'd had no interest in women, finding his relief in the bottle instead.

"Please, don't feel uncomfortable," she continued easily, her casual manner successfully hiding her fear that he would quickly leave and never return. "I have cared for you for a long time, Jacques, and I'd always hoped that we could share a closer relationship."

Jacques desperately needed a drink. Had he truly betrayed Tila's memory with Laiti? The thought screamed through his brain, but he fought against acknowledging it.

"And please, don't feel as though you've done something wrong, Jacques," Laiti went on insightfully. "I invited you here. It was my idea." From beneath lowered lids, she watched him as, at her words, his expression grew less wary. Feeling more certain that he wasn't going to bolt from her presence, she gestured to the platter of hot, appetizing food she'd just prepared. "Will you join me for breakfast?"

Bewildered by the situation he found himself in, Jacques nodded in assent. "Yes, thanks."

Jacques's manner was reserved as he sat down beside Laiti to share the delicious meal. He felt a great need for a drink, but he also wanted to know more about the past night. Guilt lurked in the back of his mind, but Laiti's constant, interesting chatter held it at bay as they breakfasted. Soon, to his surprise, he found that the meal was over, and he admitted to himself that the time had passed pleasantly. Knowing that he had to find out exactly what had transpired between them, he was about to broach the subject when he heard someone approach and looked up to see Konga drawing near.

"I had heard that you'd remained all night in the village, Duchant," Konga stated matter-of-factly, ignoring Jacques's sudden look of acute discomfort. "I am glad you are still here."

"Oh?" Jacques lifted an eyebrow as he regarded the rich young islander.

"It is time that I spoke with you. Leave us, woman," Konga ordered.

Laiti glanced from one man to the other, wondering what business Konga had with Jacques, before she moved discreetly away.

Getting to his feet, Jacques followed Konga to the edge of the forest, some distance away. When the younger man was certain that they were alone, he came straight to the point.

"I am ready to marry, and I want Espri for my wife," he stated bluntly.

Having known of the warrior's interest in Espri, Jacques was not surprised by the statement, and he nodded his understanding. "You are a fine man, Konga. Have you spoken of your desire to Espri?"

Konga answered flatly, "I have spoken to her."

"And?"

"And she says that she is unwilling to marry now."

Jacques considered the situation thoughtfully. He was well aware that Konga was rich and brave, and that many of the island maidens were in love with him. The man would make any woman a fine husband, and he would no doubt father many strong sons.

"I have no objection to your marrying Espri."

"That is good." Konga's expression grew smug now that he was sure Jacques would offer no resistance to his plan to claim Espri. "Your daughter is a prize beyond compare." His dark eyes gleamed in hungry anticipation.

"Indeed, she is," Jacques agreed. "And I would see her treated as such."

"I will cherish her as no other," the young man answered. "She will be Konga's woman."

As he watched the warrior stride away, Jacques wondered just how Konga could be so confident that he would win Espri when she had told him plainly that she had no interest in marrying. Shaking his head in confusion, he moved to rejoin Laiti.

"You have finished your discussion with Konga?"

"Yes. What he had to say did not take long," Jacques informed her.

"There is trouble between you?"

"No. He only wanted to know if I would approve of a marriage between him and Espri."

"And what did you tell him?"

"I told him that I had no objection. He is young and wealthy. She could do much worse." Jacques shrugged.

"I am not so sure," Laiti remarked under her breath.

"What do you mean?"

"While it is true that Konga is a powerful man, I have always felt that you can judge a man's heart by the way he deals with those who serve him."

"And?"

"And his servants are treated cruelly. He is a hard taskmaster, Jacques, and I feel he would treat his wife with disdain."

Not wanting to concern himself, Duchant dismissed her opinion. "It is not my concern. Whether she marries him or not is entirely up to Espri. It will be her decision. I only told Konga that I had no objection to their marriage. I did not agree to help him."

Laiti fell silent. The pleasant interlude that they had shared during breakfast was over, and they now stood awkwardly before each other, not quite sure what to say or do.

"I must go," Jacques finally declared, wanting to put an end to the stilted moment.

Laiti voiced her concern. "Will you be back?"

"I don't know," Jacques answered honestly.

She nodded wisely, accurately reading his thoughts. "I will be here, Jacques. And know that I will always be glad to see you."

Their eyes met for a moment, hers revealing her love for him and his reflecting his own deep uncertainty, before he hurried away.

The cup of rum had really helped. Mitch could almost feel the sharp edge of his pain dulling beneath the liquor's soothing onslaught. A slight sigh escaped him, and for the first time in months, he knew a moment of real peace.

Espri, ever sensitive to his well-being, heard his sigh and feared that something was wrong. "Are you all right?"

Mitch was startled to find that he'd attracted her attention. "I'm better than I've been in a long time."

Espri smiled at his words. "I'm glad. Last night I didn't know whether you were going to make it or not. Do you feel like eating something? It might help you get your strength back."

"Yes, I think so. Thank you."

She started to go to the cooking hut to prepare some food, but it occurred to her that he might enjoy sitting in the sun for a while.

"Would you like to sit outside? The day is still young and the heat is not yet intense."

The long days in the damp hold had left Mitch with a distinct aversion to the dark, and he was eager to feel the warmth of the sun again. He quickly agreed to her suggestion and was starting to get up, when the sudden drop of the blanket effectively halted his actions.

"Do you have my pants?"

"No, I'm sorry. They were all but ripped off while you were in the sea, but I can fashion you a pareu, of sorts, if you'd be more comfortable in one."

"Please."

"You'll have to stand so I can secure the cloth about your hips," Espri instructed as she came to him and grasped his arm in order to help him to his feet. Though she had known Mitch was tall, his upright male presence was overpowering her. As a quiver of excitement raced through her veins, she scolded herself for her reaction to his nearness, and she attempted to keep her touch impersonal. Trying to ignore the feel of the firm muscles rippling beneath her hands, she efficiently adjusted the cloth about him and, taking great care to avoid intimate contact, knotted the material over his hip.

In spite of Mitch's efforts to ignore her closeness, the slight press of her body to his as she fixed the material about his waist had an electrifying effect on him. He wanted to move away from her as quickly as he could before his body betrayed his desires, but a brief moment of vertigo forced him to hold onto her for support and his good intentions were undermined. He knew it was foolish to desire a woman he'd never seen, but he couldn't help himself. He bent to her, whispering her name in a hushed plea.

"Espri . . ." His lips found hers with unerring accuracy, brushing them softly in a tentative caress which became more urgent.

Espri was taken by surprise, but after a stunned instant of immobility, she responded fully, knowing that this was what she'd been wanting, what she'd been waiting for, ever since he'd touched her, thinking she was Fifi, the day before. Looping her arms about his neck, she strained nearer, needing to feel again the hardness of his manly form. When his mouth slanted demandingly across hers, a flush of heat flowed through her, sending her senses soaring. The burning hunger within her became uncontrollable, and she began to move restlessly against him, seeking some unknown, yet exciting, resolution to these feelings he'd aroused in her.

The sweetness of her scent enveloped Mitch, and he was lost in the rapture of their kiss. When she started to stir in his arms, he lost all semblance of restraint. His hands, which had gripped her for support, now moved with deliberate care down over the silken expanse of her shoulders, coming to rest at her hips and pressing her more tightly to him. Then his mouth left hers to seek out the softness of her throat, to find that place where her pulse fluttered in frantic rhythm.

The touch of his heated mouth sent shock waves of pleasure through Espri, and her breasts swelled with desire, their peaks tautening in invitation. Only vaguely did she realize that the low moan she heard was her own, and when his lips returned to hers she sighed in breathless ecstasy.

Espri's will was dissolving in the power of Mitch's embrace, but the distant sound of her father calling out to her stopped her runaway emotions. Stiffening, she pulled back from Mitch's kiss, suddenly conscious of what she'd been about. Her color heightened by the force of her desire, Espri tried to break away from the possessive encirclement of his arms, but Mitch refused to release her.

"Please . . . you don't understand . . . I must go." Her words came out in a rush, and she was relieved when he set her free.

"Espri?" Mitch was puzzled by the change in her.

"Wait here," she told him quickly as she hurried outside to greet her father.

"Espri!" Jacques's voice was louder now.

"Espri, what is it?" Mitch called out. He wanted to know why she was so nervous, why she responded so quickly to this man's call.

It occurred to him that this man must be her husband, and the thought rankled. Mitch wanted to deny that possibility, but judging from Espri's fear of being found in his arms, he knew it must be true. Anger flared. Women are all alike, he said to himself. Not one is satisfied with just one man.

Disgusted, he resented having been aroused by Espri, and he cursed the temporary sightlessness that put him at a disadvantage. He should have been more cautious. He should have realized that she was probably just as treacherous as all the other women he'd ever known.

Espri heard Mitch call out to her, but needing time to compose herself before she faced her father, she did not respond. Taking a moment to calm down, she clasped her trembling hands together in an attempt to regain control of her runaway heart; then she hurried toward the path.

"Espri!" Jacques emerged from the forest.

"Good morning, Papa!" She forced a smile as he stepped into the clearing.

"How are you this morning? Did everything go all right? How is the white man?" he asked quickly.

"Mitch's fever is gone," she confided, relieved to find her father completely sober.

"Mitch, is it?"

"Yes. Mitch Williams. It was a long night, but I think he's going to be fine now. He's awake if you'd like to speak with him," Espri offered.

"I'd like that very much. How is his head wound?"

"The bandage is still on and he was having some pain when he first awoke, but I gave him some of your rum to ease the discomfort."

Jacques nodded his approval. "Did it help?"

"I think so. He's looking much better."

"Good." Stepping into the hut ahead of her, he addressed Mitch. "Espri tells me, *monsieur,* that at last you have decided to rejoin the living." Jacques's deeply accented voice was tinged with seeming good humor. "My name is Jacques Duchant and yours, I understand, is Mitch Williams?"

"Yes, sir. I'm Mitchell Williams." Mitch extended his hand in the general direction of Jacques's voice.

Jacques shook it, and then sat down on Espri's mat while she hovered nearby. "Espri, prepare food and drinks. I'm sure Mitch could use something substantial after his long bout with the fever."

"I was about to do that when I heard you call. I'll be right back." Espri had noticed a certain tenseness in Mitch when he'd shaken hands with her father, and she wondered about that as she left to prepare the meal.

When Espri had gone, Jacques turned his attention back to Mitch.

"I'm glad to find that you're recovering," he told him. His original concern about this man being around his daughter had not lessened, and he would be relieved when Mitch was gone from their lives.

"I thank you for all your kindness. I'm sure I wouldn't have made it without your help." Mitch's words were spoken smoothly, and they revealed none of his rancor over Espri's betrayal.

Jacques was pensive as he considered Mitch. Though Mitch seemed articulate enough, he still bore the marks of the lash, and they didn't lie.

"How did you come to be washed ashore here?" he ventured.

"I was aboard the *Seastorm* out of San Francisco. We were caught in the storm and started taking on water. The seas were rougher than any I'd ever seen, and I was washed overboard while trying to get to a longboat." He paused a moment to dwell on the memory of that fateful day. "Espri mentioned that another man was washed ashore and is being tended in the village. Do you know anything about him?"

"I spoke with Anuitua, the woman who is caring for him, early yesterday and she said that the man is young and has blond hair."

"My friend Tommy fits that description. He was washed overboard at the same time I was."

"Well, you'll be glad to know that he is better too. Last night at the gathering, Kohea, Anuitua's husband, said that the man had regained consciousness and was doing well."

"Can you take me to him?"

"In a day or so, when you're feeling stronger. It is some distance to the village," Jacques explained. Then he asked, "How many men were there in your crew?"

"There were over twenty others, but they had managed to get off the *Seastorm* before we did." Mitch's thoughts darkened as he remembered the fury of the ocean and the long desperate hours he'd spent clinging to the wreckage of the demolished ship.

"I haven't heard of any other survivors. The rest of your crew was probably lost, although there is a slim chance that some of them made it to a neighboring island."

"I'm not familiar with Malika or its location. Is it part of a chain?" Mitch was suddenly anxious to learn all he could about the island.

"Not many people know of our existence," Jacques answered. "We're part of a small island group southwest of Tahiti."

Mitch nodded. "I take it from your statement you don't get many trading vessels here."

"Very few," Duchant replied. "I take it you're anxious to return home as quickly as possible?"

"Yes," Mitch answered quickly. "I've been away too long." Thinking of San Francisco and of his home lifted his spirits considerably, and he smiled at the realization that he might soon be on his way back.

Jacques was briefly puzzled by his answer. Surely, this man had known when he'd signed on for the voyage that he'd be at sea for an extended period of time. He was about to question his remark, when Espri returned.

"The food is ready," she announced. "I thought Mitch might want to eat in the dining hut. It's more open there, and sunny."

"I would, thank you," Mitch replied with cool precision.

Hearing the difference in his tone and wondering at it, Espri started forward.

"Let me help you," she said. She took Mitch's arm, and though it was totally innocent, the simple contact sent a thrill of excitement through her. Espri frowned. She had never felt this strong an attraction to a man before; and the force of it was disturbing. In the past, when she had heard the village women talk of their passion for the men they loved, their words had had no meaning for her. Now she realized this feeling was what they'd meant—this all-encompassing desire to touch and be touched.

Fear froze her heart and she glanced surreptitiously at Mitch, studying his dark, handsome features. Was she beginning to fall in love with him? No! She would not love Mitch, nor any man. Girding her emotions against such foolhardiness, she struggled to maintain her calm demeanor as she efficiently guided him outside.

The warmth of the sun was a joyous caress to Mitch as he stepped out of the hut, but even its enticing heat could not distract his thoughts from the woman who was walking beside him, guiding him to their destination. The sweet fragrance of her perfume teased his senses, and he was annoyed at his inability to casually dismiss the memory of her embrace. Though her kisses had affected him as no other woman's had, she was Jacques's wife. While he hadn't been a saint or a celibate all these years, he most certainly did not sleep with married women. The very idea repulsed him. With great effort, he forced all thoughts of how pleasurable it had been to have her in his arms from his mind and hardened his heart against her. Espri had nursed him and he was thankful for that, but he knew he would have to make sure that nothing ever came of the powerful attraction that existed between them. He was relieved when he was settled in the dining hut and Espri released her hold on his arm. He relaxed and enjoyed the meal, conversing easily with Jacques and making some plans for a trip to the village to meet the man he hoped was Tommy.

Chapter 6

It was midafternoon, a quiet time when the oppressive heat of the day slowed the pace of life on Malika. Deep within the heart of the island, secluded in a glade shaded by massive ironwood trees, was the impressive home of the *taupau*, the sacred virgin of the tribe. The *taupau*, a young woman named Tikiru, lived in this place of honor far from the village, for her lofty position forbade her from having casual contact with the islanders.

Her hut was a mansion by Malikan standards. It rested on a raised stone platform and had broad, airy verandas at the front and the back. On the front veranda, Tikiru now reclined while her servant Nelani artfully arranged her hair.

Chosen at birth for her position, Tikiru had been denied nothing during her sixteen years of life save intimacy with man. She was the vestal virgin, the chaste sacrifice to the gods, and as such she was given preferential treatment over all. She wore no clothing as she rendered herself to her handmaiden's attentions, enjoying the faint caress of the warm, gentle breeze on her smooth, untouched flesh. Her skin was golden, her features perfect, her breasts small yet inviting.

Nelani, her slave, stood behind her concentrating on the task of styling Tikiru's freshly washed hair. She, too, had been chosen at birth, but it was her lot to serve the *taupau* and keep her happy. Her earliest memories were involved with that pursuit. By virtue of her profession, she, too, was to remain celibate, forsaking the pleasures of the flesh for the honor of serving in the temple.

"I do not believe you." Tikiru glanced up suspiciously at her servant.

"It is true, Tikiru," Nelani insisted. "I have seen him myself."

"You have seen a man with hair as golden as the sun?" Tikiru frowned at the news.

Nelani nodded, her manner at once serious and excited for the man was the most handsome one she'd ever seen.

"He was pulled from the sea yesterday and is staying with Anuitua."

Tikiru was intrigued.

"Tell me about him," she commanded, and her servant hastened to reply.

"I did not speak to him. He had not yet recovered from his time in the sea, but he was young and very handsome."

"I would like to know more about him. You will go back to the village and find out for me."

"But why?" Nelani was confused by her mistress's sudden interest in a man. Never before had any male attracted her attention.

Tikiru glared at her. "It is not your place to question me! Go! And do not come back until you can tell me everything about him."

"Your hair?"

"It is fine for now."

Nelani knew better than to arouse her mistress's ire. Many times she had been whipped for something that Tikiru had considered an offense.

"I will go," she acceded, and immediately left on her quest to discover more about the stranger who was saved from the sea.

* * *

Tommy O'Ryan sat in the comfort of Anuitua's home, believing himself to be the luckiest man alive. Somehow, the fates had decreed that he be washed ashore on this beautiful tropical island, and here he was, in almost perfect health, being waited on by friendly natives who couldn't do enough to please him. His clothing had been torn from him during the long hours he'd spent in the sea so he wore only a pareu that had been given to him by Kohea, husband to Anuitua.

Alone for the first time since his rescue, Tommy sat quietly, drinking fresh water from a cup fashioned from a coconut shell. As happy as he was over his own narrow escape from death during the storm, his thoughts were drawn to Mitch and he felt an overwhelming sense of loss. The man who'd helped him so much during the torturous months at sea under Captain Warson was no doubt dead.

His heart heavy, Tommy remembered how Mitch had stood up to the brutal captain, and he was glad that he'd been brave enough to free him from the hold before the ship had been destroyed. At least, Mitch had had a fighting chance to survive. That was all anyone could ask for.

Nelani made the trip to the village as quickly as possible. She found Tikiru's interest in this man baffling. Furthermore, it worried her. The high priests did everything they could to keep Tikiru isolated, and it would not bode well for her mistress should they learn that she was becoming interested in men. That was *tapu!*

Though she often came to the village, Nelani took great care not to attract undue notice as she tried to learn more about the survivor. Little could be gleaned, however, from the idle chatter of the women. Frustrated, she realized that she would have to go directly to Anuitua, and she approached the other woman with considerable trepidation.

"Nelani! What a surprise to see you here!"

Anuitua's easy greeting eased Nelani's nervousness.

"I have come on an errand for Tikiru. She wanted to know how the man you rescued is doing." Her words were not false.

"He is doing well," Anuitua told her proudly, pleased with her own part in saving him.

"That is good news."

"Had you heard about the other man?"

"No. There was another?"

"Yes, on the far side of the island. Espri and Jacques found him, but I believe he is more seriously injured than Tommy."

"Tommy?"

"That is his name, Tommy O'Ryan. He just left with Luatu's man, Ka, to go and see this other man who was rescued."

"Oh." Nelani tried not to let her disappointment at having missed the stranger show. "I must go now. I will see you soon, Anuitua."

Instead of following the track back to Tikiru, she skirted the village and raced through the low, dense growth in an effort to catch up with Ka and this Tommy. Luckily, the men's progress had been slow, for Tommy had not fully recovered his strength, and Nelani was able to locate them after a short search. Keeping herself hidden by foliage, she watched as Ka helped the young man traverse the slightly difficult forest path.

Her first impression of Tommy had been correct, Nelani thought. He was tall and slim, and his blond hair glistened in the sunlight like molten gold. He was unlike any man she'd ever seen before. She remained unmoving until they had passed from sight; then she started back to tell Tikiru all that she'd seen and heard.

* * *

Mitch lay on the pandanus mat in the hut, trying to rest, but sleep would not come. Time and again, he recalled the illicit kiss he'd shared with Espri, and desire, unbidden, flared. He swore violently under his breath as his thoughts wandered to what might have happened had their kiss not been interrupted.

Suddenly sitting up, Mitch banished his imaginings, and with a nervous gesture, he raked his hand through his thick, dark hair. Despite his determination to resist his attraction to Espri, he could not deny that what he felt for her was strong—almost overpowering. The meal they'd shared had been an exercise in self-control, for she had sat close beside him, helping him with his food and brushing ever so casually against him while he had tried to carry on an intelligent conversation with her husband.

Cynically, Mitch reasoned that Espri was probably very aware of his desire for her and that was why she'd been carrying on as she had. And, though he had heard all the sailors' tales of just how wanton the island women were, he could not forget that she was married. Contempt for her flooded through him, successfully killing the ardor his more erotic thoughts had evoked. He would leave Jacques's home as soon as possible, thereby removing himself from temptation. When the bandage came off in the morning, he decided, he would go to the village and be free of Espri's sensuous presence.

"Jacques!" Ka, servant to Luatu, called out to the old Frenchman sitting contentedly in the dining hut, drinking from a bottle of rum.

"Ka, it is good to see you!" Jacques slowly rose to his feet as Luatu's man approached, accompanied by an unknown white man. "There's no trouble in the village, is there?" he asked quickly, wondering at the visit.

"No. All is well. I have come because Chief Luatu asked that I bring O'Ryan here to see the man you rescued."

"You must be Anuitua's man?" Jacques turned to Tommy.

"I'm Tommy O'Ryan, sir." Tommy was surprised to find a white man in residence on the island.

"Jacques Duchant. I'm glad to see that you're better."

"Thank you. I was very lucky. From what I've been told, the man you saved was the only other survivor of the *Seastorm*'s sinking."

"It seems that way." Jacques nodded.

"Has he improved?" Tommy asked hurriedly.

"Mitch is going to be fine."

"Mitch!" Tommy's excitement was undeniable. "Mitch is the man who's here with you?"

"Why, yes . . . he's—"

Having heard the sound of voices outside, Mitch got to his feet and gropingly made his way to the door.

"Mitch!" Tommy caught sight of his friend and ran straight to him. "Thank God, you're the one!"

The two men embraced heartily before Tommy asked with sudden concern, "What happened to your eyes?"

"It's not my eyes so much as the cut on my forehead, but Jacques and Espri have assured me that I will have this off tomorrow." He put a tentative hand on his carefully swathed brow.

"Good."

"Come, let us sit and have some refreshment," Jacques offered, motioning toward the shade of the nearby iron-wood trees.

Taking Mitch's arm, Tommy led him in the direction Jacques indicated, and they sat in the cooling shadows some distance from the hut while Jacques went for a bottle of rum.

"Where is Espri?" Ka asked when Jacques returned with the liquor.

"She has gone to fetch water, but she should be returning soon."

"She is a lovely woman. The envy of many," Ka remarked, and Mitch sensed possessive pride in Jacques's terse answer.

"Yes. She is."

Nelani was nearly breathless when she reached the hut, and she was dismayed to find that Tikiru was not there. Taking the path that led to their own private freshwater pool, she found her mistress sitting on the bank, nude, staring at her own reflection.

"Do you think me beautiful, Nelani?" Tikiru asked, not taking her eyes from her reflection in the still waters.

"Oh, yes, Tikiru. Very. Your beauty is honored by all," her servant acknowledged.

"And my body?"

"Is perfect." Nelani was puzzled by the questions. "I do not understand why you ask me these things."

"It is not important that you understand," Tikiru declared arrogantly.

Suitably humbled, Nelani waited silently for her mistress to speak.

"What did you discover?" Tikiru finally asked as she stood up.

"The man's name is Tommy O'Ryan."

"Tommy . . ." She smiled as she spoke his name. "What else?"

"He is healthy now. I saw him walking with Ka. He is handsome for a white man." Nelani felt her heartbeat quicken. "Tall and slim and his hair is like no other—"

"He is staying with Anuitua?"

"For now."

Tikiru smiled, her dark eyes alight with some inner excitement. "You may go."

Recognizing that her mistress was planning something, Nelani knew it was her duty to speak up. "Tikiru, you must not see this man. You must not have anything to do with him!"

Tikiru became indignant. "I do not need your advice, Nelani!"

"But—"

With all her strength, Tikiru slapped Nelani across the face, and she watched with pleasure as the girl's lip began to bleed profusely. "Do not ever tell *me* what to do! You are my slave! Now, be gone!"

Cowed by her mistress's vicious temper, Nelani fled the pool.

Tikiru shrugged indifferently as the young woman disappeared into the forest. *Nelani is a fool*, she thought. Smiling confidently, she stretched languidly and ran her hands over her body. She didn't understand exactly what was happening to her of late, but she had become restless and she was bored. True, as *taupau*, she wanted for nothing. She was pampered and spoiled, perfumed and bathed, but there was an unnamed yearning deep within her. It was making her desperate for . . . for what?

Tikiru didn't know exactly what she needed. Her unrest seemed to have begun when she'd presided over the fertility rites. She had had a vision that night. She had seen the image of a man, a man formed in gold. During the trance she'd seen him joining with a dark-haired woman, and a great emotion had swept through her, rendering her weak with an unknown longing. Then that emotion had been overpowered by a terrible sense of dread. The mystical dream had left her shaken, and now, Nelani's news of a white man with hair the color of the sun both excited and frightened her. Had the vision been a warning? Was he there to harm her or to help her?

Knowing that she could not rest until she had seen him, Tikiru began to make plans to enter the village that night, incognito. She had never made the attempt before, having always been content to follow the priests' dictates to stay aloof from the everyday life of the island, but she knew now that she must go. She had to know the true meaning of her dream.

Espri was surprised to find that they had visitors when she returned to the glade, and she was glad that she'd taken a few extra minutes to freshen up while at the pool. She had not dallied there long, though; for the memory of Tana and Konga entwined in the throes of passion had besieged her, causing her to wonder at the joy to be found in that most intimate embrace.

She did not doubt that making love with Mitch would be exciting—just being near him made her senses reel—but she felt she could not allow herself to become too involved. Attractive though he might be, he was a force to be reckoned with—a threat to her well-being—and she could not risk losing her heart to him. Still, she wanted him. She could not deny it. He'd created a firestorm of feeling within her, and his touch left her weak willed and craving more.

Observing Mitch now, as he sat with her father and the other two men, she admired again his fine masculine figure. Tall and broad-shouldered, he exuded a potent maleness, and she was certain that no village maiden would refuse him should he decide to take her to his bed. To distract herself, Espri concentrated on welcoming their guests, hurrying forward to greet them.

Mitch sensed rather than heard her return to the glade, and when Jacques called out for her to join them, he tensed.

"Espri, this is Tommy O'Ryan. The man who was rescued near the village. He is staying with Anuitua."

"So you are Mitch's friend." Espri was genuinely pleased.

Tommy gazed up at Espri, captivated by her beauty. He cast a quick glance in Mitch's direction and wondered if his friend had any idea how lucky he was to be staying here with such a lovely woman. But Mitch's expression seemed suddenly grim, and when Espri sat down at his side, Tommy could have sworn that he looked almost pained. Handing his friend the bottle of rum, he watched curiously as Mitch took a deep drink.

Espri, too, noticed Mitch's strained look.

"Has your pain worsened?" she asked.

"No, it's the same," Mitch responded, trying to keep the curtness out of his voice. *Why had she sat down next to him?* He groaned mentally. It was bad enough that when she was near he was aware of her with every fiber of his being, but to have her within reach and not be able to take her into his arms again . . .

Jacques, also, wondered why Espri had chosen to sit by Mitch, and as he watched the interplay between the two, he became concerned. It would not do for her to become enamored of this man. He was just a common sailor, and he had already expressed his desire to get off the island as quickly as possible. There would be no future for Espri with him. It would be better if she gave her heart to one of the island men—Konga, for example. Deciding to speak with her on the matter as soon as they were alone, he turned his attention back to the conversation.

"When this bandage comes off," Mitch was saying to Tommy, "I'd like to join you in the village."

"I'm sure we can arrange something," Tommy agreed, pleased at the thought of their being together.

Espri knew she shouldn't care, but Mitch's words pierced her heart and she agonized over them. Giving him a sidelong glance, she let her eyes linger only briefly on the broad, muscular plane of his chest before dragging her gaze away. He was so eager to leave . . . it was just as Tana had said it would be. He would go and stay with Tommy—and Tana. Somehow the thought of him being near the insatiable Tana filled her with conflicting emotions, and she didn't know how to deal with them. Was her heart telling her that she wanted him? Espri quickly denied this possibility. She would let Mitch go, and she would not miss him.

Happy to hear that Mitch was eager to go to the village, Jacques cast a quick look at Espri, and noting nothing different in her expression, he thought possibly he'd imagined her interest in the man. Just to be sure, though, he would talk with her about Mitch.

Ka soon suggested he and Tommy begin their trek back so they could make the village before nightfall. Leaving Tommy alone with his friend for a minute, he started off across the clearing with Jacques and Espri.

"Mitch," Tommy began earnestly, "I can't tell you how glad I am that it was you. Are you sure that you'll be coming to the village tomorrow?"

"As soon as I get this bandage off."

"Good, although you may change your mind once you do," Tommy remarked, his eyes following Espri.

"Why do you say that?" Mitch frowned.

"Believe me, once you see her, I don't know whether you'll want to leave Espri. She is gorgeous and obviously she cares about you—I mean she didn't leave your side all afternoon." Tommy sounded more than a little envious of his friend's good fortune.

The news that Espri was truly beautiful disturbed Mitch. While she'd been beside him during the visit, he'd imagined her as young but unattractive in order to remain indifferent to her nearness, but now . . . "You say she's gorgeous?"

"Absolutely." Tommy was enthusiastic. "Anuitua has a good-looking daughter named Tana, but she doesn't hold a candle to Espri. Are you sure you want to leave?"

"Positive," Mitch answered stonily.

"Well, maybe you'll change your mind once you see her."

"Don't count on me changing my mind."

Tommy was curious about Mitch's attitude, but he didn't

question him. "Ka is waiting for me now. I'd better go. I'll see you tomorrow?"

"Tomorrow."

Not wanting to be in close contact with Espri, Mitch pleaded exhaustion and retired to the hut shortly after Ka and Tommy had gone, leaving Jacques and Espri alone. After building their nightly fire, father and daughter sat before it, enjoying its welcoming brightness as darkness claimed the land. Finally Jacques tossed aside the now-empty rum bottle and, much to Espri's dismay, retrieved a container of kava.

"Papa, do you really need more?"

"Yes, *chérie,* I do," he answered firmly.

"But why?" she protested, though she knew doing so was futile.

"Because I want it." Jacques's voice hardened, and he took a drink of the highly potent liquor. He'd been thinking, not only about Espri and the possibility that she might be coming to care for Mitch, but also about his time with Laiti. The guilt he'd felt earlier in the day had not lessened.

Annoyed, Espri turned away, looking quickly in the direction of the hut.

"He's not the man for you, Espri," Jacques said coldly.

"What do you mean?" She was truly surprised by his words.

"Do you think I do not see? Never before have you ever shown this kind of interest in a man."

"I'm not interested in Mitch," she said, wanting to believe that herself.

"Then that is good." Not sure whether to believe her or not, he took a deep swallow of the kava. "He is a white man and you know nothing about dealing with them. You are an innocent."

"You're a white man," Espri remarked thoughtfully. "Is he so different from you?"

"He is an ordinary sailor, *chérie*. He plans to leave here as soon as he can, and he will not look back once he's gone. It is far better that you do not become attached to him."

While Espri listened to her father, consciously acknowledging that he was probably right, a part of her fought against the harshness of his words. "That is probably true. At any rate, he is planning on moving to the village tomorrow."

"That is good." Jacques nodded, satisfied.

"I suppose," Espri murmured, and then, feeling restless, she stood. "I think I'll go for a walk."

"Be careful, *ma petite*. The night is not always gentle," her father murmured thoughtfully as he watched her walk away.

Chapter 7

The moon cast its silvery beams across the solitary island, bathing it in gentle, glowing light, while stars spangled the sky in a surreal dusting of twinkling brightness. A faint, night-cooled zephyr floated across the land, carrying on its gossamer wings the heady scent of the tropical flowers.

The hour was late when two figures clad in voluminous cloaks crept through the outskirts of the village. Pausing often, they moved stealthily toward Anuitua's hut.

"Which hut is he in?" Tikiru whispered to Nelani.

"It's that one, but you must not do this. What if someone sees you?"

"No one will see me," Tikiru declared. "Who else would be in the hut?"

"Kohea, Anuitua, and their daughter Tana."

Tikiru nodded. "I will be careful. Wait here."

Wrapping the concealing cloak more tightly about her, she edged forward, taking care to stay as far out of the light of the night fires as she could. Undetected, she finally reached the open doorway to Anuitua's home and looked inside.

The single room of the hut was divided into three sleeping sections, each sheltered from the other by the hanging partitions commonly used by the islanders to provide a modicum of privacy. To one side, she could see Anuitua and her husband fast asleep in one another's arms. Tana, their daughter, was sleeping in the area at the center. But besides noticing their locations and how deeply they were sleeping, she paid them little attention. She was here to see her golden man. The gods had predicted this; they would protect her.

Though the divider at the far side barred the last area from her view, she stepped boldly inside, feeling certain that the man was there. Silently, her encroachment unnoticed by the resting family, Tikiru walked past Tana and then disappeared behind the partition.

A shiver of illicit excitement surged down Tikiru's spine as she saw Tommy for the first time. Though there was little light, she could make out his sleeping form, and she moved to his side, trying desperately to see the features that had haunted her since the night of her vision.

Kneeling, wanting so much to touch him, she held herself back. She could make no mistake. To touch him would awaken him, and she could not take the risk that he might speak out and rouse the others. No. Tonight, she would just look at him and commit to memory the beauty of his features, the yellow gold of his hair. Her golden man. Tikiru stayed by Tommy for some time before finally rising to go.

Tommy had been sleeping deeply thanks to the inordinate amount of rum he'd consumed that afternoon with Mitch and the others, and he didn't, at first, understand what had awakened him until he opened his eyes and gazed up at the ephemeral creature hovering above him. She was smaller and infinitely more delicate than any woman he'd yet seen on the island. He knew it wasn't Anuitua or Tana, but he couldn't see her face. He wondered if this was a woman or a ghost. Following his instincts, he sat up quickly and reached out, snaring her arm. He knew then that she was no fantasy, but who was she? And why had she come in the middle of the night? He drew her nearer, and she dropped to her knees by his side.

"Who are you and what do you want?" he asked in a hushed whisper.

Tikiru knew a moment of complete panic. She had never meant this to happen.

"You must release me. I must go." Her whisper was melodic, naturally seductive, and Tommy immediately fell under the spell of his night visitor.

"But why? I will not hurt you." He did not want to let her go.

"I cannot stay here." She emphasized the words. "Release me now and I will meet you . . . tomorrow." Desperate to flee, she would have promised anything to escape his potent presence.

"At dawn?" Tommy pressed her for an answer.

"No. At midnight, when the moon tops the trees." She was struggling slightly against his grip. "But you must tell no one."

Tommy, still in a bit of a liquor-induced haze, nodded his agreement. "Where?"

"At the edge of the beach near the cove."

"Cove?"

"It is north of the village. Please . . ."

Unable to resist, Tommy pulled her to him and kissed her full on the lips, seeing for the first time in the night's dusky cover the loveliness of her face. The touch of his mouth on hers, forbidden by ancient law, sent a shaft of intense pleasure through her. Was this the emotion she'd felt in her vision?

"You are beautiful," he told her huskily when the kiss had ended. "Do you have a name?"

"Nelani . . . I am Nelani," she lied, shaken to the core of her being by his embrace, and when he released her, she fled the hut without being detected.

Tommy started to go after her, but he stopped when he realized his actions would only awaken the others. Confused yet bewitched, he shook his head in disbelief. Who was this

Nelani that she had to come to him so secretly? He'd met
most of the islanders, yet he'd never seen her before. Where
had she come from, and how had she known about him? He'd
found her kiss unbearably exciting, and as he lay back, he was
lost in anticipation of their rendezvous the following night.

Espri sat on the beach, staring out across the moon-kissed
sea. She was not anxious to return to her home, so she had
lingered there for some time, hoping that the peace of the
night would ease the conflict within her. But, to her dismay,
she found that the silence and the solitude only intensified her
feelings, leaving her all the more perplexed.

Mitch . . . why did he affect her so? She knew many men
from the village, had even been kissed by a few, but none had
ever ignited such passions within her. As she thought of the
embraces they'd shared, first when he'd thought she was Fifi
and then just before her father had returned home, a flame of
excitement kindled.

Needing to escape the heated intensity of her wayward
thoughts, she stood and ran to the water's edge, stripping off
her sarong as she went. With abandon, she cast the garment
aside and raced into the billowing surf, hoping that an ex-
hausting swim would help to clear her mind and relieve the
unwanted desire coursing through her body.

She was here! Konga could not believe his luck as he
watched Espri dive, nude, into the oncoming wave. He had
known that Espri sometimes went for a late-night swim and
he had decided to come to the beach on the chance that he
might run into her. With undisguised excitement, he threw off
his pareu and dashed into the water after her.

The sea was tranquil, distinctly at odds with Espri's turbu-
lent emotions, and she welcomed its warm caress as she
swam steadily away from the beach, unaware of Konga's pursuit. Beyond the pull of the incoming surf, she paused to

catch her breath, rolling onto her back to float motionlessly for a moment in the ocean's cradling embrace.

Konga was a powerful swimmer, and he had no difficulty catching up with Espri. The roar of the outbreakers hid the sound of his approach, and when she stopped swimming to rest, he also hesitated, enjoying the sight of her sleek body, etched in silver by the moon's pale luster, drifting on the night-blackened sea.

He had never seen Espri unclothed before. His eyes swept over her, settling on the gentle thrust of her breasts and the dark, inviting juncture of her thighs. She was beautiful, and he was certain that she would be his.

No longer able to restrain himself, Konga silently slipped beneath the surface, his strong strokes quickly bringing him beneath her.

The change in the current directly below her alerted Espri to his presence, and she knew a moment of fear as she considered the creature that was circling her in the inky depths. The possibility that it was a shark was terrifying, but, fighting down the urge to panic and strike out for shore, Espri slowly reversed her position and with a single, easy kick directed herself toward land, hoping the surf would take her the rest of the way to the beach.

Konga understood Espri's moves, and he surfaced, out of her line of sight, only long enough to take another breath before diving deep beneath her once again. This time his intent was more bold. No longer content to observe without touching, he propelled himself up and snared her ankle, dragging her down beneath the waves.

The shock of the attack completely panicked Espri, and there was no time for her to take a breath before she was pulled down into the black water. The memory of other shark-attack victims assailed her as she fought valiantly against her tormentor, but she wondered vaguely, as her strength began to fail, why there was no biting pain in its deadly grip.

Enjoying himself immensely, Konga pulled her toward him with a caressing yet unyielding grip. The twisting of her body as she fought inflamed him, and he exulted when her struggles lessened and she became manageable in his arms. He held her tightly against his side with one arm, then brought them to the surface with one powerful stroke and made for shore.

Espri's lungs were nearly bursting when she surfaced, and she took a deep, reviving breath, only to gasp and choke as sharp pain seared through her breast. Then, as awareness of reality returned, she understood what had happened to her, and fury erupted within her. With a violent move, she tried to wrench free of Konga's hold, but he only laughed victoriously and tightened his grasp.

"You are mine, Espri. Have you not known that all along?" he told her huskily as he got to his feet and swung her squirming resentful form up into his arms.

"You're a beast, Konga!" she cried hoarsely, though she felt helpless as he masterfully carried her to the beach.

"Only because you drive me to it, woman." Konga smiled down at her coldly. "I warned you not to make me wait. I can no longer deny my desire for you. I want you, and I mean to have you. Now!"

The feral quality of his smile unnerved her, but she knew better than to show weakness. With a strength she didn't feel, she tensed against his touch as he knelt and placed her on the warm sand.

"I will not permit this. I do not want you or love you." Espri mustered what dignity she could, but her limbs were weak and she was shivering. She pushed herself into a sitting position and met his stare evenly.

The defiance in her eyes made Konga angry. "You may not love me, Espri," he rasped, "but we do not need love to share the delights of our bodies."

"No! Konga, don't do this!" Espri's eyes widened in final acknowledgment of her perilous situation.

But Konga did not heed her plea. There would be no more talk between them! He was tired of her sharp words and her ridiculous denials of the passion she had for him. He would show her how absurd her protests were.

Boldly, he cupped one of her breasts as his mouth descended to claim hers. Espri tried to get loose, but he pushed her down and covered her body with his own, pinning her in the soft sand.

Cringing away from him, Espri felt sick as he probed her most secret places, brazenly exploring her with an almost hurtful touch. When his mouth left hers to taste of her breasts, she gasped in outrage and screamed out as loudly as she could.

Her shriek irritated Konga, and he clasped a huge hand over her mouth, silencing her.

"No one will come." His voice was husky as he kissed her shoulder and throat, enthralled by his own dominance over her. For so long, he had waited for this moment . . .

Mitch awoke suddenly and lay still, listening to the night sounds and wondering what it was that had awakened him.

"Jacques? Espri?" he called, thinking them nearby, but when there was no immediate response to his call, he knew he was alone in the hut. Sitting up, he touched his forehead lightly, and he was relieved to find that the pain had lessened considerably. He was musing on the rapid improvement of his injury when he heard the scream. It was a shrill unworded cry for help that pierced him to his very soul.

"Espri . . ." Mitch murmured in frantic recognition, and he hesitated only briefly before ripping the protective covering from his brow. Getting to his feet, he hurried to the door of the hut, squinting uncomfortably as he tried to bring the glade into focus. The night fire had burned low, and it now cast an eerie reddish haze over the clearing. Mitch glanced around, trying to orient himself.

"Jacques?"

There was no answer, for the older man, unbeknownst to Mitch, had passed out long ago beneath the comfortable cover of the ironwood trees. Another, fainter cry of distress reached him and he raced from the hut heading in the direction from which it had come.

Though totally unfamiliar with the terrain, Mitch luckily discovered the path to the shore quickly, and he followed it to the crescent beach. In the dimness of the moonlight, he could make out, in the distance, the figures of a naked man and woman intertwined in what appeared to be a lover's embrace. He was almost convinced that he'd made a mistake when another shriek of outrage split the night air.

"Konga! Please!"

Recognizing Espri's voice, he started forward. "Espri?"

Konga had been so engrossed in taking his time with Espri and drawing out his own pleasure that the presence of another man, so close, startled him. For a moment he stopped mauling Espri, and in that split second, she made her move. Nauseated by his loathsome gropings, she took full advantage of his brief hesitation to grab a handful of sand and throw it in his face.

"Argh!" Konga screamed as the coarse grit blinded him. "You!"

While scrambling from beneath his heavy body, Espri accidentally brought her knee up, and a cry erupted from the huge islander's throat. Startled by what her simple acts had accomplished, Espri froze, looking at Konga in bewilderment.

"Espri! Are you all right?" Mitch was near now, staring back and forth from the prostrate form of the naked warrior to the crouching, slender, nude figure of the exotic island girl.

The sound of his voice shattered Espri's moment of immobility, and she launched herself into his arms, sobbing with fright. Mitch's arms encircled her automatically, cradling her against him in a protective, secure embrace.

Konga recovered enough from her accidental, yet incapacitating, blow to glare up at the two of them.

"I will have you, Espri!" he growled viciously. "No man on this island can keep you from me! Not Jacques and certainly not him." Konga sneered.

Mitch tensed at the insult, and putting Espri from him, he took a threatening step forward, his dark-eyed gaze unflinchingly meeting Konga's hate-filled glare.

"You'd better go while you still can," he said in a calm yet deadly tone.

Konga, still feeling the effects of Espri's devastating blow, knew this was not the time for a confrontation. Trying to maintain some semblance of his warrior's dignity, he got slowly to his feet and glowered malevolently at the white stranger.

"I go now, but this is not the end between us, white man." With one last glance at Espri, he turned, and after snatching up his pareu, he stalked away into the darkness.

No longer able to control her reaction to what had almost happened to her, Espri began to shiver uncontrollably. Seeing her distress, Mitch took her in his arms once again and held her close to comfort her.

"Mitch . . . thank you," she managed to get out.

"Did he hurt you?" he asked, his voice gruff as he suddenly became aware of her nakedness pressed so tightly against him.

"No, I don't think so." Espri looked up at him, her eyes meeting his. "Your eyes!"

"Don't worry about me. I'm fine." A heat soared through Mitch as he gazed at her alluring beauty. Tommy had been right; she was gorgeous. "But where the hell is Jacques? He should have come to your aid!" he declared furiously, angry at the other man's absence and at the uncontrollable desire flaring within him. Her husband should have responded to her call for help, not him! And what was she doing out here in the dark with that big islander in the first place? Had she been teasing Konga in the same way she'd been taunting him? His jaw tensed at the thought, but he imagined that that was probably what had happened. In his mind, contempt became mixed with concern.

Espri sighed, exhausted by her harrowing experience. "He's probably passed out somewhere," she said wearily. "After you went to bed, he started drinking kava and . . ." She let the sentence drop, not wanting to discuss her father's problem, but Mitch caught the nuance and looked down at her questioningly.

"Does he do this often? Leave you on your own this way?"

"Often enough." Espri's answer was tinged with sadness.

Mitch fell silent as he imagined her life with a man who got his greatest pleasure from a bottle, and he felt a pang of compassion for her. Her husband was a drunk. But how could Jacques possibly choose drink over Espri's love? She was so young and desirable.

Mitch suddenly wanted to soothe her hurts. He wanted to . . . As soon as the thought came, Mitch was irritated with himself for even having entertained it. What the hell was happening to him? It didn't matter what he wanted to do! She was Jacques's wife, and he would have none of her, no matter how delectable her sweet body was!

Tensing against the power of his demanding urge, he dropped his arms from her and stepped back, feeling the need to put some distance between them, to end the closeness of the moment.

"We'd better get back," he said, trying not to look at her as she stood before him, temptingly beautiful.

"Mitch?" Espri was still recovering from shock, and she

swayed weakly before him, totally bewildered by his abrupt remoteness. Reaching out to him for support, she found herself longing to be back in the safety of his embrace.

He cursed under his breath when he realized she did not have the strength to stand on her own. Then he lifted her into his arms, intending to carry her back to the hut.

"Mitch?" His name was a soft plea, and Espri gently, nervously, reached up to touch his cheek. Was this the same man who had kissed her with such passion earlier that day? There was something disparaging in his eyes, and she was at a loss to explain it. Did he find her unattractive now that he'd actually seen her? His remembered touch, so different from Konga's foul abuse, had been gentle as well as arousing, and she longed for a sign of need from him now.

"Espri . . ." Mitch wanted to find her dress so she could cover herself before he lost what little control he had.

Go ahead and take what she's giving away! his baser side urged. *After all, she's only a native girl. It's not as though she is the wife of some San Francisco business acquaintance. They do this all the time here! Take her!* He was tempted, Lord knows he was. Espri was everything he'd ever wanted in a woman—passionate and willing, her body lushly curved. Mentally, he shook himself, making one last attempt to hold himself in, but when she placed her arms about his neck and pressed herself to him, whispering, "Please," he was lost.

His mouth swooped down to claim hers. Gone were his noble intentions. Gone was his vow not to have her. He was a man driven by the demons of desire as his mouth plundered hers. Allowing her to slide down his body so she stood pressed against him, he caressed her, exploring her back and hips with a knowing, experienced touch. Then, cupping her buttocks, he lifted her to him and moved his hips suggestively against her nestling softness, letting her know exactly what his intentions were. He was on fire. He had to have her.

Espri could feel the hard evidence of his love pressing demandingly against her, and she gloried in it. She wanted him. No longer did she try to hide from that fact. His kiss was exquisite pleasure, his touch exquisite agony.

No words were spoken as they dropped slowly to the sand, together.

"You're more lovely than I ever imagined," Mitch told her thickly as he drew her down with him and kissed her with a fervency that left her breathless. His caresses traced paths of tingling excitement over her silken flesh as he explored her body. Her flesh felt sleek and supple, her breasts were succulent and inviting. Unable to resist, he bent to suckle the crest of one satin orb, and the cry of pleasure that erupted from her thrilled him. He molded her lithe, velvet form to his lean hardness as she writhed, in need, against him.

Espri could not remain still. The feel of his lips at her bosom stirred the flame of her excitement even higher until she knew she would do anything just to please him. The heat he'd created within her left her burning with desire, and all rational thought fled her mind as she drew him to her. Boldly, she reached down to touch him as she had seen Tana touch Konga, and when she heard Mitch's sharp intake of breath a victorious smile curved her lips. She would please him just as Tana had pleased Konga.

Her experience meager, she had to rely only on what she'd witnessed the other night. Quickly, she slipped her hand between their straining bodies and unknotted his pareu, pushing it aside to give her free access to his hardness. Her hands were restless as they strayed, with intimate innocence, over him, teasing and arousing at the same time.

Remembering how Konga had responded to the caresses of Tana's mouth, she decided to do the same thing to Mitch. Drawing him to her, she kissed him deeply, meeting his pleasure-giving tongue in a passionate duel. Then, wanting only to satisfy him further, she let her lips trail down his neck and across his chest. Only as she shifted lower to touch her lips to his throbbing need did Mitch react.

Up to that point, Mitch had been totally enthralled by her exquisite movements and her unhampered response to his caresses. He had felt certain, because of her seemingly practiced caresses, that she was far from innocent, and that certainty eased his still-troubled, but somewhat silenced, conscience. But, when she moved to caress him so boldly with her lips, he was stunned. The cold reality of what was coming to pass jolted him back to his senses, and he tangled his fingers in her hair, pulling her up, away from him.

Espri cried out in both pain and surprise at his reaction.

Mitch was filled with self-loathing as he realized that, no matter how wrong it was for them to come together, he still wanted her.

"This can go no further, Espri."

She heard the censure in his voice. "I don't understand."

Swearing out loud from frustration, he rolled away from her heated body and stood up.

Espri stared up at him in total confusion as he tied the pareu about his waist.

"You don't want me?"

"My body desires yours; that's all," Mitch bit out, forcing an icy control over his raging passion.

"And that isn't enough?" She frowned. Konga had said that that was all that mattered.

Mitch misunderstood her words, and his expression grew scornful for he thought her a wanton.

"No." His answer was curt and final. "For me, it isn't." Disgusted with himself for his weakness where Espri was concerned, he turned away, heading back toward the path to the hut.

Chapter 8

"What happened? Did you see him?" Nelani asked excitedly as she and Tikiru made their way through the dense foliage of the tropical forest.

"Yes, I saw the golden one." Her mistress's tone was serious.

"The golden one? Why do you call him that?" she questioned as she hurried to keep up with her mistress.

"It is not for you to know," Tikiru replied haughtily.

Frustrated by her reply. Nelani decided to use a little bargaining power. "It will be for Manti the high priest to know, if you continue to abuse my service. I am here to see that you are happy, but not to assist you in breaking your vow," she challenged, feeling possessive toward the handsome white man she had seen first.

Tikiru's eyes narrowed as she spun about and faced her slave. "I would see you dead before I would allow you to speak to Manti of this."

Inwardly, Nelani quaked at her mistress's threat, but she did not show her fear. "Then tell me why it is you had to see this man when those in the village hold no attraction for you."

Pondering the wisdom of sharing the sacred vision, Tikiru finally assented. "I had a vision of a golden man."

Nelani was stunned. It was well known that Tikiru's visions were *tapu*. "Was Tommy the man in your vision?" She held her breath as she awaited the answer.

"He was." Tikiru turned and started to walk on toward her hut, leaving her awestruck servant to follow.

"What did your dream tell you?" Nelani didn't know whether to be worried or happy; over the years, Tikiru's visions had predicted both good and bad.

"I have not yet been able to fully interpret its message."

"Did you tell Manti of your vision?"

Tikiru glanced back at Nelani and transfixed her with a commanding glare. "No. And I won't until I understand it completely. Now, be quiet. We do not want the priests to discover that we ventured out."

Nelani fell silent as she trailed after her.

Tikiru's mind was racing, trying to understand what had just happened with this one called Tommy. He had kissed her. She had seen that done often enough when couples engaged in ritual mating during the fertility ceremony, but she had never known that it could evoke such pleasurable sensations. She had tingled all over from the touch of his mouth on hers, and she would have allowed him to kiss her again, had the presence of the others not deterred her. Was there danger in this? A kiss surely did not break her vow not to know man.

And what was she to do about the meeting she'd arranged for the next night? If she did not go, he would no doubt begin to ask questions and then the truth would be out. No, she would have to meet him herself or . . . The sudden inspiration to send Nelani in her place felt right. She would do it.

Once they were safe inside their hut, she threw off her concealing cloak and faced her slave, her expression set.

"Tomorrow night, when I have returned from the sacrifice, we will go out again."

"Tikiru! It is so dangerous for you!" Nelani protested.

"Be silent! I will tell you what to do and you will do it. There is much to be considered. Leave me now."

"Shall I bathe you?"

"No, be gone. You offend me with your disapproval. I am the *taupau*."

"Yes, Tikiru. I will go." Backing from the room in total submission, Nelani disappeared to her own sleeping quarters.

Tikiru waited until Nelani had gone; then she stripped off her sarong and, after tossing it casually aside, strode, nude, across the room to step out onto the veranda. Bathed in the moonlight, she seemed an ivory statue as she stood motionlessly on the stone gallery staring out at the dark forest.

The vision came to her again, then, and she swayed in a trancelike state as scene after scene bombarded her. The golden man . . . the golden man . . . over and over she saw him, and each time he was making love with an incredibly lovely island girl. She could see their coupling vividly, but she could not identify the female whose face was always hidden from her, as it had been in the dream. Once more a strange emotion swept through her, leaving her weak and trembling. Then came the fear . . . molten and golden and swirling in a heated whirlpool of devouring death. Collapsing on the veranda, Tikiru sobbed helplessly and finally fell into deep normal sleep from which she did not awaken until daybreak.

Nelani lay on her bed contemplating all that had happened that day. She had never known Tikiru to be so secretive, and it troubled her. She felt that her mistress, whose every wish was granted, would only have the need to hide things if they boded ill. Unless she had come to desire a man . . . Nelani frowned at the possibility. Had Tikiru's vision involved passion for Tommy? That thought sent a shiver of frightened expectancy down her spine. She prayed to the gods it was not so, for if the *taupau* desecrated her body by coupling with a mere man, that could mean death at the hands of the high priest for Tikiru and the man—and herself for not having prevented it. Pushing that terrifying thought from her mind, Nelani closed her eyes, and after a long restless time, she finally drifted off to sleep.

Espri had remained on the beach, lost in troubled thought. What had happened to Mitch? One moment they had been lost in the throes of ecstasy, and the next he'd pushed her away from him. Then he'd left her after a curt dismissal.

The passion she'd felt had turned quickly to embarrassment as she'd realized that her father might have been right. Mitch was a white man, and perhaps he was not like the island men. Perplexed by all that had happened, she wondered anxiously what to do next. Her heart prodded her to go after Mitch, to try to find out why he'd rejected her, but logic dictated that she stay away from him for he obviously did not want her. Knowing that she would have no peace of mind until she fully understood, Espri retrieved her sarong, tied it securely about her, and followed the path Mitch had taken.

Mitch paced the hut like a caged animal. He was glad that he'd come to his senses before taking Espri, but the memory of her volatile responses to his every touch left him feverish with desire. He had long considered himself an accomplished lover, but not even the most passionate and learned of his past mistresses could compare with Espri. Her skin was like velvet; he couldn't resist touching it. Her lips, like the finest wine, never quenched his thirst. Mitch drew a sharp breath as he remembered the taste of her flesh. She was beautiful . . . she had wanted him. He cursed himself soundly for being a fool, and he couldn't wait for morning when he could leave the torture chamber that her home had become. His jaw tight, he slowly brought his need for her under some semblance of control. Then he stretched out on the mat and tried to rest.

Espri was nervous and unsure of herself as she crossed the clearing. The fire was only a mass of glowing embers now, and she mused that that was exactly how she felt, the blazing fire that Mitch had stoked to life within her having faded to smoldering ashes. Hurt by his rejection and unsure of his reception, she moved cautiously toward the hut. The black abyss of the doorway seemed very intimidating. Tentatively, she peered into the dwelling's concealing darkness, and she saw Mitch, lying on the mat, seemingly asleep.

"Mitch?" Her voice, though barely a whisper, seemed loud to her own ears, and she started skittishly at the sound.

Mitch had found it impossible to sleep. His body still ached with need for Espri, and he'd become more and more restive with each passing moment. Keeping his eyes closed, he gritted his teeth against his powerful longing and lay rigidly on the bed.

The sound of her voice brought him upright on the mat. "Espri?" he questioned. Then he saw her silhouetted in the doorway against the red glow of the dying fire.

"Oh, Mitch!" She wanted to tell him of her confusion, to ask him to explain everything to her, but her words were a sigh of yearning that shattered the last fragments of his iron-willed control.

All thoughts of right and wrong lost, he came to his feet and swept her into a possessive embrace, his mouth claiming hers.

Without hesitation, Espri surrendered to his lovemaking. She had found her answer. He did want her; that was enough! The confusion that had plagued her was forgotten. There was only Mitch and the moment and the desire she felt for him.

Urged on by her willingness, Mitch gave himself over to the illicit joy of her love. He wanted her and he would take her. He was a man with a man's needs, and she was the one woman who could satisfy those needs.

But what had started out as a mere lusty encounter changed in nature as their kisses grew less and less fervent and more and more enraptured. There was a wondrous element to this final acknowledgment of the inevitability of their joining, and they both experienced it, slowing their pursuit of oneness to savor every touch, every kiss.

"I need you, Espri, more than I've ever needed another woman," Mitch confessed as he broke off one heart-stopping kiss to stare down at her in the dusky half-light. Her exotic beauty could strike all semblance of sanity from his mind and leave him an unthinking creature governed only by his passion. Even before he had seen her, he had wanted her, and now . . . with a guttural growl, he bent to her again, tasting of her mouth and pulling her full against him.

Espri thrilled to his abandoned caresses, and when he encouraged her to move to the mat with him, she went without pause. What little clothing they were wearing was quickly discarded and they surged together, flesh melding to flesh, the mindless unity of love.

Mitch committed to memory each satiny curve of her welcoming body: her full, responsive breasts . . . her gently rounded hips . . . her slim, well-shaped legs. He thought of them wrapped tightly about his waist as he plunged hungrily into her, and he shivered in anticipation.

Mindless in her arousal, Espri clung to him as he positioned her beneath him and moved between her thighs. Spreading her legs wide, he pressed against her, the proof of his fierce desire for her pressing intimately at the portals of her womanhood. As his alien hardness touched her as no man had, a gasp of excited expectancy escaped her, and she tightened her grip on his shoulders, biting her lip to keep from crying out.

"Easy, love." Mitch, thinking her experienced, bent to kiss her just as his hips surged forward to penetrate her sweetness. The slight barrier he encountered was rent before he understood its significance, and the sudden, unexpected knowledge of her innocence rocked him to the depths of his being. "Espri . . ." he groaned as he lay sheathed in her feminine core, the ardor that was gripping him driving him to lay claim to that fertile ground which had previously been untouched.

"Please . . . Mitch," she whispered as the small pain she'd experienced lessened and he began to move deep within her. "I want you."

"Move with me, sweet," he urged, sliding his hand to her hips to guide her untutored movements.

Espri intuitively understood, and she began to match him, thrust for thrust. Sweat glistened on their bodies as they strained together, hips grinding against hips, legs interlocking in the throes of their passion.

Espri was filled with wonder as new sensations swelled through her and each stroke of his driving body took her nearer and nearer to that ultimate release, until in one blinding instant her world exploded into a thousand shards of exquisite delight.

Mitch had never been emotionally touched by a woman's pleasure before, but the knowledge that he'd satisfied her on their first time together filled him with mystifying joy. Entranced by the beauty of their joining, his own completion overwhelmed him, filling him with rapturous ecstasy as he gave her the gift of his love.

At last, his breathing ragged, Mitch lay still, reflecting on their coming together. It had been so spellbindingly perfect. Yet how could she have been a virgin? The discovery that she had been untouched had struck him as sharply as a physical blow. Espri was lovely . . . and so responsive. Surely any man would want her. Why had Jacques not taken her? Was he impotent?

Mitch drew a shuddering breath as rational thought slowly returned and with it the painful acknowledgment that he had taken another man's wife. He could not deny that he'd enjoyed making love to Espri, and that admission provoked guilt. He'd been no better than a rutting animal. He had wanted her, damn the consequences. Even now as she lay quiescent beneath him, Mitch knew he wanted to take her again; she was like a fire in his blood.

Suddenly furious with himself for his own part in her betrayal, he levered his weight from atop her. He didn't know why she had been a virgin, but he intended to find out.

Espri opened her eyes and started to smile blissfully up at Mitch, but the smile froze on her lips when she saw the undisguised anger in his penetrating gaze. Their lovemaking had been more wonderful than she could ever have imagined, and she could not understand why he was upset.

"Mitch?" She lifted a hand to touch his cheek in a lover's gesture.

Mitch snared her wrist, and when he spoke, his words were snarled. "I think some answers are in order."

Espri was stunned by his attitude. A chill shook her. "Answers? I don't know what you mean."

His grip on her wrist tightened unconsciously. "I mean, how is it that you came to me a virgin? Why hasn't Jacques . . . ?"

Espri's bewilderment was total as she stared up at him through the semidarkness. He sounded as though her untouched state had been loathsome. Anger grew within her. "Jacques? What has my father got to do with this?"

Mitch blanched, his lips tightening in a grim line. "Your father? Jacques is your father?"

Espri pulled away from his grasp and sat up. "Of course he's my father. Who did you think he was?"

"Your husband." The words came out slowly, painfully.

Espri gasped in righteous fury.

"You thought Jacques was my husband, yet you made love to me?" She grabbed her sarong and twisted it about her, concealing her lush figure from him before getting hurriedly to her feet. "You must have a very low opinion of me if you think I would do something so treacherous as bed you while I'm married to another!"

Her words made him realize how grossly mistaken he'd been, but he was not about to explain to her that most of the women he'd known would have had no compunctions about doing such a thing.

"I'm sorry."

"I have been nothing but kind to you. I don't understand how you could have thought me so low, so deceitful!" Espri's heart was aching for his revelation had destroyed the beauty of that night.

Mitch loomed over her, but she gave no ground, glaring up at him, hands on her hips.

"Espri," he began. Thinking that she, like every other woman he'd ever been involved with, could be distracted from her purpose by another session of passionate lovemaking, he reached out to take her in his arms. "I misjudged you and I'm sorry." He drew her against his chest, bending to kiss her deeply.

Espri submitted for a moment, but even as the flame of desire flickered to life at the sensuous touch of his lips, the fury of her indignation smothered it. Twisting away from him, she rushed to the door.

"My father was right! White men are different. I should have heeded his advice and stayed away from you."

Without a backward glance, she raced off into the night's concealing shadows.

Mitch watched her go, his emotions in turmoil. He almost went after her, but the disgust he'd read in her expression held him immobile. She had been an innocent, and he had shattered that innocence, in more ways than one.

Cursing, Mitch searched out his pareu, then tied it about his waist before lying down once again on the mat. His arms crossed behind his head, he stared blindly at the thatched roof, knowing there would be no rest for him this night.

Jacques rolled over and opened bleary, bloodshot eyes. It took a few moments for his world to right itself, and when the dizzying motion finally ceased, he sat up. Blindly, he grabbed for the bottle of kava, sighing with relief to find that there was still some of the potent liquor remaining. He tilted the bottle to his lips and drank heavily. When he'd savored the last drop, he angrily tossed the empty vessel aside.

"Espri!" His ragged voice boomed across the early morning brightness of the glade. "Damn! Where is that girl?" he muttered to himself as he struggled to his feet.

The liquor he'd just imbibed hit his empty stomach with resounding force, and he staggered as he made his way across the clearing to the hut in search of his daughter and another bottle of kava or rum. Leaning heavily against the doorway, he gazed inside the darkened hut, hoping to find Espri, but to his dismay the room was empty. He frowned at the deserted hut, then swung drunkenly around, glaring in confusion out across his domain.

"Jacques."

The Frenchman turned quickly to find Mitch coming toward him from the direction of the beach. "What are you doing up? And where's the bandage?"

"I'm feeling much better this morning. As you can see, my cut is healing nicely."

Jacques grunted in acknowledgment. "Where is Espri?"

"I haven't seen her for a while," Mitch answered truthfully.

"She must have gone to the pool," Duchant grumbled, rubbing his temples to relieve the ache. "Are you still going to the village today to stay with your friend?"

"Yes, if it's no trouble for you." Mitch was certain that his despicable actions had destroyed whatever feeling Espri had had for him, and after long sleepless hours of reasoning the situation through, he'd decided that perhaps it had all been for the best. True, she was a tempting piece; the most delightful creature he'd ever bedded, in fact, but she was also just a woman. He'd had many before, and, no doubt, he would have many more. Still, an unbidden thought encroached on his rationalizing: Espri had been a virgin. He had been her first lover. Mitch determinedly pushed the thought away. He would not allow himself to care. Caring only led to deeper feelings. He would follow through on his plan to join Tommy in the village, and as soon as possible, he would leave for home.

"We will go as soon as Espri returns and we eat," Jacques told him, eyeing him thoughtfully. "You look mighty uncomfortable in that pareu," he added, with a twisted smile. "I have several pairs of pants, if you'd like to try one of them. And a razor?"

"Thank you." Mitch returned his smile as he rubbed at his bearded chin. "I'd like that very much."

Jacques went into the hut to search out those items, and he followed.

Tikiru stood with her hands on her hips, glaring at Nelani. "You will do exactly what I tell you!"

"Yes, Tikiru." The servant girl bowed her head submissively.

"As soon as the ceremony ends tonight, we will return here as always. No one will suspect a thing. Then, when the moon begins to rise, we will leave again."

"Are you planning on seeing the white man again?"

"He will be waiting on the beach in the cove."

"Tikiru!" Nelani was truly frightened. "If the high priests find out, it could mean your life."

"Do not worry. I have done nothing that will endanger my vows nor do I intend to," she replied smugly.

"Then why are you meeting him at all?"

"I will not be meeting him. You will."

"I don't understand." Nelani was confused.

"He is expecting a woman named Nelani to be there, and you will be."

"But how could he be expecting me?"

"Because I told him my name was Nelani. He could not see me plainly in the dark of night, and since we are both about the same size . . ."

"Why do you feel the need to do this?"

"Do not question my motives, Nelani. We will speak of this no more until tonight. Then, I will tell you exactly what I want of you. Now, come and help me bathe."

"Yes, Tikiru." Though Nelani agreed easily enough, she was worried. What did her mistress intend to do? Surely this was related to her vision, but how? Knowing that she would get no answers, she gathered Tikiru's cleansing ointments and followed her mistress to their private bathing pool.

As the sun edged ever higher into the eastern sky, Espri knew it was time to return to her home. She did not look forward to seeing Mitch again, but not being one to back down, she intended to face him with as much calm as she could muster.

After fleeing Mitch's embrace, Espri had passed the last long hours of the night sitting by the waterfall in silent meditation. In all honesty, she could not deny that she had wanted Mitch since the first time he'd touched her. She had enjoyed the lovemaking they had shared that night. For the first time, she had been attracted to a man and she had gone to him willingly. She had expected their joining to be blissful, but it had not turned out that way. He had satisfied her physically, but the disturbing discovery of how he felt about her had left her feeling soiled.

Determined to have no more to do with him, she squared her shoulders in an unconscious gesture of control. They had made love, the moment had been pleasurable, and that was all there was to it. As her father had told her, Mitch would be leaving the island at the first opportunity anyway, so it was better that things went no further. *After all*, Espri thought fiercely, *I don't love him*. Yet, as she neared the glade, she couldn't help but wonder why Mitch's low opinion of her had hurt so badly.

"Espri!"

Jacques's welcoming call drew Mitch's attention, and he stopped shaving to watch Espri cross the glade to speak with her father. She looked cool and composed this morning, not like the abandoned lover who'd come to him during the night, but at the memory of their encounter, he found himself becoming aroused. No other woman had had this effect on him. Irritated, he wiped the lather from his face. Thrusting the vivid images from his mind, he set aside the razor and small mirror that Jacques had loaned him, and slowly brought his urgings under control. Glad that he had decided to move into the village, he started across the clearing.

"Must you drink so early in the day, Papa?" Espri asked as she watched Jacques lift the bottle of rum to his lips.

Her father paused thoughtfully for a moment and then set

the liquor aside. "I suppose you're right, *ma petite.* I'll refrain for now."

His response totally surprised Espri, and she could only stare at him in wonder until Mitch's good morning intruded into her thoughts. A tingle raced down her spine at the sound of his deep voice, but she dismissed it as unimportant and turned to face him.

"Good morning, Mitch. It's good to see you up and about." She swallowed nervously, and her eyes widened imperceptibly as she glanced at him. Surely, just the sight of him shouldn't cause her heart to beat faster and her legs to tremble, but it did. Gone was the rough growth of beard, and he seemed even more handsome without it. He'd shed the pareu for a pair of her father's white pants which fit him almost too well. Snug across the hips, they were molded to his taut buttocks and powerful thighs, and Espri couldn't stop herself from staring as she remembered those thighs pressed so intimately to hers. He looked so different that he almost seemed a stranger. Forcing herself to answer with casual indifference, she remarked, "I see Papa's loaned you some pants."

"Yes, and a razor." Mitch grinned easily as he rubbed his clean-shaven jaw, but he was uneasy. He wondered how she could be so aloof when hours before they had lain in one another's arms, making love. His eyes narrowed as he watched her, but he could detect no flaw in her composure. Perhaps what the sailors said about island women was true, that sex meant very little to them and that, until they married, they enjoyed many partners. The thought grated on his nerves. He had been her first, he told himself, not one of many. That had to have meant something.

He bristled at the possibility that Espri had already dismissed their encounter. Suddenly becoming aware of the path his thoughts had taken, he girded himself against them. He was moving to the village, and he probably wouldn't see her again. That was exactly what he wanted. What difference did it make anyway? He would be going home soon.

"Are you all set to go to the village?" Espri directed her attention back to her father with an effort.

"Yes, *chérie*. As soon as we have something to eat," Jacques replied. He sensed some kind of tension between them, but he had no idea as to what was causing it.

"Of course. I'll prepare something right away." Espri was grateful for the excuse to leave them. "Then you can be on your way."

"You'll be coming with us, won't you?" her father asked. "Luatu, I know, is anxious to see you."

Realizing that she didn't have a good reason for not accompanying them, she agreed. "Of course. I have missed Grandfather greatly."

"Luatu?" Mitch wondered.

"Chief Luatu is my grandfather," Espri explained. "My mother was a princess."

"Oh. And your mother . . ."

"Is dead," she answered, glancing quickly at her father, her expression apologetic. "I'd better prepare the food now so we can go. The walk to the village is a long one."

As she hurried away, Jacques slowly reached for the bottle of rum.

Chapter 9

Tana was idling away the hours until Konga returned from the day's fishing when word came to her that Jacques and Espri were on their way to the village with the white man named Mitch. She anxiously awaited their coming, hoping that what she'd said during her visit to Espri's home had had an effect on the other woman. If she had managed to stir Espri's interest in Mitch, then there was a good chance that Konga could be made to realize Espri did not want or love him. Certainly, his warrior's pride would not permit him to continue to profess love for a woman who had chosen another man over him. Then he would be hers, hers alone! Eager to see if her brazen remarks had had the desired effect, Tana kept close watch until she spotted the trio approaching her family's hut.

The tall, clean-shaven white man looked vitally alive as he crossed the clearing, and though Tana had been only half serious when she'd chided Espri about him being a gift from the sea, she was certain now that her words had been true. He was magnificent, broad at the shoulders and narrow at the hip. The pants he wore only served to emphasize the powerful strength of his thighs and the long, lean length of his legs. His skin was deeply tanned, and his hair was as dark as that of the island men. When he looked up, his gaze locked with hers, sending an animal thrill coursing through her body.

Her eyes feasting on Mitch's handsome features, Tana spoke first as she walked boldly forward to meet him. "You have recovered."

Mitch looked down at the woman standing before him. "I'm afraid I'm at a disadvantage," he told her in his most courtly fashion. "You know me, but I know nothing of you."

"You mean Espri didn't tell you that I came and offered to help nurse you?" She glanced accusingly at Espri. When she saw a quickly shuttered flare of possessiveness in the other woman's eyes, she was pleased. Her plan had worked!

Mitch was instantly aware of the subtle antagonism in their exchange, but he continued smoothly. "I'm afraid not, but then we've had little real time to talk. I'm Mitch Williams, and you?"

"I am Tana, daughter of Anuitua," she told him, turning slightly to gaze up at him flirtatiously.

Despite her breathlessness and the pounding of her heart, Espri had convinced herself that she didn't care about Mitch, and she had been in total control during the long trip to the village. But now, as she watched the other woman work her wiles on Mitch, a strange resentment filled her. How dare Tana approach him so! And in the middle of the village!

Tommy had been right the previous day when he'd said that Espri was far lovelier than Anuitua's daughter, Mitch thought.

"Tana, I've come to see Tommy. Is he here?" Mitch pretended not to notice her posturing.

Tana was about to answer when her mother came bustling forward to greet them.

"Espri! Jacques! How good to see you! Is this Tommy's friend?" She regarded Mitch with open curiosity.

"Yes. Anuitua, this is Mitch Williams." Jacques nodded toward the other white man.

Anuitua smiled widely at the stranger. "Tommy has spoken of you often. I am glad you are well."

"Thank you." Mitch returned her smile and then looked quickly around. "Is Tommy here?"

"He has gone out in the canoe with my husband Kohea, but they should be returning soon. Will you stay and wait?"

"Thank you, but no," Espri answered quickly, for she did not want to remain in Tana's presence any longer than necessary. "We are going to visit my grandfather. When Tommy gets back, please send him to Luatu's."

"I will," Anuitua promised. Then she stood by her daughter's side, watching as the others started off toward the house of the chief. "This Mitch is a very handsome man, Tana. You did not mention that when you came back from your visit the other day." Anuitua looked up at her daughter, questioningly.

"He was heavily bandaged then and I could not see all of his face," the girl explained, adding, "Perhaps if I did not love Konga so much, I would take this one to my heart."

Her mother nodded, her agreement complete.

Espri had tried to maintain some distance between herself and Mitch on the way to the village, but as they started up the narrow path that led to Luatu's isolated homesite, she was forced to walk closer to him. She found his proximity most distracting. Every nerve in her body seemed to be aware of his nearness, and she found herself growing more and more tense.

What does this uneasiness mean? she wondered. She had never felt this way about a man before, but she had never made love to a man before, either. She had talked herself into believing that what had happened with Mitch had been nothing out of the ordinary, and she thought, with a tinge of bitterness, that it certainly had been that way for him. He had given no indication that there was anything different between them. He'd been cool and polite, and, if anything, he seemed quite pleased to be moving to the village.

Puzzled by her feelings, Espri was glad when they reached the large clearing at the top of the incline; there she could move away from him. "This is my grandfather's home." She gestured toward a large, spacious hut and two smaller open-sided structures that served for cooking and dining.

Chief Luatu had watched their approach, and he was overjoyed to see them. He embraced both Espri and Jacques with much affection before turning to Mitch.

"It is as I told your father"—he nodded his imperial approval of Mitch's good health—"you have saved him."

"You give me too much credit, Grandfather," Espri demurred.

"Nonsense." His eyes were warm as he looked upon her. "You are as gifted at healing as your mother was, and this man is proof." Luatu was obviously proud of her accomplishments. He turned to Mitch. "Ka told me of his visit with you yesterday. I am glad that you are well."

"Thank you, sir."

"My name is Luatu as yours is Mitch. Come, sit down, and we will talk and eat before the afternoon heat grows too oppressive," he invited.

"Thank you."

Luatu led them to an open-sided dining hut, where they all reclined in comfort as the serving girls brought refreshments.

Being a man who prided himself on being perceptive, Luatu sensed a depth of feeling between Mitch and Espri, but since they were cool and distant to each other, he wasn't sure whether their feelings were amorous or antagonistic.

"So." Luatu faced Mitch, and wanting to know more about him, he asked, "Tell me of your home."

"I'm from San Francisco."

"You have family there?" the older man inquired as he offered Mitch a cup of coconut milk.

"Only Jon, my younger brother," Mitch replied as he took the proffered drink. "My parents died some years ago."

"Have you always been a sailor?" Luatu questioned, sensing that there was more to this man.

Mitch gave a short, joyless laugh. "No. My life at sea was not of my choosing."

"I don't understand."

The chief frowned, and Espri could not disguise her sudden interest in Mitch's reply.

"I wasn't aboard the *Seastorm* of my own will," he told them, his tone cutting. "I was shanghaied."

"Shanghaied?" Espri had never heard the word before.

"Captains who don't have a full crew when they are ready to leave port buy the men they need," Jacques offered as an explanation.

"Buy them?" She was aghast as she met Mitch's gaze.

"Ships can't sail without enough men, so, for a price, they buy men from crimps," Mitch explained.

"Crimps?"

Mitch nodded. "Crimps drug or ambush any able-bodied men they can find and then deliver them to ships' captains for a price."

"You were sold to a ship's captain? How terrible!"

"It was." Mitch looked grim. "Many a man has disappeared that way, never to be heard from again. Now I understand why."

"And your brother?"

"I'm sure Jon must think I'm dead," he responded bleakly.

Jacques regarded Mitch with growing respect now that he knew he was not a common sailor. "Then he will be all the more excited when you return," he said.

Mitch managed a smile. "It will be good to get home. I am looking forward to it."

"When I learned of your rescue, and Tommy's, I sent word

out to the other islands to see if there had been any other survivors," Luatu told him.

"Have you heard anything?"

"My messengers will not return for another week or so," the chief answered. "I also had them pass the word that if any ship comes near the shore, it is to be signaled to alert the captain of your plight."

"Thank you, Chief Luatu." Mitch was pleased by the old man's efficiency. "When Espri told me where Malika was located, I wondered if any trading ships put in here."

"It does not happen often," the old man explained. "But we will be prepared, just in case." Changing the subject then, he went on. "Kohea mentioned, when I spoke with him earlier today, that you want to stay here in the village with your friend O'Ryan."

"Yes. It seems the best solution."

Luatu nodded. "There is an old deserted hut near the end of the beach. It is in some need of repairs, but it should serve you well while you are with us. You could share it with your friend. Would you like to take a look at it?"

"Yes, I would," Mitch agreed. "Thank you."

"Espri. Do you know the place?"

"Yes, Grandfather."

"Then take Mitch there and see if it will meet his needs." The old man commanded with the authority of one used to having his directives obeyed.

"Yes, Grandfather." Espri knew she could not refuse, but she did not find the thought of spending time alone with Mitch appealing. "Are you ready?" she asked Mitch quickly, anxious to get it over with.

"If you are," he agreed.

Luatu watched them go and he was most pleased with himself. They looked good together, Espri and Mitch, and though the white man had expressed a desire to go home, maybe when that time came he would change his mind.

* * *

Low, rolling waves raced up the wide expanse of beach as Espri escorted Mitch to the abandoned dwelling. They hadn't spoken since they'd left Luatu's, and she felt uncomfortable for her thoughts kept straying to the previous night and how arousing his embrace had been.

Mitch, too, was feeling the strain of her nearness. Every time he glanced at her, now that they were by themselves, he was reminded of the passion they had shared and of how she had felt in his arms. *God, she is lovely*, he thought, gritting his teeth against the desire that threatened to overwhelm him and cursing himself for his vulnerability to her.

She is just another woman, Mitch kept telling himself; but his reasoning had little effect on his craving for her. Despite his convictions, he wanted her. The sound of her voice . . . the curve of her hips . . . the swell of her breasts . . . he found every aspect of her enticing. Indeed, he could hardly keep his hands off her. Scowling blackly, he stared out to sea, searching for something else to concentrate on, something that would take his mind off of Espri.

"There is the hut." The cool tone of her voice cut through his brooding thoughts, and he looked up to see a ramshackle dwelling nestled at the edge of the forest. "No one's lived here for several months, but I don't think you'll have too much trouble putting things back in order," she declared as she led the way into the small structure.

Rays of softly filtered sunbeams drifted through the gaps in the neglected thatched roof, bathing the interior of the hut in swatches of golden light. It was hot and humid inside, and the musty smell of disuse permeated the air.

Mitch's gaze followed Espri as she moved about, and a sense of unexpected intimacy assaulted them when she looked up and caught him watching her. Espri flushed as she noted the craving in Mitch's eyes, and she couldn't prevent the shiver of desire that shook her at the remembrance of his touch, his kiss. How handsome he was! So tall and virile.

"Well? Do you like it?" she asked hurriedly, trying to end the tense moment.

"Very much," Mitch growled, the double meaning in his answer obvious.

"Good," Espri responded briskly, eager to get away from him. "Then I'll go on back and—"

"Espri." Her name was a caress. "We need to talk."

"There is really nothing to say," she replied almost primly.

"But I think there is." He walked slowly toward her, his gaze holding hers.

"I can't imagine what. Everything was said last night and—"

The gentle touch of his hand on her cheek stopped her rash flow of words, and when she lifted her eyes to his, they were shining with desire.

"I don't want you, Mitch," she stated, not believing the words even as she spoke them.

"I know." His voice was low and harsh as he cupped her chin and lifted her face so their lips could meet in a sweet-soft exchange. He felt her tremble as his mouth moved slowly over hers in a nonthreatening exploration, and the passion he'd controlled with such fierceness surged to life. He wanted to deny that he wanted her, but his need swept him on.

Now that he had her in his arms, there was no stopping. She fanned the sparks of his desire into an all-consuming conflagration. Governed only by his senses, Mitch kissed her hungrily as his hands stripped away the barrier of her sarong, baring her tender flesh to his arousing touch.

Espri had not meant to surrender to him. She had fought the attraction between them all morning. But here, alone in the shadowed stillness of the abandoned hut with him, she could no longer resist the temptation to join their bodies. Though she might hate Mitch for the cruel things he'd said to her, she couldn't deny that she wanted him, for her senses seemed to have a life of their own when he was near.

Their mouths touched and blended, and their bodies strained together, driven by a hunger that was as old as time. They abandoned themselves to the moment, their caresses frenziedly seeking completion as they dropped to the floor, wanting only to touch and be touched in the most intimate fashion.

Breeches shed, Mitch moved against Espri, letting her feel his readiness, but refraining from taking her too soon. He wanted her completely aroused and mindlessly eager for him.

Delighting in the exquisite sensations coursing through her as Mitch trailed burning kisses over her throat and bosom, Espri moved restlessly against his hardness, needing that joining that would make them one. His mouth was a searing brand as he tasted of her glorious breasts, teasing, in turn, each taut peak with hot caresses until Espri cried out in her need of him.

Rising above her, his weight braced on his arms, Mitch fit himself to her sweetness, seeking the center of her love as he gazed down at her passion-flushed features. Then he thrust slowly forward, impaling himself in the heat of her and groaning in agonized ecstasy as her tightness gripped him and held him.

"Mitch . . ."

His name was a sigh, and he kissed her then, passionately; the deep, sensuous thrust of his tongue simulating the slow, steady rhythm of his hips as he began to move within her.

Tana stood transfixed by the sight of Mitch and Espri entwined in love's most intimate embrace. She had caught sight of them as they'd started across the beach and had been following them in the hope of discovering that there was more to their relationship than met the eye. It both surprised and delighted her to find that they were actually lovers. She only regretted that Konga wasn't there to see for himself where Espri's affections lay. Hurrying away from the lovers, Tana headed back toward the village, hoping that Konga had returned early. She had to convince him that Espri was not the woman for him, and she could think of no better way than to show him that Espri had chosen the white man for her first lover.

Sated, Espri lay in Mitch's arms. Their coming together had been explosive and wild, and she was reflecting, almost fearfully, on the power of the emotions he aroused in her. He had only to touch her and she was his. Could this be happening to her? No other had stirred her so. Was this love, the emotion that had brought her father so much joy and so much pain? The realization that it probably was settled uneasily upon her.

Mitch was resting atop Espri, relishing the feel of her silken body. How delectable she was! And how exciting! At no time in his past had a woman driven him to the brink as she did. When he was possessing her, he forgot everything but the driving need to take her, body and soul.

He tightened his arms around her and rolled onto his back, drawing her above him. The long, sleek black curtain of her hair surrounded them as her lips curved in a contented smile.

"You're beautiful," he murmured, his eyes meeting hers in heated understanding.

"You make me feel beautiful," Espri answered, her voice soft and lilting.

His hand tangled easily in her hair, drawing her down for a soft, almost cherishing kiss. Mitch felt in that moment that he could hold her forever, and though that feeling should have troubled him, he felt oddly satisfied. She would be his until it was time to leave Malika.

Last night Mitch had known that they shared something

special, and now that she was no longer upset over his mistaken opinion of her, Espri realized it, too. She had come to him willingly; there was no reason why they couldn't continue in this way. She was an island woman, used to open relationships.

He was about to caress her when Tommy's distant call sent him scrambling for their clothes.

"Mitch!" Tommy was outside the hut now.

Mitch was dressed first so he casually stepped outside to greet his friend.

"I see you found the hut with no problem." He smiled. "It's good to see you."

Tommy laughed, knowing Mitch referred to the removal of the bandage. "It's good to see you too," he returned. "Your cut looks better."

"It is."

"Are you still planning on—" Tommy broke off his sentence as Espri emerged from the hut. "Espri, I didn't know you were here."

"I brought Mitch out from the village so he could take a look at the hut my grandfather has offered you."

Tommy's gaze lingered a bit too long on her lush curves; then he became aware of censure in Mitch's regard.

"Well"—he quickly walked ahead of them into the hut—"how is it?"

"I've seen worse in San Francisco." Mitch smiled wryly as he looked around the dwelling again.

"You're right," Tommy agreed, remembering some of the shanties near the waterfront.

"Chief Luatu said it was ours as long as we remain on the island, and since he's already put out the word to signal any ships spotted in the area, hopefully that won't be too long."

His words, though meant to be conversational, sent a shaft of sudden pain through Espri's heart.

"All we have to do is make it livable again," Tommy agreed.

"We might as well find out how to repair the roof and get started," Mitch was saying.

"Kohea has already offered to help," the younger man declared. "He'll be here soon."

"Good."

"I will be going." Espri's tone revealed nothing of the intimacy that had passed between herself and Mitch or the heartache she was now experiencing.

Mitch wanted to take her in his arms and kiss her, but the coolness of her tone held him back. Attributing it to Tommy's presence, he asked easily, "Will I see you again soon?"

"There is the Ceremony of the Sacrifice tonight. If you like, I will take you."

"A sacrifice?" Both Mitch and Tommy were surprised at the prospect. "I thought there were missionaries here."

"The priests come occasionally, but they have so many islands to visit and so little time to spend with the people, the ancient gods are still important here," Espri explained.

"But a sacrifice? Surely not human?" Mitch had heard of the cannibalistic tribes that inhabited some of the islands in the South Pacific.

"No. The missionaries were successful in eliminating the more bloodthirsty practices, but many of the old ways still live on, no matter how hard they try to change them."

"I would like to see the sacrifice," Mitch declared.

"Me, too," Tommy agreed.

"When the drums begin at sunset," Espri explained, "come to the village. I will meet you by the path that leads to my grandfather's home."

"Until then." Mitch's eyes were dark with remembered passion as he watched her start back across the sunswept beach.

* * *

Jacques stood hesitantly before Laiti's hut, a half-empty bottle of rum clenched tightly in his hand. He had been drinking since that morning, but for some reason the liquor was having little effect on him.

Anxiously, he looked around. A part of him was eager to see Laiti, yet another part fought against his growing need to be with her. He did not remember the night they'd spent together, but he did not doubt her word. When he'd consumed so much kava, it was not unusual for him to forget everything that occurred. It had happened before, and it would probably happen again.

"Jacques!" The island woman stepped from her hut and smiled delightedly up at him. "I am so glad you've come."

"Hello, Laiti." His answer to her greeting was stilted, reflecting his nervousness.

"Come, sit with me." She took his arm and led him to her dining hut. "It is good to see you. How is Espri? And your white man?"

"Espri is fine, and Mitch is well enough to move into the village with the other white man."

"That is good." She sat down beside him.

Jacques started to take a drink, but Laiti put a hand on his arm.

"If you are going to be with me, then you will not drink." Her usually carefree expression suddenly became serious.

Her words penetrated to the heart of his dilemma. He looked from Laiti to the bottle. Emotions warred within him. With liquor, he could forget everything miserable about his life. Without it? . . . He glanced at her again and stood up.

"I'm sorry," he mumbled.

"Tila is dead, Jacques," Laiti snapped at him. "It is time you accepted that and went on living."

"Laiti . . ."

Turning, he took the coward's way out, and he left the woman who loved him staring after him sorrowfully.

Chapter 10

The low throbbing of the drums drew the natives from all parts of the island. They hurried forth to the temple, not wanting to be late for this most important ritual. The Ceremony of the Sacrifice was held only twice during the year to atone for their transgressions against the gods, and they knew it was important that they attend.

The temple had been carved out of the forest. Open-air and circular in construction, it was guarded by massive stone figures of the Malikan gods, and the huge altar rose high above the clearing where the worshippers sat. Torches flamed brightly about the glade, casting quivering shadows in all directions, and the deep-voiced chanting of the natives gathered in this sacred place lent an eerie feeling to the whole event.

Konga had arrived at the temple early to pray before the stone altar and to offer his own sacrifice to Tane, the god of manhood. All of his life, Konga had known what he'd wanted, and he'd gotten it. Now, for the first time, he was being denied his heart's desire, and he could not bear the humiliation. Fury and frustration had filled him all day. He had relived the moments he'd spent with Espri the previous night, and he knew he could not rest until he'd wreaked revenge on the white man who had dared to interrupt them. With reverence, he ended his chant before the altar, feeling certain that the god who had always guided him wisely would do so again.

Nelani adjusted Tikiru's skirt for what seemed like the hundredth time as they waited out of sight of the villagers for Manti to appear and to signal the beginning of the sacrifice.

"Is he out there?" Tikiru asked.

"Manti?"

"No . . . the golden one. Tommy," she hissed. "Go and see."

Nelani was taken aback, but she hastened to do as she was bid. Slipping away, she stayed in the darkness beyond the brilliance of the torches, her eyes searching the crowd. At last, she saw Tommy enter the clearing and sit with Espri and another white man she hadn't seen before. Hurrying to return before the ceremony began, she rushed back to Tikiru.

"Well?" she demanded impatiently.

"He just arrived."

"Where is he sitting?"

"With Espri, near the back."

Tikiru smiled strangely at the news. "Good. Manti is here. We will begin soon."

Tana had been frustrated in her efforts to locate Konga all afternoon and she lingered near the fringes of the crowd, hoping to find him and be with him this night. It was with great relief that she finally saw him sitting alone on the outskirts of the temple grounds. She rushed to his side, eager to speak with him.

"I have been looking for you, Konga." She was almost ebullient in her happiness. As soon as she told him the truth about Espri and the white man, he would be hers!

"Why?" His tone was not welcoming, and he did not even bother to look at her.

Dropping down beside him, she smiled her most beguiling smile and reached out to touch him. "I have not seen you all day and I missed you."

Konga had no desire to talk with Tana, much less be with her. He was obsessed with making Espri his own, and he did not want to be distracted from his purpose.

"I have not missed you," he said bluntly, wishing she would leave him to his dark thoughts of revenge.

She gasped slightly at his rude reply, but was not deterred by it. "Shall I make you miss me?" Her voice was sultry, but he drew away when she moved nearer.

"You needn't try. I do not want you anymore."

"What?" Tana could not believe her ears. "You can't mean that. I love you."

He shrugged. "You have known from the start that I do not love you."

"But I can change that," she told him desperately.

"There is no point. Espri is the only woman I've ever wanted, and she will be mine, very soon."

Knowing that she was losing him, Tana cried heatedly, "She will never be yours! She does not want you!"

Konga glared at her sharply. "What do you mean?"

"Mitch and Espri are lovers."

"Do not speak lies!" he hissed threateningly.

"I saw them today."

"Where? Doing what?" Konga had to know the truth. Had Espri given herself to the white man?

"They were at the old hut Chief Luatu has given the whites. I saw them, Konga. They were naked and they were kissing and their bodies were joined." She emphasized her words.

Konga's jaw tensed at the thought. He wanted to kill the white man who had claimed his love. "She will still come to me."

"Surely, you don't still want her, now that you know she cares for him?"

He leveled a deadly, obsidian gaze on her. "As I have said, she will still be mine."

"Konga, you are a complete fool if you believe that. I am the woman who loves you. Espri does not want you. She loves the white man."

Holding himself under rigid control to keep from throttling her, Konga stood up. "Be gone from me, woman. I do not ever want to speak with you or see you near me again."

"I don't understand. I love you," Tana pleaded, completely confused by his attitude. "Since Espri does not want you and I do—"

"It does not matter to me what your foolish feelings are!" He was seething. "Compared to Espri you are nothing. She is the only woman I have ever loved and I will have her yet."

All of her plotting had been for naught. Konga would never love her. Tana was devastated. In one last, desperate plea, she started toward him, but he pushed her away.

"Espri will be mine!" he swore vengefully, and he stormed off, leaving Tana in tears, her hatred of the other woman soaring to new heights.

Tommy sat with Mitch and Espri, watching the preparation for the ritual with fascination, and when another chant arose from the crowd he looked questioningly at Espri.

"What are they saying?"

"They are calling for the *taupau*," she explained.

"What is a *taupau*?"

"The *taupau* is the temple priestess," Espri started to explain, but just then Tikiru appeared. "Look."

Tommy turned and was completely spellbound by the sight of the partially clad woman on the altar. He had found many of the native girls attractive but this one was beyond compare. Her hair—long, black, and glossy—fell past her waist in a silken cascade, and the skirt she wore tied loosely at the side rode low on her hips, baring one leg almost completely. Her skin glistened from the oil with which she'd been anointed, and her breasts, tempting and succulent, were bared for all to see. Around her neck, she wore a single medallion. About her wrists were bracelets of multicolored shells. To the ankle of her exposed leg was strapped a very lethal looking, gold-handled knife.

"She's beautiful," he said breathlessly. He watched in awe as the priestess was lifted onto the altar, where she acted out a sequence in the story of life on Malika.

When the tempo of the drums reached a frenzied pitch, Tommy waited in expectation, and he was shocked when the priest handed her a snake that was at least three feet long. When the priestess lifted the reptile above her head and began to dance, he felt his blood stir. Though Tommy knew this was a religious rite, there was something so pagan and wanton about her movements that he was aroused. His eyes never left her as she wrapped the snake about her in what seemed a lover's embrace, and he was startled when her eyes met his across the distance. She stood poised, holding the reptile to her breast, and when the drums suddenly stopped, she plunged her knife into the creature, killing it instantly. Soaked in the blood of the snake, the *taupau* glanced at him once more, then she collapsed on the altar. A tall, muscular servant was summoned by the high priest, and he silently carried her away.

"What happened? She's not hurt, is she?" Tommy asked Espri quickly when the man disappeared into the back of the temple with the priestess.

"No," Espri assured him.

"When can I meet her?"

"I'm afraid that's impossible," she explained as the priest came forth to end the ceremony. "She is forbidden contact with the islanders."

Tommy's spirits sank at her words, and he fell silent.

Driven to emotional heights by Tikiru's sacrifice, the Malikans were ready to celebrate, and they left the temple, their mood exultant. Only Tommy lingered behind, staring up at the now-darkened altar and remembering the woman who had stared at him so boldly during the climax of her performance.

The erotic nature of the ceremony had only enhanced the desire Mitch had been feeling as he'd sat so close to Espri, and he felt a searing need to be alone with her as they followed the crowd from the temple.

Espri, too, had felt the stirrings of passion as she'd watched the *taupau's* performance, and she was eager to be with him. All afternoon she had pondered the revelation that had come to her during their lovemaking. It was true, she decided. She loved him. And that discovery had left her alternately ecstatic and frightened.

The words he had spoken so offhandedly to Tommy, about leaving the island, were branded in her mind. He had meant them, of that she was certain. He wanted to return to his home in San Francisco. Her only hope, she realized, was to try to win his heart, to make him want to remain on Malika, for she did not want to think of losing him.

"Espri . . ."

"Come." She took his hand and led him down an obscure path, away from the others.

"Where are we going?" he asked with a smile of anticipation as the forest closed around them in a warm, green cocoon, heightening the intimacy between them.

"To my favorite place on the island." Espri's voice was breathless as she directed him through the dense growth. "I hope you will enjoy it too."

Mitch stopped and pulled her into his embrace. "If you are

with me, it will be heavenly." His lips met hers in a fervent caress.

"Hurry!" She laughed lightly as she pulled away and darted ahead of him.

Mitch caught up with her just as they reached the pool, and he pulled her back to him for a passionate kiss. Only when he released her did he look around.

"I see why this is your favorite place," he agreed, taking in the sparkling glory of the waterfall and the blossoms that brightened the deep green foliage adorning the bank.

"Will you swim with me?" she asked enticingly, as she untied her sarong and tossed it aside.

In a quick motion, she dove into the warm, inviting pool and swam easily from him, her sensuous movements holding Mitch spellbound as they revealed only an occasional, teasing glimpse of a rounded breast and sleek thigh. Totally captivated by her loveliness, he stood, transfixed, as she climbed onto the ledge beneath the waterfall. The sight of her standing in shimmering splendor beneath its splashing cascade galvanized him into action, and, shedding his pants, he dove cleanly into the water, swimming to her with hard, powerful strokes.

Espri chuckled throatily as he pulled himself up next to her, and her eyes skimmed his strongly muscled body approvingly. She went into his arms without waiting for an invitation, and beneath the warm caress of the laving waters their lips met, tasted, then blended in soft enchantment.

The moment was sublime. Time ceased to matter. All that existed was man and woman and the breathtaking rapture that nature intended their coming together to be. Love swept over them in a rush of feeling, and they held tightly to one another, bewitched by the surging emotions that possessed them.

Enraptured, Mitch pressed cherishing kisses on her lips, while Espri wanted only to be his, forever. They moved behind the flow of the waterfall then, to stretch out together on the narrow ledge, their bodies united in perfect harmony.

No words were spoken. No words were needed. Each touch, each caress said it all as their hands explored with loving reverence. And, when Mitch could no longer hold back the gift of his desire, he moved between her willingly parted thighs, merging with her in a timeless pattern.

Each stroke of his lean body lifted Espri to greater heights, and she wrapped her limbs about him, drawing him deeper into her as the thrill of his lovemaking sent her spiraling to paradise and beyond. The shuddering of her body as she achieved her pleasure added to Mitch's own excitement, and he lost himself in her velvety depths, reveling in that possession which left him spent yet euphoric.

Cradling Espri in his arms, Mitch lay quietly, sheets of water curtaining them from the real world. It was as though they had transcended time and space, and they surrendered to the beauty of the moment, savoring its perfection.

Espri's senses were alive with love for Mitch as she curled tightly against him. Their joining had been wonderful in every way, and she yearned to stay in his embrace forever.

Tikiru lay prostrate on the mat in her hut as Nelani tended her, washing the vile blood from her limp body. When the gore had been cleaned away, Nelani lifted her mistress's head and pressed a cup of kava to Tikiru's lips.

"Drink," she urged, hoping the potent brew would help to revive her.

Slowly, Tikiru sipped from the cup and then lay back, too weak to move.

"Did I do well?" she asked, without opening her eyes.

"You were magnificent, as always, Tikiru," Nelani reassured her, remembering how the villagers had been entranced by her dancing.

"Good." Tikiru's lips curved slightly. She lay unmoving for a time and then looked up. "The time . . . how late is it?"

"The moon is beginning its ascent."

"Then we must go. Now." She struggled to a sitting position.

"You should rest a little longer and get your strength back."

"There is no time. He will be waiting."

Nelani had hoped that she'd forgotten about the meeting with the white man, but she knew now that was not so. "Are you sure you must do this?"

"Yes." There was certainty in Tikiru's voice. "Bring me a sarong—one of yours. I must not be noticed."

"Yes, Tikiru," Nelani agreed, and she went in search of the garment.

Getting slowly to her feet, Tikiru ran her hands over her body, feeling chilled and slightly nervous over what she was about to do. Never before had she met with a man; she wasn't sure how to go about it. She only knew that she had to be with him.

Nelani returned quickly and wrapped the soft white garment about Tikiru's slender body. "Will we need the cloaks again?"

"Yes, we will wear them until we are far away from the temple."

Minutes later, concealed in the wraps, the young women left their hut and headed in the direction of the cove where Tommy would be waiting.

Tommy stood on the beach, gazing out across the moonlit sea, pondering everything that had happened to him over the past few months. First, he had been shanghaied in San Francisco, then the shipwreck, and now this—a rendezvous with a mysterious woman who had sworn him to secrecy. He wasn't quite sure what to make of it all, and he wondered if anyone would believe him if he did get back home to tell his story.

The thought of his family saddened him, for he knew that they had probably given him up for dead. He'd left the farm in the valley to go into San Francisco on an errand for his father. It had been his first time alone there, and he now regretted that he hadn't followed his father's advice, avoided the saloons and gambling houses. Knowing it was too late to worry about it, he sighed and pushed those thoughts from his mind.

Tommy wasn't sure what caused him to glance back over his shoulder, but when he did, he saw a woman approaching cautiously from the forested edge of the beach.

"Nelani?" he called out softly as he stood up.

"Yes. I am Nelani." She stopped before him.

Tommy frowned as he stared down at her. He sensed that this wasn't the same woman he had kissed last night. Not that he could remember exactly how she'd looked—it had been very dark and he'd been more than a little drunk—but he was almost positive that this was not her.

"I am glad you came." His tone was warm.

"You are to come with me." Her voice was stilted as she repeated Tikiru's instructions.

"I am?" he asked curiously. "Where are we going?"

"I cannot tell you that," Nelani replied curtly. Then she walked away, leaving him to follow.

Tommy was intrigued. Why all the mystery? And if this was Nelani, who was the woman he'd seen last night? Quickly, he went after her, not speaking as they traversed the beach and started up a steep trail that led to an isolated palisade he'd only seen from a distance. The top of the bluff was stark compared to the rest of the lushly forested land, and he looked down at Nelani, wondering what he was supposed to do next.

"She is there waiting for you," Nelani directed; then she turned away, leaving him to venture forth alone.

"Who?" he asked, but Nelani had already disappeared from sight, heading back the way they'd come.

Stepping forth from the protective cover of the trees, Tommy walked across the top of the moonlit bluff, and he couldn't believe his eyes when the woman he'd worshipped from afar earlier that evening appeared before him.

"The *taupau*!" he breathed in awe.

"Yes, I am Tikiru," she answered. "You are Tommy, the golden one."

"I am Tommy." He wasn't quite sure what to say. "Golden one . . . ? You mean my hair?"

"I have never seen such hair before. It is as vibrant as the sun." Boldly she lifted a hand to touch his hair.

Snaring her wrist in a firm yet gentle grip, Tommy stared down at her. "What do you want of me?"

Tikiru's blood was pounding at just that simple touch and her eyes widened at the question. "I do not know. I only know that I needed to see you again."

"Why did you tell me your name was Nelani?" he questioned.

"It is forbidden for me to go into the village." She told the half-truth easily. "If I had been discovered, there might have been trouble."

"Are we safe here?" He looked around.

"Yes, for now, but you must never reveal my identity to anyone." Nervously, she wet her lips with the tip of her tongue, and, though he was not an experienced lover, he recognized the invitation.

Without speaking, he drew her close and kissed her, his mouth taking hers softly at first. He savored the thought that the *taupau* was actually here with him. She was to be cherished. He released her wrist as he deepened the kiss, and instinctively, Tikiru locked her arms behind his neck. Sensations more powerful than those that had assaulted her the night before claimed her now, and she was afire with a strange need she could not name.

Tommy lost track of everything except the woman in his arms. She clung heatedly to him, moving against his hips in an innately sensuous rhythm that was pushing him over the edge of control.

"I would touch you," he murmured as he pressed kisses against the slim line of her throat.

Without thought, Tikiru untied the sarong and let it drop. She was accustomed to nudity and found great pleasure in rubbing her breasts against his chest, but when Tommy suddenly stopped, she looked up at him wonderingly.

Tommy was looking down at her, totally bewitched. Things were happening so fast that he wasn't sure it was real. Before him stood the woman he'd desired from the first moment he'd seen her, and she, it seemed, wanted him. The memory of her seductive dance with the snake on the altar destroyed the last of his restraint. Swinging her up into his arms, he searched out a small grassy spot and lay down with her.

Tikiru was enthralled. She had no idea what she was doing, but she knew it felt right. His lips blazed a trail of fire over her more than willing body and when he lingered over the taut peaks of her breasts, she cried out in ecstasy. Many times during her ritual dances, Tikiru had experienced these same feelings, but she had never known what they'd meant. Now, it all came together . . . the heat . . . the tingling . . . the love . . . and when Tommy moved to mount her, she was ready.

Wrapping her legs about his hips as she had seen the island girls do with their mates during the fertility rituals, she urged him closer, wanting him to take what she was so urgently offering. Gone were all thoughts of her vow of chastity, or of the high priests and the possible consequences of her actions. She knew only a burning desire and a throbbing emptiness deep within her that clamored to be fulfilled.

Lost in the rapture of her sweetness, Tommy positioned himself and plunged deep within her. He did not realize that she was untouched until he broke the barrier of her innocence. The cry of agony that erupted from her as he breached her tight sweetness was like a knife to his heart, and he froze in horror.

"God, Tikiru, I didn't know . . . I'm sorry . . . I didn't mean to hurt you."

"It is good, my love. Do not worry. Take me to your fullest passion. I would know it now." She framed his face with her hands and kissed him, but Tommy was immobilized by what had just occurred.

How could it be that she was still a virgin? Surely every man on the island wanted her. He had seen that tonight at the ceremony. How had she remained untouched all this time?

"Please, golden one." Tikiru kissed him again, this time boldly slipping her tongue between his lips and challenging him. "Love me."

Tommy shuddered as his desire stirred to life, and when her hands moved lower to caress his back and buttocks, he could no longer deny his need. His movements were swift and sure as he possessed her completely, and moments later, he achieved his peak, emptying himself deep within her.

Tikiru lay still beneath his welcome weight, wondering at what had just taken place. Though he seemed totally content, she still felt a burning passion that had not been satisfied. Her breasts were throbbing, her nipples alive with the need to be touched. Deep within the womanly core of her, a pulse was beating that had only increased in tempo since Tommy had ceased his movements.

"Tommy . . . please touch me again. I need to know more of you. My body is still on fire," she pleaded.

Though his own desire was quenched, he kissed her deeply, and feeling her need, with great tenderness he began to rouse her to completion. His mouth sought her breasts, teasing them with heated caresses, while his hands stroked her lower limbs, skimming lightly over her hips and thighs before centering on her most vulnerable place. Tikiru began to move wildly as the flame within her grew, and when her world exploded in the blinding flash of feeling that pulsed through her body, she collapsed, sobbing, against him, no longer an innocent, but a woman well loved.

Together they drifted in languid peace, each having found total fulfillment in the other.

"I love you, Tikiru. From the moment I saw you at the temple, I knew I must have you."

The mention of the temple sent a chill through her, and she shivered.

"Are you cold?" he asked, concerned.

"No. I am warmed by the strength of your love, but I must go. Will you meet me again?"

"Of course, but can't you come to me in the village?"

"No. It is not allowed."

"Then when?"

"I will send word through Nelani."

"Do not make me wait too long." He leaned over her to kiss her again. "My desire for you has only grown more intense since we have been together."

She responded willingly to his kiss and then drew away.

"It will not be long, but you must promise never to tell anyone of our meetings."

"I would do nothing to endanger what we share. If you want my silence, you have it."

Tikiru took his hand and placed it on her breast, enjoying the feel of it on her body. "Your hands do marvelous things to me. It is as if we were made to be one."

"Yes, love. It seems that way."

Their eyes met and held in the moonlit darkness. Then, as she watched, he shifted his hand to cup her breast and gently kissed the peak, running his tongue across its sensitive flesh.

Throwing her head back in rapturous wonder, she arched to him and surrendered briefly to the working of his lips and tongue. What joy! Only the realization that time was slipping away kept her from giving herself to him again.

"I must go." She tore herself from him and quickly rose to her feet, lest her body completely betray her.

"I will be waiting." His voice was solemn as he looked up at her, standing so beautiful and proud before him.

She nodded, then hurriedly picked up her sarong. She did not even bother to put it on, but hastened into the protective seclusion of the forest where Nelani waited, holding her cloak. She slipped it on.

"Your sarong?" Nelani asked.

"I do not need it," Tikiru replied quietly. She wanted only to return to the safety of her home.

Nelani bundled the garment under her arm, and they started off in the direction of their hut. They arrived there without incident, and when they were safely inside Tikiru stripped off the concealing cloak. It was then that Nelani gasped, terror on her face.

"What . . . ?" Tikiru looked at her quizzically.

"By the gods! You have broken your vow!" Nelani pointed at the blood smeared on her slender thighs.

"If you value your life, you will hold your tongue," Tikiru hissed.

"But why? You have everything! Why risk it all? Even your life?"

"I love him, Nelani. Now, speak no more of this. What has happened is my choice. You will say nothing," she ordered.

"Yes, Tikiru." Nelani was dazed by the realization of what had just happened. She had suspected that it might, but she had never believed the other woman would truly forsake her vow. "Shall we go to the pool? It would be best to bathe the scent of the man from your body. Then I will anoint you again."

"All right," Tikiru agreed. She was nervous now that she

was away from Tommy and the protective warmth of his embrace.

Together, the two women walked through the moon-kissed darkness to the private bathing pool, and in the quiet of the predawn hours, Nelani washed all traces of the man's possession from Tikiru's body.

Much later, when Tikiru lay alone in her sleeping quarters, she had time to think of her joining with the golden one, to remember the glorious splendor of his touch. Nothing in her young life had prepared her for the joy of their union, and she meditated on it as the birds began their morning song to welcome the dawn. Perhaps, she thought as she listened to their exultant song, she would feel that way about each new day now that she had Tommy. And with a smile curving her lips, she drifted off to sleep, exhausted in mind and body.

Chapter 11

The low-lying clouds that scudded across the moon in a gauzy veil momentarily blocked the purity of its light as the two lovers walked hand in hand along the path that led from the pool. Pausing occasionally to kiss and whisper endearments, they savored the intimacy of the evening they'd just passed, alone and isolated from the revelry that was going on in the village.

Espri's heart sang as Mitch's lips met hers in a tender exchange. No words could describe the perfection of what they'd shared, and any doubts she'd had about loving him had been erased. She wanted him with a passion that surprised her, and she vowed to find a way to win his devotion.

It was with much regret that Mitch ended the kiss. As he smiled down at her, he saw desire flare once again in her dark eyes. How sweet she was, and so giving. Her lovemaking had been so uninhibited that the memory of intimacy with any other woman faded. Caressing her cheek with an adoring touch, he pressed soft kisses to the corners of her mouth before drawing back.

Then he studied her face intently, wondering what it was about her that fascinated him so. She was beautiful, but he'd known other beautiful women. He frowned slightly at the realization that Espri touched him deeply, made him want her beyond all reason. It was becoming difficult for him to consider leaving her when a ship came.

"Mitch, is something wrong?" Espri saw his frown and wondered about its cause.

"No, love, nothing's wrong," he murmured.

His use of the word "love" thrilled her. "You are not unhappy?"

"No." Mitch grinned boyishly. He'd never been more content in his life. "I'm not unhappy."

"Good." Espri flashed him a bright, coquettish smile, and they started off in the direction of the village.

Even though she was surrounded by happy, celebrating islanders, Laiti was unhappy. Jacques had not returned to her since she had asked him not to drink that morning, and she had come to realize as the hours passed that there was little hope he would. He had used liquor as a crutch too long to be able to give it up now. She had thought that her offer of love, of a new beginning, might lure him away from it, but she had been wrong. Sighing in disappointed acceptance, she rose and walked toward her hut. She had had enough of the revelry. It was time to be alone.

Laiti did not see the man standing in the night's deep shadows, and only as she was about to enter her home did she hear his call.

"Laiti."

"Who is it?" She squinted into the darkness, but could only make out a male form.

"Jacques." He stepped out into the flickering firelight.

"You've come?" Happiness surged through Laiti.

"I've come," he said somberly, coming to stand before her. "I've done a lot of thinking today."

"I'm sorry if I was cruel this morning."

"Everything you said . . . was true," he admitted haltingly. "You were right . . . Tila is dead."

"Oh, Jacques!" She went tearfully into his arms. "Everything will be all right now, I know it!"

He lifted her chin, and though he smiled down at her, it was a smile tinged with sad acceptance. "I think so."

Konga had been drinking steadily since he'd argued with Tana, and he was now quite drunk. Sitting alone amidst the crowd of merrymakers, he stared leeringly into the flames of the massive bonfire, fantasizing about what he was going to do to Mitch. He hated him! Never before had he felt such unbridled bloodlust, and he was determined to kill the white man the first chance he got!

His hand moved exploringly to his waist, and he smiled viciously as he touched the knife strapped there. A quick death would be too easy for that man. Perhaps he would carve him into little pieces.

Konga did not see Mitch and Espri enter the village. Though it was very late and most of the islanders had had far too much to drink, the celebration showed no sign of abating, and the pair were immediately caught up in the revelry. Drums pounded out a wild, sensual rhythm, and many of the Malikan women danced before the men, proud to show off their talents.

"Look! There's Espri!" one of the dancing women called out. "Come, Espri! Join us!"

Espri wanted only to stay by Mitch's side, but the women giddily grabbed her by the arms and pulled her into their midst. They knew she was one of the finest dancers on the island so they wanted her to join them in the joyous fertility dance. Unable to escape them, Espri gave Mitch an apologetic look.

Mitch, however, was intrigued at the prospect of watching her dance, and he smiled his approval.

The drums switched to a different rhythm, their pagan

beat arousing all the primitive urges Espri tried so carefully to control. She had always enjoyed dancing, and she found herself swept away by the sensuous music. Her body moved as one with the throbbing beat, drawing breathless approval from those watching and envious glances from the other females. Though they were good, Espri outshone them, her lithe figure taunting and retreating before some unseen lover in bewitching, erotic movements. When at last the drums rose to a crescendo and then suddenly ceased, she fell to her knees in supplication, her arms outstretched, her eyes, fixed on Mitch, leaving no doubt as to her feelings.

There was a clamor of excited adulation when she finished, but it stopped abruptly for Konga roared to his feet, throwing his bottle of liquor into the fire with crashing, explosive intent. Nervously, the hushed villagers backed out of his way as he stalked toward Mitch. They knew Konga was a force to be reckoned with, and they did not want to incur his wrath.

"I let you go easily last night," the huge warrior declared as he approached his rival. "But you will not be so lucky now. I challenge you to prove yourself, white man." He eyed Mitch with obvious disdain.

A challenge, so issued, was rare on Malika for it usually meant that the fight would be to the death. The carefree islanders generally enjoyed life too much to get embroiled in such heated confrontations, and Konga's dare shocked them. They all knew how he felt about Espri, but they had never suspected that he would go to such lengths to try to win her.

Espri gasped. "Konga, no!"

"Shut up, woman." His words were a snarl.

Mitch was caught off guard by Konga's dare, but he showed no sign of it as he faced the warrior, his stony gaze subtly gauging the islander's strengths and weaknesses. Though he and Konga were about the same height, Konga outweighed him by at least fifty pounds, and Mitch knew that could be a deadly difference.

"I have no reason to prove myself to you," he replied with disdain.

Konga colored at Mitch's taunt. "Then you are less than a man!"

Mitch leveled a frigid gaze upon his flushed-faced adversary as he shrugged with seeming indifference.

"There are those who would argue the point."

Taking him to mean Espri, Konga lost control and started to launch himself at Mitch, but Espri threw herself before her lover.

"You allow a mere woman to protect you?" Konga chided. "It is as I said—you are no man."

"Espri," Mitch said quietly, "move. This is something I should have taken care of last night."

"Mitch . . . please . . ."

She looked up at him pleadingly, but she found his fierce expression frightening.

"Ha!" Konga laughed. "He listens to the counsel of women! He is a fool!"

A hushed silence fell over the group as Mitch gently shoved Espri to the side. "You are the fool, Konga. You are like a wild dog, baying at the moon. You want something that will never be yours. A wise man knows the difference between that which he can and cannot have, and he accepts his lot without anger."

Konga drew his knife and tried to lunge at Mitch, but two of the island men restrained him.

"You have issued a challenge, and according to custom, it must be dealt with as such," one of the men proclaimed. "Form the circle."

The crowd stepped back until they were standing in a circle, the fire at its center. Then one of the men thrust a long-bladed knife, similar to Konga's, into Mitch's hand.

"There are no rules," the man explained.

Mitch nodded his understanding. He felt no fear as he

stared at Konga. During his younger days he'd been involved in many a brawl in the saloons on the waterfront, and he was quite familiar with knife fighting. His advantage over Konga would be his ability to move, and move quickly. He intended to make the most of it.

The two men who'd been holding Konga released him and stepped back, clearing the circle.

"Come, woman," Konga mocked. "I am waiting."

"Mitch, be careful," Espri whispered as she watched him move cautiously toward Konga.

As soon as Mitch took a step forward, Konga threw himself at Mitch, hoping to fell his opponent immediately, but Mitch nimbly dodged the heavier man, then returned his jeering laugh.

"You are the woman, Konga. You are fat and slow!"

A low chuckle came from the people, but it was quickly silenced when Konga turned a threatening eye on them. Tossing his knife from hand to hand, his movements more deliberate now, he advanced toward Mitch once more. But Mitch was ready, and when Konga launched another attack, he kicked out, knocking the charging warrior's feet from under him. Completely enraged, Konga rolled to his feet, bellowing furiously. Maddened by his rival's unexpected prowess, he lashed out with the knife again and again, backing Mitch toward the crowd, who, according to custom, were forced to shove him back into the fray. Then Konga feinted to the right, but hurled himself to the left. Caught by the ploy, Mitch fell beneath his opponent's great weight. He tried to throw him off, but Konga laughed at his attempt.

"If you were not a woman before, perhaps I should make you one now, eh?" He laughed.

"You'll not have the chance," Mitch scoffed as he freed a hand and chopped at Konga's unprotected throat.

The warrior choked at the surprise blow and grabbed at his

neck. In great pain, he could not stop Mitch from slipping free of his weight. It only took Konga a minute to recover, and he was more infuriated than ever as he again circled Mitch. Death gleamed in his eyes as he thought of how wonderful it would be to sink his knife into the white man's heart.

Mitch read the change in Konga and tensed, sensing that a headlong assault was coming.

"Now!" Konga bellowed as he lashed out with his weapon and lunged forward. His anger helped him this time; he made contact with Mitch, shoving him to the ground and wickedly slashing his upper arm. Then he fell upon him and they struggled fiercely, brawn against brawn, as they rolled about the arena; each desperately seeking an advantage; each determined to win.

Mitch could feel his strength ebbing as his blood flowed freely from the wound Konga had inflicted. He knew he had to do something, and fast, before he lost any more of his agility; but Konga, sensing that he was weakening, increased his ferocity.

Savagely they wrestled, their struggle bringing them closer and closer to the fiery blaze. As Konga rose above him, Mitch gave one last desperate twist, then surged upward in an effort to dislodge him. The strategy worked and the warrior fell heavily to his side, his knife hand exposed to the searing flames. He screamed in agony as he snatched his hand away from the fire, and in that instant Mitch was free. Konga did not allow the burn to stop him, though. Since he'd lost his knife, he grabbed a blazing log from the fire, and holding it with his good hand, he came after Mitch.

Knowing that it was now or never, Mitch dove at Konga. Knocking the fiery weapon away and pinning him to the ground, he placed his knife at the warrior's throat.

"With one thrust I could kill you, Konga," Mitch rasped raggedly, and the islanders fell silent as they waited to see him complete the fight. "But I will not."

Konga glared up at Mitch as he moved off his chest, wishing that the white man had done the deed. By sparing his life, he had disgraced him before his friends.

"Go ahead. Kill me!"

But Mitch merely tossed the knife aside, and favoring his injured arm, turned to Espri, who awaited him.

Tana had heard the commotion and had rushed over to find out what was going on. It had disgusted her that Konga was drunk and challenging Mitch to a fight, for she had known that in his condition he didn't stand a chance to win. Mitch was not as big as Konga, but he was strong and no doubt faster, and Tana had felt certain that he would be victorious.

Now, as she watched Konga slowly rise, cradling his burned arm, she felt nothing but revulsion for him. The man was an idiot, and he deserved what he'd gotten.

Glancing over toward Mitch, Tana was irritated when she saw Espri hovering over him. How unfair it was that she had won again! Everything Espri wanted she got. A firm resolve took hold of Tana. Somehow, she was going to find a way to ruin Espri's happiness.

"Mitch! Espri! What happened?" Jacques pushed his way through the gathering with Laiti following close behind him.

"Konga challenged Mitch to a fight, Papa," she explained quickly.

"And Mitch won?" Her father was astounded.

"Yes. We have to do something about his arm."

"Bring him to my hut," Laiti offered. "I will tend him there."

And as they walked off, they did not see the baleful glare that Konga directed their way.

It was late when Tommy arrived at the hut. He needed desperately to talk with Mitch about what had just happened, but he knew he could not. Tikiru had made him promise to keep silent about their meeting, and he had to respect her wishes. He entered as quietly as possible, not wishing to disturb Mitch, and he was surprised to find that his friend had not yet returned from the celebration in the village.

Stretching out on one of the sleeping mats Anuitua had provided, he tried to sleep, but sleep proved elusive. Time and again he envisioned the perfection of Tikiru's body and he remembered the overpowering joy he'd felt when he'd made love to her. He loved her. He wanted her. Nothing else mattered to him. At that moment, if he'd been given the choice between returning home to the bosom of his loving family or staying on the island in the hope of meeting Tikiru again, he would have stayed. Tossing restlessly, he finally managed to doze off, but his dreams were troubled by confusing visions of snakes and Tikiru and the altar.

Espri stood with her father outside the hut and near the small fire he'd built while inside Laiti set about binding Mitch's arm.

"It is not a good thing that he defeated Konga," Jacques said worriedly.

"What do you mean?" Espri cried. "You would rather he had been killed?"

"No. Of course not, but we both know how ferocious Konga's temper can be. Mitch has humiliated him before most of the tribe. It will not sit well with him."

"We must warn Mitch then. Although Konga is an honorable warrior—"

"Konga was an honorable warrior. He has never been beaten before, and we do not know how he will react."

Espri nodded in agreement and then, as her thoughts moved to other things, she realized how unusual it was for her father to be with Laiti—and to be sober. "What are you doing here with Laiti? I thought you would be with Grandfather."

"Laiti is a good woman," Jacques answered slowly, glancing toward the hut. "I have grown fond of her."

Espri was startled by the news. "You have?"

"We have talked, she and I, and we have much in common."

"I had noticed that you . . ." Espri wasn't quite sure how to mention his sobriety, but he laughed and answered for her.

"That I haven't been drinking." At her nod, he went on. "Laiti has asked that I not drink while I am with her, and I've agreed." The feeling of being fully alive as a man once more was a heady experience for him and far more potent than any intoxicating brew.

"Papa, that's wonderful." Espri smiled delightedly. "I'm so happy for you!"

"Are you?" Jacques wondered.

"Yes!"

"But your mother . . ." A trace of guilt still hovered in the back of his mind.

"My mother has been dead for many years. She would not begrudge you happiness, Papa. She would insist upon it!"

Jacques smiled at that thought. "And you, Espri. Are you happy?"

She stared solemnly at the doorway to the hut. "I care about him deeply."

"I have seen it in your eyes, *chérie,* but be careful. Although he is not the ne'er-do-well I'd originally thought, he is not one of us."

"I know." Espri released a small sigh. "I know."

It was midmorning when Tana strolled excitedly across the beach in the direction of Mitch's hut. She had just spoken with her father at length, and at her suggestion, Kohea had agreed to loan Mitch and Tommy a canoe so they could join the island men on the fishing excursions. That excited her for if they accepted the offer, twice a day she would have the chance to talk with Mitch.

Mitch had not yet arisen. He'd returned to the hut just before dawn after spending a few hours talking with Jacques and Laiti and Espri. His arm had been sore, but the cut had not been too deep. It would heal. Relaxing on his mat, he had closed his eyes and had soon fallen asleep, his injury and the excitement of the night having taken their toll.

Tommy had awakened early, however, his mind filled with thoughts of Tikiru. He had not been an innocent where women were concerned, yet his night with Tikiru had opened up a whole new vista for him and he yearned to see her again. He was in love. He was certain of it. What else could it be? His soul longed for her closeness, his body ached to be joined with hers.

He had been up for several hours before Mitch emerged from the hut to join him on the beach.

"What happened to your arm?" he said. He'd seen the bandage when he'd awakened and had wondered about it.

"There was a fight in the village last night. It's nothing serious." Mitch dismissed his injury, for he did not want to discuss his altercation with Konga.

"Oh." Tommy sensed that there was more to the matter, but he did not pursue it. "Have you ever been in love?" he asked quickly as he idly tossed a shell across the sand.

Mitch was startled by his question, but he smiled knowingly. "No. Why? Has some little island girl caught your eye?"

Tommy couldn't prevent the flush that spread across his features. "You could say that."

"Who is she?"

"I don't think you've met her yet. Her name is Nelani," he lied, knowing that to reveal Tikiru's identity might get her into trouble. "I think she is the most gorgeous woman in the whole world and I can't seem to get her out of my mind. Don't you feel that way about Espri?"

"Espri is a beautiful woman." Mitch suddenly felt uncomfortable under the younger man's probing questions.

Tommy was puzzled. "I don't understand. You want her, don't you?"

"Of course I want her." Mitch was irritated. He did not want to explain himself. "I'd be a fool not to."

"But you don't love her or want to marry her?"

"No! You will find as you grow older that wanting and loving are not necessarily related," Mitch snapped. The younger man's simplistic logic disturbed him.

"If you loved her, though, wouldn't you want to stay here? I mean, Malika is a virtual paradise."

"But I don't love Espri," Mitch declared, with more vehemence than was necessary.

"But suppose you did"—Tommy was trying to find the answer to his own dilemma—"wouldn't you want to stay on Malika and be with her?"

"No. I could not stay here. I have too many responsibilities at home. I must get back," Mitch explained. "When a ship finally does arrive, Espri and I will go our separate ways."

It sounded reasonable enough, but as he said the words, Mitch felt slightly disgusted with himself.

Tana could not believe what she was hearing as she approached the two men. The sea breeze was carrying their words directly to her, and Mitch's statement that he did not love Espri, his plan to leave Malika, made Tana smile to herself. She wondered what Espri would think if she knew how indifferent her lover really was.

"Good morning." She greeted the men brightly, and they looked up, surprised. They had been too intent on their conversation to notice her approach.

"Hello, Tana."

"Mitch, how is your arm? I have worried all night."

"There was no need to concern yourself. It will be fine."

"That is good," Tana responded, and sensing that they wondered why she had come, she went on. "I have news from my father."

"What is it?"

"If you are able, he is willing to take you out in a canoe so you can learn how to fish our shores."

Knowing that it was important to learn all they could about the way of life here, they readily accepted the offer.

"Good. The canoes will be going out later this afternoon. Father suggested that you share our midday meal before going out, so he can tell you what you need to know."

"Tell him we would be honored," Mitch said.

"Fine." Tana's smile was warm. "I will see you then."

Espri had spent the night at Luatu's, and she had fallen asleep almost immediately upon retiring. She had longed to spend the balance of the night with Mitch, but since he was sharing the hut with Tommy, such intimacy was impossible. Perhaps someday they would never have to part. She sighed dreamily as she hurried from her grandfather's to seek out her love.

Her heart was light as she raced lightly over the path that led to the beach, but her happiness wavered as she emerged from the trees to find Tana with Mitch and Tommy. What was she doing here? Her mistrust of the other woman went deep, and she was instantly on guard. Had Tana gone to Mitch last night after he'd left the village? That thought sent jealousy flaming through Espri, but she forced herself to put it from her mind. Still, she couldn't help but remember Tana's interest in Mitch, and she was relieved to see that the other woman was taking her leave of them.

Tana was surprised and vindictively pleased when she saw Espri heading her way.

"Good morning," she purred. "It's a wonderful morning, isn't it?"

"Yes, it is," Espri responded, smiling through clenched teeth as she walked by her.

Tana, having noted Espri's misgivings, merely chuckled throatily as she continued on her way.

"Espri!" Mitch called as he caught sight of her. He was struck by her natural beauty, and a thrill of emotion charged through him. Remembering that he'd just emphatically denied any real interest in her, he suddenly felt like a blackguard. It jarred him to realize that he'd come to care deeply for Espri and that it would not be a simple matter for him to leave her.

Faced with the truth, he wondered what to do. His relationships with women had followed a predictable pattern. He would court them, woo them, bed them, and when they began to indicate a desire for marriage, he would discard them for a new conquest. But Espri wasn't like those women. They had been worldly. They had entered into a liaison with him, knowing that he wasn't interested in a permanent attachment, and though a number of them had tried to maneuver him to the altar, his wishes had prevailed.

But Espri . . . where did she fit into his life? She had saved him from almost certain death. She had given him the gift of her innocence with no thought to the consequences, and she continued to give, though he'd never professed love for her or made any promises. Oddly enough, that made him want to possess her even more; yet he had vowed never to allow any woman to become so important to him that his own happiness depended on her well-being.

Confused by his feelings, he pushed his perplexing thoughts away and rose to go meet Espri.

Chapter 12

It was midday and Anuitua with Tana's help had prepared a sumptuous feast. The older woman was surprised by her daughter's enthusiastic assistance.

"Why this sudden interest in cooking?" she asked.

"I have decided that Konga is not the man for me," Tana answered coolly. "And there is no man on the island I would rather have than Mitch."

"He is an *upalu kane*," her mother agreed. "Were I not an old woman . . ." She laughed ruefully as she imagined herself in the arms of the virile younger man.

Tana gave Anuitua a quick incredulous look, amazed that her mother would harbor such thoughts.

"But what of Konga? You have wanted him for so long," Anuitua pressed, wanting to know more about this unexpected change in her daughter's feelings.

"I grew tired of waiting for him to realize the depth of my love," the young woman lied, not wanting her mother to know that Konga had callously rejected her.

"That is good. You are at the age when you should be considering marriage, and with Konga's feelings for Espri, he would not have made you a good husband."

"I know."

"This Mitch . . . he cares for Espri, doesn't he? After all, he fought with Konga over her last night," Anuitua said shrewdly.

Tana's eyes brightened as she recalled Mitch's conversation with Tommy that morning. "He is only using her. I overheard him talking with O'Ryan when I went to visit them this morning. He does not love her and plans to leave her behind when he goes."

Her mother frowned. "Even so, wouldn't he do the same to you, were you to win his affections?"

"Espri is an idiot. She knows nothing of men or how to please them, whereas . . ." Tana let herself imagine the joy she would experience in stealing Mitch from Espri.

"They are coming now with your father," Anuitua advised, and Tana went to welcome them.

"Come, join us. Mother and I have prepared the meal and it is ready for you," she invited.

Ignoring her father's amazement at her domesticity, she led them to their dining hut, where Mitch and Tommy sat down in the shade of the open-sided building as Anuitua approached carrying a platter of steaming food.

Tana positioned herself next to Mitch so that she could serve him, and she took great pleasure in leaning near and brushing her breasts against him at every opportunity. He accepted her attentions passively, making no move to encourage her, and she grew more and more frustrated when each tactic she employed to provoke his interest failed.

Mitch was aware of Tana's sensuality as she sat beside him, but he was not in the least affected by it. Espri was the only woman he desired. He concentrated on the instructions Kohea was giving regarding the canoe they would be using.

When, at last, the meal was ended and the men rose to be about their business, Tana was sorely vexed, for her attempts to get closer to Mitch had been unsuccessful. Deciding on a new strategy, she smiled grimly. If she couldn't entice Mitch to come to her, perhaps the best way to destroy Espri's happiness was to manipulate her. Espri was inexperienced, and Tana was confident that she could turn the conversation she'd over-heard that morning to her own advantage. Intent on her goal, she headed into the village to find her rival.

Skirting the splashing waters of the waterfall, Espri swam slowly across the width of the pool. After leaving Mitch, she'd come there to think and to try to make some sense out of her runaway emotions. Seeing Tana with him that morning had aroused a sense of jealousy in her, startling because of its fierceness. It was not like her to be so volcanic in her reac-tions to people, and it worried her to find that she had so little real control over what she was feeling. When the sound of someone coming drew her attention, Espri was dismayed to see Tana standing at the edge of the pool.

"Why, Espri, I didn't know you would be here," Tana ex-claimed convincingly; though in truth, after fruitlessly searching the village she listened to women's conversations to discover where Espri had gone.

"I was just leaving, so you can have the pool all to your-self," Espri remarked before she started to swim back to the bank.

"Don't leave on my account," Tana told her as she settled on the moss-covered ground. "I just wanted to come here and enjoy the quiet for a while."

"It is a peaceful place," Espri agreed.

"I'm sure you needed some quiet too, after all the excite-ment last night. Konga certainly made a fool of himself and Mitch . . ." Tana sighed exaggeratedly. "Wasn't he wonderful? I'm so glad that his arm wasn't badly hurt. With any luck, he'll be fine in a few days."

"Yes, he will." Espri was finding her remarks most irritat-ing. How long had Tana been with Mitch that morning? she wondered bitterly. And what had passed between them in the afternoon while he'd been at her home?

"He and Tommy have gone out with the men, fishing, you know," Tana went on. "My father is teaching them to use the canoes so they will be able to provide for themselves while they are with us. I just wonder how long he'll be here . . ."

"I imagine he'll be here for some time. Ships rarely come to Malika." Espri was voicing her real desire.

"Ah, but when a vessel does come, he will leave." Tana's statement held a finality that chilled Espri. "Why, only this morning, he was telling Tommy how important it was that he return to his home and how he will leave Malika without a regret when it is possible to do so."

Espri's eyes widened a bit at this last news.

"You look surprised, Espri." Tana's gaze narrowed as she prepared to deliver her most devastating line. "Did he tell you that he was going to stay?"

"No."

"I'd thought not, but I suppose you were hoping . . ." She read the answer in Espri's eyes and gave her a consoling look. "Your innocence may have intrigued Mitch in the beginning, but—"

"But, what?" Espri demanded, suddenly furious that this woman should know something about Mitch that she did not.

"Mitch is a man used to dealing with experienced women. I assumed you understood, but being as naïve as you are—"

"What are you talking about?"

"Well, it's obvious to me how you feel. You love him, and you want to marry him. You even turned down Konga for Mitch. But, Espri, you're being foolhardy. Mitch doesn't love you."

"You don't know that!" Espri cried. She had already been drawn into Tana's malicious game.

Tana suppressed a victorious smile. "Oh, but I do." She stood up slowly, smoothing her sarong sensuously over her thighs. "This morning, he denied it before both Tommy and me."

The color faded from Espri's perfect features. "Oh." She remembered Mitch's slightly distant mood when they'd been together. At the time, she had thought it was because Tommy was with them, but it was not. He did not love her, and he had proclaimed it openly. What he felt for her was simply lust. Espri felt embarrassed by her childish dreams of winning his affections.

"He said he didn't love you and that he intended to go home just as quickly as he could." Tana enjoyed the sense of power she was feeling.

"As I told you that first day, Tana, Mitch is free to make his own decisions." Espri tried to seem indifferent, though Tana's statements had shattered her. "I have no hold on him."

"Obviously," Tana said tauntingly as she started down the path. "And I'm glad."

When the other woman had disappeared from sight, Espri dove beneath the surface and swam to the bank underwater. Pain, sharp and agonizing, was tearing at her as she stepped from the pool, and her tears fell unheeded as she wrapped her sarong tightly about her. Mitch did not love her . . . he planned to leave . . . he was used to sophisticated women. Now she understood her father's warning. Mitch was a white man, different from the islanders.

Espri found her own innocence humiliating. How trusting she'd been! She had given her heart far too quickly. She should have remembered her resolution never to fall in love. She should have exercised more control over herself.

Anger overcame her, and with it came some semblance of rational thought. While it was true that Tana's news hurt, perhaps it was not such a bad thing to find it out now. Now that she'd been made aware of Mitch's intentions, she could protect herself.

There is no point in continuing to see him, Espri thought.

Why spend more time with him and risk deepening my strong attraction when I know there is no future for us?

It was better to end the relationship. No doubt, Mitch would not be troubled overmuch by her refusal to be with him anymore. As Tana had said, he didn't love her, so it would be easy for him to find another to satisfy his needs. Still, the prospect of never knowing his love again tore at her heart. His touch . . . She knew it would take a long time to forget the bliss they had shared. Sadder but wiser, Espri left the pool.

As was their custom, the island men met on the beach to make the preparations for the afternoon's catch, and Mitch and Tommy were warmly welcomed by them. When Mitch was congratulated for his stunning victory over Konga, he accepted the praise coolly. He had not wanted to fight the man, and he was glad that it was over.

"Is Konga going out?" he asked Kohea as they readied the boats.

"He'll be along, but it is difficult for him right now. He lost much face last night, and he's in danger of losing his status as a mighty warrior."

"He was drunk."

"True, but *he* issued the challenge and he lost. It is our way," the older man explained.

Mitch said no more as they completed their preparations, and when all was ready, Kohea gave the order and they set forth.

Under the expert guidance of the islanders, the canoes moved swiftly out to sea, and Mitch and Tommy were pleased that they managed to hold their own with the proficient natives. Though they knew the basic fundamentals of maneuvering the outriggers, it was their first time out and it was a challenge.

Tommy was glad for the diversion the outing provided, for

he was hoping that the fishing trip would help keep his mind off Tikiru. She had been in his thoughts all day; she was becoming an obsession with him. Each minute away from her seemed like an hour, and he could hardly wait to see her again. Forcing himself to concentrate, he followed Kohea's instructions carefully, helping Mitch paddle the vessel through the dangerous, narrow channel in the barrier reef and out into the open, unprotected waters of the Pacific.

Having made the passage safely, Mitch and Tommy felt more confident about their abilities, and they settled easily into the islanders' ways, relaxing and truly enjoying the adventure of the catch.

Konga had watched from afar, waiting until the outriggers were in the water before joining them. Even then, he trailed slightly behind, for he wanted to avoid drawing attention to himself. Revenge was his motive on this day; he fully intended to pay Mitch back for the humiliation he'd suffered the night before.

Taking great care to conceal his resentment, he waited for the opportunity that he knew would come. It would take a while for the blood of their catch to attract the sharks, but invariably the gray, sleek monsters of the deep would come. In the distance, they would circle menacingly, awaiting the chance for an easy meal. And today Konga hoped that easy meal would consist of the two white men.

His plans made, Konga busied himself with fishing. It was difficult for him to maneuver his nets and spear because of his injured hand, and the pain served as a vivid, angry reminder of his purpose. Mitch had taken his woman. He had embarrassed him before the entire village. The white man would pay with his life!

As the hours passed and the sun dipped low on the western horizon, the sharks appeared. At the sight of them, Konga knew it was time to make his move so he maneuvered himself within striking range of Mitch and Tommy's canoe. When they were both standing to pull in their nets and could not see what he was doing, Konga reached out with his paddle and tipped their canoe, sending them both splashing headlong into the sea.

The sharks, ever aware of vibrations in the water, homed in on their thrashing. With lightning speed, they darted toward the floundering men. Though the canoes were spread out over a goodly distance, Kohea saw their plight and sent out the warning cry. Immediately, the islanders abandoned their nets and set out to aid the men in the water.

Gasping for breath, Mitch surfaced first. Unaware of the danger, he treaded water for a moment, waiting for Tommy, and when his friend came up, they struck out for their canoe together.

"What happened?" Tommy was obviously disturbed by the unexpected upset.

"I'm not sure," Mitch ground out as he latched onto the side of their outrigger. "But I've got a feeling it was no accident."

Tommy's expression grew pensive. "Konga. But why would—"

He didn't finish his statement for the cries of the islanders interrupted him.

"Konga! Help Tommy while I get Mitch!" Kohea was shouting as he paddled full speed in their direction.

"What the—" Mitch grasped the older man's hand and was hauled unceremoniously into his canoe just as the attacking sharks darted past.

Konga was thoroughly disgusted. His plan had failed and yet . . . He decided that he could still turn the situation to his benefit. By rescuing Tommy, he could save face, so he grudgingly paddled nearer and extended a saving hand to the panicked young white man.

What happened next was so unexpected that for years to come the natives would speak of it in terror.

Tommy had just grasped Konga's hand and had levered himself halfway over the side of the outrigger when a shark struck at Konga's vessel. Konga had been standing in order to pull Tommy into the boat, and the blow of the lethal creature catapulted him into the water and made him a hapless prey for the already frenzied sharks.

His horror-filled scream echoed across the open waters as the sharks attacked. Tommy managed to throw himself the rest of the way into the canoe, and he watched in terror-filled frustration as Konga's blood stained the turquoise sea. It was over almost as soon as it had begun.

Dazed, the men left the scene to return to the safety of land. Though Konga had died a hero's death and there would be a celebration in honor of his bravery, none of them would soon forget the grisly spectacle they'd just witnessed.

It was late afternoon and Tikiru was pacing her hut like a caged tigress. Though she was nude and had just returned from the bathing pool, she felt hot and restless. Memories of the previous night with Tommy burned within her, and she craved him. Consumed by her need, she strode out onto the veranda, hoping that a cooling breeze would end her torment, but the air was still and she grew more and more distraught with every passing moment. She had to have him. She had to be with him.

"Tikiru!" Manti's imperative call sliced through the haze of her desire, and she looked up questioningly.

Affecting a look of regal disdain, she faced the high priest. "Manti, I had not expected you."

The old man stared at her, his eyes narrowing. There was something different about her, but he wasn't quite sure what it was. "There has been a death," he stated baldly. "Your people will need you tonight."

"A death? Who?" She suddenly feared that it might have been Tommy.

Manti saw the flicker of emotion in her eyes and wondered at it. "Konga, son of Autiki."

"How?" Tikiru breathed an inward sigh of relief.

"An accident while fishing . . . a shark attack."

A shiver ran through her. "I will celebrate the ceremony of death at the midnight hour."

Mitch and Tommy walked slowly toward the village. Their mood was grim for they realized just how close they had come to death.

"He tried to murder us, Mitch!" Tommy finally voiced his thoughts.

"I know," Mitch answered. "I should have watched him more carefully. I should have realized that he was out to kill me, but the whole afternoon had gone so well that I let my guard down."

"I'm glad he's dead!" Tommy declared vehemently. "He deserved it, but the others think he died trying to save me!"

"At that moment, he was trying to save you. I guess he thought by helping in the rescue he could regain stature with the villagers."

"Shouldn't we tell them what really happened?" Tommy demanded.

Mitch was thoughtful. "There is no point, now. He's dead."

Tommy was still outraged at the islander's cowardly trick, but he had to agree that no real purpose would be served by revealing Konga's treachery. It was over.

Mitch thought of Konga and his obsession for Espri. The Malikan had wanted her and had been willing to go to any lengths to have her, and for that he'd paid with his life.

"I'd better find Espri and tell her all that happened," he said. "Are you going to the temple tonight?"

"Yes." Tommy responded quickly, for he hoped that Tikiru would be present at the ceremony.

"I'll see you there," Mitch called back as he headed off to locate Espri.

When Espri had returned to the village after her conversation with Tana, her resolve had been firm—she would have no more to do with Mitch, no matter how badly she might want him. Jacques had sensed a change in her and had questioned her about it, but her feelings had been too raw at the time to discuss it. She had told him only that she was going home.

Jacques and Laiti had been confused by Espri's decision to leave, but had not tried to press her for an explanation. And when Jacques had considered going with her, Laiti had discouraged him, her womanly instincts telling her that Espri needed some time alone.

Now, as they watched Mitch approaching, they wondered what to say to him.

"Laiti, Jacques." He greeted them easily as he glanced around in search of Espri. "Do you know where Espri is?"

"Yes," Jacques said curtly. "She's gone home."

Mitch was startled. "Home? Why?"

"She did not say," Laiti put in. "She left some hours ago."

"She did?" He frowned. "I guess I'd better go after her. Have you heard the news about Konga yet?"

"Konga? No."

"He was killed during the catch. A shark."

"How could that be?"

"One of the sharks upset his canoe and he fell in." Mitch paused as he remembered the gory scene. "I'll talk with you about it later. I want to find Espri right now."

And before Jacques or Laiti could mention her strange mood, he hurried off.

* * *

Espri had hoped that a vigorous swim would tire her so she could sleep that night, but after only half an hour in the water, she was exhausted physically while her mind still refused to rest. Turning back toward shore, she allowed the surging waters to do the work for her. Floating easily, paddling only occasionally, she drifted toward the beach on the crest of the low-rising waves.

In the shallows, she walked from the water. In the moonlight, the surf swirling about her hips, she seemed a mermaid or a naiad of the sea. Her slender, naked body glistened in the subdued light as she strode forth un-self-consciously, believing herself to be alone.

Mitch reached the glade just as darkness claimed the island. He had been surprised not to find her at the clearing, and he then began to suspect that something was not right. Taking the path to the beach, he stopped, mesmerized, at the edge of the forest when he caught sight of her emerging from the sea. Her beauty was undeniable. With unaffected grace she moved to pick up her things, and his body came alive with need for her.

"Espri . . ." His voice was low and hoarse as he started forward, eager to hold her once more.

Startled by the unexpected interruption of her solitude, she clasped her sarong to her breast and whirled about to face him.

"Mitch, I had not thought that you would come," she said quickly as she tied her sarong about her. She didn't care that she was still wet, or that the cloth clung to her revealingly; she only knew that she could not face him, nude, and maintain any semblance of composure.

"You didn't think I would come after you?" He was puzzled by her statement. "Why?"

"I thought you would understand why I left the village."

"What are you talking about?"

"I'm talking about not being together any longer."

"What?" Mitch was shocked.

"I have decided to end this thing between us before it becomes any more complicated."

"It isn't complicated. You want me and I want you. What we share is special."

Espri flinched inwardly at his callous summation of their relationship. It was that simple for him because he didn't really care. Though it was the most difficult thing she'd ever done in her life, she met his questioning gaze levelly.

"We have shared only the joining of our bodies. Many others on the island do the same every day." She managed a convincing shrug.

"Didn't our coming together mean anything to you?" he demanded in stunned disbelief.

"I enjoyed the experience, it was pleasurable, but it meant no more to me than that," she lied. "Did you feel differently?" Espri gave him one last chance to declare his love.

"No, of course not." His reply was out before he thought about it, and it strengthened her determination to break off with him.

"You see, there was no more to it."

Mitch felt for a moment that she sounded almost wistful, but he quickly discarded that possibility as ridiculous when she continued.

"I know that you intend to leave the island as soon as you can, so I think it's best that we stop this thing between us now."

"Espri, why throw away something that pleases us both?" he challenged, pulling her into his arms and kissing her before she had a chance to protest.

She did not fight his embrace, but remained rigid in his arms until he ended the kiss. "I am sure that I can find the same pleasure with an island man," she answered with a calmness she did not feel.

Her casually spoken words staggered Mitch. He clenched his hands into fists, angry at the thought of her in another man's arms. "I'm afraid you'll find yourself sorely disappointed if you think the joy we found is shared in every lover's embrace."

"I am sure you will be able to find another woman to satisfy you," Espri remarked offhandedly.

"Espri," he protested, moving to hold her once more, but she put up a hand, stopping him from coming any nearer.

"There is no future for me with you, Mitch. You plan to leave Malika as soon as you can, so there is no reason for us to continue. Please, go."

"I see," he said slowly when she'd finished speaking. He felt as if someone had struck him a physical blow, but he maintained a calm façade. "If that's the way you want it . . ."

Espri looked at him steadily, trying to read some emotion in his expression, but his features were inscrutable. Realizing that her dream of being loved by him was not going to come true, she answered, "It is."

"If you ever change your mind . . . you know where you can find me," he told her, and then without another glance in her direction, he turned and walked away.

Chapter 13

Mitch was filled with frustration as he left Espri standing on the beach. He had thought that everything was perfect between them. Why, the love they'd shared at the pool the previous evening had been unmatched by any he'd experienced, and he'd been anxious to see her again after spending the day apart. But now it was over, almost before it had begun.

Mitch reviewed their conversation over and over again as he made the long trek back to the village, and a burning fury grew within him as he imagined her seeking sensual pleasure with another man. Suddenly aware of the intensity of his reaction, he wondered at it. Hadn't he vowed never to let any woman become that important in his life? Surely he was reacting this way only because she was the first woman to end an association with him. In all his previous encounters, he had been the one to end the involvement when it had grown too tedious. This was the first time it had been done to him, and he was finding it extremely irritating.

Yet, as he tried to put her from his mind, the memory of her unblemished perfection taunted him, making him realize just how much he still desired her. Feeling the need for a drink, he picked up his pace and hurried back to the village,

hoping liquor would dull the knot of pain centered in
his chest.

Espri remained on the beach long after Mitch had gone.
She felt empty inside and colder than she'd ever been in her
life. It was as if a vital part of her had died.

The memory of Mitch's last desperate kiss assaulted her,
and she remembered how difficult it had been for her to hold
herself aloof, not to respond. She still wanted him, she could
not deny it, but she fully intended to overcome that need. She
had been happy before she knew Mitch, and she knew she
would be happy again, somehow.

The low, staccato beat of the native drums came to her
then, as they resounded through the darkness and echoed
eerily across the hills and beaches of Malika. The news they
carried—Konga's death—shocked Espri. Jarred from her
misery, she listened carefully to the message, knowing that,
since she was a princess, her presence would be required at
the ceremony. With little time to lose before the ritual was to
begin, Espri raced back to the glade to prepare herself to
attend.

Mitch was glad that Tommy was not at the hut when he got
back for he was in great need of solitude. Searching out the
bottle of rum Kohea had given them, he took a fast, deep
swig, enjoying its fiery potency. Bottle in hand, Mitch drew
a shuddering breath and walked over to the doorway.

He supposed that the unobstructed view of the sea and the
star-dusted sky was beautiful, but tonight he found no appeal
in it. Instead, he longed to be gone—to be free of the island
and the spell Espri had cast upon him.

His last thought startled him, and he considered it carefully
as he took another big swallow of rum. What did he really feel

for her? He had enjoyed their lovemaking. She had been the most exciting woman he'd ever had, and she had been a virgin. From the first moment they'd touched, he had wanted her. She was still a fire in his blood—an unquenchable thirst. But what did it mean? Was this love? Mitch hastily discarded the thought. This was not love, but desire. With time, it would fade to a pleasant memory. He took another swig, hoping to reach the point of forgetfulness soon.

Tommy was surprised to find Mitch alone at the hut, drinking, when he returned. "Where's Espri?" he asked easily.

"At home, I believe," Mitch replied brusquely.

"Is something wrong?"

"No."

"Oh." He could tell that Mitch was not in the best of moods so he decided to change the subject. "Are you going to the ceremony at the temple?"

"Ceremony?"

"Konga's funeral, I guess," Tommy explained. "When the drums stop, it will be time for it to begin."

Mitch shrugged.

"Well, I'm going to go. Maybe I'll see you there." When Mitch didn't bother to respond, Tommy started off in the direction of the temple.

The drums suddenly ceased their throbbing tempo and a hush fell over the expectant mourners gathered before the altar. Then the beating began again, in a pulsing regular rhythm that built to fever pitch before exploding into a violent roll as Tikiru appeared. Draped in a white, flowing robe, she wore an ornate headdress styled of fresh flowers, and about her waist was a belt of polished shells.

Tommy was mesmerized as he watched her from afar. How beautiful she looked tonight, how desirable! His gaze followed her every movement, and when she raised her arms to the sky in a gesture of supplication, he gasped, for in each hand she held a skull.

When Tikiru heard the stunned exclamations of the people gathered before her, a thrill went through her as it always did when she performed the rituals for them. Chanting the death song, she placed the skulls of Konga's ancestors on the altar and then began the dance that had been handed down from generation to generation since the beginning of time as the Malikans knew it.

Having just arrived at the village, Espri took her place at Luatu's side among the mourners. She looked most regal as she sat there, and she appeared to be concentrating solely on the ceremony, taking little notice of those around her.

Mitch arrived late, and he remained at the rear of the crowd, watching the ritual with little real interest. He laughed silently over Konga's pernicious foolishness, for had the warrior waited one more day, he would have had Espri all to himself.

Glancing around, he spotted Espri sitting with Luatu and Jacques in a place of honor near the front. His gaze lingered on her and he willed her to look his way, but Espri seemed oblivious to his presence.

Tana was overjoyed when Mitch arrived by himself, and when he sat down at the rear, alone, she felt confident that her little discussion with Espri had worked.

Despite her sedate manner as she sat with her father and grandfather, Espri had noted Mitch's arrival, and the sight of him, so tall and darkly handsome, had shaken her to the depths of her being. She longed to turn and look at him, but she refused to give in to the impulse. With great strength of will, she kept her gaze fixed on the altar and tried to concentrate on the ceremony, but the memory of the sweetness they'd shared tore at her heart.

"Espri?"

She looked up quickly at the sound of a man's voice and was surprised to see Ka, Luatu's servant.

"May I sit with you? Chief Luatu will need me when the ceremony ends."

"Of course," she replied, giving him a welcoming smile as he sat down next to her.

Mitch had been watching Espri's every move, and when she smiled at the islander who sat down beside her, a surge of rage swept through him. Furious, he stalked from the temple, wanting only to get away from the sight of Espri with another man.

Tana watched as Mitch left, and without a second thought she followed him from the temple, taking care to keep out of sight until she knew where he was bound.

Every fiber of Espri's being had been aware of Mitch's presence, and when she sensed a movement in the area where he was seated, she couldn't stop herself from glancing up. To her disappointment, she discovered that Mitch had gone, but she saw Tana hurriedly go after him. Jealousy flared through her at the thought of Mitch with the other woman, and she turned back toward the altar, fighting back the tears that threatened.

Mitch idly lifted the nearly empty bottle of rum to his lips, then drank deeply as he settled in on the beach before his hut. He was drunk and he knew it and he didn't care. Alone, he sat near the water's edge, watching the ebbing of the tide with a semblance of fascination. The copious amount of liquor he'd consumed since leaving the temple had quelled his rage, and he was feeling far more philosophical now about his attraction for Espri.

Laughing in self-derision, Mitch told himself that there'd been nothing special about her.

"Not a thing," he growled out loud.

Tipping the bottle to his lips, he drank once more of the wine of self-deception. There was nothing special about Espri except that she had come to him untouched and she was beautiful and she had stirred him as no other woman.

In a sudden flare of frustration, he was furious. First with Espri, for having ended something so perfect. Secondly with himself, for allowing her to become so important to him. Hadn't he seen what this kind of involvement with a woman could do to a man? Wasn't that why he'd always taken care not to allow any woman to get too close? He'd been a fool to let his guard down with Espri, and now he was paying the price.

In a burst of painful logic Mitch decided it was far better that Espri had ended their interlude for she had saved him the trouble of doing so when the time came for him to head home. He hadn't wanted any commitments. When a ship arrived, he would leave Malika without a regret, and never look back . . . yet the thought of never again being with Espri left him feeling very empty and very alone.

"Good evening, Mitch." Tana's tone was sultry and more than a little suggestive. She had watched from a distance as he'd settled down in the warm sands. She knew he'd been drinking, but she didn't care. If Espri was foolish enough to let this man go, she certainly wasn't going to pass up the opportunity to entice him into her own bed.

Mitch was surprised to see her for he had thought all the islanders would be at the temple. "Tana." His reply was neither inviting nor dismissing.

"You are alone tonight?" she questioned coyly.

Mitch grunted in response and took another drink. He had known since the first time he'd met Tana that she wanted him, but he'd made it a point to ignore her invitations. She was attractive; he just wasn't interested. He'd had the best the island could offer in Espri, and he wanted no substitute.

Not in the least discouraged by his unresponsive attitude, Tana sat down beside him as he finished off the last of the rum.

"The night is a lovely one," she purred in an attempt to draw him into conversation, but Mitch, in no mood for pleasantries, didn't bother to answer.

"Is there a reason why you're drinking so much?" she finally asked when he tossed the empty bottle aside.

"I'm celebrating," he told her, thinking to himself that it was best he and Espri were through, that he was glad he hadn't gotten more involved with her.

"I would celebrate with you." Tana leaned closer in the hope of establishing a certain intimacy between them.

"No, Tana." Mitch got unsteadily to his feet. "This celebration is a private one."

Tana feigned a pout as she considered what to do next, but Mitch didn't give her a chance to act. Swaying, he trudged across the sands and disappeared into his hut.

After the ceremony ended, Espri was completely miserable as she made her way back to her grandfather's home to spend the night. Since she'd seen Tana go after Mitch, she had been haunted by a vision of the two of them together, making love. It was driving her to distraction.

Espri had thought that ending their involvement was the right thing to do to save herself from future heartache, but she realized now that she had set herself up for misery. Mitch was a virile man who enjoyed women, and now she would be forced to watch as he became close to other, more willing, island maidens. The prospect unnerved her. Suddenly she remembered his parting words: *"If you ever change your mind . . . you know where you can find me."*

Wouldn't it be better to share what little time they had left rather than to deny herself that small portion of happiness? Without Mitch, life stretched ahead of her in an unending series of bleak and lonely days. As she decided to take that risk, she smiled for the first time that night. She loved him, and though she was painfully aware of exactly what the future held, she would have to be satisfied with whatever Mitch would offer her. She hastened through the village, determined to find him and to set things straight between them.

Tommy sighed as he glanced around the deserted bluff. He knew he hadn't mistaken Nelani's hastily relayed message at the end of the ritual, but he'd been waiting for a long time on the windswept cliff and there had been no sign of her. He grew more and more worried, but when he finally saw her rushing toward him, he opened his arms in ecstatic delight.

"You came!" he declared gratefully before claiming her lips in passionate desperation.

"I could not stay away from you, my golden one!" she told him breathlessly as they broke apart.

"I have been wanting you all day—needing you," he whispered before kissing her again.

"When Manti told me that a man had been killed during the catch, I was so afraid it had been you." Tikiru gazed up into his beloved face. "I love you, Tommy, and I would not want to go on without you."

"You'll never have to, Tikiru," he told her huskily as he held her close.

"I tried not to look for you during the ceremony tonight, but it was as if my eyes were drawn to you. Love me now, my golden one, for there is little time and I have great need of you." She moved from his embrace and released the cloak, letting it fall to her feet. She stood before him, proud in her nudity, then took his hand and led him to their bed of sweetgrass.

They came together in a cataclysmic joining, both fierce and exciting. Ecstasy claimed them both quickly, and when they lay satisfied in one another's arms, they knew the joy of perfect union.

"Marry me, Tikiru, and I will spend the rest of my days

making love to you." Tommy rose above her, worshipping her with his eyes, but he felt her tense at his words. "Is something wrong?"

"No," she hedged. Then, feeling that he deserved to know a part of the truth about her, she told him, "I cannot marry you, Tommy."

"But why?" He was shocked by this news. It had seemed the perfect solution to their secret trysting. He would marry her and stay here with her, forever.

"As *taupau* I must never marry," she explained as simply as possible without lying.

He nodded slowly in understanding and then bent to kiss her. "I want no other as my wife, Tikiru, so I will love only you for all of our days."

The beauty of his declaration moved her, and she began to cry softly as their lips met, sealing his pledge. She wanted nothing more than to spend her every waking moment with him, but she knew that was not to be. Fearful of Manti and of what might happen if he learned of her love for Tommy, Tikiru knew she could not linger with him. Denying her own desires, she tore herself away and hurried back to the haven of her home.

Reluctantly, Tommy let her go, but he stood alone on the bluff for a long time after she'd gone, savoring the joy they had shared that night.

It was late when he returned to the village, and he was surprised to find that the celebration in honor of Konga was still going on. When he joined Kohea and Anuitua near the big bonfire that had been built on the beach, Kohea pressed a full cup of kava into his hand and then smiled in approval as Tommy downed it quickly.

"Did you go to the temple for the ceremony?" the older man asked as he refilled Tommy's cup.

"Yes," Tommy replied as he took another deep drink of liquor.

"How do you find our ancient ways?"

"In many things, our societies are much alike. Where I come from, when someone dies, though there is sadness, there is also happiness. Many times there are gatherings such as this one. We call them wakes."

Kohea nodded thoughtfully. "It is good."

"The *taupau* is very beautiful," he added thoughtfully, unable to resist mentioning his love.

"Yes. Tikiru is her name. She lives in the temple with the high priests and presides over all the ceremonial functions."

"Does she ever come to the village?"

"No!" Kohea was scandalized by the thought. "That would be *tapu!*"

"*Tapu?* I don't understand."

"It is strictly forbidden. The *taupau* must stay in the temple. She is never permitted to meet with mere mortals for there is always the danger that she would be defiled."

"Defiled?" Tommy was suddenly growing concerned.

"As *taupau*, she must remain inviolate. It is her vow. It is her sacred duty," he explained.

Tommy nodded numbly, awestruck by what he'd done. Taking the cup of liquor with him, he started off down the beach, his thoughts in turmoil. If Tikiru was forbidden to meet with men, then she had risked everything to come to him. He worried about what would happen to them, should they be found out. Unable to send a message to her, he knew he would be forced to wait until they met again for answers to the questions bothering him.

Tana stood just outside the door of Mitch's hut, trying to decide what to do. She wanted Mitch badly, but his dismissal of her had been discouraging. Determined to make one last try, she glanced inside and was disappointed to find that he'd already fallen asleep. An unladylike Malikan curse escaped her as she started to turn away. Then a distant movement at the far edge of the beach caught her eye. A lone female was heading toward the hut, and Tana knew instinctively that it was Espri.

At the sight of her archrival, Tana assumed that her original plan to separate them hadn't worked, so decided to try one last vicious trick. Stepping into the darkened interior, she stripped off her sarong and stretched out carefully beside Mitch, placing herself in a wanton position. Then, smiling vengefully, she awaited the coming showdown.

It had taken Espri some time to reach Mitch's hut, but she didn't care. She needed to see him, to talk with him, and more than anything to be held in his arms. How she loved him! She felt almost free since she'd acknowledged her need for him, and she could hardly wait to tell him of her desire.

The moon was low in the blackened sky, and its harsh light seemed to coat all things in stark shades of black and gray as Espri eagerly approached the hut, her heart filled with gladness.

"Mitch?" Having called out his name softly, she hesitated briefly before peering inside the hut. What she saw there caused Espri to gasp and silently back away. She had never thought it would happen so soon. She'd felt he'd cared for her a little, but obviously she'd been wrong. Mitch had replaced her as quickly as he could—and with Tana!

Turning away, Espri raced toward her home, and when she reached the beach where she'd met Mitch earlier that night, she collapsed on the warm sand. Her dreams crushed, her innocence devastated, she sobbed brokenly, the vision of Tana lying naked in Mitch's arms tormenting her.

Dawn found Espri huddled on the sand, awake but no longer naïve. An icy protective shell had formed about her heart that night, and, as she watched gold streaks washed across the horizon proclaiming a new day, she felt that she, too, was ready to face her future without Mitch—without love.

Chapter 14

Like a brilliant emerald, Malika rose majestically above the silken blue depths of the Pacific, and the men approaching the island in the massive, high-prowed canoe shouted their joy at having safely completed their journey. For the better part of four days, the three natives and the missionary had been navigating the open sea on the return leg of their voyage to the outer islands. Now their odyssey was at an end. They were home.

Comfortably seated in the rear of the vessel, Father Pierre Papin watched as the lush tropical paradise came into view. Of all the islands he visited, only on Malika had he had a modicum of success in spreading the Word, and for that reason, returning here always seemed like a homecoming.

Absent from the island for many months now, Father Pierre was eagerly looking forward to a reunion with his old friends Jacques Duchant and Chief Luatu. He was also anxious to meet the two white men who, according to the Kikini natives, had been washed ashore on Malika after the bad storm several weeks before. Spotting the children waving to him from the beach, he stood up and returned their greeting.

The little ones, recognizing the priest even at a great distance, ran excitedly to the village with the news. The drums quickly spread the word of his imminent arrival, and the people, always glad to see the gentle missionary, turned out en masse to greet him. Jumping into their canoes, they paddled quickly out to sea to meet his canoe.

Delighted with his welcome, when the boats had at last pulled into the shore, Father Pierre quickly climbed from his own outrigger to embrace each of his joyous followers. Glancing up, he saw Luatu at the edge of the beach. Taking a baby in his arms and holding another child by the hand, he led the way to the chief.

When Luatu had heard of Father Papin's imminent arrival, he, too, had hurried down to the beach and had waited at the edge of the forest in dignified restraint for the priest to come to him.

Surrounded by the welcoming throng of villagers, Father Pierre crossed the sands to greet Luatu.

"It has been a long time, my friend." Father hugged him.

"Too long," the chief agreed. "Were your visits to the other islands successful?" he inquired as they started off toward his home.

"The Lord only knows," Papin answered, his eyes twinkling.

"Word of your arrival has already been sent by the drums, so I am sure Jacques will be here soon."

"Thank you. Is he well? And Espri?" Father Pierre had a special fondness for Luatu's granddaughter. He had watched her mature, and he knew that the man who captured her heart would win a prize of untold value.

"Jacques is fine and so is Espri," Luatu informed him.

"I have greatly missed Malika's beauty and its love," Father Pierre declared as he kissed the baby and handed her over to her smiling mother. Then, with a quick blessing, he dismissed the crowd, promising to spend time with each of them later, after his visit with their chief.

"It is good that the people love you," the chief remarked as he watched his people disperse.

"It is an unbroken circle," Pierre responded sincerely as they settled in at the dining hut. "Now, tell me what has happened on my favorite island. I am sure I have missed much during my time away."

And Luatu began to regale him with tales of the island's happenings.

Some distance away, Manti heard the message of the drums and grew livid. The interloper had returned! Hatred filled him, for the white priest's preachings of one loving God had begun to erode his own power over the Malikans. Furious, he stormed off to the village, determined to try to prevent Father Pierre from gaining any more influence over his people.

His expression hostile, his arms folded defensively across his chest, Manti approached his chief and the priest. "Luatu."

Looking up, Luatu gestured to his friend. "Come. Join us, Manti. I was just telling Father of the village news."

Aware of the native high priest's intense dislike and distrust, Father Pierre smiled. "Please, Manti."

Manti eyed the priest malevolently as he sat near Luatu. He had no use for this white man who had come to the island for the sole purpose of turning his followers away from their tribal worship. Listening in bitter silence, Manti was pleased to learn that the man had met with little success during his journeys.

"Have there been any births while I was gone?" Father Pierre asked as he accepted a cup of fresh, sweet coconut milk from a serving girl.

"There were two fine babies born, one boy and one girl," Luatu informed him. "But there was one death."

Papin was shocked by the news. "Who? One of the old men?"

"No. It was Konga, son of Autiki. He was killed in a shark attack."

"But he was a strong young man . . . how did it happen?"

"He was trying to save another who had fallen into the sea, and lost his own life in the struggle."

"And the other man?"

"He was saved."

The priest nodded. "I had heard, on Kikini, that two men had been recovered from the sea. Did they survive?"

"Yes. Jacques and Espri found one and nursed him back to health."

"Tommy O'Ryan is the other man. He is well, too."

"It is a credit to your Christian kindness that you cared enough to help them," Father said approvingly.

"It has always been our way," Manti sniped.

"Indeed, it has." Papin refused to be intimidated by the powerful native. "And you as a people are to be commended for it."

Manti sat back rigidly.

"The two white men are basically good men," Luatu continued, "although I am certain they are growing restless in their desire to return to their own homes. They have been here for nearly two months now."

"I have no news of any ships, but perhaps there will be one soon," Papin said encouragingly. "It is never good to be away from loved ones for too long." Then, remembering Konga, Father Pierre asked, "It is a noble thing Konga did. Was there a funeral?"

"No, there was no need; his body was lost," the chief explained. "But Manti did perform the ceremonial death ritual."

Trying not to offend the pagan priest, Father looked over at Manti and answered tactfully, "Then I am sure Konga has been well served, but I will also add my prayers to Manti's in order to insure his eternal salvation."

A flicker of emotion showed in Manti's eyes at the white

man's proclamation, but he held his tongue, though his thoughts were vicious. So! The arrogant white priest thought his prayers were not powerful enough to save Konga, did he?

"Father Pierre!" Jacques's call rang out across the clearing, interrupting Manti's malicious musings.

"Jacques! Mon vieux ami!" Pierre lapsed into French for a moment as they hugged one another. "How have you been? And where is that beautiful daughter of yours?"

"Espri will be here later," Duchant explained. "You've just arrived?"

"Just a short time ago. Much has happened since I've been gone, and Luatu and Manti were just telling me the news of Konga's death."

Jacques sat with them. "It was a horrible thing."

The men then became involved in conversation, discussing all that had occurred since their parting.

Mitch and Tommy were working with Kohea when word of the missionary priest's return reached them. Mitch was anxious to speak with the priest, for he might have news of a ship in the area, so when Kohea urged them to quit work for the day and go to Luatu's to meet him, he was glad to do so.

Mitch was eager to leave the island. Though he had immersed himself in work, helping Kohea and the other men with any and every task, the six weeks since he'd last been with Espri had passed slowly, each hour seeming long and empty. Consciously, he denied feeling anything for Espri, yet he took great pains to avoid seeing her; and, though he had ample opportunity to indulge himself with the eager Malikan maidens, he felt no desire for any of them. So it was that he had marked time quietly, anticipating the day when he would finally be off the island and on his way home.

Tommy outwardly went along with Mitch's enthusiasm for a meeting with the priest, but he was far from eager to leave

Malika. Even though he was aware of Tikiru's *tapu* status and the fact that she could never marry, his love for her had grown. Caught in the grip of their powerful feelings for one another, the pair had cast all thoughts of the danger of discovery aside. They continued to rendezvous whenever possible, cherishing each forbidden moment. Consequently Tommy hoped desperately that there was no news of a ship for he did not want to be forced to make a painful decision. To go would mean leaving his love behind; to stay might raise questions and ultimately put her in peril.

As they passed through the village they found that a pig had been slaughtered and set to roast in preparation for the welcoming feast that would be held that night. Luatu saw them approaching and called out to them.

"Father Papin, this is Mitch Williams and Tommy O'Ryan." Jacques nodded toward each man as he said his name.

"Father," Mitch said.

Both men shook hands with the priest and then sat down.

"It is my understanding that you are two very blessed men."

"That's very true, Father," Tommy agreed. "And we've been made most welcome here."

Father Pierre smiled benignly. "I understand from Chief Luatu that you are anxious to be on your way home, and I regret that I have not brought you the good tidings that a ship is on its way. But the word is out on the other islands to send any vessel here."

"That's good to know, thank you." Mitch was not at all encouraged by the news.

"Here comes Espri now," Luatu announced, happy to see his granddaughter.

Espri was excited at the prospect of seeing Father Pierre, for his arrival seemed the answer to the fervid prayers she'd been saying over the past month. She loved the priest dearly and valued his counsel. Running toward him, she was swept up in his affectionate embrace, and it was a moment before she realized that Mitch was among those gathered around. She greeted him distantly.

"Espri," Mitch replied curtly.

His gaze was so cold as it raked over her that she was un-nerved by it and quickly turned away. "Tommy, it's good to see you again."

"Hello, Espri," the younger man replied.

Although Mitch did not betray his feelings to the others, he was furious, and he cursed himself silently for the sudden surge of desire he'd felt when he'd first seen her. Damn! He'd stayed away from Espri all this time, yet his need for her was as powerful as it had ever been. He had thought that the at-traction would lessen, but it hadn't. Try as he might, he could not deny the passion she aroused.

Espri was stricken. How could she have been so foolish to think that she could come to the village and not see Mitch! It had been only six weeks, but it seemed a lifetime. It took all of her self-control not to stare at him. She had thought her feeling for him was dead, killed the night she'd seen him with Tana, but she realized that was not so. She needed desperately to leave, to get away from his overwhelming presence.

Disguising her very real distress behind a façade of total absorption in what Father Pierre had to say, she tried to dwell purposefully on his every word. Yet time seemed to drag, and it was with great relief that she finally managed to excuse herself, telling the men that she had promised to help Laiti with preparations for the feast that night.

Mitch's eyes glowed with a fierce inner light as he watched her walk away, and he couldn't help but remember how perfect they'd been together.

The rest of the day had passed in a flurry of activity for Father Pierre. He had celebrated Mass for the natives, baptized the infants who had been born since his last visit, and met with several islanders who were professing an interest in his teachings. Now, as the moon rose over the darkness of the sea, the feasting began. Food and drink flowed freely, and everyone partook, save Manti, who stayed on the fringes of the festivities watching all the happenings with a jaundiced eye.

Mitch ate with Tommy and then disappeared into the shadows. From his vantage point just beyond the light of the big bonfire, he could watch Espri, unobserved. Driven by emotions that seemed out of control, he remained in the darkness, dwelling on her every laugh, every frown. Suddenly realizing what he was about, he became annoyed and stalked away into the night.

Although Espri sat in a place of honor near Father Pierre, she had had little opportunity to speak with the priest privately. He was surrounded by well-wishers. As the evening had passed in a continuous flow of greetings and loving exchanges, she had grown weary of the happy façade she was forced to maintain. She was not happy, and she doubted she would be for some time to come.

She had made every effort not to pay attention to Mitch, but his presence had seemed almost a tangible thing. Every time she'd looked up, he'd been there, his eyes resting on her with disturbing intensity. Then, just as disturbingly, he'd gone, leaving her to wonder where and with whom.

Father Pierre had known Espri since childhood, and he sensed a sadness about her that he'd never witnessed before. She had always been lighthearted and loving, and it bothered him that her gaiety was strained. It was during a lull, late in the evening, that he first had the chance to question her.

"Espri? Is something wrong?" His words, so accurate in their perception, caught her unaware for she had been trying her best not to allow her distress to show.

"Is it that obvious?" she returned, smiling with a certain grimness.

"Only to me, *ma petite*." He frowned. "Would you like to talk?"

"I do need your advice, but I don't want to take you from your feast. Perhaps you could come home with us tomorrow?"

"Of course, I had planned on spending time with you and your father, and that will give me the chance to do both."

Relief washed over her. Soon she would be able to unburden herself. Father Pierre was the wisest man she'd ever known; he would be able to tell her what to do.

"Why do you insist on taking these foolish chances?" Nelani raged at Tikiru, who was readying herself for another meeting with her lover.

"Manti is in the village. It will be safe," she answered easily.

"But it's foolhardy for you to continue this way. Don't you realize what could happen if you're found out?"

"And how will I be found out?" Tikiru turned on her servant. "Who would ever suspect?"

"You are taking a great risk."

"It is my risk," Tikiru told her haughtily as she started to leave. "And it is worth any price to be with Tommy."

Manti was disgusted. All night, he'd watched the islanders fawn over the white missionary. Such folly! Didn't they know that the gods of their ancestors were the only true gods and that their behavior was angering them? Unable to witness any more, he left, intent on returning to the temple and offering up a sacrifice of his own to appease the deities.

Hidden behind a bank of clouds, the moon offered little light at this late hour, and for that reason Tikiru was not clearly discernible on her way back to her hut. Slipping silently through the forest in her concealing wrap after her meeting with Tommy, she did not see Manti as he walked the path to the temple.

Manti, however, saw the cloaked figure of a woman, and noting the direction of her flight, he followed her, thinking something amiss. Forbidden to barge into the *taupau's* quarters, he called out her name in fierce inquiry.

"Tikiru!"

Having heard footsteps behind her, Tikiru had darted around to Nelani's sleeping room and had entered there, waking her slave and sending her out to meet with Manti.

"Where is Tikiru?" he demanded imperiously.

"She is sleeping, Manti." Nelani bowed humbly before her high priest.

"If she is sleeping, then who did I just see running through the forest?" he asked cagily.

"It was I, O Most High," she lied, to protect her mistress.

"Is there a problem, Manti?" Tikiru suddenly emerged from her own hut, looking very much as if she'd just been awakened from a sound sleep.

"Your servant has been leaving you unattended while you slept," Manti informed her.

"Nelani! Haven't I forbidden you to meet with that man?" she asked harshly.

"Yes, Tikiru."

"And you defied me?"

"Yes."

"I will leave you to handle this." The high priest turned to leave the glade, relieved that his concern had been unfounded.

Tikiru nodded and watched until he disappeared into the forest. Then she herded Nelani back inside, and they stared at each other, terribly aware of what had almost happened.

"You will take a note to Tommy in the morning." Tikiru began to shake as fear of discovery gripped her heart, for she knew the horrible punishment Manti would deal out, should he find that she'd defiled her vows. "I will not be able to meet with him again. It will be too dangerous . . . for both of us."

"What?" Father Pierre looked at Espri in stunned surprise as they sat talking the following day.

Eyes downcast, she nodded. "I'm going to have a baby."

"Who's the father?" he demanded, standing up authoritatively in front of her.

"It doesn't matter, Father Pierre," she responded dejectedly.

"It most certainly does matter, Espri," he insisted, and then the dreaded thought struck him. "Was it Konga?" he asked sympathetically, touching her shoulder lightly to comfort her.

"No!" Espri looked up at him quickly.

"Then, who?"

Sighing, knowing that she wouldn't be able to hide the truth much longer, she confessed. "The father of my child is Mitch Williams."

"The white man I met yesterday?"

"Yes."

"Have you told him?"

"No!" She was stricken at the thought.

"Then you must. He has a right to know if it is his child you are to bear," he explained logically.

"I can't tell him. He doesn't love me, Father. What happened between us . . . well, it was a mistake."

"You're calling your unborn child 'a mistake'?" He was outraged. "Surely, you loved this man if you gave yourself to him. I know you that well, Espri."

"I did love him."

"Did?" His searching gaze rested on her pale, tense features.

"I don't know anymore. It seemed so right at the time . . ." Tears fell unheeded as she finally gave in to the desperation that had been haunting her since she'd first realized her condition.

"It is his duty to care for you and the child, Espri," Father Pierre pronounced authoritatively. "I will handle this from here on."

"But I don't want to marry him if he doesn't want me!" she protested, in anguish.

"He wanted you enough to make love to you, Espri. Besides, it's too late to worry about that. You are having his child." He patted her hand reassuringly. "I will speak with your father, and we will see what can be arranged."

Espri groaned. How had this ever happened to her?

"Will you trust me to do what's best for you?"

She nodded, unable to speak.

"Good. Why don't you stay here while I go talk to Jacques?" Father Pierre suggested, then started off to plan her future.

Shocked, Jacques stared at the priest. "You're serious?"

"Very. She has just confided everything to me."

"There is only one thing we can do. He'll have to marry her," Jacques declared instantly.

"I agree," Father Pierre told him solemnly.

"I will speak with him myself," Jacques went on. "I may not have been the best father to her, but I love her and I will not allow him to use her this way."

"I understand. Do you want me to come with you?"

"No. This is something I must do alone."

The priest watched Jacques walk stiffly toward the village.

Chapter 15

Espri was tremulous as her father escorted her toward Mitch, who stood before Father Pierre. Though she had had three days to come to terms with the fact that he had agreed to the marriage, her anxiety had not lessened. Mitch did not love her, and she knew that he never would. Even her father's and Laiti's comforting reassurances that she was a beautiful bride did nothing to ease her panic at being joined with a man who did not, she was sure, really want to marry her.

The ebony silk of her hair had been artfully styled, delicate tropical blossoms having been woven among the thick tresses, and the white sarong she wore was almost Grecian in form, fastening over one shoulder and falling in flowing folds over her slender body. Nervously, she clung to Jacques's arm; sensing her distress, he patted her hand encouragingly.

Espri's eyes were focused on Mitch as she drew near the altar. *He looks so tall and forbidding*, she thought as she took in the stern line of his dark, angry features. No man likes to be forced, and she was certain that Mitch was not an exception. Furthermore, though she had thought herself immune now to his potent masculinity, his dominating presence still affected her. Her heart pounded in her breast, her limbs quaked as Jacques handed her over to Mitch's keeping. His hand engulfed hers in a warm, steady grip, and Espri looked up at him quickly, questioningly. Her impetuosity cost her her pride, though, for his eyes mockingly met hers. Glancing quickly away, she tried to pull her hand free without drawing any attention to herself, but Mitch refused to relinquish his hold on her.

Her mind full of agonizing thoughts, Espri tried to listen to the words Father Pierre had begun to speak over them. How had this come to pass? In a few short minutes her fate would be sealed; she would be married to Mitch. It seemed so long ago when she had wanted nothing more than to be his wife, but now . . . so much had changed. He wasn't marrying her because he loved her. He was marrying her to claim the child that nestled contentedly deep within the protection of her womanly body.

"Do you, Espri Duchant, take this man to be your wedded husband?"

Father Pierre's question stormed the meager defenses Espri had tried to erect against the happenings of the day, and though it seemed an eternity before she could answer, she paused only an instant.

"I do." Though she spoke softly, her voice quavered.

"Do you, Mitch Williams, take this woman to be your wedded wife?"

"I do," he rasped harshly, and Espri shivered at the impact on their lives of those two small words.

"Then by the power vested in me by God, I pronounce you man and wife." Father Pierre beamed.

The islanders who had gathered for the wedding erupted in a cheer of delight, showering the newlywed pair with flowers as the final words were spoken. Espri cast Mitch a sideways glance and found his eyes on her again, but this time their expression was cold and inscrutable. She tensed as he took her in his arms, and when he bent to kiss her, she trembled violently.

His mouth slanted across hers in a passionate demand that left her weak and breathless, and when he finally released her, she stared up at him in bewilderment. She had expected hatred—fury—but never this passion!

"I never said I didn't want you, Espri," he taunted softly. Then he coolly turned away to speak with the others.

Luatu smiled to himself as he observed the kiss from a distance. Mitch, though he had protested against the marriage before finding out about his child, proved by his actions that he did still want Espri, and the chief felt certain that, given time, they would find together the joy they deserved. It was good.

Knowing that the blessing of the ancestors was an important part of any Malikan wedding, Luatu led the celebrators up the path to the temple, where Manti awaited them. After instructing Mitch and Espri to sit on the cloth that had been spread in front of the altar, the island priest chanted praises to his gods and invoked Espri's ancestors, whose skulls were displayed in honor before them, to bless the marriage. Tikiru came forth, finally, to perform the fertility ritual that would ensure the happy couple the gift of many offspring.

Espri sat rigidly at Mitch's side as she watched Tikiru's dramatic, sensual dance. Never before had she been aroused by the fertility ceremony, but now, sitting so close to Mitch and feeling the heat of his presence, the priestess's explicit movements created a stirring of awareness within her. Uncomfortably, she finally shifted her position to try to quell the disturbing surge of feeling that was racing through her. Mitch, however, seemed unaffected by the lustful exhibition of the lovely *taupau*, and the glance he directed at Espri, when he noticed her restlessness, was sardonic. Embarrassed to find that he was aware of her agitation, she prayed that the wanton portrayal would soon end.

When at long last Tikiru completed the performance, she fell in supplication at Manti's feet. At Manti's signal, a servant came forth and carried her back out of sight into the temple. Then, turning to Espri and Mitch, Manti bid them stand, and he ended the ceremony with an exhortation to the newly married couple never to let their love for one another die.

Manti's commandment seared Espri's heart. Her love for Mitch would never die, she knew that, but she saw little hope for her future with him. He wanted her, he'd never denied that, and she was his, now and forever, by the decrees of God and man; but there would be no love in his coming to her. Espri only hoped that, with time, he could forget the circumstances of their marriage, that he would come to feel some warmer emotion toward her. *Maybe after the baby is born it will happen*, she thought; and a flicker of happiness lit her face.

As Espri's features were transformed by the radiance of her smile, Mitch scowled blackly at her obvious happiness. It irritated him to think that she was perfectly content with the arrangement, but then why shouldn't she be? She'd gotten almost everything she wanted. The only thing she didn't possess was his love, and he would do his best to see that she never did. He might be married to her, but he would not allow her to have any power over him.

His eyes glittered as they skimmed over her loveliness, missing nothing in their intimate perusal of her; not the slightly fuller thrust of her breasts or the gently rounded swell of her stomach beneath the clingingly soft material. Mitch knew a moment of awe as he silently considered that his child was alive and thriving within her. As soon as he'd learned of its existence, he'd become resigned to the marriage, for he had never doubted for a moment that the baby was his. Despite his protestations that he did not want to marry, the decision had been made for him. He'd been caught, well and good, by Espri's tender innocence.

Passion swelled within him at the thought of possessing her again, and he lifted his gaze to hers, allowing her briefly to see his desire for her reflected in his eyes. Espri was stunned by the smoldering heat of his glance, and her eyes widened in nervous anticipation of the time when they would finally be alone.

"Espri! Mitch!" Luatu's voice broke through the sensual web that had been woven about them by Tikiru's performance, and they both looked up at the chief. "It is time for the feast!"

She quickly glanced back at Mitch to see if what she'd witnessed had been real, but Mitch's expression was once again shuttered, revealing nothing. At Luatu's encouragement, they led the way to the beach, where a big bonfire had been burning since that morning in honor of their upcoming nuptials. Once they'd taken their seats in the flower-strewn place of honor, the procession of the gifts began. As a princess of the Malika, Espri was due tribute from every family, and a representative from each clan came forth with presents. Cloth and mats, utensils and livestock were all brought forth for their approval, then taken to the hut which Jacques and Luatu had given them earlier that morning.

Tana was bitter as she watched the procession from a distance, her heart wrenched by Espri's happiness. Konga was dead and Mitch had married Espri in spite of her ploy in his bed that night! She remembered with some embarrassment how angry Mitch had been when Tommy had come back and found them. He had been furious with her; he had denied her insinuation that they had slept together, telling her that he could recall everything that had happened that evening. Grimacing at the hateful memory, she wondered if there was ever to be any joy in her own life.

"Tana?" A deep male voice interrupted her thoughts, and she looked up to find Ka standing nearby.

"Ka . . . what do you want?"

"I saw you standing here alone and thought you might want to come to the celebration with me." His dark eyes looked upon her appreciatively.

Tana paused, her previous misery forgotten. "I would like that, Ka, very much." And turning her best seductive smile on the chief's most important servant, she went with him to join the merrymaking.

Tommy stood in the crowd near Mitch, watching with interest all that was transpiring. In his heart, he wished that this celebration had been his—a wedding between himself and Tikiru—but he knew that would never be. In fact, he was desperate for he feared he might never be with her again after receiving her cryptic letter telling him that the danger of discovery had become too great and they could no longer risk meeting. He did not know what had happened to cause her to break off their rendezvous, and at first, he'd refused to accept it, returning nightly to their meeting place in the hope that she might have changed her mind. But long, lonely hours on the bluff had convinced him that she'd been serious. Being apart from her was driving him into despair, and he wondered if they would ever have the chance to be together again.

Drinking from the cup of kava that someone had pressed into his hand, he surveyed those before him. He realized that if Manti was here there was no one at the temple to prevent Tikiru from slipping away. An expectant thrill surged through him, and he excused himself from the merrymakers to head for the bluff, where he hoped his love awaited him.

Tikiru had seen Tommy in the wedding party at the temple, and it had taken all of her inner strength not to betray her feelings for him. She loved Tommy, yet because of that love she knew she could not allow herself to put him in danger. She had to continue to deny her own passion in order to protect him. Sitting on the veranda of her hut, Tikiru stared out into the darkness, listening to the distant sounds of revelry and knowing that she would never have such a chance for happiness. Tears fell silently as she mourned the loss of her love.

* * *

Tommy was furious as he stalked across the deserted bluff top. Why hadn't she come? Did she not care for him anymore? Surely, she realized that he needed to be with her! Despondent, he sat on the ground where they had made love so many times and prayed for her to come, but his prayers were for naught. After waiting nearly an hour, he gave up his vigil and decided to take action. Tommy wasn't quite sure where her hut was located, but he knew it was somewhere in the *tapu* section of the island near the temple. Setting out, he followed the path she'd taken when she'd left him after their meetings. Though the way was obscured, guided by his instincts, he finally came upon a structure which appeared dark and deserted in the darkness of the moonless night.

"Tikiru?" he called out softly when he saw a lone figure reclining on the veranda.

The woman sitting there stiffened at the sound of his voice, then flew from the porch into his arms. "Tommy! My love!"

They embraced with pagan wildness in the shadows of the night until Tikiru came to her senses and drew away from him.

"You must go. Manti will kill you if he finds you here."

"That does not matter to me anymore, Tikiru. My love is like a living thing, hungering for your touch and the sound of your voice. I thought I would go mad tonight at the wedding ceremony. You looked so beautiful and I needed you so badly."

"I feel as you do, but there is nothing I can do. We must remain apart."

Tommy clasped her to him and kissed her hungrily before she again freed herself from his arms.

"If you love me, you will go, Tommy. Now!" she ordered, her fear heightened by the intensity of the feeling he had aroused within her.

"When will I see you again?" he asked recklessly.

"We cannot continue to meet." Her answer was cold and

final. "Our only contact can be through the temple ceremonies. Anything else could mean your death, and I could not bear it."

Tommy began to protest, but she turned her back on him. "Go. Now."

"I will go, but I will never give up the hope of someday being with you." Turning away in bleak despair, he left her.

As was the tribal custom, the women of the village stole Espri away from Mitch to prepare her for the wedding night. Escorting her to her new home, they stripped off her wedding sarong and combed the flowers from her hair. When she'd been bathed and anointed with *monoi,* they hastened to leave, knowing that at any moment the groom would arrive to claim his husbandly rights.

When the women left the feast, the festivities became far more raucous and Mitch was almost glad when the time came for him to go. Accompanied by Jacques and Luatu, he started up the path that led to the secluded hut where his bride awaited him.

Although he had not wanted to marry, he could not deny that the night ahead held great appeal. *Espri is mine,* he thought possessively.

Mitch had tried to deny his passion for Espri during their long weeks apart, and he'd almost convinced himself that he didn't want her; but after seeing her again the night Father Pierre returned, he'd realized that he was still very much attracted to her.

When Jacques had first approached him about the marriage, he had been adamant in his refusal. He did not want to marry, had no intention of doing so. But when Jacques had told him of the baby, his whole perspective had changed. No longer were his wishes of paramount importance. A child was involved, and there was no doubt that it was his.

The news had surprised him. Through all the years and

all the mistresses, he had never before sired any offspring, and he knew that marriage was the only way to deal with this situation. He would have a son or daughter, and he would proudly accept the responsibility.

Mitch had wondered about Espri's attitude toward their prospective union, but he had not ventured to question Jacques about it. And, since she had made no effort to see him since the wedding had been arranged, he had felt certain that she was pleased by the prospect. He frowned now at the thought.

Jacques glanced at Mitch. Noticing his suddenly ominous expression, he knew it was his duty to speak. Though the man may not have wanted to marry Espri, he was the father of her child, and as such, he should hold to his duties as husband and parent.

"Mitch." Jacques's harsh tone penetrated the younger man's thoughts, and he turned to his new father-in-law. "Espri is my daughter, and I love her very much. I won't abide any cruelty to her."

Pinning Jacques with a glacial glare, Mitch was about to give a heated reply when Luatu interceded.

"Do not worry, Jacques. Mitch loves Espri, and he will do well by her." The chief smiled serenely.

Knowing there was no point in denying the old man's words, Mitch faced Jacques. "She will come to no harm."

"She is your wife now," Duchant said pointedly.

"And I am her husband," Mitch retorted sharply just as they came to the edge of the glade near the newly constructed hut.

"We will leave you here." Luatu put a restraining hand on Jacques's arm when the other man would have gone on with Mitch. "May your marriage be a strong one, bonded in love," he said, and then he and Jacques turned away, leaving Mitch to face Espri alone for the first time since the wedding.

Espri was apprehensive as she waited for Mitch. They had

not spoken since the marriage had been arranged, and she had no idea how he felt about their situation.

Though her father had been reluctant to speak of it, she had forced him to tell her what had transpired when he'd gone to Mitch, and what she'd learned had not been particularly encouraging. According to Jacques, Mitch had refused to marry her at first, but, after learning of her delicate condition, he had agreed. She sighed heavily. Many of the island men would have joyfully taken her to wife, but she was now married to the one man who had let it be known from the beginning of their time together that he did not want to be bound to her. Espri felt sure that Mitch resented their marriage. Certainly, he'd indicated by his passionate kiss after the ceremony that he desired her physically, but beyond that their union would be empty, save for their child.

A slight sound drew her attention, and she looked up to see Mitch silhouetted in the doorway.

He stared down at her as she sat in nude splendor before him.

"You look very lovely, my dear," he said casually as he stepped inside the hut.

Espri swallowed nervously and watched him walk toward her. She could not see his expression in the darkness, but the coolness of his tone frightened her. Mitch, however, could see her clearly, and he noticed how wide her eyes were and how tensely she held herself.

Kneeling beside her, he reached out and cupped her chin, asking coldly, "Why do you look so afraid? Could it be you realize that a man doesn't like to be forced?"

"No one forced you!" she snapped, jerking free of his grip.

"Did you plan this?" he jeered as he ran his hand down her shoulder to her breast.

"Plan?" Espri was suddenly furious with him. So, he thought because she'd told him of her love that she'd connived to wed him! "Hardly. This baby was as much a surprise to me as it was to you."

Her sharp words gave him pause and he looked at her with new interest. "Do you want the child?"

His question stunned her, and she was too open to lie about such an important thing. "Of course I want our child. It's you I didn't want! Did you think for one moment that I desired to marry a man who doesn't want me?" she demanded, brushing his hand away.

Though her words astonished him, he shrugged and kept his expression guarded. "Neither of us wanted this union, Espri, but since we are married, there is no reason to deny ourselves the few pleasures the situation offers."

"But I don't want you!" she declared heatedly, standing up and turning her back on him, but in her unclad state she was vulnerable and he knew it.

Drawing himself up to his full height, he stood behind her and ran a warm, gentle hand down the curve of her spine until it rested on her hip. She shivered beneath the caress, but didn't move.

"We both know that's not true, don't we, Espri?" he taunted, but she only stiffened at his gibe. "Look at me," Mitch insisted. "Tell me to my face that you don't want to make love with me."

Straightening her shoulders, her arms crossed protectively over her breasts, she turned to him to refute his words, but when her eyes met his, time was suspended. Emotions, deep and dark, shone in the depth of his gaze, and she was caught up in the intensity of the moment.

Her heart pounding in her breast, Espri stood motionless as he took the final step toward her and crushed her against his chest. Savagely, his mouth took hers, trying to force from her the response he knew she was capable of giving.

Espri held herself rigid in his arms, fighting the excitement that was sweeping over her as he parted her lips and thrust his tongue deep within the honeyed sweetness of her mouth. She didn't want to reveal to him the sensual power he had over her, but her body was betraying her and she swayed weakly against him as he thoroughly dominated all of her senses. When his hips ground against hers in an arousing invitation, Espri couldn't suppress a gasp of expectancy as she felt the hardness of his desire.

Mitch sensed the fire within her and he pressed his advantage, trailing his hands arousingly over her silken flesh in an attempt to break down her defenses. Masterfully, he exploited her weaknesses until Espri was writhing against him, needing to know the fullness of his possession once again. Seemingly of their own volition, her arms looped around his neck, and Mitch held her close, savoring the softness of her breasts crushed to his bare chest.

"Tell me you want me, Espri," he whispered as he nuzzled at her throat.

"No . . . I . . ." She suddenly began to struggle weakly to be free of him. "Mitch . . . no . . ."

"Oh, yes, *wife!*" he countered harshly. "Yes." Taking her up in his arms, he lowered them both to their marriage bed and pulled her tight against him. "Can you feel how much I want you? Do you remember how it felt to be as one?"

His hands roamed over her, and his lips followed in an erotic foray that left her panting and devastatingly defeated. When he bent to kiss her breast, she clasped him to her, crying out in ecstasy as his hand dipped between her thighs to tantalizingly touch the center of her womanly need. As pleasure pulsed through her, he ceased his love play and drew back slightly to gaze down at her flushed features.

"Shall I stop?" he asked coolly. "Or shall I make love to you? The decision is yours."

Even though she loved him, Espri hated Mitch at that moment for forcing her to admit to her need for him and for so easily establishing his domination of her.

"Love me, Mitch. Please . . . love me." Her plea was heart-felt, and her fingers clutched at him in desperate desire, urging him nearer.

Smiling in triumph, he stripped off his pants and came to her without delay, spreading her thighs and positioning himself above her. Lowering his hips to hers, he probed gently, intending to enter her slowly, but Espri could wait no longer and she surged upward, impaling herself on his strength. The velvet heat of her body surrounded him, holding him a willing prisoner of her love. Enraptured, Mitch began to move, savoring the delicious sensation of that intimate caress.

Espri matched his rhythm, eagerly accepting his every thrust and glorying in his possession. It no longer mattered that he had forced her to respond; it only mattered that she was holding him and loving him. The weeks they'd spent apart seemed only a distant memory as their bodies melded and merged. This was her heaven and her hell—to have his physical love, but nothing more. Abandoning all thought, Espri gave herself over to the passion of the moment, responding instinctively to his every urging and reaching the peak of her pleasure just as Mitch achieved his own pinnacle.

He lay still briefly, resting heavily upon her, and then raised up on his forearms to look down at her, mockingly.

"Maybe being married to you will have some benefits after all." He sneered. "You did enjoy it, didn't you, dear wife?"

Stung by his flippant treatment of something she'd considered beautiful, Espri shoved at his unwelcome weight. "I hate you!"

"Oh, really?" Mitch smiled at her smugly as he remembered the abandon with which she'd just given herself to him. Shifting away, he regarded her with a casualness she found unnerving, but when he cupped her breast and gently teased the taut crest, her breath caught in her throat. Lifting an eyebrow derisively, he glanced at her stricken features. "I love the way you hate, Espri."

He came to her again then, hot and demanding, creating within her an undeniable need for him, then slaking that need with a practiced precision that seemed more punishment than passion. When he'd finished, he levered himself away from her slender form, turned his back to her, and seemed to fall asleep almost immediately.

Silently sobbing, Espri lay unmoving as she listened to the even tenor of Mitch's breathing as he slumbered peacefully beside her. She had not wanted to be just a plaything to him, but it seemed that the bed would be the only thing they would be sharing in their marriage. She hadn't wanted to settle for that, but he'd left her no alternative. Turning on her side, Espri closed her eyes and tried to rest, but many hours passed before she finally drifted off.

Chapter 16

Jacques's mood was somber and his expression troubled as he joined Luatu and Father Pierre for breakfast the following morning.

"Jacques? What is wrong?" Father Pierre inquired, noticing his friend's anxiety.

"I am concerned about Espri," he answered flatly as he started to partake of the food set before him.

"There is no need," Luatu told him confidently. "She has a husband now."

"But what kind of a husband?" Jacques demanded quickly. "I know nothing of this man, yet I have entrusted to his keeping that which I love most in this world—my daughter."

"You must trust in the Lord's guidance," Pierre advised. "Many times things do not go as we would wish, but"—his gesture indicated human helplessness—"who are we to dictate the happenings of life? And you are forgetting that soon you will be a grandfather."

Though the Father's words were spoken with humor, Jacques glared up at him. "Had she not found herself *enceinte,* she would not now be married to Mitch!"

"Jacques." Luatu's calm gaze met Jacques's angry one.

"You must accept what has come to pass. It is good. Mitch will make a strong husband and a good father to their child."

"I hope you're right, Luatu. I only want happiness for Espri, and I fear that she will find none with Mitch."

"It may take time, but it will happen," the chief predicted. "Why not think of your own situation? You are going to be very lonely, living by yourself so far from the village. Perhaps it is time you looked for a wife? I am sure there are many women who would want you."

Jacques smiled as he remembered the night he had just passed in Laiti's more than willing arms. "There is only one woman I care to be with."

"And I am sure she is willing." Luatu's eyes were twinkling, for he was aware of Laiti's feelings for Jacques. "Maybe, Father, there will be more than one wedding for you to perform while you are with us."

According to Malikan tradition, the newlywed couple usually spent at least three days in seclusion enjoying each other to the fullest before returning to their normal activities, so Tommy was surprised when he found Mitch waiting for him on the beach the following morning.

"I hadn't expected to see you for several days," he chided, wondering why Mitch would want to be away from his beautiful bride even for a minute. "I thought it was the custom for newly married couples to spend their first few days alone."

Mitch dismissed his observation with what seemed a casual laugh. "We were alone—all night," he told him meaningfully.

"But there was no reason for you to rush back here to help me."

"I was restless, and since she was still sleeping"—he shrugged indifferently—"I thought you could use a hand."

"There's never any doubt about that." Tommy was glad

for his company as they set out together to make their day's catch.

More than restlessness had driven Mitch from Espri as she lay sleeping that morning. When he'd awakened to find her slumbering beside him, he'd been stricken with remorse over his behavior the night before. He had never taken a woman who wasn't willing, and in spite of the fact that she had responded to him, he felt he had abused her, especially after he'd heard her crying. She had told him that she didn't want him, yet her wishes had meant nothing to him. Methodically, using all of his considerable expertise, he had aroused her, then forced her to admit a desire she hadn't wanted to feel. The fact that he'd enjoyed their coupling only made his guilt that much more unbearable.

Ashamed, Mitch knew he was the one who'd been defeated by the victory he'd so craved. By conquering Espri's resistance and taking her body despite her express wishes, he had caught himself up in a web of passion from which there seemed no escape. In proving his point that she would respond to him, he had forced the issue and lost the advantage. He found now, after taking her, that he wanted more than a manipulated response to his touch. He wanted to recapture the spontaneous joy they had known in their first encounters, encounters that were branded in his memory as the most perfect he'd ever known.

But Espri had left no doubt in his mind as to her feelings about their marriage. She had not wanted it, and now that she had professed her hate for him, Mitch knew that he'd lost far more than he could ever have hoped to gain by his lustful taking of her. He would have to bide his time, and never again, he resolved, would he force her to surrender that which she would not freely give.

* * *

Espri awoke. The sun, high above the horizon, told her that she'd slept well; far better, in fact, than she'd hoped. She had just started to stretch in languid contentment when the actuality of what had transpired between herself and Mitch during the night came to her. Mortified, she sat up, burying her face in her hands. How could she have come to him so willingly? She hadn't wanted to love him . . . but she had. He had mastered her senses completely, and as much as she hated to admit it, she had gloried in his domination.

Suddenly needing to see him again, Espri got up and, wrapping a sarong about her, hurried outside, thinking to find him waiting for her in the glade. To her dismay, the clearing was deserted. Panic filled her—had she so displeased him that he'd gone?

She briefly considered going to the village to find him, but pride held her back. She could not admit her marriage was a failure. Somehow, she would have to find a way to draw him to her. He had cared about her once, and perhaps she could arouse those same feelings in him again. When he approached her the next time, she was determined not to refuse him, but to go to him willingly. After all, he was caught in a marriage he clearly did not want, and it was up to her to prove to him that their joining would not be such a bad thing. Though it upset her that he only wanted her physically, she realized that could be a basis to build on. Maybe with time, things between them would improve.

The hours passed interminably as she awaited his return, and she began to wonder, as the morning ended, if he would come back to her. Finally, when she could stand the suspense no longer, she left the hut and followed the path that led to the sea, hoping that an invigorating swim would ease her tension.

The fishing had gone well that morning, and it was afternoon before Mitch returned home. He was expecting a major confrontation with Espri, and knowing that he deserved whatever censure she would lay upon him, he was surprised to find her gone.

Had she left him? Mitch had never considered that she might, and the thought jarred him. His invitation to her to enjoy the advantages their marriage gave them had been a disguised statement of his need for her; her denial of that attraction had been a challenge he could not ignore. But by proving that her desire did still exist, he might possibly have driven her away from him completely.

Frustrated and angry over the situation he found himself in, he was just starting back toward the village to look for her when she returned from her swim. When their eyes met, Espri quickly shuttered her expression lest he witness the joy she'd felt at seeing him again.

Mitch saw the change in her and felt that she did hate him. She had seemed almost happy as she'd entered the clearing, but upon seeing him, she'd turned cold and distant.

"I see you're back." It was all he could think of to say.

"I went to swim," she explained, then added almost casually, "Are you leaving again?"

"No." Mitch quickly turned away from the path to the village. "In fact, I just got back."

"Oh?" Their polite conversation was ridiculous, but Espri knew of no way to break through the rigidness of the moment.

"I went out with Tommy this morning. The catch is in the cooking hut." His eyes were warm as they feasted on the sight of her, but he held himself in check.

Espri felt that he was totally indifferent to her, and her spirits sank. "I'll go clean them," she offered, her defeat complete.

Mitch watched her go, feeling that the chance for any real intimacy between them was gone. Whatever good feelings she'd had for him in the beginning had now turned to hate, and he had to accept full responsibility for that. Their future together seemed to loom like a grim specter before him.

Angered by the entire situation, he stalked away, hoping that they could at least come to some kind of understanding by the time their child was born.

Sundown. Night. Espri had been anticipating its arrival with both excitement and trepidation. All day she had recalled the thrill of being in Mitch's arms, and she could hardly wait to be with him again. He had said the previous night that it was the one part of their marriage they should enjoy. Tonight, Espri fully intended to do so. She would not fight him. She would meet him more than halfway and try to convince him through her actions that what they shared was still special.

Mitch had been uncommunicative all afternoon, and when she'd announced to him after they'd shared a silent meal that she was going to bathe, he had made no effort to come with her. Now she was ready for bed and she hoped he was too.

"Good night," she said as she rose from where she'd been sitting by the fire and started to enter the hut.

Mitch nodded briefly in response, then watched her go from beneath lowered lids. Desire flared within him at the memory of loving her, but he refused to act upon it. She did not want him, and he would respect her wishes.

Espri tossed restlessly, waiting for Mitch to come to her, but as the hours passed, she slowly came to realize that he no longer wanted her. No doubt her struggles and vows of hatred the night before had killed the last shred of feeling he'd had for her. She almost went out to him to ask him to make love to her, but fear held her immobile. Mitch could be cruel—he'd proven that the night before with his barbed comments—and she didn't think she could stand it if he belittled her desire to please him.

Mitch remained outside for a long time. He did not join Espri in the hut until he was certain that she'd already fallen asleep. Though his self-imposed exile from her bed would be difficult for him, he knew he had to do it, for to make love to her when he knew how she felt about him would be degrading for both of them.

That day and night set the pattern for their time together. They each went their separate ways during the day; then, at night, Espri retired first and Mitch followed when he was sure she was sleeping. He made no sexual overtures toward her, and though the tension between them became almost unbearable, neither would make the first move to rectify the situation.

It was a week after the wedding when the news came.

"Espri!"

She looked up to see Laiti rushing across the clearing toward her. Noticing the woman's stricken expression, Espri was concerned. "What is it? Is my father all right?"

"There is news." Laiti panted, and her next words shattered what little peace Espri had managed to salvage from the shreds of her marriage. "A ship has made landfall in Kikini!"

Her eyes widened in disbelief. "A ship? In Kikini?"

The island woman nodded quickly. "It's true. I just heard the messenger from the chief of Kikini telling Luatu. He said that after the ship takes on water and supplies it will be coming here to pick up the survivors of the shipwreck."

Espri found herself speechless. What could she do? On occasion she had admitted that this might happen, but she had never really believed it would. Naïvely, she had counted on giving birth to her child here among her loved ones, with Mitch at her side, but now . . .

"Espri?" Laiti had noticed how pale she'd become and she grew concerned. She touched Espri's arm.

"I'm sorry." Espri blinked and forced a small smile. "How soon did he say the ship would get here?"

"Possibly by tomorrow," she answered.

"Did you see Mitch in the village? Does he know yet?"

"No. The men had not yet returned from the sea, but I am sure that he will know before he returns home to you this day."

Espri nodded. "I must go to my father and tell him the news."

"Would you like me to go with you?"

"It's not necessary, but thank you for offering." She hugged Laiti affectionately.

"If you need me for anything . . ."

"I know. I'll come to see you as soon as I find out what is going to happen."

Laiti pressed her friend's hand reassuringly and then headed back to the village, leaving Espri to start on her way to see Jacques.

Mitch and Tommy returned from their fishing to find Luatu waiting for them on the shore in the company of a native they didn't recognize. They frowned in expectation as they nimbly jumped from their craft and came forward to greet him.

"Luatu, this is an honor and a surprise," Mitch called as he came up the beach.

"The surprise will be yours and Tommy's," the old chief told him as he gestured to his companion. "This is Haki, a messenger from my friend Chief Kinatu on the island of Kikini."

A thrill of hope surged through Mitch as he suddenly realized the nature of Luatu's news.

"There is news of a ship?" He was incredulous.

Luatu nodded. "It is one of the China trade ships on its way back to San Francisco, so I am told. It is taking on supplies and water at Kikini, and will be here to pick you up within the next day or two."

Stunned, Mitch stood silently for a moment as conflicting emotions washed over him. A ship! Home! But what of Espri? He knew he had to go to her.

"Has Espri heard the news yet?" he asked.

"I don't think so. It would be best, I'm sure, if she heard this from you."

"You're right. Thank you, Luatu. I'll be back to speak with you later. And, Haki, thank you." He glanced at Tommy, who had remained strangely quiet throughout the entire conversation. "Tommy? What's the matter?"

As if jarred from deep thought, the younger man faced him, assuming a pleased expression. "Nothing. You go on."

Mitch knew that this news would be traumatic for Espri, but he was determined to try to make the transition as easy as possible for her. He was disappointed when he returned to their hut, though, for she was not there. Eager to tell her about the ship, he searched for her on the beach and at the bathing pool, but he could find no trace. Expecting her to return at any moment, he settled in to wait for her.

Espri looked at her father worriedly. "But what am I to do?"

"Since you have no idea what Mitch's plans are, I think you should ask him."

"What if Mitch plans to leave me behind?" Her panic was very real. The way he'd been treating her lately, she had wondered if there was a future for them even on Malika . . . but in San Francisco?

"Do you honestly believe that's a possibility?" Jacques gave her a measured look.

She thought long and hard before answering. "I don't know, Papa."

"He's your husband, Espri. You are bound together in God's eyes. Mitch took that vow seriously, and I don't think he would consider leaving here without you."

"But I'm not sure I want to go."

"Espri." Jacques's voice contained condemnation. "You are his wife. You must go where he leads; it is your duty."

She paled at his words. "I know you're right."

"You love him, don't you?"

Sighing, she reflected on the tenseness of her relationship with Mitch, then answered honestly. "Yes."

"Then your place is at his side," Jacques told her. "Has he heard this news yet?"

"No, I don't think so. He was out fishing with Tommy."

"Don't you think you should be there when he finds out? I'm sure he will be excited at the prospect. It is, after all, what he's been waiting for all these long months."

Nodding, she hugged him. "I love you, Papa."

"And I love you." He returned her embrace. "Now, go to your husband."

As Jacques watched her leave, a great sadness overcame him. She had been his entire life for years. He did not want her to leave Malika, but he knew it would be wrong to encourage her to stay. He only hoped that Mitch was the man Luatu believed him to be.

Uneasy, Espri returned home, and she was surprised to find Mitch already there.

"You've heard the news?" she inquired quickly, not looking at him.

"Yes. Luatu met us on the beach. He said the ship should be here within two days to pick us up."

"You will be glad to go?" she ventured, wanting him to tell her his plans.

"Malika is very beautiful, but it's important that I return home," Mitch stated determinedly. He was becoming increasingly excited by the thought of going home.

Espri paled at his use of "I" and not "we." She knew then that her worst fears were coming to pass—he intended to leave without her.

"I know it won't be easy for you, but with time . . ." he

continued, hoping to ease any anxiety she was feeling about leaving her home and going to a strange new world.

"I'll be fine." Espri was becoming angry at his seeming unconcern for her plight.

"Good." Mitch had expected to find her reluctant to go with him, and he was pleased by her seeming willingness to do so.

Good! she thought furiously. He was going to desert her and their unborn baby, and because she'd said she'd be fine, in a stroke of perverse independence, he was willing to drop the subject that easily! Her pride surging forth, she stiffened and started to walk away.

"Espri? Is something wrong?" He frowned as he noticed that she seemed upset.

"No. Nothing's wrong." She tried to keep her tone steady. "What things do you plan to take with you? Shall I start getting them together now?"

A cold dread filled him as he listened to her words. She sounded as if she wanted him to leave, alone, and that she couldn't wait to see him off. How she must hate him—but hate or not, she was married to him.

"We will pack our things together," he stated emphatically, his dread turning to icy fury. She was his wife, and by God, she was going with him! He'd be damned if he'd leave her behind.

"Our things?" Espri glanced at him quickly in disbelief.

"Don't say a word." His voice was cold. "You will be ready to go with me when the boat comes. Do you understand?"

"But . . ."

Needing to get away before he said something in anger that he might regret, Mitch turned from her. "I'll be back."

Espri watched him go, her heart heavy. His obvious anger convinced her that he resented taking her with him, yet she silently prayed for a chance to make their marriage work.

* * *

Tommy was desperate. While the news of his imminent rescue should have made him ecstatic, it had only filled him with despair and confusion. What was he going to do? He loved Tikiru deeply and he couldn't bear the thought of being separated from her. It was difficult enough being here on the island and knowing that they couldn't meet, but if he returned to California, he knew with a certainty that he would never see her again. Tormented by the decision he was being forced to make, he knew he had to see Tikiru once again.

Biding his time, he nervously anticipated nightfall, for when darkness enshrouded the land, he intended to go to Tikiru, dangerous though it might be. The hours passed slowly, and when at last it was reasonably safe, he started off toward the sacred temple.

Nelani was shocked when she saw Tommy approaching, and she rushed forward to try to send him back to the village.

"You must leave," she ordered, attempting to keep him from Tikiru.

"I have to see her. Where is she?" he demanded in a lowered voice.

"She's not here. Now, please go," Nelani pleaded, knowing that if they were discovered the price they would pay would be high.

"I will wait."

Nelani was about to say more when Tikiru appeared nude on the veranda of her hut.

"Nelani? Where are you?"

Tommy brushed past the servant and hurried up the few steps to take Tikiru in his arms. Holding her close, he kissed her deeply before she had a chance to protest his coming.

Overwhelmed by his unexpected appearance, Tikiru permitted herself to enjoy his forbidden embrace briefly before struggling to break free.

"Tommy! You must go. Manti could come here at any time!"

"Tikiru, I have to talk with you. I can go on like this no longer." He kissed her again desperately.

"No . . . not here." She pushed away from him with all her might. "Please, Tommy, go. I will meet you later on the bluff, but it will have to be the very last time that we see each other."

Knowing that it very well might be, he stepped back, his passion-darkened gaze sweeping over her heatedly. "I'll be waiting for you."

After Tommy had disappeared into the forest, Nelani rushed to Tikiru. "You don't really plan to meet him there, do you?"

Tikiru's expression was troubled as she turned to her slave. "I must."

"Let me go in your place. I will tell him that you hate him and never want to see him again."

"He would know that to be a lie," she answered sadly. "I love him, Nelani, more than my own life."

"You'll be careful?" Nelani insisted, and Tikiru nodded.

It was well after midnight when Tikiru finally felt she could slip safely away. Wrapping the concealing cloak about her slender figure, she hurried off into the night to rendezvous with her love.

Tommy had not bothered to return to the village. Tense and on edge, he'd gone straight to the bluff in anticipation of Tikiru's coming, and when he finally saw her racing across the stark open terrain toward him, he opened his arms to her and clasped her to his chest.

"Ah, my love . . ." His words were heartfelt, and his mouth claimed hers in a devouring kiss that told her of his hopeless passion.

Swept along by the power of their need, they moved in unison to seek out the soft grass that had served them so well in the past, and their clothing was hastily discarded as they lay upon that natural bed.

"I want you so, Tikiru," Tommy told her huskily as he pressed fevered kisses to her throat and bosom.

"Oh, yes. Please love me, Tommy," she urged him, intertwining her legs with his and moving wantonly against him. "I have missed you, and I need you so."

The flame of her desire consumed him in a fiery frenzy, and he mounted her quickly, seeking and finding the heated depths of her body. Tikiru trembled with the force of the emotion that surged through her as she clung to him, insatiable in her passion. Each powerful thrust of his driving hips brought her closer and closer to the edge of ecstasy, and she arched in abandon as the pleasure took her, pulsing through her in endless waves of exquisite bliss.

Tommy felt her shudder, and he knew a moment of male pride. He had pleased her; he had given her the gift of his love. Continuing to move in steady rhythm, he cupped her hips and lifted her tightly to him, penetrating her to the fullest and eliciting a groan of sensual excitement from her. He peaked then, emptying his life-giving seed deep within the fertile depths of her body, and they collapsed together, sated and fulfilled.

Reason returned as they lay side by side, and it was with deep regret that Tikiru faced him.

"Tommy . . ." She reached out to touch his cheek.

"I know, Tikiru." His voice was toneless as he captured her hand and kissed the palm. "I have news that I must tell you."

"What is it?" She was instantly alert.

"There is a ship at a neighboring island. It's coming here next."

"A ship? You will be leaving Malika?" Her eyes widened at the possibility.

"You tell me, Tikiru"—he pierced her with a serious look—"should I stay?"

Stricken, she looked away. She knew it had to end. If he were to leave the island . . .

"We can never be together, Tommy, and I should not have come tonight. The only reason I did was to tell you that it cannot happen again," she told him, though it pained her to do so. "You should go with the ship when it comes because both of our lives would be at stake if we were discovered and the risk of that is growing too great."

"Come with me." The idea suddenly occurred to him. "Since we cannot share our love openly here, run away with me. We could sneak you onto the ship, and no one would ever have to know. By the time they'd discovered you'd gone, we would be far out to sea and on our way to America. Marry me, Tikiru, and I will spend the rest of my days loving you."

Her eyes brightened with hope. Could she do it? "I don't know . . . you want me to leave my people?"

"I love you, Tikiru. I will let no harm ever come to you. Say you'll come with me."

"I'll come," she agreed hastily, knowing that the rest of her life would be empty and meaningless without him.

Overcome with joy, Tommy embraced her excitedly. "When the ship arrives, I will send word. Until then, do nothing."

She nodded, her heart pounding at the thought of being with him forever. "I love you, Tommy, and I will do whatever you want if it means we can be together."

"Good." He kissed her tenderly, understanding the sacrifice she was making so that they could be together. "You'll never regret this, Tikiru. I promise."

She wrapped her arms about his neck, and they clung together, oblivious to the tragedy the future held for them.

Chapter 17

Manti awoke suddenly. The dream he'd been having had seemed so real and so threatening that he was confused and disoriented. He tried to remember all that he'd envisioned, but could recall only fragments of it. Upset and unable to go back to sleep, he began to restlessly pace his chamber. Something was about to happen; the sense of foreboding he felt was almost overwhelming.

It was not often that he sought out Tikiru, but knowing that she was gifted with the power to interpret such visions, he went to her then, without pause, in the middle of the night. It was dark and quiet as he made his way to her hut, but he was so intent on discovering the meaning of his dream that he did not notice. And when he reached her abode, he stood before her hut as was customary, calling out to her a chanted, authoritative summons to which she could not, by law, fail to respond.

Nelani had been resting in her own bed when she heard the high priest invoking Tikiru to come forth. Sitting up panic-stricken, she quickly debated the chance of finding Tikiru and bringing her back before Manti would get suspicious, but she knew there was no time. Manti was here, now, and he was demanding an audience with the *taupau*. Rising, she dressed, lit a torch, and went out onto the veranda to speak with him.

"Oh, High Priest, why do you summon the *taupau*?" she asked, bowing in homage before him after she'd placed the torch in a rack.

"I must see her," he answered without hesitation.

"But she is resting and bade me not to disturb her," Nelani lied, she hoped convincingly.

Manti's eyes flashed with anger. "I am the high priest. She will see me—*now!*"

Nelani was afraid, but her years of training to be faithful and submissive to Tikiru steadied her. She knew she could not abandon her mistress now. Turning, she disappeared into the hut and knelt down beside the deserted bed to pray to the gods to save Tikiru from Manti's wrath.

Manti waited impatiently before the hut, and as the minutes slipped by, he became increasingly suspicious. By sacred law, he was forbidden to violate the sanctity of Tikiru's hut, but he knew he had no choice.

"Nelani! Bring forth your mistress!" he ordered, and when there was no response to his call, he entered the hut.

Manti stared incredulously at the slave girl praying beside Tikiru's empty bed.

"Where is she?" he asked as he stood rigidly behind her.

"I do not know," she answered truthfully.

His hand snaked out to grasp her by her hair, and he pulled her back against him, holding her so tightly that her neck arched painfully. Nelani gasped as he lifted his sacrificial knife from his belt and ran the sharpness of the blade softly yet threateningly down her cheek, then pressed the point to her throat.

"I would know where Tikiru is," Manti demanded again, letting her feel the prick of the bodkin. He watched with cold indifference as blood began to flow freely from the cut.

Nelani shuddered in fear more than pain, but her loyalty

held her steadfast against his cruelty. "Perhaps at the bathing pool," she finally offered as she felt the warmth of her own blood on her breast.

Manti nodded in silence and shoved her back to the floor. "I will see."

Stalking from the hut, he covered the distance to the secluded pool quickly and was infuriated to find it deserted. Tikiru was gone . . . but where? His patience at an end, he raced back to the hut to get the answer to his question.

"Your mistress is not at the pool, Nelani, and I have a feeling you are not telling me all you know." He smiled lethally at the cowering slave. "I want to know where she is. You know it is forbidden for her to have contact with anyone. Has she been meeting someone?" He delved deeper into the mystery of her disappearance. "Was that really Tikiru I saw the other night on the path?"

"I do not know where Tikiru is," Nelani insisted again, refusing bravely to give him the answers he so craved.

"Then you will die for your ignorance," he declared calmly, dragging her to her feet. Violently he stripped off her sarong, and tearing the fabric, he bound her wrists and ankles with it. Pushing her roughly to the floor, he left the hut and returned to the temple to summon his male servant Nahi.

"Go to Tikiru's hut and bring her slave girl to me, here," he ordered.

"Manti!" Nahi protested quickly in outrage. "It is forbidden for me to go there!"

"By my decree, you are free to enter without punishment. Go now, and hurry."

"Yes, Manti." Nahi rushed to do his bidding.

Nelani lay where Manti had left her. Shaking and helpless, she realized that there was little hope of rescue, that only Tikiru's return could save her from certain death. When Manti's servant entered the hut, she was startled, and she became more frightened.

"What are you doing here?" she asked desperately, but he ignored her question and bent to pick her up. "No! Please don't do this! I have done nothing to displease the gods!"

Nelani tried to struggle free of the man, but he only tightened his hold on her, his vicious grip bruising her tender flesh. Sobbing, she collapsed against him, knowing that her struggles were futile.

Nahi displayed no emotion as he carried her to where Manti waited at the altar, and at the priest's instruction, he placed her carefully atop the stone slab.

Vulnerable and guiltless, Nelani lay before the high priest. "I have done nothing to deserve this, Manti."

But his glittering eyes conveyed only contempt. "Perhaps if Tikiru comes in time, you will live," he told her casually. "Begin the drum."

Nahi pounded out the message loudly on the ceremonial drum, and the throbbing tones swelled across the island, alerting all to come to the temple. Manti turned back to the slave, and pouring a potion into a cup, he lifted her head and forced her to drink of the bitter brew.

"Swallow all of it," he commanded, and, helpless, she obeyed. "If you move, I will kill you now," he told her coldly as he cut away her bonds, his hands idling unfeelingly on her body as he positioned her.

The effect of the drug was immediate; Nelani couldn't have protested had she dared to.

"Where is Tikiru?" a distant commanding voice demanded, and Nelani had no will to resist it.

"With the white man," she mumbled.

Manti was totally shocked. The white man? Surely not the husband of Espri . . .

"Which white man?" he pressed.

"The golden one . . . the one called Tommy." Nelani was not aware of her betrayal.

"Where are they?"

"I don't know . . . I don't know . . . maybe the bluff . . . I don't know." Her answer became fainter as darkness finally overwhelmed her completely, sweeping her into the blessed relief of unconsciousness.

At the first sound of the drum, Tikiru tore herself violently from Tommy's arms. "No!"

"What's wrong?" he asked quickly, trying to take her back into his embrace; but she pushed him away.

"Somehow, we have been found out! I must go. I must leave now!"

"But how do you know?" he persisted, disbelieving.

"The drum . . . Manti has taken Nelani to the temple to sacrifice!"

"Sacrifice? What are you talking about?"

"He is going to kill her!" Hurriedly, she donned the sarong she'd worn, and forgetting her cloak, she started to race from the bluff top.

Tommy wrapped his pareu around him and went after her, but as he reached her side, three of Manti's servants stepped from the forest.

"Seize them!" the leader ordered.

Tommy managed to knock down two of the men, but the third one struck him from behind and he fell heavily at Tikiru's feet, unconscious. The men then grasped her by the arms, but she glared at them and spoke with authority.

"There is no need to use violence on me," she said calmly. "I will come with you without a struggle."

Kneeling beside Tommy, she kissed him quickly and then stood, ready to follow the men back to Manti. They led her to a private chamber deep in the temple. Then one man stayed behind to guard her while the others went to fetch Manti.

"My servants have led me to understand that you were

found in the company of the white man," Manti declared as he entered the chamber.

"It is true." Tikiru would not deny the obvious.

"Hold her down," he directed, and despite the fight she put up, the three brawny men soon had her immobile on a mat on the floor. Kneeling down beside her, he brushed aside the skirt of her sarong and curtly ordered, "Hold her legs far apart. I must examine her to see if she has defiled herself with a man."

She twisted and strained against his humiliating touch, but his cold hands explored her expertly, finding in her breached womanhood the answer to his quest.

"She has forsaken her vow of chastity." He sneered in disgust as he stood up and looked down upon her. "Strip her of her garment and bring her forth to the altar to witness the terror her fleshly ways have caused."

Espri was awakened by the sound of the drum and was horrified by the message it conveyed.

"What is it? What's the drum saying?" Mitch asked when he awoke to find Espri up and preparing to leave.

"Evidently there has been some kind of trouble and Manti the high priest is summoning all the islanders to the temple."

"What kind of trouble?"

"I don't know."

"Wait, I'll come with you," he offered, sensing an urgency in the situation.

"We'd better hurry."

Espri leading the way, they headed for the temple.

The villagers had already assembled, and they were shocked by what they'd found. The *taupau*'s servant Nelani lay naked and unconscious upon the sacrificial altar while Manti prayed over her, offering up her soul to the gods as appeasement for the transgression that was, as yet, unknown to the islanders.

Espri gasped when she realized what was about to happen. "Where are my grandfather and Father Pierre?" She glanced around, desperately trying to locate the only two men on the island powerful enough to stop the ritual sacrifice.

"What is it? What's he going to do?" Mitch asked as he watched the priest in fascination.

"Kill her," Espri answered succinctly. "And soon. I have to find Luatu."

Rushing from Mitch's side, she ran back toward the village with him following behind, and she was grateful when she found her grandfather and the missionary just starting up the path to the temple. "You must come at once!"

"What is it, Espri?" they asked.

"It's Manti. He intends to sacrifice Nelani."

"What?" Luatu and Father Pierre glanced at each other in outrage.

"There have been no human offerings here in years! Why is he reverting to that savagery?" Father Pierre asked worriedly. "What could have happened?"

"We don't know, but we'd better hurry," Mitch urged.

Luatu and Father Pierre led the way, bursting into the temple just as Manti ended his chant. Startled by the disturbance the two men caused, the pagan priest looked up, his fiery eyes meeting those of the missionary in a haughty, hate-filled glare.

"Manti!" Luatu's voice rang out across the temple as he hurried forward to the altar with Pierre close behind. "What is the cause for this?" he demanded imperiously.

"The sacred vows have been defiled. They must pay for the desecration with their lives," the high priest answered fiercely, his bloodlust obvious.

"What sacred vows?" Luatu asked, noting the fresh blood on the young girl's throat and breasts.

"The *taupau* . . . it is because of her wicked actions that Nelani must die."

"I do not understand," Luatu ventured. "What has Tikiru done?"

"She has forsaken her vow and has joined with a man."

"Who?"

"The white man, Tommy."

"Tommy?" Mitch had followed them to the forefront, and he now looked worriedly around for his friend. "Where is he?"

"The defiler has already been dealt with," Manti declared. "Now it only remains to punish the women." He gestured to the men who were standing in the shadows behind the altar, and they came forth, pushing Tikiru before them. "Witness, people of Malika! Your priestess has forsaken you. She will pay with her life for her wickedness!"

The crowd murmured excitedly at the sight of Tikiru.

"Grandfather! You must stop him! You can't let him kill them, no matter what they've done!"

But it wasn't Luatu who stepped forward to challenge Manti as he raised his knife to cut the drugged girl's heart from her chest; it was Father Pierre.

"You must not do this, Manti. Killing is wrong—always," he declared loudly.

"Be gone, white man. You know nothing of our ways. It is just punishment for the defilement Tikiru has wreaked upon the temple. Only with these deaths will the gods be appeased."

"And only with their lives will my God be satisfied," Pierre returned fearlessly, and he reached out to touch Nelani. "You will have to kill me before I allow you to harm these two women."

The priests' eyes met and clashed over the young woman's motionless body, but Manti was not intimidated. Viciously, he slashed downward with the deadly weapon, but Father Pierre blocked his lethal blow, deflecting with his own arm the knife that would have ended Nelani's life. Luatu moved then, and with Mitch's help he managed to restrain Manti and to knock the knife from his grip. Manti and Pierre faced each other again as the blood dripped to the altar from the deep cut on the missionary's forearm.

"Nelani and Tikiru must die!" the pagan priest insisted, trying to break free from Luatu and Mitch.

"Take them, Father," Luatu ordered, and Father Pierre nodded as he lifted Nelani's limp body from the altar and motioned for Tikiru to follow him.

Luatu and Mitch did not release Manti until they were certain that Father Pierre and the two women were safely away. Then, addressing his people, Luatu spoke.

"The old ways are no more," he declared imperiously. "Return to your homes now!"

Manti stood, silently seething, behind his chief.

Luatu turned on his one-time friend. "You are welcome to remain here, but I will hear no more of your desire for killing. Remember this." He was fierce as he glowered at Manti.

"You cannot end our ancestors' ways so easily." Manti sneered.

At this comeback, the chief's expression hardened. "It is only because of Father Pierre that I do not see you dead now," Luatu told him mercilessly.

Blanching at the threat, yet very aware of Luatu's power to have him killed, Manti was distraught. "I will not stay here and face the ridicule of the people!"

"I would not bid you to go, but I will not accept your presence on Malika if you cannot be at peace." Luatu had always been aware of the antagonism Manti had for the missionary, but he had never realized the depths of that resentment until now.

Manti stormed away without answering.

"I must see to Father Pierre," Luatu said gruffly as he watched the man who'd once been his friend walk off.

"If you have no objection, Luatu, I'd like to come with

you," Mitch offered. "I'm worried about Tommy, and I think one of the women may know where he is."

"Both of you, come. I am sure Father's arm will need some attention," the old chief told Mitch and Espri.

When they had returned to Luatu's home, they found Pierre gently caring for both of the women, unmindful of his own injury. He had covered them with blankets and was trying to rouse Nelani from her drugged stupor.

"How are they?" Luatu asked.

"I think they will be all right, although I'm not sure what drug Manti gave Nelani."

But even as he spoke, the girl began to stir. With a soft groan, she opened her eyes and was startled to find herself safely ensconced in the chief's hut. "What happened? How do I come to be here?" When Nelani saw Tikiru sitting beside her, she gasped audibly. "You came!"

"He was going to kill you, Nelani, because of me," Tikiru told her brokenly. "I'm sorry."

"Father, come out for a moment," Luatu said quietly, and Pierre stepped outside, wondering what he wanted.

"Yes, Luatu?"

"Espri will bind your wound for you," Luatu explained.

For the first time Pierre noticed the ugly knife wound on his forearm. He smiled crookedly in wonder. "I am certain that it will hurt tomorrow, but right now I feel nothing." Joining Espri by the fire, he sat patiently while she cleansed the injury and wrapped his arm in soft, clean cloths.

When Mitch and Luatu went inside the hut to talk with the women, they found that Tikiru was trying to wrap a piece of cloth around her in some semblance of dress so she could leave.

"Where do you think you're going?" Luatu asked.

"Tommy . . . he's injured, maybe dead . . . have to go to him . . ." She was visibly trembling.

"You know where Tommy is?" Mitch broke in anxiously.

"On the bluff top."

Luatu looked at Mitch. "Have you been there? Do you know the path?"

"I haven't been up there before, but I know how to get there," Mitch answered.

"Go, then, and try to find your friend." The chief glanced at Tikiru before he stepped outside with Mitch. "If he is alive, do not bring him back to the village. These are a good-hearted people, but the *taupau* has always been sacred and pure. It will not rest well with them that she has forsaken her vows and taken a lover. They would resent Tommy's presence, no matter how willing a partner Tikiru was."

"I understand," Mitch answered, praying all the while that Tommy had come to no serious harm.

Luatu watched him go and then returned to face the two women.

"Tikiru, I want to know exactly what happened tonight," he said.

She lowered her eyes submissively. "I have failed to keep my vows and am not worthy of your respect or consideration."

"Tell me everything."

Tikiru faced him resolutely. "There is little to tell. I had a vision many nights ago. A vision of the golden-haired white man. When Nelani told me that a man with hair the color of the sun had been rescued from the sea, I knew I had to see him, to find out the meaning of my dream. I fell in love with him."

"And despite your vow not to join with a man, you had relations with him?"

"Yes, Luatu." Tikiru considered apologizing, but did not. She was not sorry for the time she'd spent with Tommy, and she knew that she would probably do the same thing again if she had the chance.

The sound of voices distracted the chief from his inquisition, and ordering her not to leave the hut, he went outside to see what the disturbance was. An angry group of torch-bearing islanders was crowding the path to his home so Luatu went forth to speak with them.

"What do you want?" he demanded, standing firm and strong at the end of the path. "Why have you gathered here?"

"Manti was right!" one man cried out. "The *taupau* has abused her vaulted position and has been defiled. She deserves death! It is so written by the ancestors!"

Luatu folded his arms across his massive chest and scowled at them. "The old ways are dead. You have accepted Father Papin, have you not?" At their answering murmur, he continued. "What does Father tell us about forgiveness?"

"But she took a vow!" another yelled heatedly.

"Who are you to judge?" Luatu thundered. "Leave."

Knowing the fury their chief was capable of when angered or defied, they turned, grumbling, and headed back to the village.

"The natives are restless tonight." Pierre spoke cautiously to Espri as she finished tying the bandage about his arm.

"Grandfather will settle everything. He always does," she told him with great confidence, although in her heart she worried. There had never been a situation like this before, where there was a direct conflict between new and old.

"They are gone for now," Luatu said with some measure of relief as he joined Pierre and Espri. "I think, Father, it will be best for everyone if you take the women to another island."

"I was thinking the same thing," he agreed. "Are there men you can trust to send with me?"

"My own personal servants will accompany you," the chief pledged. "There are some who fanatically follow Manti and would think nothing of capturing Tikiru and Nelani and taking them back to him for sacrifice. For that reason, I want no word of their whereabouts revealed."

"I understand, and I will take the utmost caution." Father Pierre stood up and shook Luatu's hand. "It will be best if we leave immediately."

"Come. Let us tell the women of our plan."

The two men reentered the hut.

"You will be leaving the island with Father Pierre," Luatu told Tikiru and Nelani. "It is the only way I can ensure your safety."

"What of Tommy?" Tikiru asked fearfully. "Is he alive?"

"We have not heard anything yet, and we do not have time to wait. There are those among the islanders who would not hesitate to hand you over to Manti."

"But I don't want to leave Tommy," Tikiru protested.

"There is no way I can allow you to stay. To save your life, you must go," Luatu pronounced. "If Tommy is still alive and you were to be seen together by the villagers . . ." He did not say more; there was no need.

Tikiru was devastated. "I understand, but, Luatu, please, could you send me word of Tommy? I could not exist, not knowing his fate."

"I will send word through Father Pierre," he agreed. "Now, you must go, while it is quiet."

Ordering his men to lead them to the secluded beach across the island from the village, Luatu bade them safe journey.

"I will look forward to our next meeting, old friend," Father Pierre told the chief as they clasped hands.

"It will be good."

"Espri," Pierre called out, and she came across the clearing. "God bless you, *ma petite,* and may your journey to your new home be a safe and happy one."

She hugged him tightly, knowing that they would probably never meet again. Her eyes misted at that thought, and her smile lacked conviction. "Thank you, Father. Please . . . be careful, yourself."

"I will," he assured her, and then he disappeared with the others into the darkened forest.

Mitch raced up the narrow path that led to the bluff. Manti's words rang in his mind—*"The defiler has been dealt with"*—and he dreaded what he might find.

"Mitch!" Tommy's call pierced the silent darkness as he stepped from the overgrowth to the side of the path.

"Tommy! Thank God you're alive!" He embraced the other man with great relief.

"They've taken Tikiru . . . I must find her and help her." He was desperate to rescue his love from her fate at the hands of the high priest.

"It's over, Tommy," Mitch told him solemnly.

"What are you talking about?" he demanded, his soul freezing at the thought of her possible death.

"Tikiru is safe. The chief and the missionary saved her and her servant girl."

Tommy shook with relief. "Then I must go to her." He started to rush past Mitch, but his friend restrained him.

"Luatu insisted that, if you were alive, I was to keep you away from the village. Despite their Christian conversion, the islanders were still upset when they discovered that their *taupau* was no longer sacrosanct."

"Mitch, I love her . . . I need to see her."

"Perhaps tomorrow, we can arrange a meeting, but for now it's safer for both of you if we stay as far away as possible."

Tommy looked lost. "All right," he finally agreed, knowing that the only alternative was to overpower his friend, and, the way he was feeling, that would be impossible.

"Are you hurt?" Mitch suddenly asked, noticing how unsteady the younger man suddenly seemed.

"I don't know," Tommy admitted, grimacing as he touched the back of his neck. "I was out for quite a while."

"Let's head back to my hut. It's far enough from the village for us to be safe."

The desperation of the night over, they headed slowly in the direction of Mitch's home.

Tikiru was crying quietly as she followed Luatu's men through the forest and out onto the beach. The horror of what she'd just been through had stripped her of her dignity, and she was lost in a sea of confusing emotions. Her selfishness in ignoring Nelani's warnings and doing only what she wanted cost her more than she'd ever imagined. Tommy was probably dead and Nelani had suffered most cruelly, all because of her. Her guilt nearly unbearable, she regretted that she had not died on the altar. It would have been far better, she reasoned, to have ended her life at the same time as Tommy rather than face the rest of her days knowing she was responsible for his death.

"Tikiru!" Nelani's excited whisper broke through her sorrowing thoughts, and she looked up at her slave. "Look! There. Down the beach!"

Glancing in the direction in which the slave girl was pointing, she gasped in stunned amazement. Coming toward them were two men and one was unmistakably Tommy. Her joy at seeing him was so great that at first she could not speak. Breaking away from the others, she ran toward him.

Tommy and Mitch had decided to follow the shoreline back to the hut, and initially they had been cautious when they'd seen the small group of men and women emerge from the forest. But it had only taken Tommy an instant to recognize his love, and he'd rushed forward to meet her.

"Tikiru!" His voice was strangled with emotion as he swept her into his arms and kissed her.

"Oh, Tommy! You're alive!" She clung to him, unable to believe that he'd been spared Manti's deadly wrath.

"Tikiru! We must go!" Nelani called as she and the others waited by the outriggers for her to come.

"Go?" Tommy asked quickly as Mitch caught up with them. "Where are you going?"

Father Pierre came forward to speak with them. "There is much ill will toward Tikiru among the islanders, and Luatu is fearful for her life. We are leaving Malika tonight. It is the only way we can be sure nothing will happen."

"I'll go with you," Tommy offered without pause, but Father Pierre curtly refused.

"No. As she is, she can settle on another island without being recognized, but if you were to come along it would only be a matter of time before someone discovered the truth."

"Then Tikiru can come with me," Tommy countered, trying to find a way for them to be together. "The ship should be here at any time."

"You both might be dead before it arrived," Father Pierre informed him flatly.

"No, Tommy." Tikiru faced him, her eyes dark with concern. Now that she knew him to be safe, she would not let him endanger himself again. "I must go and you must stay."

"Tikiru . . ." His agony was evident.

"It is the only way. Do you think I would be able to live with the knowledge that you had died because of me?" she told him, her pain tearing her apart. "In these past few minutes, when I thought you were dead, I did not want to go on living." She smiled faintly. "Now, knowing that you are well, I can face my future."

"There has to be a way!" he insisted, but she stepped away from him, turning to Father Pierre.

"No, Tommy. I'm sorry. She must go now, before we are discovered." Father Pierre put an arm around Tikiru and started to lead her away.

"Tikiru!"

Breaking away from the priest's supportive grip, she rushed back to her love, throwing herself into his arms for one last kiss. "I shall love you forever, golden one." She smiled at him sadly and then returned to where Pierre was waiting to assist her into the canoe.

Tommy watched in heartbreaking agony as the outrigger disappeared from view beyond the barrier reef.

Chapter 18

"I'm Captain Clark, owner and master of the *Providence*," the gray-haired man declared as he greeted Mitch and Tommy when they boarded his vessel the following afternoon.

"I'm Mitch Williams." Mitch took the captain's hand and found the big man's grip warm and strong.

"And I'm Tommy O'Ryan."

"Welcome aboard."

"Thank you, Captain Clark. We appreciate your taking the time to come to Malika for us." Mitch surveyed the tall-masted ship with interest.

"Have you been stranded here long?" Clark inquired, curious as to the story behind their being here.

"Several months," Tommy supplied. "Yours is the first ship to come to the area since the *Seastorm* went down."

"You'll have to tell me about it later, after you've settled in," the captain encouraged.

"We'd be glad to," Mitch agreed.

"Ah, here's my wife now. Mildred," he called out, as a short, plump woman appeared on deck.

"Your wife travels with you?" Mitch had not expected to find another woman aboard.

"Always." Captain Clark smiled affectionately as she came

toward him. "Mildred, these are our new passengers—Mr. Williams and Mr. O'Ryan."

"It's a pleasure to meet you," Mildred said pleasantly.

"Well, if you gentlemen will get the rest of your gear aboard, we'll be making sail," Clark told them.

"Captain, one more person will be coming with us," Mitch declared quickly. "My wife will be joining us shortly."

"Your wife was sailing with you on the *Seastorm*?" Mildred was thrilled at the prospect of having another female to visit with during the long trip back to California.

"No. Espri and I have only just married." Mitch glanced toward Malika and saw Luatu's outrigger coming their way. "She's coming now."

Captain Clark and his wife were both astounded to see a beautiful young girl, clad in the native mode of dress, riding in the position of importance at the front of the ornate canoe. "You've married an islander?"

"Yes," Mitch answered somewhat defensively; but noticing that there had been no malice behind their words, he softened his reply. "Espri is the granddaughter of the chief and her father is a Frenchman who decided to make his permanent home on Malika."

"She's lovely," Mildred confided.

"Thank you."

They watched from the deck as Espri said her final farewells to Jacques and Luatu and then began to climb up the ladder that would take her to her husband. Mitch went to her aid immediately and helped her aboard.

Espri was surprised and secretly pleased by his unexpected display of attentiveness, and she allowed him to draw her forward across the deck to meet the Clarks. The feel of his hand at her waist sent a shiver of excited anticipation through her, causing her to hope that, indeed, this would be a new beginning for them. But feeling her reaction to his touch, Mitch tensed, thinking her response one of aversion to his nearness. Espri noticed that his expression suddenly darkened, and her hopes were dashed.

"Captain Clark, Mrs. Clark, this is my wife Espri." Mitch introduced them, outwardly displaying none of the anger Espri sensed he was feeling.

"I'm delighted to meet you, Mrs. Williams." Mildred took Espri's hand as she studied her with twinkling brown eyes. *This woman is lovely*, she mused thoughtfully. *No wonder the handsome Mr. Williams married her*. "It will be wonderful to have another woman to visit with during the rest of our voyage."

"Please, call me Espri," the younger woman invited, taking an immediate liking to the captain's wife.

"And I'm Mildred." She patted Espri's hand with welcoming reassurance. "Have you brought all your things with you?" She had noticed only the single sea chest that Mitch had hauled aboard.

"All of our things are here," Mitch answered, smiling wryly.

"Oh." She was surprised. "Well, then, let's go below and get you settled in, shall we?"

As Captain Clark went to the helm to get the ship underway, Mildred led them below deck. After directing Tommy to a room amidships, she opened the door to a cabin at the stern and turned to Mitch and Espri.

"I hope you find this will suit your needs."

"Thank you, Mildred." Mitch placed their trunk on the floor and looked around with interest. Though small, the room did boast a porthole and a convenience. "It is much more than I expected."

"You're more than welcome. If you need anything, please let me know."

"We will," Mitch assured her.

"I'll look forward to seeing you both later, then," Mildred said as she left the cabin.

"Fine," Mitch answered, and Espri flashed her a quick, grateful smile.

When she'd gone, Mitch closed the door and Espri stood in silence, surveying the tiny room that would be her home for the long months at sea. She had never been aboard a ship like this before, and she found most of the furnishings quite curious. The bed was large, and it dominated the cramped, white-walled room. Pegs for hanging clothing lined one wall. A narrow shelf was on the other. A washstand equipped with a china pitcher and bowl stood in the corner near the bed-stead, and above it was a small, round mirror.

"Mrs. Clark seems very nice," Espri remarked to break the silence.

"Yes," he replied tersely as he busied himself with their sea chest.

"Do wives usually sail with their husbands?" she ventured.

"It isn't done often," he explained without looking up. "Mainly because of the hardships suffered at sea. Things can get pretty rough during a long journey, and a lot of women would rather wait in the comfort of their homes for their men to return."

Espri knew that if Mitch were a ship's captain she would most certainly sail with him, for she found the prospect of being apart from him for months unbearable. Dismissing that thought as ridiculous because he didn't care if she was near or not, she turned her attention to the bed, her curiosity aroused. Unable to resist temptation any longer, she touched the mattress.

"This is soft!" she exclaimed in wonder, and then sat down on it for the first time. "I had no idea . . ."

Espri was beaming with delight at her discovery, and her innocence still had the power to amaze Mitch. Realizing it would not be easy for her to adapt to his way of life in San Francisco, he felt a driving need to protect her, to shield her from all they would have to face in the coming months. Mitch's gaze warmed as he took in the ebony length of hair cascading down her back, and he noted the way her sarong clung tightly to her perfect figure. His desire for her, so long denied, stirred to life as he imagined them making love on the comfort of the bed, and he swore silently to himself as he stood up. Fighting the urge to take her, then and there, he scowled blackly, knowing that he had to get away from her tempting presence.

"Stay in the cabin until I return," he barked, without preamble, and he stalked from the room, shutting the door tightly behind him.

Espri stared after him, her eyes wide. She did not understand what she'd done to anger him. Sighing, she lay back, testing the comfort of the bed, and she couldn't help but try to imagine what it was going to be like to share its wide softness with Mitch.

His desire for Espri under control, Mitch searched out Captain Clark, and he found him on deck, directing the setting of the sails.

"Mr. Williams, I'm about finished here." The captain issued several more orders and then gave Mitch his full attention. "Would you care to join me for a drink in my quarters?"

"Yes, I'd like that, and please, I'd appreciate it if you'd call me Mitch."

"Done." Clark started off toward the passageway that led to his cabin. "What's your preference? Rum? Whiskey?"

"Whiskey."

"Fine." They entered the captain's more spacious quarters, and Clark went to his massive desk, motioning Mitch to take a seat across from him. Opening the bottom drawer, he extracted two glasses and a nearly full bottle of bourbon. After pouring them both a healthy draft, he handed Mitch his. "To your health," he toasted, and they downed the liquor easily.

Mitch savored the taste of the potent bourbon. "It's been a long time." He sighed.

Clark eyed him with interest. "You don't seem a common sailor. How did you come to be aboard the fated craft?"

Mitch's smile was sardonic as he met the captain's gaze steadily. "I was shanghaied in San Francisco."

"I had suspected as much." The captain nodded as Mitch's declaration confirmed his original suspicions. "Your friend, too?"

"Yes. I imagine our families have given us up for dead by now." Mitch stared pensively at the amber liquid in his glass.

"Well, I'm sure they'll be glad to have you back. What did you do before going to sea?" Clark's wry sense of humor brought a cynical chuckle from Mitch.

"My *chosen* profession as opposed to my *enforced* profession?" He grinned. "I run Williams Shipping."

The captain started in surprise, and his eyes narrowed. "You're *that* Williams?"

"At your service," Mitch acknowledged, amusement in his voice.

"A fine business you run," Clark complimented.

"Thank you. I'd be honored to have you sign on, once we're back. The *Providence* seems a tightly run ship; I think we could do well together."

Pleased by the offer, Clark nodded as he refilled their glasses. "So, tell me of the *Seastorm* and your time on Malika. Who was the captain?"

"Warson, and a more villainous man I've never encountered." Mitch recalled the man, and after all this time, his hatred for him was a powerful thing.

"I'd heard rumors to that account. It's no wonder the man had to buy a crew."

Mitch sighed as he leaned back in his chair, stretching his long legs out before him and sipping slowly of the whiskey. "Tommy and I were very lucky. The *Seastorm* went down in a cyclone, and we were the only survivors."

"You were washed up on Malika?"

"Yes. Espri and her father took care of me. Tommy was found by a family in the village."

"Mildred and I were hoping you would join us tonight for dinner."

"You're most kind. We would be delighted to accept." Mitch was pleased by the invitation. He had decided to seek Mildred's aid, if she was willing, in helping Espri adapt to her new way of life. "Considering the position I now find myself in, I was wondering if I could enlist your aid."

"Of course. What can I help you with?"

"As you've seen, my wife is far from suitably clothed for her arrival in San Francisco. Would it be possible to purchase any extra clothing you might have aboard?"

"We do have some cloth we were bringing back from the Orient. Is Espri talented with a needle and thread?"

"Yes, but she has little idea of our fashion."

"If you have no objection, I'll suggest to Mildred that she help her. She may even have a few gowns that could be altered to fit your wife."

"I'd be most grateful."

"I have some extra things too, and I've spoken with my first mate, who is more your friend Tommy's size. We should be able to find at least a change of clothes for the both of you."

"Thank you." Mitch was relieved that the clothing issue had been so easily dealt with. "I know this transition is not going to be easy for Espri."

"I'm sure Mildred will do all she can to help. She is very happy about having Espri's company. I think they'll get on well together."

"You've been most kind."

"Nonsense. It's the least I can do for you."

"I'd better be getting back to see how Espri is faring. What time would you like us to join you tonight?"

"We generally dine after sunset. I'll send the cabin boy for you."

"Fine. Until then . . ." Mitch rose and they shook hands before he left the captain's cabin.

Espri had remained in the stateroom as Mitch had bid, but when she felt the vessel get underway, she knew she had to have one last look at Malika. Hurrying up on deck, she positioned herself at the rail and stared out across the blue-green waters, watching numbly as Malika faded from view. So much had happened to her in such a short period of time that she felt almost anesthetized against this final separation from her family and her lifelong home.

It was not easy, this saying good-bye to the security of the life she'd shared with her father and grandfather, but both men had emphasized her duty as Mitch's wife, and she knew she was obligated to go with him. Suddenly feeling very alone, Espri fought a moment of panic. Knowing she would soon have her child, she rested her hand on her slightly rounded stomach as if to confirm the reality of the baby's existence.

Mitch entered their cabin fully intending to explain to Espri his reason for telling her to remain in the room, but when he discovered that she'd left despite his instructions, he was furious. Storming up the companionway, he strode out on deck. As he had expected, all the sailors were watching Espri, who stood at the railing. Their leering expressions clearly revealed their carnal thoughts, and a surge of protective jealousy propelled him toward her.

"I thought I told you to stay below!" Mitch suddenly loomed over her, his expression dark and ominous.

Startled by his unexpected appearance, Espri stumbled over her explanation. "You did, but I wanted to watch."

"It doesn't matter to me what you wanted. When I tell you to do something, I expect you to obey without question," he growled, gripping her arm tightly. "Especially while we are on this ship." He glared ominously at the randy seamen, and they quickly turned back to their duties.

Though his fingers dug painfully into the soft flesh of her upper arm, Espri did not protest his lead, and she accompanied him without any resistance. But when he opened the door to their small stateroom, she turned on him, her anger equaling his.

"What do you think you're doing!" she demanded, shaking off his hand and staring up at him angrily, hands on her hips in defiance of his manhandling.

"I want you to stay below deck in our cabin unless I'm with you," he answered curtly.

"Why?" she challenged. "Are you ashamed of me? Do I embarrass you now that you're back among your own kind?"

She looked beautiful in her rage, her dark eyes flashing fire, her breasts heaving in indignation. Mitch wanted to hold her and kiss her and love her, to tell her that he'd be proud to claim her as his anytime, anywhere; but once more he thrust the desire from him. And when she spoke again, he knew he'd been right to refuse to act upon his feelings.

"If you feel that way, then why don't you leave me here? I could be happy on Malika. I don't need you." She had taken his silence to mean her words had hit their mark.

"Obviously," he drawled mockingly. "I'm just to leave you here to raise my child without a suitable father."

"Jacques and Luatu would be wonderful fathers for the child. Leave me here, Mitch. I don't belong with you!" Espri hardened her voice so he wouldn't hear the desperation she was feeling.

"Your pardon, my love." Mitch's eyes were cool as they drifted over her. "You are my wife in the eyes of God and man. Your place is with me. I'm sorry if that doesn't please you, but you may as well accept it. You will be mine until we are parted by death."

Tears glittered in her eyes; she couldn't go back and she

didn't want to stay with him—not if she was to be despised. "Very well. If I am to play the part of your wife, I shall expect the consideration due my position."

"Meaning?" he derided.

"Meaning, I won't tolerate such treatment at your hands."

"My dear," he said icily, "I apologize for my thoughtlessness in trying to protect your virtue, and I bid you to enjoy the freedom of the deck whenever you feel so disposed. Don't let it bother you that every jack-tar aboard will lustfully watch your every move and think how pleasant it would be to spread your thighs and mount you."

Espri blanched and then flushed at his crudity. Mitch noted her distress, but continued.

"They know you are my wife and under my protection, but that could be conveniently forgotten should the opportunity arise for them to take their pleasure of you. And that, my love, is why I bade you to remain in our cabin until such time as I could escort you on deck."

"I'm sorry," she murmured.

"You should be." He did not intend to let her off that easily. "From now on, trust my judgment as to what's best for you. There is usually a very sound reason behind everything I ask you to do."

"Yes, Mitch."

"As the voyage lengthens, no doubt the strain upon the men will increase. A pretty woman is always a temptation on board a ship, but after months at sea their needs will be strong. I advise you now, plan your excursions on deck when either Tommy or I can accompany you."

"Yes, Mitch."

"I need to speak with Tommy." He started to leave, but turned back. "By the way, we've been invited to dine with the captain and Mildred tonight." Her expression brightened considerably at the news, and Mitch, very aware of her beauty, quickly left.

Espri listened to his retreating footsteps as she stared at the closed portal. The prospect of spending most of her time during the next long months within this confining space unnerved her, but she understood Mitch's reasoning now and could more easily accept her lot. She had just stretched out across the bed when a soft knock came at the door.

"Yes?" she called, sitting up quickly.

"Espri, it's Mildred."

"Oh." Espri hastened to admit the gentle woman. "Come in."

"I'm not disturbing you?"

"No, not at all. Mitch left to speak with Tommy, and I was just going to rest for a while."

"If you'd rather I came back later—"

"No. I really would appreciate your company now."

"Good." She came bustling into the room, her arms filled with what looked to Espri like a jumble of multicolored cloth. "I thought we could take this time to talk and get better acquainted."

"I'd like that." Espri's smile was open and genuine.

"Your husband mentioned to the captain that you were in need of clothing, so I've brought a few things along to see if we can fashion you something suitable."

"Suitable?" Espri's knowledge of clothing was severely limited.

"Yes, my dear. As much as your sarong is comfortable, it just won't do when we reach the cooler climes," Mildred told her thoughtfully.

"Is it very cold in San Francisco?" Espri asked a bit timidly.

"Compared to what you're used to, yes, but don't you worry. We've several months before we reach your new home, and by then, we'll have you well outfitted. Stand up for me now and let's see what we can do here."

The rest of the afternoon passed in a whirl of activity, for

Mildred introduced Espri to the fundamentals of women's fashion.

"Why must we wear all this?" Espri gestured in wide-eyed wonder at the various garments Mildred had spread out on the bed.

"Why?" Mildred looked perplexed for a moment and then laughed in genuine amusement. "I've never considered the 'whys' of it before; in fact, I don't know. I just know that no lady of substance can be properly dressed without the correct underthings and over-things and in-between things."

They laughed in easy camaraderie. Though Espri thought the clothing looked confining and more than a little ridiculous, a part of her looked forward to dressing up for Mitch. *Maybe*, she thought, *if I look more like the kind of woman he's used to, he might change in his feelings toward me*. With that in mind, she wholeheartedly participated in Mildred's attempts to instruct her in the proper apparel, and she was excited when the older woman promised her an altered gown by late the following day.

"You can do it that quickly?"

"Maybe sooner," Mildred told her, studying her trim figure. "I've got your measurements and hopefully enough extra length in the hem to make up for our differences in height."

"Thank you, Mildred." Espri was overwhelmed by her generosity and patience.

"Don't be silly. This has been fun for me. It's exciting to introduce you to a whole new world."

"I just hope I'll be able to adapt to it." This was the first indication she'd given Mildred of her insecurity, and the older woman understood.

"I don't think you have a thing to worry about. Just stay as sweet as you are and hold your head up proudly. You're a very lovely woman. Changing the way you dress will never change that," she declared with almost motherly affection. "Now, I'll see you at dinner tonight with your handsome husband."

Espri nodded. "I'll look forward to that."

Since the ship's stores had been restocked during their stopover at the islands, dinner aboard the *Providence* was particularly sumptuous that night, and the Clarks ate heartily, enjoying the variety of island fruits now added to their diet. When the cabin boy had taken away the dirty dishes, Captain Clark brought forth a bottle of fine brandy and poured a snifter for each of them.

"Brandy?" He held out the globular glass to Espri.

She glanced quickly at Mitch, and at his encouraging nod, she accepted the delicate-looking snifter, holding it in both hands.

"It's called an after-dinner drink," Mildred offered. "But you mustn't drink it quickly for it's quite potent. Just sip at it, so." She demonstrated, smiling at the other woman's very natural grace as she mimicked her. "Wonderful. Espri is a very quick learner, Mitch."

His dark eyes upon his wife, he responded, "Yes, I know."

Espri felt the heat rise to her cheeks at his unspoken meaning, and she was grateful that neither Mildred nor Captain Clark sensed the undercurrent of his words. She studied her husband, feeling for a moment as if she really didn't know him. Since he'd donned the white shirt, dark trousers, and boots that the captain had sent down to their cabin, Mitch seemed a different man, his manner having somehow subtly changed.

"I understand you two ladies were discussing fashion this afternoon," the captain said with interest.

"Yes, and while I was aware that it wouldn't be acceptable to wear my island clothing in San Francisco, I had no idea how much was involved. Mildred's going to help me sew a few things so I have something to wear when we reach your home." Espri glanced at Mitch.

"*Your* home too, now," he told her, his gaze meeting hers over the rim of his snifter.

"We have some silks from the Orient and some other material, so I think we should fare quite well," Mildred informed them.

"Good," the captain said approvingly. "I'd invited O'Ryan to join us this evening, but he declined. He seems like a personable young man, but is something bothering him?"

Mitch answered. "The last few days have been rough for Tommy. It was painful for him to end some associations he'd made on Malika, but I'm sure he'll come around soon."

Clark nodded. "With luck and favorable winds, I estimate we should make landfall within four months."

"Sounds good to me." Mitch smiled broadly. "I've traveled before, but this is one homecoming I am really anticipating."

Growing more and more aware of his love for his home, Espri made up her mind that by the time they reached San Francisco, she was going to know everything Mildred could teach her about being a "lady of substance."

It was much later when they returned to their own cabin. The fiery liquor had sharpened Espri's senses, and she'd become acutely conscious of Mitch as he'd sat so close to her during their dinner with the Clarks. Painfully acknowledging to herself that he did not feel the same way toward her anymore, she was careful not to have any physical contact with him. It was going to be difficult enough to share the bed with him, but if he openly rejected her again, she didn't know what she'd do.

Mitch followed Espri into the cabin, his emotions in turmoil. Sitting next to her all evening and knowing that they would soon be sharing the single bed in their stateroom had left him unsettled. There was nothing he wanted more than to spend the night making love to her, but if he took her, he knew she would only hate him more. All evening, she had seemed to go out of her way to avoid touching him, and the remembrance of her earlier shiver of distaste when he'd helped her aboard only served to reaffirm what he believed to be the truth.

Espri felt his eyes upon her, and she glanced back over her shoulder at him as she untied the sarong and let it drop. He had seen her unclothed so often that she had no idea her natural gesture had taken on a new meaning under these different circumstances.

Mitch's desire soared as he stared at her. God! How he wanted her. Hungrily, his gaze raked over her slim body, devouring the tempting beauty of her breasts and the rounded curve of her shapely hips. All thoughts of restraint fled and he took a step forward, intent only on tasting of her charms once more.

The sudden tension in the room had made Espri nervous, and when Mitch started to walk toward her, his eyes devoid of expression, she became frightened. The startled look she gave him halted his progress and his passion chilled. Scowling at his own momentary loss of control, he turned and stalked back toward the door.

"I'm going to check on Tommy. I'll be back later." Without even glancing in her direction, he quit the room.

Chapter 19

"Well? What do you think?" Espri faced Captain Clark's wife anxiously. They had spent the entire morning together, fitting the dress Mildred was altering for her, and now the work was done.

The older woman stood back from the younger one and studied her with mock impartiality before breaking into a wide smile. "You look marvelous . . . but I knew you would."

"Do you really think so?" Espri twisted around, trying to get a better view of herself in the small mirror over the washstand.

"Absolutely. Do you want to go show your husband?" Mildred asked.

Espri wanted nothing more than to impress Mitch with her appearance, but she was hesitant about trying to walk in public in the shoes Mildred had given her. Though they were comfortable enough, she found them terribly awkward. "I don't know. Maybe it would be better if I waited here for him."

Mildred clucked like a mother hen and took Espri by the arm, urging her toward the door. "Are you worried about walking?"

Espri gave her a wondering look. "How did you know?"

"I know because you seem to be afraid to move. Come on,

now. I'm sure he'll be delighted with your appearance. And don't worry about falling; it'll only take you a minute to get used to the shoes."

"I don't know. They feel so cumbersome . . . barefoot is so much easier. How can you stand wearing these all the time?" Espri laughed ruefully as she took a few steps.

"Necessity, I suppose. You may not appreciate them now, but you will when the weather turns." Mildred opened the door and led Espri from the cabin. "Let's see your brightest smile," Mildred encouraged. "Good girl. The most important lesson you can learn is that a lady must always seem to be enjoying herself, even when she's miserable."

"Really? Why?" Deception was not part of Espri's personality.

"Appearances, my dear, are everything in polite society," the older woman confided. "Things are very different in your husband's world. Very little is as it first appears."

Espri nodded solemnly. "Do you think I'll ever be able to remember everything?"

Mildred laughed easily. "Don't worry. I'm sure you'll do just fine when the time comes, and perhaps your honesty will start a new, refreshing trend."

They went up the steps slowly, giving Espri time to accustom herself to the novelty of balancing on the low heels, and then stepped out on deck.

Mildred gave her a reassuring hug as they looked around for their husbands. "Let's see what the menfolk have to say about this," she said.

Strolling the deck slowly, they headed for the helm, where the men were deep in conversation. Mitch had his back to the women as they approached, but when the captain indicated that he should turn around, he glanced over his shoulder and started in surprised fascination. He found it hard to believe that the sophisticated creature walking toward him was his wife. Dressed in a shirtwaist daygown with her hair pinned back in a sedate bun at the nape of her neck, she bore little resemblance to his wild island beauty. Gone was her sweet naïveté. Before him stood a strikingly attractive female who looked worldly and mature—a woman to be reckoned with. And despite its high-necked, long-sleeved conservative style, her dress was amazingly flattering, for the soft cotton material fit snugly across her bosom, hinting subtly at the fullness beneath, while the skirt flowed in graceful lines all the way to the floor. Moving away from the other men without speaking, he went to Espri and kissed her cheek.

"You look marvelous, darling," he told her gruffly as her eyes met his searchingly.

"Thank you." She flushed with pleasure.

"Espri, you're beautiful!" Tommy, too, was surprised by the transition.

"Mildred, you've done a wonderful job of advising her," Mitch declared.

"It's been a pleasure." Mildred read the men's expressions correctly, and she knew that Espri had impressed them. "We still have a few other things to put together, but I think she's going to do very well in San Francisco."

"I do too," Mitch agreed wholeheartedly.

Taking Mildred's counsel on the manner of a lady seriously, Espri smiled at him in spite of the fact that her feet were aching and the dress was confining. "I'm glad you approve."

"Most assuredly." Unable to help himself, he reached out and touched her cheek with a gentle hand as their gazes met and held.

Excitement trembled through her, and had they been alone, Espri knew she would have thrown herself into his arms, regardless of the consequences. The past night had been a miserable one for her. She had been expecting things to change between them now that they were on the ship, but Mitch had followed the same pattern he'd taken to on the island, staying away from their cabin until long after she'd already fallen asleep. Espri was determined that as soon as she could, she was going to put an end to it. Even though their marriage had been forced, he was now her husband and he had been right—there was no reason why they couldn't share a mutually satisfying physical relationship. Eagerly, she looked forward to the time when they could at least be that close again.

"Well, we have more sewing to do, so we'll leave you gentlemen to your duties." Mildred drew Espri along with her as she started back toward the companionway.

Espri couldn't resist one last backward glance at Mitch, and she was surprised to find his gaze still upon her. Giving him one last fleeting smile, she disappeared with the other woman, out of sight below deck.

Espri had been anticipating going to bed that night, and she was thoroughly disappointed when, after dining with the Clarks, Mitch left her at the stateroom door, saying he was going to speak with Tommy for a few minutes. It took all of her inner strength to play the lady and not let him see her disappointment. Frustrated, she stripped off the uncomfortable "civilized" clothing, pulled the pins from her hair, and lay across the bed, lost in thought.

Mitch knocked briefly at Tommy's door, and when there was no answer he went up on deck to see if he could locate his friend. As he had suspected, Tommy was standing at the rail, staring out across the blackness of the sea.

"You didn't join us for dinner again," he said easily as he went to stand beside him.

Tommy gave him a quick, apologetic look. "I'm afraid I wouldn't be good company right now."

Mitch was quiet for a moment, sympathetically understanding. "You may not think so now, but the pain will lessen with time."

"I should have stayed with her to help protect her."

"Tommy"—Mitch's tone was serious—"as difficult as it was, you made the correct decision."

The younger man slammed his fist down on the rail and faced his friend, his eyes bleak with the knowledge that his love was lost to him. "But I love her, damn it! Could you have gone off and left Espri?" he demanded. Then, remembering their earlier conversation on the island, he said disgustedly, "Oh, never mind. You told me yourself you would have. Probably the only reason you brought her along was because you had to get married. God! I wish Tikiru had been pregnant; then I could have kept her with me."

Mitch had become furious because of Tommy's derisive statement, and he had been about to respond to it when he'd realized that every word his friend had said was true. He had said those things only weeks ago. Funny, he thought, they sounded so cold and callous now. He frowned as he wondered if he had really changed so much.

"You're wrong about that," he said with a calmness that surprised him. "For all that I professed indifference, I couldn't have left Espri behind, child or no child."

"I'm glad," Tommy remarked. "I have to admit that I'd wondered how you could even think of it. Espri is so beautiful, and certainly very much in love with you."

Mitch found Tommy's observation perplexing—Espri, in love with him? Then he remembered that "love and hate are but a wit apart," and he frowned at the thought.

"Do you have time for a drink in my cabin?" Tommy suggested. "Captain Clark gave me a bottle of whiskey, and I could sure use a shot right now."

"Sure. Let's go." Mitch clapped Tommy on the back as they went below. It was strange but he was feeling lighter of spirit.

* * *

Espri was angry. She had been waiting hours for Mitch's return, and she would wait no longer. Getting up from the bed, she quickly dressed in the clothes and shoes Mildred had given her. She didn't know why Mitch was so determined not to come to her, but she had had enough. It was time he knew exactly how she felt. If he didn't like it, at least they would know where they stood. Things had been miserable between them since that first night, and she knew the only way to rid their marriage of that painful memory was to replace it with more beautiful ones. Set in her resolve and completely forgetting his warning about being alone on deck, she left the cabin, intent on locating Mitch.

Espri paused at Tommy's door, but hearing no conversation within, she felt certain that the two men had gone topside. After hurrying up the companionway, Espri was surprised to find no sign of them. She stood quietly, listening for the sound of Mitch's or Tommy's voice, and when she thought she heard them talking near the stern, she started in that direction.

Davis and Harcourt could hardly believe their eyes when they spotted the island wench coming their way. They stared lustfully at the long-haired lovely, and gave only a fleeting, quickly dismissed thought to her able-bodied husband. If she was here, strutting around the deck at this time of night, then she must be lacking something from her old man. They exchanged heated, knowing glances and waited quietly for her to come closer.

Espri didn't realize her mistake in wandering about alone until it was too late.

"Evenin', missy." Harcourt gave her a wide smile that revealed uneven, blackened teeth.

"Oh . . . hello . . ." She started to back away, but they took several steps forward until they were towering over her.

"Lookin' fer somethin?" Davis moved even closer.

"Yes, I was looking for my husband," Espri replied, trying to maintain an even demeanor with the two threatening seamen.

"You mean he ain't gracin' your bed?" Harcourt leered. "If'n I was married to you, I'd sure be beddin' you good and proper every night!"

"Excuse me. He's probably with the captain. I'll check there." She started to rush away, but a hamlike hand grabbed her by the arm and jerked her back. Pulled off balance, Espri stumbled against Harcourt's wide chest. "No!"

"Ah, c'mon, sweetings, give me a taste of that island magic, what d'ya say?"

When he groped at her bodice, Espri knew she could not fight them off alone. She needed help.

She screamed, but Davis quickly clamped a hand over her mouth. "Now, that wasn't nice, dolly. Hold still."

Espri twisted and struggled as the seamen sought to rip her dress and expose her breasts.

Below, Mitch paused as he heard what sounded like a muffled call for help. He stood up quickly and opened Tommy's cabin door. "What was that?"

"I think someone screamed up on deck," Tommy said as Mitch rushed from the stateroom.

At top speed, they ran the length of the corridor and then charged up the steps and onto the deck. Briefly, they stood immobile until the sounds of the struggle taking place near the stern jarred them into action.

"My God! It's Espri!" Mitch caught sight of her fighting against the overpowering strength of two men. If anything were to happen to her . . .

Rage filled him, and he ran toward the sailors, Tommy close on his heels. Hearing their approach, Harcourt and Davis released Espri, and attempted to get away. But Mitch launched himself at Davis and tackled him about the waist.

Then he viciously pummeled the man with his fists, not letting up until he ceased to struggle and lay unconscious beneath him. Davis subdued, he turned to help Tommy restrain Harcourt, but the younger man already had things well under control. Only then, when his vengeance had been wreaked, did his thoughts turn to his wife.

Espri had been relieved and thankful when Mitch had appeared, and she had watched in horrified wonder as he and Tommy had quickly dispatched her two assailants. When Mitch started toward her, she was filled with love for him, and she wanted to tell him of her gratitude for his timely rescue.

"Oh, Mitch! It was horrible!" Without thought, Espri threw her arms about him and hugged him. "Thank you . . . thank you."

But there was no answering response. He rigidly accepted her embrace. "You are all right?" he asked coldly, and when she looked up, she was stunned to find that his expression was thunderous.

"Yes, I'm fine, thanks to you and Tommy." She wanted to tell him of her feelings. "I'm so glad you came. I was so afraid."

Once he was assured that she was uninjured, however, Mitch took her by the shoulders and held her away from him, his glittering eyes revealing his deadly anger. He was still in the grip of an explosive rage.

"Didn't I tell you at the beginning of the voyage to stay in our cabin?" he demanded. "I even went so far as to explain my reasons, did I not?"

Espri wanted to explain why she had dared to venture out on deck. "Yes, but—"

Giving her a disgusted look, Mitch let her go. "Then get back there, now!" he thundered.

He started to walk away from her, but she grabbed his arm. "Wait, Mitch. Listen to me! I only came out here because—"

He shrugged off her hand, impaling her with a frigid glare. "I don't care why you came out here. The point is, you did and you were almost raped. Now, get below!"

Unshed tears glistened in Espri's eyes as she stared up at his stony expression. "I will not!" she cried defiantly. "Not until you listen to me."

Mitch's jaw tensed. "Madam, since you care so little for your own safety, I withdraw my protection. You may stay or go as you please." He left her, then, striding away without looking back.

Espri suddenly became aware that Tommy was watching her sympathetically. Embarrassed by his concern, she whirled about and fled. Blinded by her tears, she hurried down the dimly lit companionway, but in her haste, her long, unfamiliar skirts became tangled and she lost her balance. Espri tried to grab the banister, but she missed and tumbled to the bottom of the steps. Wracking pain gripped her when she landed heavily, and she clutched her stomach.

"Mitch . . ." She called his name in soft desperation as the spiral of welcoming darkness slowly overwhelmed her, freeing her from the excruciating torment.

Mitch sighed as he stood at the rail, staring with unseeing eyes out to sea. The truth had come to him tonight as he had fought to defend Espri, yet, at the time, he'd been unable to face it. Running a nervous hand through his windblown dark hair, he grimaced at his own ridiculous self-deception. It all seemed so clear now—and so simple. He loved Espri.

The jealous frenzy he'd experienced when he'd seen the other men trying to harm her had been unlike anything he'd ever felt before, but it had been that emotion which had forced him to acknowledge, at long last, the truth. He knew now that he could not live without Espri. He loved her more than life itself, and he would do all in his power to protect her for the rest of their lives, despite his recent disavowal. Briefly he thought of Andrew, but he dismissed such reflections. No longer would he let his friend's misfortune shape his own future. He would spend the years to come with Espri and their child, and they would be happy. He would see to it.

Mitch knew he should tell Espri now he felt, but he wondered how she would react to his declaration. Certainly with disbelief at first, he mused. He'd given her absolutely no reason to think that he felt anything but contempt for her since the moment of their union, and now it was up to him to prove to her that his feelings for her were true. Somehow, he knew that was not going to be an easy task.

"I've turned the seamen over to the first mate," Tommy told Mitch as he joined him.

"Thanks, and thanks for helping me."

"No problem. Is Espri all right?" He had seen the way she'd hurried from the deck, and he'd feared that she might be injured.

"Espri was frightened, but otherwise unharmed," Mitch told him flatly.

Tommy paused thoughtfully for a moment before saying, "This may not be any of my business, but I couldn't help but overhear what you said to her on deck. Why were you so hard on her?"

"I had told her not to come topside by herself," Mitch replied tersely.

"Even so, if she was frightened by their attack, why aren't you with her now, comforting her?"

Mitch knew Tommy was right, and he had the good sense to feel ashamed. He was resisting returning to their cabin because he dreaded the upcoming interview. He'd never professed his undying love to a woman before, and he was more than a little unnerved at the prospect of facing Espri.

"You're right," he answered, pushing away from the rail. "I'll see you in the morning."

"Wait. I'll walk as far as my cabin with you."

"Fine."

They crossed the deck in silent companionship, but when Tommy entered the companionway, he suddenly stopped.

"Mitch . . ." His voice was hoarse as he reached back and grabbed Mitch's arm to pull him forward.

"Oh God, no . . ." Mitch took the steps two at a time and then knelt beside Espri. Seeing the blood that stained her skirts, he ordered, "Get Mildred, Tommy. Quickly."

"Right." Tommy raced away to the captain's cabin as Mitch tenderly touched Espri's pale cheek.

"Espri . . . darling, can you hear me?" he murmured, bending over her to make sure she was still breathing. Satisfied that she wasn't dead, he decided to move her from the corridor. Carefully, he lifted her in his arms, and though she moaned softly, she did not come to as he carried her swiftly to their stateroom. Kicking the door open, he placed her, fully clothed, upon the bed. Then he dampened a washcloth, sat beside her, and pressed it to her brow. Taking her hand, he stayed at her side as he waited for Tommy's return. It seemed an eternity before he heard footsteps clattering down the companionway. He rushed to the door and threw it open just as Mildred raised her hand to knock.

"Thank God, you've come," he declared. Then he stood aside to allow her to enter.

"How is she?" Tommy asked, though he remained in the passageway.

"She's alive," Mitch answered distractedly. "I'll speak with you later."

Tommy nodded and then turned toward his own cabin as Mitch closed the stateroom door.

"What happened?" Mildred asked as she moved to the bedside and quickly began to unfasten Espri's clothing.

"She must have fallen down the steps."

"You didn't see it?" She glanced at him sharply.

"No. I was on deck with Tommy and she was returning to the cabin," Mitch answered. "What can I do? There's so much blood. Has she lost our baby?"

"Espri was pregnant?" Mildred looked up in surprise.

"Yes, she was about three months along." Mitch stared down at his wife's colorless features.

"I see. Why don't you wait outside? I told my husband to bring the ship's surgeon, and they should be here any time. Will you let them in when they arrive?"

"I'd like to stay with her," Mitch argued.

"No." Mildred's reply was firm and brooked no comment. "Wait outside."

Mitch felt that his chest was in a vise as he left the cabin to stand in the narrow corridor, awaiting the ship's doctor.

When he'd gone from the room, Mildred hurriedly unbuttoned Espri's gown and carefully stripped it from her. Then, just as she was covering her with a blanket, Dr. Canfield arrived. Mitch admitted him right away, but when he started to follow the doctor into the room, Mildred again barred him, bidding him to join the captain for a drink before she closed the door.

Mitch stood in the hall, staring at the closed portal, uncertain of what to do. The idea of staying there, yet not being allowed in with Espri, left him frustrated, but it seemed a better alternative than leaving to search out the captain. He wanted to be there, just in case Espri awakened and needed him. Leaning against the wall, he stood in silent vigil, determined not to move from that spot until he'd found out what her condition was.

Mildred waited anxiously as the ship's doctor examined Espri. His expression was grim when he looked up.

"I'm afraid the baby's lost," Dr. Canfield concluded.

"Oh, no." Mildred was saddened by the news. "How terrible . . . but Espri . . . will she recover?"

"There are no bones broken," the doctor said, "and her

bleeding has stopped, but she suffered quite a loss of blood. She will no doubt be weak for a while."

"And children?"

"I think she will be able to conceive again. This was just an unfortunate accident. I feel certain that, with time, she'll make a full recovery."

"Thank heaven."

"She should be coming around soon." Dr. Canfield took her pulse again to reaffirm the steady, regular beat of her heart.

"Shall I go fetch her husband?" Mildred asked. "I'm sure he's anxious to know how she is."

"Yes. I'd like to speak with him."

Mildred expected that she would have to search the ship for Mitch, and when she opened the door and found him waiting outside, she was deeply touched.

"You didn't go to the captain?"

"No. I thought she might need me." Mitch looked haggard as he quickly stepped forward. "Is she awake? How is she?"

"Dr. Canfield wants to talk to you. Dr. Canfield, Mr. Williams is right here."

"Good." The doctor left Espri's bedside and stepped out into the hall. "Stay with her," he instructed Mildred.

"I will," she assured him as the two men faced each other in the narrow expanse of the corridor.

"How is she?" Mitch asked. He tried to see into the stateroom, but Mildred shut the door as she reentered.

"I'm afraid there is bad news," the doctor began, and Mitch knew a moment of panic.

"She's not going to die, is she?" he asked, horrified.

"No. I'm sure her recovery will be complete, but she has lost the baby."

As much as he'd dreaded the news, Mitch had known that was a possibility because of the heavy bleeding. "But she will be well?"

"I believe so, yes," Dr. Canfield replied. "As I was telling Mildred, she did lose a substantial amount of blood during the miscarriage, but there was no permanent damage."

"Then we'll still be able to have children?"

"I would think so."

Mitch was saddened by the loss of their unborn child, but the knowledge that Espri was going to live filled him with joy.

"Can I be with her now?" he asked anxiously.

"Yes. She hasn't regained consciousness yet, but it's just a matter of time."

Mitch nodded in understanding as he shook Dr. Canfield's hand. "Thank you."

"Call me if she seems to be worsening; otherwise I'll just look in on her tomorrow."

Mitch watched until Canfield had gone. Then, girding himself, he quietly opened the cabin door and went in. Espri lay unmoving on the bed, her eyes closed, her color ashen. Mitch was stricken for a moment—she looked dead—but the comforting touch of Mildred's hand drove that unbidden thought from his mind.

"How is she?" His voice was gruff and just above a whisper.

"She hasn't stirred yet, but she will. Why don't you sit by her? I'm sure you'll be the one she wants to see when she awakes," the older woman said encouragingly.

Mitch hesitated. He wondered if Mildred was right in her assessment. Espri might despise the very sight of him. After all, wasn't it his fault that she'd lost the child? If he hadn't been so cruel to her on deck, this would never have happened. Riddled with guilt, he started to refuse, but Mildred drew him forward.

"You sit with her while I go back to my own cabin and put on something a little more appropriate." She gave him a reassuring smile, and Mitch noted for the first time that she wore a dressing gown and slippers.

"All right," he agreed nervously, and she bustled from the room, leaving him alone with Espri.

Mitch stood uneasily in the silent room. The hour he'd just spent waiting in the hall had been the longest of his life, and now that it was over, he wasn't quite sure what to do next. His prayer that Espri's life be spared had been answered, and he knew he would be thankful forever.

Soberly, he moved forward and, unable to resist doing so, sat down on the edge of the bed, taking great care not to disturb her. Espri looked so pale and delicate that he hesitated to touch her, but his need to reassure himself was strong and he took her hand, pressing a devoted kiss to it before holding it over his heart.

"I love you, Espri," he told her softly, choking over the intensity of the emotion that assailed him. "I was on my way to tell you when I found you at the foot of the stairs . . ."

Gently, with his free hand, he brushed a stray dark curl from her cheek, then grimaced when he saw the vivid bruise that had been hidden beneath it. The contusion was a forceful reminder of his part in her accident, and as guilt, heavy and damning, swept over him again, Mitch knew he could never forgive himself for the pain he'd caused her.

Standing up, he wished Mildred would return so he could leave. The cabin was now a torture chamber as memories of their time together assailed him. He had known almost from the first how innocent she was, yet he had not treated her with the tender respect she'd deserved. He berated himself silently. He couldn't lose her now—now that he'd discovered his love for her!

Some minutes later, the sound of Mildred's soft knock came as a relief, and Mitch let her in without hesitation.

"Is she any better?" Mildred asked as she glanced uncertainly at the bed.

"No, she hasn't regained consciousness yet," Mitch told her hoarsely.

Sensing his despair and wanting to encourage him, she patted his arm. "She will, Mitch. Don't worry."

He felt a sudden urge to unburden himself to this sweet, understanding woman, but his pride held him back. His jaw tensing as he fought for control, Mitch nodded tightly.

"I'll be up on deck."

Mildred glanced at him quickly, surprised. "Don't you want to be here when she wakes?"

"I'll be close by. Just call me if she wants to see me," he answered curtly as he opened the door to go.

"Mitch?"

He froze and looked back questioningly.

"I'll call you as soon as she begins to stir," Mildred said quietly.

Again he nodded, and without speaking, he quit the room. Mildred had been about to protest his departure, but when their eyes met, she had witnessed such torment in his expression that she'd realized he desperately needed the time alone to pull himself together. Though this was a terrible situation, Mildred couldn't help but smile as she thought of the love these two shared. Espri obviously adored her husband, and Mildred knew, after watching Mitch in his sorrow, that her feelings were fully returned.

Setting aside the small bundle of bedclothes she'd brought along for Espri, Mildred settled in, anxiously awaiting a sign of progress in the young woman's recovery.

Chapter 20

Mitch was holding her and kissing her, and she was arching against him in ecstatic need . . . wanting him . . . loving him . . .

"Mitch . . ." Espri stirred slightly, whispering the name of her love.

Mildred, who'd been sitting close by the bed, quickly came to her side and gently touched her hand. "Espri? Can you hear me?"

Distantly, Espri was aware of someone calling her name, but she didn't want to awake. She wanted to keep dreaming of Mitch. She loved him so, and in her dream, he loved her.

"Espri!" The voice was more persistent, penetrating the safe warmth of her fantasy, dragging her back to the present.

Though she fought against it, clinging with all her might to the last wispy shreds of her mind's vivid illusion, the grimness of reality intruded. She shuddered and took a deep breath before opening her eyes. Blinking against the light that assailed her, she closed her eyes again for an instant and lay still, trying to collect her thoughts. It had been so peaceful in her dream . . .

"Mitch?" she finally asked, hoping to find that he was there and that her dream hadn't been a fantasy.

"No, it's Mildred."

"He's not here . . ." Espri's tone was sad as she opened her eyes to find her friend hovering worriedly over her.

"He was, but he wanted to wait up on deck."

"Wait? For what?" Espri was momentarily confused. Nothing seemed right . . . and why was she in bed?

"For you to awaken. You had a serious fall and—"

"Oh, God." It all came back to her then and panic swept through her. "My baby . . ." Espri looked up at Mildred, wildly. "I remember now. I lost my balance on the steps . . . and I was bleeding. Mildred . . . did I lose my baby?"

Mildred had not wanted to be the one to tell her of the lost child, but she had no choice. "Yes." She nodded solemnly, her eyes downcast.

Dry sobs wracked Espri as she curled on her side and clutched at her stomach. "Not my baby . . ."

"I'm sorry." The older woman couldn't stop her own tears as she witnessed Espri's grief.

"No . . ." She groaned. "The baby was all I had."

Mildred sat down beside her and gathered her in her arms, hugging her tightly. "Nonsense," Mildred scolded lovingly. "You have your husband."

Espri lay back when her friend released her, her emotions numb. Dry-eyed, she looked at Mildred and said very calmly, "That's where you're wrong. You see, I don't have my husband."

Mildred was shocked by Espri's statement, but she quickly discounted her words. "Of course you do. Mitch was here and I could see how upset he was."

"No," Espri said dispassionately. "He really doesn't care." Espri had no doubt that Mitch was upset, but not for the reason Mildred thought. Mitch had no feeling for her; he'd made that perfectly clear when he'd sent her from him without a word of comfort after her ordeal with the sailors. He had told her he was withdrawing his protection of her, and judging from his anger, she was certain he had meant it. Their marriage had been difficult enough, but now, without the baby to bind them, Espri felt there was little hope for their future.

"You'll see for yourself. I'll go get him for you. I know he's worried."

Espri didn't bother to answer as the older woman left the room.

From his position on the foredeck, Mitch stared emotionlessly at the pink- and gold-streaked Eastern horizon. He had been hoping that the advent of a new day would give him a better perspective on everything that had happened, but the dawn only served to reveal his loss more clearly.

He rested his forearms on the rail, his broad shoulders slumped in weary defeat. He knew he would have to face Espri as soon as she awoke, and for the first time in his life, he was truly afraid. He loved her. No one had ever meant as much to him as she did; yet he felt helpless to salvage any part of their relationship. Espri had made it clear from the beginning that she didn't want him, and now that she'd miscarried, he had nothing with which to hold her. Steeling himself against their upcoming encounter, he awaited Mildred's summons.

"Mitch . . ." Mildred's soft call broke through his introspective thoughts and he wheeled about anxiously.

"She's conscious?" He strode hurriedly across the deck toward her.

"Yes." Mildred saw the flare of hope in his eyes and she smiled, more sure than ever that Espri was wrong about Mitch's feelings.

"Does she know about the baby?" he wondered, looking suddenly haggard.

"Yes. She asked me pointedly about the child and I didn't want to lie."

"I understand and I thank you. I was dreading being the one to tell her. How did she take the news?"

"She wanted your baby very much," was all Mildred would say for she felt it was not her place to tell him of Espri's anguished reaction.

Mitch nodded, his eyes growing dark with concern. "I wanted our child too." He started past her, tensing in expectation.

"Mitch?"

"Yes?"

"Espri needs you," Mildred declared simply.

He was tempted to deny her observation, but he didn't want Mildred to know the pitiful state of their marriage. He nodded tightly and then moved off down the steps toward their stateroom.

The closed door loomed before him and Mitch paused only long enough to school his features into a mask of self-protective, polite detachment before entering the cabin. The brightness of the lamplight revealed Espri unmoving on the bed, her face turned away, her eyes closed. She looked so pale that he feared briefly that she'd once again lapsed into unconsciousness. Only when he closed the door and took a step farther into the room did she stir.

An unexpected wave of anger swept over Espri as she looked up at Mitch; though he looked tired, he displayed no signs of grief or remorse. In fact, he seemed calm and unaffected by it all.

His heart lurched as his eyes met hers, taking in her darkly shadowed, wary expression. She was awake, but little color had returned to her face and the bruise on her cheek still stood out. Mitch came forward with calculated slowness.

"Espri . . ." His voice was gruff and deep.

"Hello, Mitch."

He drew the chair Mildred had been using nearer and sat down. Despite his seeming control, he was on edge.

"I'm sorry about the baby," he said abruptly, then silently cursed himself for blurting it out.

"Are you really?" Espri retorted in disbelief, her tone brittle, her eyes flashing anger.

Her words were like a physical blow, and though outwardly Mitch appeared unmoved, inwardly he flinched at her accusation. "Yes, I am."

"Forgive me, but I find that difficult to believe."

Mitch blanched under her attack. "I understand, but it is the truth, Espri. In fact, I was on my way to you when I found you at the foot of the stairs."

She felt his protestations bordered on the absurd. Surely, it was his guilt speaking, and that annoyed her. "Please, spare me any apologies," she told him contemptuously. "I've known from the beginning how you felt about our situation. As you will recall, you have never hesitated to tell me exactly how you felt about our marriage."

"That was true in the beginning, but—"

She cut him off. "I don't want to hear it. My life is a shambles, and you think a few comforting words are going to help? I told you I didn't want to come along. If you'd listened and left me behind, my child would still be alive!"

"*Our* child would still be alive," he countered, but she only shrugged and looked away, blinking back tears.

"It doesn't matter now," Espri said quietly, all of her energy expended on her burst of fury.

"It does matter. We are still man and wife."

Her eyes narrowed as she regarded him. "Have you ever really considered us as such?"

Her barbed comment hurt, but he knew it was justified. He had not wanted this marriage in the beginning, but now . . .

"Espri," he began haltingly, his eyes searching hers for some indication of her feelings, "neither of us wanted this union, but we are married and it's up to us to make the best of it." He paused. There was so much he wanted to say to her, but he knew this was not the time. He would have to wait. "I intend to try," he assured her.

Espri's thoughts were bitter. Why had it taken the death of their unborn child for him to realize that their marriage was worth the effort it took to make it work? Suddenly exhausted, she drew a shuddering breath before saying woodenly, "I think I'll rest now."

"Think about what I've said, Espri." Mitch reached out to take her hand, but she withdrew from his touch. Refusing to admit defeat, he smiled tenderly at her as he stood up. "I'll be back."

Espri stared dully at the closed cabin door. She had wanted Mitch for so long, had prayed that he would come to want their marriage, but now she couldn't help but wonder if he'd said these things only because he felt responsible for her accident. Too exhausted to think on it more, she sighed and nestled deeper into the softness of the bed, drifting off into a deep dreamless sleep.

Though the night had been long and he was mentally and physically exhausted, Mitch had no desire to sleep. Pain filled him as he strode the deck, and he wondered what he was to do next. He longed to return to the cabin and hold Espri close, to share the burden of their loss, but he was barred from doing so. He vowed to himself, then and there, that he would somehow convince Espri of his love before they reached port.

When Espri awoke long hours later, Mildred was sitting with her.

"Well, good afternoon," she said, with a warm smile. "I'm glad to see you've decided to join us again."

"Have I been sleeping long?"

"Oh, yes. It's afternoon already, but I must tell you, you

look much better. There's even color in your cheeks now." She got up and came to sit on the bed. "How do you feel?"

"Better," Espri admitted.

"Good . . . good." Mildred touched her bare arm tenderly. "I was worried last night, but I can see now that the doctor was right. You're going to be just fine." Her relief was obvious. "Do you think you could eat something? I'm certain you could manage to get down some tea."

"Yes, please." Espri stirred beneath the blanket, testing her bruised muscles and finding them sore.

"I'll go get it for you right now, and I'll see if I can find Mitch. He was here just a short time ago, checking on you," Mildred told her.

"He was?" Espri was surprised.

Mildred nodded as she bustled about the room, picking up a folded garment and bringing it to the bedside. "I've brought you a nightgown. I don't know if you're accustomed to sleeping in one, but since you're to be restricted to bed for a while, I thought you might be more comfortable wearing one."

"A nightgown?"

Mildred held up the high-necked, long-sleeved white cotton gown. "Would you like to wear it?"

"Yes, I think so." Espri's unclad state made her feel exposed and vulnerable.

Mildred helped her to take care of her needs; then she held the gown so Espri could slip it on. When Espri finally lay back, she had become slightly pale from the exertion.

"I'm weaker than I thought," she murmured.

"You've been through a lot, and that's precisely why you're to do nothing but rest," Mildred declared with gentle firmness. "Now, you just take it easy while I fetch you something to eat."

"Yes, ma'am." Espri smiled faintly at the other woman's motherly concern.

Mildred went first to the galley to order some food for her

patient, and then, while the cook prepared it, she sought out Mitch. She finally located him in her own cabin, deep in conversation with her husband. Pausing in the doorway, she studied him for a moment, noticing how exhausted he looked and realizing that the ordeal had taken a toll on him.

"They've already received twenty-five lashes each and will be confined for the next four weeks," Captain Clark was saying. "I can't tell you how sorry I am this happened, Mitch."

"I know," he replied, and then added, "and if you need my help, I'd be more than willing to do whatever I can."

Clark nodded. "I'll keep that in mind." Glancing up, he saw his wife waiting in the doorway. "Mildred, come in. How's Espri?"

"She's doing much better. That's why I was looking for Mitch. I thought he'd want to know that she had awakened."

"Thank you, Mildred," Mitch said quickly. "I'll go to her right now."

"I'll be bringing her some food, shortly," she told him. "Would you care for anything?"

"No, I'm not hungry, but thank you."

She watched him go and then went into her husband's waiting arms. "It's so sad."

"I know. He's taking it very hard."

"So is Espri," Mildred confided; then she sighed. "I wish there was something I could do to make it easier for them."

"You've done everything you can. It's a private matter and something they have to work out for themselves."

Mildred nodded thoughtfully, and then, remembering a part of the conversation she'd overheard, she asked, "What was it you were saying about some of the men receiving lashes?"

Her husband held her away from him. "You haven't heard the whole story yet, then?"

"No. What story?"

"Espri went on deck late last night and two of the men accosted her."

"Mitch wasn't with her?"

"Not at the time. I think he was below with Tommy. Anyway, Mitch heard her scream, and he and Tommy rescued her just in time. She must have fallen on her way back to their cabin."

"You've seen to the sailors' punishment?"

"First thing this morning. They behaved like animals and I won't permit that type of behavior among my crew," he answered sternly.

"I'm glad, darling." She kissed him quickly. "Now, I must get Espri's food. I'll be back later."

Mitch had had all morning to think, and he was determined to make every attempt to convince Espri of his sincerity. He knocked softly before entering their cabin, but any anxiety he'd had about her condition was greatly eased when he found her awake and much improved. "Mildred told me that you'd wakened. How are you?"

"Much better." She was aloof. She had been expecting him and had steeled herself against revealing any emotion.

"You're looking better," he told her.

"Thank you."

"I see Mildred brought you a nightgown," Mitch noted, finding that bit of civilization not to his liking.

"Yes, it's quite comfortable."

"She'll be here shortly with your meal." Mitch turned away and went to the washstand, then stripped off his shirt. "I'll just get cleaned up before she comes."

"Fine." Espri's voice sounded remote, but her gaze followed him about the cabin. She noted how tired he looked and she watched him from beneath lowered lids.

"In deference to your condition," he began, turning to face

her as he dried himself, "I checked with Captain Clark to see if there was some way to rig a hammock in here for my use, but there isn't. If you think my sharing the bed will disturb your rest, I can sleep out on deck."

"There's no need for that."

He nodded thoughtfully and then sat down on the edge of the bed, capturing her hand in a warm grip before she had time to pull it away. "There's much that needs to be said between us, Espri."

"What do you mean?" she countered warily. Though the touch of his hand and his open expression stirred her heart, she hardened herself against any possible deception. Her hurt was too deep.

"I meant what I said to you last night. I don't want things to be as they were before."

Caught up by the intensity of his gaze, Espri didn't move as he leaned forward and touched his lips to the bruise that stained her otherwise flawless cheek. "We'll make a new start, you and I."

Disturbed by the sweet, gentleness of his kiss, she snapped defensively, "Suppose I don't want to?"

"Then I'll just have to convince you that you do. Our vows were ''til death do us part,'" Mitch said patiently. He was tempted to take her in his arms and kiss her, but he sensed it was not the time to press her. He was grateful when Mildred's knock gave him an excuse to end the conversation. Shrugging into one of the clean shirts the captain had given him, he buttoned it quickly, and after admitting Mildred, he excused himself and left.

Espri watched Mitch go, puzzled by this new side of him. His tender devotion had been so convincing that she'd almost believed it. Was there hope for them? Not wanting to be hurt again, she willed herself not to remember the feelings that had surged through her when he'd taken her hand in his.

When the sound of Mildred's voice interrupted her thoughts, she looked up quickly.

"Espri? You look a little flushed. Are you feeling worse?" Mildred's inquiry penetrated her musings as she set a tray laden with food before her.

"No. I'm just tired, I guess." Espri avoided meeting the other woman's eyes.

"Well, let's see if you can eat something and get your strength back." Mildred remembered Espri's earlier statements about Mitch and wondered about his haste in leaving. Was there truly trouble between them? She hoped not, for they made such a handsome couple and this was a time when they really needed one another.

Sunset . . . the hour Mitch had been looking forward to all afternoon. He knew he had to go below and get some sleep, but he wondered if he really could. How in God's name was he going to get any rest, lying in bed next to Espri? Loving her as he did, he knew it was going to be difficult. It was for that reason that he had volunteered to work on the *Providence*. Mitch reasoned that after a hard day's physical labor, he might be able to fall right asleep as he had during the long months on the *Seastorm*. Girding himself, he went below, hoping that he would find some way to cope with the enforced intimacy.

The cabin was bathed in the pale glow of the single hanging lamp when he entered, and Espri appeared to be sleeping. Carefully, he closed the door behind him, then set about getting ready for bed. Quietly, he washed and changed into the comfortable pants he had brought from the island. He wanted to share the bed with her, but, unwilling to disturb her slumber, he extinguished the light and sat on the chair near the foot of the bed. Stretching his long legs out before him, he sought sleep in that awkward position.

Espri stirred, coming awake slowly. She was surprised to find that she had slept the afternoon away and it was dark. Shifting positions, she groaned aloud as her bruised, cramped muscles protested.

Mitch heard her moan and sat up with a start. "Espri? What's the matter?"

She had not known that he'd returned and she gasped, jumping slightly at the unexpected sound of his voice. "Mitch?"

"Just a minute; I'll light the lamp again."

She saw the flare of the match and watched as he adjusted the wick.

"There." He turned to her, his expression worried as he regarded her from across the cabin. "Are you ill?"

"No," she replied, her breath catching in her throat as she returned his regard. How handsome he looked, so tall and virile. Espri couldn't help but remember the first time she'd seen him wearing the pants she'd fashioned and how happy they'd been for a short while. "It's just that I've grown quite stiff from the fall."

"Let me help you. Do you want to sit up?" He started toward her.

"No," Espri answered almost too quickly. She didn't want him any closer than necessary. "I'll manage."

"I hope I didn't frighten you just now."

"No. I just hadn't expected you to be here," she said skittishly. "What time is it?"

"About an hour after sundown," he told her as he settled back in the chair.

"You were in the chair? Why? I thought we'd agreed to share the bed."

"We did," he acknowledged. "But you seemed to be resting comfortably and I didn't want to risk waking you."

"That was very thoughtful of you. Thank you." Espri was quite touched by his consideration.

"Sleep, I'm sure, is the best thing for you right now."

"I suppose. I know the doctor has ordered bed rest, but I don't know how I'm going to stand being in this cabin for very long. I'm not used to being so confined."

"Since your health depends on it, I will make sure that you do as Dr. Canfield ordered," Mitch stated firmly. "Now, if you've no objection, I need to get some rest. Do you want to try to go back to sleep or would you like me to get you something to eat?"

"No, I'm not hungry. Please, come to bed if you're tired."

As casually as Mitch could, he turned the lamp back down and joined her on the bed. Then, in a move that was totally unexpected, he leaned over her and quickly brushed his lips to hers.

"Good night, Espri," he said huskily as he lay back.

"Good night," she answered, stunned. As she lay next to him, listening to the even sound of his breathing, she recalled other nights they'd shared and the joy she'd found in his arms. Closing her eyes, she fought against the memory of his embrace, but thoughts of his loving assailed her and she longed to share that bliss again. Resignedly, she closed her eyes and tried to blot out the disturbing memories.

Mitch's every nerve was aware of Espri resting by his side, and it took a supreme effort to control his desire to hold her. He understood the delicacy of her condition and had no intention of making love to her; he only wanted to comfort her and demonstrate the depth of his feelings for her. Rolling onto his side, he faced away from Espri and finally managed to relax enough to fall asleep.

Chapter 21

The pale light of the morning sun was just filling their cabin with a cozy golden glow when Mitch awoke. The sight of Espri sleeping next to him brought a slow smile to his handsome features, and he grew resolute in his purpose. He would win her love, and when he did, he would once again taste of her body's joys. The memory of caressing her silken flesh and kissing her until she was wanton with desire caused his body to crave her, and he fought down the urge to take her. Trying to relax, he lay still, savoring the intimacy of the moment.

As if sensing his heated gaze upon her, Espri stirred restively in her slumber, accidentally brushing away the blanket. Mitch stared ruefully at the long, concealing gown she wore and he wished for a moment that Mildred had never given it to her. Still, the thrust of her breasts against the soft, white material was so enticing, it took all of his willpower not to reach out and fondle those inviting curves.

Levering himself up on an elbow to look down at her, Mitch murmured a deep, "Good morning, darling."

Espri's eyes flew open at the sound of his voice, so near, and she stared up at him in bewilderment. In all the time they'd slept together since being married, he had never lingered in bed in the morning and she wondered why he was starting to do so now.

"Good morning," she answered hesitantly, feeling most vulnerable under his warm, probing gaze.

"Did you rest well?" he asked, his gaze dwelling on the sweetness of her mouth suggestively before lifting to meet her eyes.

"Yes. I did," she told him, growing more nervous with each passing moment.

"Good." Mitch bent toward her easily and pressed a gentle kiss to her forehead. He felt her tense as he kissed her, and though he sighed inwardly, his grin was wide and slightly mocking when he drew back. "I'll bring breakfast to you shortly, but is there anything I can help you with before I go?" he asked, solicitous of her delicate situation.

"No. I'll be fine." Espri did want to take care of her more personal needs, but she felt uncomfortable doing so in his presence and wanted him to leave her.

She watched as he rose and efficiently began to dress, pulling on his dark pants and then shrugging into a shirt. The rough fabric was pulled taut across his wide shoulders, and, strangely, she suddenly wanted to run her hands over their broad, thickly muscled expanse.

Mitch glanced up as he buttoned the shirt and then sat back down on the edge of the bed to pull on his boots. "I'll be back with your meal. You just stay in bed," he ordered as he rose to leave the cabin.

But Espri was not inclined to follow his directions, and as soon as he had closed the door, she swung her legs over the side of the bed in an attempt to make her way to the convenience. She had just stood up and taken her first unsteady steps when a wave of dizziness left her reeling. Her knees began to buckle, and she was reaching out blindly for some support when the door swung open.

"Damn!" The harshness of Mitch's curse resounded

through the cabin even as he scooped her up in the warm strength of his arms. Striding angrily toward the bed, he laid her gently upon it, then glowered at her. "I thought you were supposed to stay in bed!"

Espri flushed beneath his condemning glare. "I had to use the convenience," she said lamely.

"I offered to help you in any way I could, didn't I, madam?" he pressed, irritated that she would refuse his aid and then risk her health by trying to walk on her own.

"Yes." Espri was mortified.

"And you didn't trust me enough to allow me that privilege?"

"I'm sorry," she muttered, embarrassed.

Having made his point, Mitch once again took her in his arms and carried her easily across the stateroom to the privacy of the small bathroom. "There. Now, just call me when you've finished and I'll carry you back."

"Thank you." It irritated her to have to rely on him for anything, but she knew he was right. She was definitely still too weak to be up by herself.

A few minutes later, she was tucked safely back in bed, and she couldn't resist a small smile as Mitch gently tended her person. How wonderful it felt to be so cherished, but what did it all mean? Was he really this concerned about her and their future together, or was he just assuaging the guilt that she knew must be haunting him? That last possibility dulled the pleasantness of the moment and her smile faded.

"Now, is it safe for me to go for your breakfast?" he asked, his eyes glowingly upon her.

"Yes," she replied coolly.

He glanced at her sharply and, seeing her closed expression, knew that their brief moment of closeness was over, that she had retreated behind her shell of indifference. "I'll be back," he said curtly, his good mood shattered.

Mitch was frustrated as he stalked from the room. As rich

and successful as he was in San Francisco, he had never had to make much of an effort to win a woman's affections. Women had always sought him out and had been more than willing to share his bed. Now, he was the one doing the pursuing, and he found this reversed situation more than a little frustrating. Still, he wouldn't have it any other way. Espri was the only woman he wanted, and she was definitely worth the effort. He would take his time and win both her trust and her love. Determined, he went straight to the galley for her breakfast.

When he returned to their stateroom, he was pleased to find Espri still comfortably ensconced in bed. She looked up as the door opened, and her eyes widened at the sight of the food-laden tray.

"I won't be able to eat all that," she protested.

"You won't have to. Some of it's for me. I've decided to breakfast with you." He set the tray on the bed beside her, then pulled up the chair.

"You're staying?" Her surprise was evident, for he had never lingered with her in the past.

Mitch's expression was strained as he looked at her. "I told you we were making a new start. Do you have an objection to my company? Would you rather I leave?"

"Well, no, but . . ."

Mitch felt a surge of victory over that one concession. "Fine. Then let's eat before everything gets cold." He took a napkin from the tray and spread it across her lap in a gesture that seemed impersonal, yet it left Espri oddly breathless. Setting her plate before her, he took up his own and sat down next to the bed to eat.

Espri's emotions were in turmoil. Confused, she turned her attention to her food. Mitch's nearness set her nerves on edge and she ate mechanically, neither tasting nor enjoying the fare. What she felt for him was powerful. She longed for his touch and kiss, but she was no longer willing to risk inviting hurt. His last rejection had nearly crushed her, and she doubted that she would be able to go on, should he cast her aside again. Hardening herself against the temptation to give in to his sweetly offered attentions, she knew she would have to fight him with all her strength.

"Full?" His question startled her from her thoughts.

"What? Oh, yes, thank you." She handed him her plate as he stood up.

"I've offered to help Captain Clark, so I'll probably be gone for several hours. I spoke with Mildred while I was in the galley, and she said she'd be coming to visit you some time this morning," he explained. "Would you like me to stay until she gets here?"

"No. It's not necessary. I think I'll just try to sleep a little more." Espri huddled down under the covers, hoping to convince him of her need to rest.

"Then I'll be back to check on you as soon as I can." Mitch placed their plates on the tray, which he set on the chair. Turning back to her, he sat on the bed, his rock-hard thigh pressed tightly to her softer one. "I'll try to hurry." His eyes were alight with promise.

Espri nervously watched as he leaned forward, intent on kissing her. She knew she should turn away, or cough, or something, but she wanted that kiss. It seemed an eternity before his lips finally touched hers in a light, impersonal caress, and she felt extremely disappointed. Though she tried to mask it, Mitch saw the frustration reflected in her eyes, and he knew a moment of unsurpassed joy. She did feel something for him! Giving her a warm smile, he stood up.

"I'll be back," he said easily, and taking the tray, he left the room.

Although Mitch was physically busy all morning working with Captain Clark and Tommy, his thoughts were constantly on Espri. He felt certain that he was making progress with her and that it was just a matter of time before he won her over.

It was near noon when he finally managed to break away to check on her, and he was disappointed to find that she was asleep. Returning to the duties the captain had given him, he passed the afternoon in a haze of anticipation, and he was greatly relieved when sundown finally came.

Espri had spent the day either napping or visiting with Mildred, who'd spent most of the morning with her. As the hours had passed and Mitch had not come back to see her, she had become slightly depressed. She was reluctant to admit it to herself, but she missed him, and when he finally came through the door, at dusk, she couldn't repress a smile of gladness.

Mitch saw her smile and his heart grew light. "Good evening, love." He wanted to go straight to the bed and kiss her, but he stifled the urge and set about stripping off his shirt so he could bathe.

"Good evening, Mitch," she replied, unable to take her eyes off of him as he strode about the cabin, naked to the waist.

"You look lovely tonight," he told her as he moved to the washstand and poured his bathwater.

"Thank you. Mildred helped me bathe, and she combed out my hair."

Mitch stared down at the black silken length of her hair and without conscious thought, he reached out to lift one heavy strand, rubbing it sensuously between his fingers. Espri lifted her eyes to his and she gasped slightly when she saw the heated intensity of his gaze.

Held captive by the wonder in her expression, he almost told her that he loved her, but he held back.

Tearing her gaze away from his with a determined effort, Espri decided she wouldn't give in to the urge to tell him of her feelings. It was not easy to fight her attraction for him when he was being so kind and loving, but she had to do it. She wasn't at all certain that the attention he was giving her was real, and she couldn't take the chance that it wasn't.

Their brief interval of intimacy gone, Mitch reluctantly returned to his bathing.

"Captain Clark said he would have a cabin boy bring dinner to us tonight." Mitch spoke again just as he finished washing.

"I think I'd prefer to eat alone tonight." Her tone was cold, and he stopped what he was doing and turned to look at her.

"I see," he said slowly, stiffening as he saw the coldness of her expression. "In that case, my dear, I shall leave you to your solitary meal." He donned clean clothes and left.

Espri had not expected Mitch to agree to go so readily, and perversely, her heart sank as the door closed behind him. When the cabin boy came with the food a short time later, she found she had no appetite and could only pick at the offered dishes.

Mitch's first reaction to her pronouncement had been anger, but when he'd had time to think it through, he realized that Espri had suffered much in the last few days. He knew that, had he been in her position, he, too, would have found it difficult to believe his profession that he wanted to make the marriage work. Resigning himself to giving her more time, he partook of a late meal in the galley with the crew.

The hour he was gone was torturous for Espri. She wondered if he would return that night, and though she disguised it when he finally did return, she was almost delighted to see him.

"I trust you enjoyed your dinner?" Mitch asked politely as he quickly undressed.

"Yes, I did," she replied.

"Good. Shall I turn the lamp down?" He was standing nude before her, waiting for her answer.

"Yes. I suppose I am ready for bed," she told him as aloofly as she could.

He nodded and, after extinguishing the light, he joined her on the bed. Not at all deterred by her refusal to dine with him, he bent over her masterfully and took her lips in a long, sweet kiss before lying back to sleep.

"Good night, Espri." His voice was deep, a sensuous caress upon her already frazzled senses, and when she didn't respond, he smiled in the darkness as he rolled over to go to sleep.

That first day established the pattern for the days to come. Every morning, Mitch would awaken Espri with a tender kiss and then help her with her ablutions before bringing her breakfast. He would pass the day working with the captain, and then return to her in the evening after she'd eaten her late meal. He had not attempted to join her again for dinner, having decided to wait until she invited him back. Each night he kissed her before going to sleep, and while his need for her was growing, so far he had managed to keep his desire under control.

As Espri regained her strength, her days became a blur of activities. Mildred visited often and kept her entertained with stories of life aboard the *Providence* while they both worked diligently on sewing new garments for her. It was during one of these visits, during the second week of her recovery, that Mitch returned unexpectedly.

"Good morning, ladies," he greeted them cheerfully, his teeth flashing whitely in his deeply tanned face.

As much as she didn't want to be attracted to him, Espri found herself thinking of the kiss they'd shared before he'd left her earlier that day, and her cheeks flushed in remembered pleasure.

"I have a surprise that I think my wife might enjoy," Mitch said, catching her attention.

Puzzled, Espri wondered what kind of surprise he could find in the middle of the ocean. "A surprise?"

"I've just spoken with Dr. Canfield, and he has no objection to your going up on deck for a while," he explained.

"Really?" Her excitement was obvious.

"Really." He grinned, glad that his suggestion to the doctor had pleased her. "Is there something suitable she can wear, Mildred?"

"Of course. Just give us a few minutes and we'll be ready," the older woman answered, and when Mitch stepped from the room, she hastened to help Espri into a daygown appropriate to wear on deck.

Though the ship's doctor had allowed Espri out of bed a little more each day, she had been confined to the stateroom, so the prospect of sitting in the sun and enjoying the freshness of the sea breezes thrilled her. Espri was ready to hurry from the room on her own, but Mildred overruled such foolishness.

"Sit down, Espri. You're not walking anywhere," she ordered firmly. "I'll get Mitch."

Her spirits buoyant, the young woman dropped down onto the bed to await her husband's return.

"You're ready?" Mitch asked as Mildred brought him into the room.

"Yes," Espri told him happily, thinking he would only be helping her up. When Mitch lifted her into his arms and held her snugly against his broad chest, she was amazed. "You're going to carry me?"

"Absolutely," he answered, thinking how wonderful it felt to have her near him once again. "The doctor said you were to take no chances on the steps."

"But it's really not necessary," she protested, feeling helpless.

"It most certainly is," Mildred put in, her eyes aglow as she observed them together. What a fine couple they made, Mitch so dark and handsome and Espri so lithe and beautiful. "Now, relax."

Obediently, Espri looped her arms about Mitch's neck, and his grasp tightened at her innocent gesture. When Mildred left the room before them, Mitch glanced down at his wife.

"Ready?"

Espri was so enthralled by the piercing, passionate look he gave her that she only nodded.

Mitch had told himself repeatedly that he would take his time with her and not press her in any way, yet he couldn't resist the opportunity to steal a quick kiss. His head dipped; his mouth hovered briefly over hers, giving her time to reject him, before his lips claimed hers in a searing, possessive exchange.

Espri had been hoping that he would kiss her, and her heart soared at the touch of his mouth. She knew she shouldn't respond, that she should keep herself aloof, but it was no use. Her desire for him was as strong as ever. The revelation dazed her, and she stared up at him, mesmerized, when he broke off the embrace.

Their gazes locked in a heated, unspoken exchange, and Mitch would have kissed her again, had not the sudden remembrance of Mildred waiting in the companionway forced him to suppress his need for Espri. "Mildred . . ." Smiling in apology, he hurried from the room, holding his wife close.

The day was a glorious one, the sun high and warm in the cloudless sky, the wind brisk yet comfortable. Espri relished the secure feeling of being in Mitch's arms again, and she was sorry when he reached the foredeck, where seats had been arranged for her outing.

"Thank you, Mitch," she said delightedly as she settled in next to Mildred.

He gave her a roguish grin as his gaze raked over her, leaving no doubt in her mind about his enjoyment of their brief intimacy. "You're welcome."

Her pulse was racing from his lusty look, but as the reality of her situation returned, she silently berated herself for her continuing desire for him. She wouldn't love him! She wouldn't!

"I'll be back for you later. Mildred." He nodded to the captain's wife before striding off across the deck.

Mildred watched him as he walked away, and she gave a deep, heartfelt sigh. "He's such a handsome man, Espri. You are so lucky."

"I am?"

"Of course. He's very devoted to you. I can tell he loves you very much." The older woman gave her a knowing look. "Why, when I think about that night you were injured and how worried he was."

"That was guilt, Mildred," Espri declared, suddenly bitter at the memory of that night. "Not love."

"Don't be silly," her friend chided. "Why would Mitch feel guilty?"

"Because we'd had an argument that night," Espri said tightly.

"All couples argue," Mildred said dismissively. "The first several years of marriage are always the most difficult. He loves you, Espri, of that I'm certain . . . and he wanted your baby."

Her last statement shocked Espri. "He wanted the baby? How do you know?"

"He told me so. He was crushed by your miscarriage, and one of the first questions he asked the doctor was whether or not you'd be able to conceive again."

"He did?" Espri's eyes rounded in surprise, and some of her rancor died.

"Absolutely." Mildred patted her hand. "Did you think he didn't want the child?"

"Oh, it's all so complicated." Espri sighed, wanting to speak of her feelings, yet not knowing where to begin.

"Why don't you tell me about it? Maybe I can help," Mildred urged.

The younger woman nodded slowly. "I think I do need to

talk, but I don't know how much help you can be. You see, Mitch really doesn't love me."

"Balderdash!" Mildred snorted in the first outburst of temper Espri had seen her display.

"No, it's true. We've been together almost since he was first washed up on Malika, but he has never told me that he loves me. He never intended to marry me or take me with him." The words came out in a rush of torment.

"What are you saying? Why don't you tell me everything from the very start," Mildred encouraged gently.

"It began several months ago, when he was shipwrecked. I took care of him and we . . . we became lovers." Espri paused, expecting condemnation from Mildred, but there was none. The older woman's expression was sympathetic. Sensing that she truly did understand, Espri continued. "But while we were close, I learned that Mitch intended to leave Malika as quickly as he could and that he had no desire to make any commitments. That was when I decided to end our relationship. I loved him, Mildred, with all my heart, but I couldn't go on, knowing that he meant to leave me at the first opportunity."

"I understand." Mildred nodded. "Go on."

"Well, a month or so after I stopped seeing him I discovered I was going to have the baby." She sighed. "My father and Father Papin, the missionary, insisted that Mitch marry me and . . . here I am. He didn't do it out of love for me. He did it because of the child." Espri paused dejectedly. "And now I don't even have the child to offer him."

"You think he doesn't want you anymore just because you miscarried?"

"Yes," Espri answered numbly.

"You're wrong. I'm certain that he loves you."

"No. He's just feeling responsible for me since the accident."

"Quite the contrary. I think your tragedy upset him so

much that he finally realized just how much you really mean to him."

A flicker of hope flared within the depths of Espri's soul, and her eyes filled with tears as she admitted the truth. "I love him so much, Mildred, but I'm so afraid."

"Oh, my darling." Mildred hugged her quickly. "Why don't you give him a chance to prove his love to you? Mitch is not like the men you've grown up with on the island. As I was telling you earlier, in the white society, things are not always as they seem."

"I want to." Espri turned haunted eyes to her friend. "But what if he doesn't love me? I don't think I could stand it."

"He does," Mildred insisted. "Wait and see. And remember, the loss you've just suffered affects him as much as it affects you but in a different way."

Holding her breath, Espri gave Mildred a quivering smile. "I will try it."

"Good," her friend answered happily. She felt positive that they would work things out.

The discussion with Mildred had altered Espri's perception of Mitch. Searching the deck for him, she observed him covertly, allowing herself to again see him as the man she loved—the man who was now her husband. Exhorting herself to go slowly, she hoped that Mildred was right, that there truly was a future for them.

Chapter 22

San Francisco

Outside the Williamses' mansion the street was crowded with carriages as guests arrived to attend the lavish ball being given by Jonathan and Catherine. In less than a year, Catherine Chamberlain Williams had gained a reputation for being the most innovative and entertaining of hostesses. Her popularity was so great that invitations to her galas were greatly prized.

"Darling," Catherine drawled to Jonathan as she stared at her reflection in her full-length mirror. "How do I look?"

Jonathan turned to look at his wife as he shrugged into his coat. "You look ravishing, as usual, but . . ." He surveyed the low-cut, turquoise taffeta gown with its innovative slim-line skirt approvingly; then he took in the single strand of diamonds that graced her throat and frowned.

Always desirous of his complete admiration, Catherine was disturbed by his expression and she wondered what had caused his displeasure. "Is something wrong?" she asked quickly.

"No. Nothing is wrong. I just think something is missing." He walked to his armoire and took out a jeweler's case. "I had not planned to give this to you until our first anniversary, but I think it should grace your loveliness tonight."

Catherine took the box from him and opened it, gasping in astonishment at the exquisite necklace and matching earbobs within. "Jon . . . they're beautiful."

"Not nearly so beautiful as the woman who will wear them," he said gallantly as he took the diamond necklace from its velvet-lined case. Moving to stand behind her, he released the clasp on the necklace she was wearing and then placed his gift about her neck. When he'd completed that task, Jon bent and pressed an ardent kiss to her bared shoulder. "Thank you for all the happiness you've given me, darling."

Suppressing a shiver of distaste at his touch, Catherine casually moved back to the mirror on the pretense of putting on the earbobs. "These are magnificent. Thank you."

"You're more than welcome." Jon smiled, glad that he'd pleased her. "Shall we join our guests? I'm sure they're eagerly awaiting your arrival so they can remark on what new fashion trend you're introducing tonight."

Catherine laughed with pleasure and turned to face him, her eyes brightening in anticipation of the envious stares she knew she'd be receiving from the other women. "I'm glad you enjoy entertaining. I do love it so."

"My darling, I am yours to command," Jonathan assured her. "I find great satisfaction in your successes and will always back you in any endeavor."

She went to him then, willingly, and kissed him, knowing that by teasing him a little before the party she would have his undivided attention all evening. "I'm now ready to face our guests."

A stunned, admiring hush fell over those assembled as Jon appeared at the top of the wide curved staircase with his trendsetting wife on his arm, and a smattering of applause greeted their descent.

The handsome pair greeted their guests cordially as they

made their way down the hall to the ballroom. Then, with a single gesture, Jon indicated that the music should begin, and the lilting strains of a waltz soon filled the air. Taking Catherine in his arms, he led her skillfully about the floor, drawing appreciative glances from all who, by courtesy, allowed them the first dance.

Standing to one side, heavy with child, Susan Stuart held her husband's arm possessively and sighed. "Catherine is so gorgeous."

"That she is," Roland agreed blandly, his expression non-committal though inwardly he was wishing he were the man entitled to squire the lovely Catherine about the floor.

When the waltz came to an end, everyone applauded their graceful display; then the ball really began.

"Look, darling. Roland and Susan are here." Catherine pointed them out to Jon. "Let's join them, shall we?"

"Of course," he agreed, taking her arm and leading her to the other couple.

"Good evening, Jon . . . Catherine." Roland shook hands with his business partner.

"Roland," Jon replied. "Susan, you're looking lovely tonight."

She blushed prettily as she demurred. "Thank you for being such a gentleman, Jon, but I'm well aware of my size."

"The months have been flying by, haven't they?" Catherine remarked coolly.

"Yes, and the doctor insists that this be my last social event for the year."

"Well, I'm glad you came," Jon assured her gallantly.

"I'd like to talk over some business dealings with you later, Jon, when you have the time," Stuart interrupted, not wanting to hear about babies and confinements. He found his wife's pregnancy tedious, and could hardly wait until the child was born. The sight of her swollen, misshapen body disgusted him; he'd be relieved when she finally delivered.

Thank God, Catherine hadn't done anything so foolish as get with child.

"That'll be fine," Jon was agreeing. "We have yet to greet our other guests, but as soon as I can break away, I'll meet with you in the study."

"Good." Business dispensed with, Roland turned to Catherine, and bending over her hand in courtly fashion, he said, "Mrs. Williams, if I may have the honor?"

"Of course you may," Catherine said quickly, and she stepped onto the dance floor, leaving her husband at Susan's side.

Roland whirled her away into the dancing couples, thrilled to have her in his arms, held close to him. "My God, Catherine, that dress is positively sinful."

She laughed throatily. "Why, Roland! My husband thought it quite intriguing."

"Ah, but your husband doesn't know how I'd like to strip it from you and take you right here in the middle of the ballroom floor!"

Again she laughed. "I don't think I can arrange the ballroom floor, but perhaps later . . . in one of the less frequented rooms . . ." She let the sentence trail off and felt the instant response of his body.

"Don't tease me, Catherine. As you well know, I am not a man who appreciates being taunted."

She feigned an innocent look. "But darling," she protested, "who said I was teasing?" The thought of making love to Roland under her own roof, with his wife and her husband nearby, fascinated and excited her. How stimulating it would be to be so illicit!

Roland growled low in his throat. "Don't tempt me!"

"I'm not tempting, I'm inviting. Do you think we'd be missed a little later? It's been days since we've been together and I need you, Roland."

His body tensed as he imagined himself deep within the hot, silken confines of her lovely body. "We'll manage—somehow." The music ended, and not a moment too soon as far as he was concerned. Escorting her back to Jon, he smiled leisurely. "Your wife is as graceful and charming as ever."

"She is a treasure." Jon gave Catherine a tender look. "Darling, I think we should mingle. I'll speak with you later, Roland."

"Until then." He nodded and Catherine knew his answer was meant for her.

The evening passed in a whirlwind of dancing, drinking, and eating. The sumptuous buffet Catherine had arranged provided enough delicacies to please even the most discriminating gourmet—consommé à la bonne femme, cantaloupe, fried mountain trout, pigeon pie, roast lamb with mint sauce, asparagus, watercress salad, apricot tarts, charlotte russe, and assorted gâteaux and bonbons—and everyone ate accordingly, not hesitating to compliment their host and hostess on setting such a grand table.

Midnight found Susan seated along the side of the ballroom in the company of the other matrons, while Roland stood in the now-deserted hall, deep in conversation with Alan Harris.

"It's true," Alan insisted, draining his glass of champagne nervously. "He was there day before yesterday."

Roland stiffened at the news. "And?"

"And it seems to me that he might just be getting a little suspicious."

"Does he have any reason to be? Every angle's been covered, hasn't it?" Stuart demanded.

"Yes. There's no way he could find out anything unless he's there when a shipment of our 'merchandise' arrives. The manifests are all altered on board so there can be no possibility of discovery through the paperwork."

"We'll just have to make sure that he's never in the warehouse when the merchandise arrives." Roland leveled a piercing glare at his colleague. "Do you think you can handle that?"

"I'm not sure. You two are dealing together, but the company is still his, you know."

"I know; believe me, I know." For a moment Stuart was lost in thought. "I'm meeting him later and I have a proposal that I hope he'll accept. If he does, we will have the solution to our problem."

"Really?"

Roland nodded. "I've acquired enough capital to buy him out, and that is exactly what I intend to do."

Alan pondered that for a minute. "What if he won't sell? I mean, the company has been in his family for generations. He might not want to part with it."

"I'm not saying he has to get out entirely. I just want to own a controlling share of the company so I no longer have to keep up this subterfuge." His eyes were glittering as he thought of the riches awaiting him once he gained complete control of Williams Shipping.

"Well, let me know how it goes. I'll be anxious to hear." Harris smiled ferally then, as a thought came to him. "There is a shipment due in at any time. Could be here tonight or tomorrow. I've left word that I'm to be notified as soon as it arrives. Would you like to join me in inspecting it?"

Roland masked his feeling of distaste over Alan's obvious lust. "No. I'm afraid young Chinese girls aren't my style, but feel free to sample whatever merchandise you want as long as you don't permanently damage it."

Alan nodded, his eyes glowing feverishly as he anticipated the arrival of the ship. They were interrupted then as Laura and Catherine stepped out into the hall.

"There you are." Laura came forward to kiss her husband's cheek. "I've been looking for you."

"You have?" Alan looked at her questioningly.

"Yes, darling. I'd love to dance . . . please?" She gave him a pleading look.

"Of course, my pet," Alan answered smoothly, and he escorted her from the hall, leaving Catherine alone with Roland.

She cast him a heated glance from beneath lowered lashes. "Well, Mr. Stuart, have you been enjoying yourself?"

"Don't flirt with me, Cat," he gritted out, his gaze lingering on the daring swell of her breasts above the low-cut bodice.

"Meet me in the study in fifteen minutes. We won't have much time, but it will be a delightful challenge, don't you think?" She was heady with a feeling of sensual power.

"You're really willing to risk everything?"

"Only for you, my love. Only for you," she told him throatily as she walked away to rejoin her guests.

Roland returned to his wife's side and doted on her tenderly. Susan was such a trusting woman that he knew she would never miss him when he went to meet Catherine, and if she did, it would never occur to her that he might be with another woman.

Catherine drifted gaily among her guests, finally locating Jon.

"Darling, we haven't danced for hours," she complained prettily as she drew him from the group of men he was speaking with, and Jon, ever susceptible to her charms, followed her gladly onto the floor.

"You've missed me, have you?" he asked good-naturedly as they glided about.

To all those looking on, they seemed the perfect couple, he tall and dark, she slender and fair—and obviously in love with each other. Little did anyone suspect that Catherine was alive with a frenzied desire to meet with Roland in a few minutes.

"Abominably, but I know I shall have you all to myself later, when our guests have gone." She gave him a smoldering look and Jon smiled in response to her unspoken invitation.

"I shall be looking forward to 'later.'" He gave her an easy, confident smile.

Catherine played her part to the hilt, as she had during the months of her marriage, and Jon, besotted as he was, never doubted her for a moment. When they parted after the waltz, he returned to his business discussion with his friends and Catherine excused herself, pleading the need for a brief respite.

Only one lamp was alight in the study, and Catherine strategically turned it down until deep, concealing shadows enveloped the room. Pulling the drapes at the two floor-to-ceiling windows, she then reclined on the full-length over-stuffed sofa to await Roland's arrival.

Roland had no trouble breaking away from Susan, and he strode down the hall casually, entering the study unobserved. His passion for Catherine being fierce as ever, he could hardly wait to pierce the sweet tightness of her. Closing the door behind him, he glanced about the darkened room.

"Cat?" He said her name softly; then he heard her delicious gurgle of laughter coming from the direction of the sofa.

"Yes, darling? I told Jon that I needed to rest for a moment. Would you like to join me?" She sat up slowly, her expression inviting.

"I'll join you," he said in a low voice, as he soundlessly locked the study door. "But I guarantee you won't be getting any rest."

She immediately rose and, with eager fingers, began to

strip, not wanting to risk ruining her gown. Within seconds, she stood before Roland clad only in a sheer, strapless chemise.

As Roland had watched Catherine disrobe, he'd felt the familiar rise of his desire. The taut peaks of her full breasts teased the gossamer fabric of the garment and seemed to beg for his caress. The darkness of her feminine delta was a vague outline beneath the sensuous material.

"As always, I find you more beautiful without all the trappings of femininity," Roland growled, and he started to unbutton his shirtfront when she stopped him.

"No, don't. I want you to make love to me with your clothes on." She came to him and wrapped her arms about his neck, rubbing herself sinuously against him. "It feels so much more . . . stolen, that way."

"You steal nothing from me. I give it to you freely," Roland told her, kissing her passionately.

Catherine responded fully, excited by the danger in their coupling. Her hands were never still as she stroked him expertly through his clothes, all the while moving restlessly against his hardness. Aware that time was of the essence, Roland led her to the sofa and pushed her gently down upon its welcoming softness. Kneeling beside her, he freed her breasts and kissed them greedily. The touch of his mouth sent a shaft of desire through her, and she arched in frenzied abandon as his hand slipped between her thighs to explore and stimulate. He brought her to full arousal easily, knowing just how to please her, and when she could wait no longer for their joining, Roland released himself from his pants and mounted her. The faint sound of muffled voices in the hall only intensified their feverish mating, and ecstasy claimed them quickly. Roland wanted to keep Catherine in his arms forever, but he knew that they could be found out at any moment.

"Darling . . ." he whispered.

"I know. We have to get back, but Roland . . ."—there was anguish in her voice—"I love you so."

"And I you." His mouth sought hers again in a heated kiss before he lifted himself from her. He quickly straightened his clothing and then helped her to her feet. "Shall I help you?"

"Please." She sighed, regretting their return to the ball. When Roland had finished fastening her gown for her, he turned her to face him and slid his hand within the bodice.

"This is what I wanted to do to you while we were waltzing," he said as he lifted her breast from the restrictive bodice and kissed the taut nipple. "You are so enticing," he murmured against her tender flesh.

Then Catherine gasped as his teeth tugged painfully at the throbbing peak. "You're hurting me!" she cried softly, wanting to pull away, yet somehow finding enjoyment in the pain.

"I want you to think of me when you're dancing with your husband," he told her punishingly.

"I think of you always," Catherine said with a small sob as her knees weakened and she swayed against him.

Roland slipped a supporting arm about her waist. "Do you want me again, Cat?" he asked as he finally stopped his tormented play and covered her sore breast.

"Oh, Roland . . ." Her body was on fire with desire for him.

He chuckled deeply and released her. "Good." He strode toward the door then, and she watched him through a passion-filled haze.

"Roland?"

"Monday afternoon, dear, while your husband is at his office," he said curtly, and unlocking the door, he was gone.

Trembling from the power of her need, she sat back weakly on the sofa, trying to regain control. She was certain that her cheeks were flushed and she hoped Roland had left no telltale marks on her body. As excited as she was, she knew she would entice Jon to her bed just as soon as the guests took their leave.

When she finally felt composed, Catherine stood, and

smoothing her skirt, she left the study only to come face to face with Jon and Roland in the hall.

"Darling." Her husband greeted her easily, giving her a quick, adoring kiss. "Did you manage to get a bit of rest?"

"Yes. Those few minutes in the study were just what I needed," she reassured him without so much as a glance at Roland.

"Good, because our guests seem to have no inclination to leave and this might turn out to be a long night."

Catherine gave him her brightest smile. "But, Jon," she drawled, "that's exactly why we entertain."

"I know, love, but when you're looking so irresistible it's difficult for me to remember that I invited everyone here."

She laughed delightedly. "I'll see you later, darling. Roland." She nodded at him with cool cordiality as she started off down the hall.

The two men, drinks in hand, continued on into the study, and after turning up the lamp, they sat opposite each other in comfortable wing chairs.

"So, tell me, Roland, what is it you wanted to discuss with me tonight?" Jon asked as he took a drink of his bourbon.

"I have a proposition for you."

"Oh? Regarding what?"

Roland leaned forward, intent on what he was about to say. "Jon, I want to buy into Williams Shipping."

"What?" Jon was astonished. Their dealings were very profitable as they stood, and he couldn't imagine why the other man would want to change the situation. "Why?"

"I feel that the company needs to expand to keep up with the times, and I can provide you with the capital you need to enlarge your fleet and thereby turn a bigger profit," he explained logically.

Jon didn't even bother to consider his offer. Standing, he strode to a window and threw back the drape to stare out at the night. "I'm sorry, Roland, but the answer is no."

"Now it's my turn to ask. Why not?" By forcing the issue, Roland hoped to catch the younger man at a disadvantage.

Sighing, Jon answered, "It's a family operation, Roland. It always has been and it always will be. Someday, I hope to have a son to carry it on, just as Mitch and I did for our father."

"But, Jon," Stuart argued. "This is a heavy responsibility for one man to handle."

"Mitch did it and I can do it."

"And you are doing an admirable job with what you've got, but why not expand? The time is right. The China trade is just beginning to boom. There are millions to be made in it."

"And we'll make our share," Jon informed him levelly.

"But we could dominate the market. Don't you realize what an opportunity we have here?"

"I do, but I have no intention of selling any part of Williams Shipping. I'm sorry, Roland. That's my final answer."

Roland gritted his teeth in exasperation. "Well, just remember that the offer is there, should you decide to take me up on it."

"I certainly will."

It was only a short time later when Roland cornered Alan in the ballroom.

"We need to talk," Roland declared.

"What is it? Did you meet with Jon?" Alan was eagerly awaiting the news.

"Yes, I met with Jon, but he refuses to sell any part of the company." Roland was quite irritated.

"What do we do now?"

"We definitely don't panic. Just make damn sure that the merchandise is out of the warehouse as fast as possible. It certainly wouldn't do for him to discover that we're using his boats to import nubile Chinese girls to work in the cribs."

"He might enjoy participating in our endeavor." Alan smiled thinly.

"I doubt it. If anything, he'd inform the authorities and start an investigation that could ruin us."

Alan nodded, his mood serious. "We don't want to chance that. I'll do my best, and if he comes snooping around, I'll give him the guided tour myself."

"Good thought. Keep me informed." Roland paused thoughtfully. "And, if there is any way I can possibly arrange it, I'm going to have a controlling interest in Williams Shipping by the end of the year."

Catherine had been mingling with her guests, accepting their congratulations on another outstanding ball, when she spotted Roland and Alan on the far side of the ballroom. Excusing herself, she made her way to them.

"Good evening, Alan. Roland, I believe this is our dance."

"How could I have forgotten?" He immediately accepted her offer. "Alan, I'll speak with you later."

He escorted Catherine onto the floor, where they blended with the other dancers.

"How did your private talk with Jon go?" she asked, curious as to the nature of their conversation.

"Not well. Not well at all," he answered. "I think I may need your help."

"With what?" She was intrigued.

He gave her a measured look. "I want Williams Shipping."

"You what?" She was stunned.

"I want to buy Jon out. I've got the money, but he's refused to sell. He wouldn't even offer me an interest in it."

Catherine didn't respond as he went on.

"I want you to try to convince him that the company needs to expand. Do it subtly, of course. We wouldn't want him to suspect that I'd coached you."

"I'll do my best, but I don't guarantee I'll have any influence. Lately, he's become more sure of himself and more determined to be in charge."

"He is becoming more like his brother every day. That's why I have to keep one step ahead of him. Gaining control of the company is the only way I can guarantee that my business deals will continue to be as profitable as they have been in the past."

"Don't worry, Roland. You always win."

"This time, my darling, I hope you're right."

Chapter 23

Espri gazed at herself in the mirror with disbelieving eyes. Was this beautiful woman really her?

"Mildred"—she turned to her friend, smiling bewilderedly—"I can't believe it."

"I told you how lovely you were," Mildred told her approvingly. "This style suits you perfectly." She hurried to adjust the skirt of the gown they had spent the past two weeks making. "And the color."

"Do you really think so?" Espri stared at her reflection again, this time frowning as she searched for flaws in her appearance, but there were none. The rose silk gown fit her superbly in a demure yet enticing manner, and Mildred had arranged her hair in an upswept style that emphasized the sparkling beauty of her dark eyes and drew attention to the slender arch of her throat.

"I know so, and this is the perfect night to wear it, don't you think? What with the news the doctor just gave you—"

"I am so glad Dr. Canfield finally said I'm completely recovered." Espri flushed excitedly. The last six weeks of enforced inactivity had been very difficult for her to bear.

"I'm sure Mitch will be glad too," Mildred teased good-naturedly. "Have you told him what the doctor said yet?"

"No, not yet."

"Well, why not?"

Espri looked nervous. "I've been waiting for the right moment, I suppose."

"Oh? I've always heard that good news is always welcome." The older woman smiled and then let the smile fade as another thought occurred to her. "Or haven't you decided what you're going to do about your marriage?"

"Well, I think I've decided, but—"

"Have you admitted your feelings to him?"

"I've been afraid," Espri offered lamely.

Mildred nodded sagely. "It's time you told him, Espri. He's been so patient and giving these last long weeks, and with little encouragement from you, I might add."

"I know."

"Believe me, if he didn't love you, he would have tired of the game by now, guilt or no guilt."

Espri nodded her head in agreement. "I know you're right, Mildred. I do still love him and I think perhaps tonight is the time to tell him, maybe even to show him. It's been so long since we've been close." She sighed wistfully.

"Let's have dinner together in the captain's cabin, shall we? There's more room there and you can show off your dress to a better advantage."

"I'd like that. Thank you."

Mitch was tired and his nerves were on edge as he headed back to his stateroom later that day. It had been weeks since he'd gotten a good night's sleep, and the thought of another night of tossing at Espri's side positively unnerved him. Didn't she know what she was doing to him? Didn't she know how much he wanted her and the price he was paying for holding himself back? He laughed mirthlessly to himself as he realized the answer. Though she was very much a woman,

Espri was not knowledgeable in the ways of coyness or coquetry. Any enticements he imagined she was using were, no doubt, just imagined.

She had given little indication that she was warming to him over the weeks. Although she had invited him back to the cabin for their evening meal, there had been no additional intimacy between them. Every morning and every evening they would kiss at his instigation, but that was as far as it went. The situation was taking a toll on him.

Mitch wanted Espri more than he'd ever wanted another woman. He had not practiced celibacy, not since he'd discovered the joys of female companionship in his much younger years, and to try to avoid intimacy with his wife while he was sleeping in the same bed with her every night was becoming unbearable.

Somehow, very soon, they were going to have to come to an understanding, for he knew he couldn't go on this way for the rest of the voyage. His desire for her was too great to be denied much longer.

Espri was standing before the small washstand mirror when he came into the stateroom, and he did a double take when he saw her.

"Espri?" He gave her a quixotic smile. "Why are you all dressed up? Shouldn't you be resting?"

"I'm dressed up because we're having dinner with Mildred and the captain," she told him, turning away from the mirror to come stand before him. "Well, what do you think? Do you like it?"

Mitch surveyed the attractive gown that was tastefully revealing. "Yes, I like it. You look marvelous. Is this the dress that you and Mildred have been working on all week?"

She nodded. "We finished just in time for the celebration."

"Celebration?" He frowned good-naturedly. "Why is it I have the feeling that I've missed something here?"

"Because you have." She laughed lightly. "I spoke with

Dr. Canfield today, and he feels that I've made a complete recovery."

"That's wonderful." He swept her into his arms and hugged her excitedly. "Why didn't you come and tell me right away?"

"I thought it would be nicer to tell you here, in private."

"Well, it doesn't matter when you told me; all that matters is that you're well." He released her when he realized how unkempt he was.

"Let me wash and change. What time is Mildred expecting us?"

"In about half an hour, so you've got plenty of time."

"Good." He took another prideful look at her and then kissed her softly. "I'm so glad that you're recovered."

"So am I," she said softly, her eyes dark with emotion.

"Isn't Espri's news wonderful, Mitch?" Mildred asked as they lingered contentedly at the dinner table.

"Yes," he answered, his gaze warm as he looked at his wife, who was sitting by his side. "I'm very thankful that everything has worked out so well. I'll always regret the loss of our child, but perhaps in the future we'll be able to have more children."

Espri met his eyes, her expression guarded. Mitch sounded sincere, and she knew on this night she would find out whether he was.

"I always wanted children, but we weren't blessed," Mildred admitted a trifle sadly.

"You were blessed with each other," Espri put in, knowing the depth of the love the captain and Mildred shared.

"That's true," she replied, and she and her husband smiled tenderly at one another. "And so are you."

Beneath the table, Mitch boldly took Espri's hand from

her lap and brought it to his knee. "That we are," he agreed, heartened when she didn't try to withdraw from his loving grasp.

It was almost an hour later when Mitch and Espri started back to their cabin, he attentively guiding her with a comforting hand at her waist.

"Would you like to go out on deck for a while?" he suggested, knowing the beauty of the night and hoping to woo her more gently beneath the stars.

"I'd love to, thank you."

Twinkling, diamondlike stars encrusted the darkened heavens and a golden wedge of a moon smiled down on them as they strode across the deck of the *Providence* to pause at the railing.

"It feels so wonderful to be moving about again." Espri sighed contentedly.

"I know how hard it's been for you," he agreed. "Being on a boat is confining enough, but to be forced to remain in a cabin in bed—well, I'm sorry it ever happened to you."

"Mitch?" she asked quickly before she lost her nerve.

He looked down at her questioningly.

"Did you mean what you said about our baby? Are you really sorry I lost it?"

"God, Espri," he growled, pulling her to him. "How can you ask?"

"I have to hear it from you. I have to know. Did you really want our baby?" She pushed free of his arms.

"I wanted that baby very much. It was a part of you and of me," he told her solemnly. "Why is this so important to you now?"

Tears glistened in her eyes. "Because I don't want a future based on lies and half-truths. I don't want to continue our marriage if you feel you've been entrapped, and without the baby to hold us together . . . Well, I just needed to know how you really felt."

"Espri, I haven't been lying to you for these last weeks. I want our marriage—very much. I just regret that it took the accident to make me acknowledge how I really feel about you." He slowly drew her closer. "I love you, Espri. I think I have from the very first time we were together."

"Oh, Mitch!" She went to him then and they embraced as lovers long parted do. "I love you too, and I was so afraid you didn't care about me."

"I know . . . I know . . . and I'm sorry I've hurt you." He held her near, but didn't kiss her. He was savoring the joy of their reconciliation. "I'll never hurt you again," he vowed fiercely. As she nestled against him, he groaned. "I have waited so long for this."

"So have I," she admitted. She lifted her head then, her lips parted in soft invitation, and he bent to her, his mouth claiming hers, gently.

"Shall we go below?" Mitch asked huskily as he broke off the kiss, and she nodded in silent response. Keeping an arm about her slim waist, he led her across the deck and down the companionway to their stateroom.

Though the cabin was dark when they entered, they didn't bother to light a lamp, treasuring instead the quiet seclusion that the darkness offered. It was a time of sensual reawakening, of intimate renewal. Theirs would be a joining, not only of bodies but of hearts and minds as well.

Their clothes were shed with calm precision—Espri's first, with his assistance. Then Mitch disrobed while she stretched out on the bed to await him.

"I've fantasized about this often," he confided as he moved to join her on the wide softness of the bed.

"You have?"

"Um . . ." he murmured as he slid down beside her and kissed her tenderly. "Every night for the past six weeks."

She laughed softly. "I've been wanting you too." She reached up and wrapped her arms around him, drawing him down to her. "Let's never let anything come between us again," she urged.

"Madam," Mitch replied dryly, moving suggestively against her. "There's nothing between us now."

"I know," she purred.

The time for talk was over, for their mutual desires swept them away. As their mouths met time and again in wonder and passion, their hands explored and teased, tracing arousing patterns over bare, sensitive flesh. Limbs intertwined, feminine softness against masculine hardness, silken flesh against muscularity, they made love. Mitch could feel the taut crests of her breasts boring into his chest, and he moved lower to taste their succulent buds, in turn drawing each into his mouth and suckling gently.

Espri arched in heated abandon at the touch of his lips, and she held him tightly, experiencing rapturous feelings. "I love you," she breathed, caressing the width of his shoulders and moving her hips erotically beneath his welcome weight.

Mitch had wanted to cherish each second of their lovemaking, but his long-denied need for Espri was so strong that when she started to buck wildly beneath him, he lost all control. Grasping her hips firmly, he pinned her to the mattress and, spreading her thighs, he slid smoothly into the heart of her womanhood. He lay quietly atop her for an instant, relishing the hot tightness surrounding him and holding him a willing captive.

Before he began to move, Espri wriggled her hips in encouragement, wanting to know once again the joy of his driving possession. She was afire with desire for him, and her movements grew frenzied as she tried to entice him to take her.

"Please, Mitch . . . love me now," she begged, linking her legs over his lean hips and pressing eagerly against him.

He began to move then, thrusting powerfully into her and, groaning ecstatically, Espri held him tightly and met his every thrust. They mated feverishly, trying to wipe away in that one joining all the long months of distrust and loneliness. The end came explosively, rocking them with sensations so perfect and so breathtakingly beautiful that they clung together, fearful it had all been a dream.

Their hearts pounding, their breathing raspy, they lay clasped in each other's arms, enraptured with what had just passed between them. Mitch, well-versed in the art of love, knew that nothing he'd known before had surpassed this moment, and Espri, untutored though she was, knew that what they'd shared had been magnificent.

Shifting slightly to relieve Espri of his weight, Mitch kissed her devotedly. "My love, if we weren't already married, I would propose to you right now."

She smiled in the darkness. "And I would accept."

Totally fulfilled, they slept, rousing occasionally to reassure themselves that they were indeed together. Soft kisses were exchanged, along with whispered pledges, and as night passed into day, they both knew they'd forged a love that would withstand any strain. A love for all ages . . .

Dawn . . . that unwelcome light that puts an end to the night's intimate embrace. Stirred to wakefulness by its unwanted presence, Mitch lay quietly lest he disturb Espri, who was curled up at his side, sleeping soundly. He smiled in memory of the hours that had just passed. How wonderful it felt to hold her close, and how beautiful it was to have her love and her trust. He would do his best to see to it that nothing hurt her, ever again.

Mitch frowned as he thought of their future. It would not be easy for her to adapt to life in San Francisco, but he hoped to make it as easy as possible for her. He suspected that there might be some initial prejudice against her because of her Polynesian blood; however, he would make it known from the moment they set foot on California soil that any slight against his wife was a slight against him. Few were brave—or stupid—enough to cross Mitchell Williams.

He smiled again, but it was a smile of grim determination. With his social standing and his money, he would see to it that Espri was accepted.

"Mitch?" Her soft inquiry startled him back to the reality of the moment. "You look angry. Is something wrong?"

"No, love. Absolutely nothing is wrong. In fact, as far as I can tell, everything is perfect." He drew her near and kissed her. "Good morning."

Espri surrendered to his embrace more than willingly, but when their kiss ended, she was still curious about his mood. She had seen him frown. "If everything is as perfect as you say," she continued, slightly breathless from his ardent good-morning kiss, "why were you frowning?"

Knowing that she wouldn't be deterred, he decided to answer her truthfully. "I was thinking about home."

"San Francisco?"

He nodded. "I was wondering how you're going to enjoy living there. It's not like anything you've ever known."

"I know, but I'll be all right. I'll have you." She rested her head on his shoulder and ran a bold hand over the firm muscles of his chest.

"I'll do all I can to help you adjust."

"I know that, and with what Mildred's been teaching me, I don't think it will be all that hard. Now that I've learned all the intricacies of dress"—she gave him an impish smile—"I think the rest will just come naturally."

"I'm sure of it." He drew her near, caressing the velvet swell of her breast.

"Have you missed your home greatly?" She sighed, loving the way he was touching her.

"I've missed some aspects of the life I was leading," he confessed. "The shipping company I own was very successful, and I enjoyed the challenge of business dealings. And, I've missed Jon."

"Your brother?"

Mitch nodded thoughtfully. "We weren't on the best of terms before I was shanghaied, and I'm looking forward to making amends."

"You fought?"

"I wouldn't exactly call what happened a fight, but I do know he was furious with me."

"Why?"

"He wanted to get married, but I refused to give him my permission."

"Why did he need your permission?" Espri found the news perplexing.

"Jon's much younger than I am, and until he turned twenty-one I had complete control of his money."

"So you threatened not to give him any money if he married?" she deduced astutely.

"Something like that." Mitch grinned.

"Did it work?"

"I don't know. The last time I saw him he stalked out of my office in a fury."

"Why didn't you want him to marry? Did you think he was too young?"

"No, not really. I just didn't approve of his choice."

"Who was she?"

"Her name was Catherine Chamberlain, and I know for a fact that she was out to hook the richest man she could, as quickly as possible. She didn't love Jon."

"How can you be sure? If he's anything like you, I'm sure many women wanted him."

"Thank you for the compliment, but that's exactly my point." Mitch glanced down at her, his expression bemused. "Two months before she got involved with my brother, Catherine was after me."

"Oh." Espri was surprised. "I guess that's what Mildred meant when she told me that in your society things are not always as they seem."

"You're right." He sighed. "Catherine was in dire straits financially, and I guess her only way out was to marry money. I don't like gold diggers." He sounded unusually vicious.

"Gold diggers?"

Mitch explained. "Women who marry only for gain. I had a friend once named Andrew. He fell madly in love and had the misfortune to marry the woman who was the object of his affection. She played him false and, in the process, she destroyed him."

"How?"

"After she'd taken him for every penny she could get, she told him she was leaving him for another, richer man. Andrew killed himself, because he didn't want to face life without her."

"How terrible."

"It was," Mitch said soberly. "It was then that I vowed never to fall in love. I refused to give a woman that kind of power over me, and I made a special effort to avoid all females who were eyeing my bank account. That's why I never allowed myself to get too involved." He kissed her quickly. "You are the only woman I've ever felt I could trust completely."

"Thank you, darling. It means a lot to me that you chose to tell me these things." Espri's lips brushed his in a delicate caress. "I understand now why you fought so hard against what was between us."

He smiled in self-derision. "It was all a matter of self-defense, but I lost anyway."

"Lost?" she asked in mock outrage.

"Lost my heart," he declared.

"That's better," she purred as he pulled her near and began to kiss her passionately. "Much better . . ."

Chapter 24

San Francisco—Two months later

Jon descended from the carriage, and after ordering the driver to wait, he entered the main warehouse of Williams Shipping. Alan Harris, whose office was situated near the main entrance, saw Jon at once and hastened forward to greet him.

"Good morning, Jon."

"Alan," he replied. "Have you received any word on the *Aurora*?" The *Aurora,* a steamer noted for her punctuality, was the pride of the Williams line, but Jon was concerned about her for she was now two weeks overdue.

"No, there have been no sightings," Alan informed him. He, too, was anxiously awaiting the steamer's arrival, but for far more personal reasons.

Jon nodded in frustration. "Keep me informed of any developments."

"I will," Alan assured him, and he was greatly relieved when Jon left. Though there was no danger of discovery that day, he fervently wished that Roland would hurry with his plan to buy Williams out so there would be no need for secrecy.

Alan waited until Jon had gone before leaving the warehouse himself; then he headed straight to Roland's office, entering by the well-guarded back door.

Roland looked up as he entered, and he immediately sensed that something was amiss. "Alan? What's wrong?"

"Jon was at the warehouse again."

"So?" He quirked a brow at the other man's panic.

"He's worried about the *Aurora* and wants to know the moment it puts in."

"Well he should be," Roland remarked sarcastically. "That damned ship is over two weeks late, and my customers are growing restless. They want the new girls desperately. We should be able to get top dollar for them."

Alan's eyes brightened at that thought. "Good, but how do I keep Williams out of the way while we get the merchandise off the ship?"

"You worry too much, Alan. Captain Mallory is on my personal payroll, and I'm sure he'll keep our shipment under wraps."

Roland's nonchalant attitude did little to ease Alan's nervousness, but he knew better than to argue. "Perhaps you're right."

"That's better." Roland favored him with a confident grin.

"How are your dealings with Williams going? Have you made any progress in taking over the company?"

A grimace was his answer. "The man's a stubborn fool, and he may be writing his own death warrant if he dares to cross me. It would not pain me in the least to see him out of the way. Catherine would inherit everything."

"You deal well with Catherine?" Harris asked pointedly, his insinuation obvious.

Roland pinned him with an icy glare, for he was determined to keep his liaison a secret. "She would be far easier to manipulate than her husband."

"Oh, I see," Harris said humbly, realizing that he had unexpectedly incurred Stuart's wrath.

"Now, go on back to the warehouse, and when word comes that the *Aurora* has been sighted I want to be the first informed, not Williams."

"Yes, Roland." Alan retreated hastily from the man's anger.

He hurried down the back stairway and out into the alley where his carriage awaited him. As he was about to climb into his vehicle, he noticed another conveyance parked a short distance back, its driver sitting in readiness. There was something vaguely familiar about the man, and though he signaled for his own driver to leave, as soon as they had turned the corner, he ordered him to stop.

Jumping down from the carriage, he returned to the entrance of the alley and watched with avid interest as the other conveyance pulled up to Roland's door and discharged its passenger. He could not readily identify the woman who descended for she was dressed in a nondescript fashion and was wearing a veil, but when the carriage came forward, he knew. Catherine Williams, in disguise, had gone to see Roland!

Alan's mind was racing. Was this all part of Roland's plan to gain control of the company, or were they lovers? Either way, this knowledge gave him some leverage should his own safety ever be threatened. Pleased with his discovery, he returned to his carriage and headed back to the warehouse.

Espri stood at the rail of the *Providence* staring out in wonder at the city that would be her new home. A brisk breeze swept across the bay, and despite the long-sleeved gown she wore, she was chilled. Shivering slightly, she moved to stand a little closer to Mitch.

"Cold?" he asked, tearing his gaze away from his beloved San Francisco to smile down at her.

Espri nodded. "And nervous, too."

"Don't worry." Mitch took Espri's hand and squeezed it reassuringly. "Everything is going to work out just fine. In a little while we'll really be home."

"You're excited, aren't you?"

"Very," he admitted. "It's been almost a year since I was shanghaied. I just hope everything has gone well for Jon."

"Why wouldn't it?"

"He hadn't shown much interest in the business before I disappeared. I just hope all the responsibilities didn't over-whelm him."

"Don't worry. If he's anything like you, he's managed it well," she assured him, slipping her arm through his. Al-though the weeks since their reconciliation had been blissful, Espri had sensed a growing tension in Mitch as they'd neared port, and she was sure it was related to his coming reunion with his brother.

"Not too well." He chuckled. "I'd hate to return and find out I'd been so successfully replaced that I'm no longer needed."

"No one could ever replace you, Mitch." Espri's words were heavy with hidden meaning, and he drew her arm against his side.

"They'd better not," he growled for her ears only.

Knowing how hot the fires between them burned and how easily they were stoked to life, she purposely changed the subject. "How soon will we be going ashore?"

"Vixen!" he muttered, understanding her tactic. "I imag-ine it will be at least an hour before Captain Clark can lower a launch for us. Have you heard any differently, Tommy?" Mitch suddenly drew the younger man, who stood apart from them, into their conversation.

"No," Tommy replied.

"Will you be glad to get back home, Tommy?" Espri asked. He had been quiet and withdrawn for most of the trip, and she wondered if he would ever get over his separation from Tikiru.

Tommy sighed. "I know my parents have been worried. In fact, I'm sure by now they think I'm dead. It will be good to put their worries to rest."

"Would you like to come and spend the night with us before you start back?" Mitch offered.

"Thank you, but no. It's a three-day ride to my home, and the sooner I get started the better. I'll be leaving as quickly as possible."

"How are you going to travel?"

"The captain has loaned me enough money for transportation and lodging, so I'll have no problem." Tommy seemed happy, but Espri and Mitch both sensed the sadness deep within him.

"I'm sorry things didn't work out better for you," Mitch told him consolingly. "But at least you're back and you have your whole life ahead of you."

"I know," Tommy agreed. "It's just that without Tikiru the future looks bleak."

"Just remember that she did escape with her life," Mitch said.

"I know," Tommy responded. "If she had been killed, I wouldn't have wanted to go on at all."

Tommy fell silent then, remembering the trauma of those last few days on the island. He knew that Mitch and Espri were right, but he also knew that he would never love another woman the way he'd loved Tikiru. The remembrance of her supple body and sweet innocence were burned into his mind, and he was certain no other woman could touch him so deeply. *I love you, Tikiru*, he whispered to the wind, and his shattered heart hoped that she knew it.

"Since it's almost time for us to disembark, why don't you go say your good-byes to Mildred?" Mitch suggested to Espri.

"I'll go find her right now." Espri started off, then paused. "Will you be here?"

"Yes, I'll wait for you."

Espri hurried to the captain's cabin, eager for a last visit with her dear friend. She knocked softly. "Mildred?"

Mildred called out for her to enter. "Are you all ready to go ashore?" she asked, her eyes alight with curiosity.

"I think so." Espri smiled tremulously. "Mitch certainly is."

"I'll bet he's excited to be going home after so long at sea," Mildred observed.

"Yes. He's looking forward to seeing his brother again."

"You will let me know how you're doing on shore, won't you?"

"Of course!" Espri hugged her quickly. She valued Mildred's friendship and fully intended to remain as close to her as possible. "I want to thank you for all your help. Can you imagine what this would be like for me if I hadn't had your wise counsel and your help with my clothing?"

"I was more than glad to assist you." Mildred smiled a bit sadly. "To tell the truth, I'm going to miss you when we set to sea again."

"Maybe I should go with you," Espri teased.

"No way. You stay right here with that husband of yours. He needs you just as much as you need him."

"I know. But I'd never have discovered that if you hadn't urged me to confess my love to him. Why, I'd probably be making plans to return to Malika right now." That thought sent an unwelcome chill down her spine.

"Well, you aren't, and I have the feeling that you and Mitch are going to have a long, happy life together right here."

"I hope you're right," Espri fervently declared. Then they embraced once more.

"You'll be going ashore soon, won't you?"

"As soon as the captain can get a boat away."

"Are your things all packed? Is there anything I can do to help you?"

"No. I got everything done last night. All we have to do now is wait."

"Let's wait up on deck, then. There's a lot to see, and you'll be ready to go when Mitch is."

"A good idea."

"I have a present for you." Mildred held out a tissue-wrapped package.

"A present? Oh, thank you. What is it?" Espri asked excitedly.

"Open it and see." Mildred chuckled and then watched happily as the younger woman unwrapped the shawl. "It's a shawl and you wear it . . . so." She put it about Espri's shoulders. "There."

"Thank you. It was chilly out on deck."

"This will help," her friend told her.

Then they started up on deck. Their last minutes together flew by in easy companionship, and before she knew it, Espri was hugging Mildred in final farewell

"I'll send you news as often as I can," Espri promised.

Mitch, who was watching their affectionate parting, added comfortingly, "I've invited the captain and Mildred to join us at the house for dinner, two nights from now."

"You have? Oh, thank you, Mitch." Grateful for his thoughtfulness, Espri turned back to Mildred and pressed her hand. "I'll see you then."

"I'll be looking forward to it."

After words of parting to Tommy and the captain, they were ready to descend. With Mitch's help, Espri managed to descend the ladder to the skiff and then sat nervously by his side as two seamen rowed them to shore. Mitch bade her to wait with the boat until he'd procured a carriage for them.

When he returned with an equipage, he handed her into it, and after giving his address to the driver, he climbed beside her. When the carriage started up with a lurch, Espri gasped and clutched at Mitch's arm for support as she almost lost her seat.

He laughed softly. "That was a smooth start for one of these hired conveyances. Wait until you've ridden in the rough ones."

"They get worse?" Her eyes were wide with a mixture of astonishment and excitement.

"Definitely," he confirmed. "But, hopefully, you'll never have to worry about it."

"I won't?"

"No, we have our own carriages and horses."

"Are you very rich, Mitch?"

He grinned at her. "I was when I last departed this fair city, and I hope to find that we still are."

"I don't care about the money. It just seems so extravagant to travel this way."

"Believe me, traveling by carriage is one of the necessary evils of living in 'civilized' cities. There are many places in San Francisco where it's not safe to walk."

"Oh." Espri turned to look out the window. She stared with interest at the construction underway and at the people who crowded the streets. "It's so busy here."

"That it is, sweet. It's a boomtown that's been booming since '49," he told her.

"What happened then?"

"Gold was discovered nearby, and San Francisco's been growing ever since."

She nodded. "Is it far to your home?"

"'Our' home," he corrected good-naturedly. Then he added, "We should be there shortly."

"Do you think your brother will like me?" she blurted out, suddenly insecure about meeting Jon for the first time.

Mitch smiled understandingly. "I think he'll love you, darling."

She smiled weakly at his reassurance as the carriage drew to a halt.

"Here we are," Mitch told her anxiously. "Come on." Throwing open the door, he climbed down and then turned back to help her descend.

Cautiously, Espri took his hand, and holding her skirts, she stepped carefully from the carriage. Only when she had safely, and gracefully, alighted did she allow herself a glance at the imposing, three-story brick structure she would now be calling home.

"Mitch! It's so big!" She regarded the twenty-room mansion with nothing less than awe.

"Let's go in," he urged. Then he addressed the driver. "Bring the trunk."

Mitch led her up the sweeping front stairway and, without pause, opened the front door and went in. He directed the driver to place their trunk inside the foyer and then paid him with the money the Clarks had lent him.

Mabel, the downstairs maid who had been with the Williams family for years, heard the commotion in the front hall and hurried forth, thinking it was the mistress returning early. She frowned when she saw a tall man standing there with an unidentified woman, and she was about to protest the intrusion when Mitch turned. "Oh my God!" she cried, and as she swayed dizzily, Mitch hurried to support her.

"Calm down, Mabel. It's just me. I've come home."

"But Mr. Mitchell, you're supposed to be dead."

He chuckled as he steadied her. "I assure you, Mabel, that I am quite alive."

She looked up at him then, and as she grew more composed, she smiled broadly. "Yes, sir. Yes, you are. But how? . . ."

"I was shanghaied, Mabel, not murdered."

"Thank heavens! But poor Mr. Jonathan thinks you were killed."

Mitch frowned. He wondered why Jon would have come to that conclusion, but he quickly dismissed the thought, adding lightly, "Well, we'll just have to convince him that I wasn't."

"Yes, sir." Mabel beamed and then turned to look at Espri for the first time.

"Mabel, this is my wife, Espri. Espri, I'd like you to meet Mabel. She's been with the family for longer than I can remember." He held his arm out to Espri and she went eagerly to his side.

She greeted the short, plump, elderly maid warmly.

"Your wife? My, my, there certainly have been changes here." Mabel was stunned by the news that he'd married. She well knew that Mitch had taken great care to avoid matrimony. "It's a pleasure to meet you, Mrs. Williams."

"I'd appreciate it if you'd call me Espri, Mabel."

"Yes, ma'am," the maid agreed, finding the young woman's dark, exotic beauty quite breathtaking even in her plain day-gown. "I'd like that."

"Is Jon here?" Mitch interrupted their pleasantries.

"No, sir. He's at the office."

At that news, he turned to Espri. "I think I'll go down to the office to see Jon. You can come with me, or you can stay here with Mabel and get settled in."

"I think I'll stay here," she replied.

"I'm sure I won't be long." He kissed her tenderly before speaking to the maid. "Mabel, my wife needs to be outfitted completely, so see if you can arrange appointments for her with the dressmakers. The sooner, the better."

"Yes, sir. I'll send word out to the carriage house for a buggy to be brought around for you," Mabel told him.

"Fine. I'll show Espri around while you're gone."

When Mabel had disappeared into the back of the house,

Mitch guided Espri through the maze of rooms on the first floor. The parlor . . . the ballroom . . . the study . . . the music room . . . Her head was spinning as she tried to take in the splendor of the house. The furnishings, Queen Anne in style, were exquisitely worked in inlaid walnut. Heavy velvet draperies adorned the massive floor-to-ceiling windows, and the ornate patterns of the wallpaper bespoke subdued elegance.

"Do you like it?" he asked, grinning, when they'd finished their whirlwind tour.

Espri's smile was bemused as she answered. "I think so."

Mitch laughed heartily at her answer and hugged her close. "I know it's different for you, but I think you'll get used to it."

"I'll just have to force myself," she teased, knowing that he wanted her to like his home.

Mitch was about to say more when Mabel returned. "The buggy is being brought around, Mr. Mitchell."

"Thanks, Mabel. I just showed Espri around the downstairs, but I'll leave the upstairs to you."

"I'd be delighted to show her around." The older servant was pleased at the chance to get to know his wife. Things hadn't been the same in the Williams household since he'd been declared dead and Mr. Jonathan had married Miss Catherine. Mabel hoped with all her heart that Mr. Mitchell's return would signal a change for the better. "Is there any particular bedroom you'd prefer to occupy?"

"It doesn't matter. My old suite of rooms will be fine," Mitchell directed.

"Fine." Mabel was relieved that he hadn't insisted on the master suite for she was certain that Miss Catherine would not have given up her sumptuously appointed quarters without a fight. She wondered if she should tell him of his brother's marriage, but decided he should hear of that from Mr. Jonathan.

At the sound of the carriage drawing up at the front of the house, Mitch gave Espri a quick kiss and then started out the door. "I'll be back," he declared. Then he was gone to the long-awaited reunion with his brother.

The ride to the main office of Williams Shipping seemed to take forever, and Mitch jumped eagerly to the ground when the carriage finally pulled up in front of the building. Without hesitating, he strode into the office. Caleb, the clerk who usually sat out front, was away from his desk, so Mitch pushed the swinging half gate open and admitted himself.

"Jon?" he called out.

Jon was at his desk reviewing the latest manifests when he heard someone call his name. The person summoning him sounded so much like his brother that Jon stiffened instinctively, but he hurriedly dismissed that thought for Mitch had been dead for almost a year. Realizing that Caleb had left the office on an errand, he pushed away from his desk and started to go to the front office. Just as he stepped around the desk, the door to his office opened and Mitch walked in.

"Mitch?" Jon's gaze locked with his brother's, stark disbelief in his eyes. "Dear God! Mitch! You're alive!" He all but flew across the room to embrace him.

"Very much so." Mitch laughed as they hugged each other.

"What the hell happened to you? Where have you been? I thought you were dead."

"That's what Mabel told me, but I was shanghaied, not murdered."

"Shanghaied?" Jon was astounded. In the beginning, when Mitch had first disappeared he'd suspected shanghaiing, but when the body had been found . . .

"Yes, I was taken aboard the *Seastorm*."

"But how did they get you? You weren't down on the coast, were you?"

"No, I'd just left Lucinda's. The crimps were waiting for me in my carriage," he explained. "By the time I regained consciousness, we had already put to sea."

"So you've been at sea this entire year?"

"No," Mitch went on. "The *Seastorm* was lost during a tropical storm, and I was washed up on the island of Malika in the South Pacific."

Jon shook his head, perplexed. "Thank heaven for that."

Mitch nodded. "I was very lucky. Only two of us survived."

"I'm just glad you did." Jon's words were heartfelt, and the brothers embraced again. "I think this calls for a celebration drink; how about you?" he asked as they moved apart. "Sit down."

Jon took a bottle of bourbon and two tumblers from the bottom drawer while Mitch settled himself in the chair in front of the desk. Pouring them each a liberal amount, he handed Mitch one glass and then raised his in a toast. "Here's to your return."

As they touched glasses, their eyes met in mutual love and respect; then they drank the amber liquid down in one long swallow. Jon quickly refilled their tumblers and, leaving the bottle out, sat down behind his desk.

"This has got to be a miracle." He grinned. "It's so good to see you. God, when I thought you'd been killed . . . Jon shook his head as he remembered his despair.

"Why did you think that?" Mitch frowned.

"The police contacted me several days after you'd disappeared. They had pulled a body from the bay and they wanted me to try to make an identification."

"That's not an unusual occurrence. Why did they think it was me?"

"The clothing on the body was yours, Mitch," Jon told him.

"My clothes . . ." Mitch was puzzled. He could recall coming to on the ship and finding that he was wearing rough sailor's garb, but he had no recollection of what had happened to his own things. At the time, he had assumed that the crimps had stolen them. "What about the body?"

"It had been in the water for some time and was badly decomposed. The height was about right, and the hair color." He paled as he remembered the gruesome ordeal. "Whoever it was, was killed by a blow to the head."

"What about Nelson, my driver?"

"He disappeared," Jon explained. "At the time, we thought he might have been the one responsible, but we never found a trace of him."

"Nelson and I were about the same height," Mitch suggested. "Could the body have been his?"

Jon considered the possibility for a moment. "Yes, but why would he have been wearing your clothing?"

Their eyes met in shared confusion. "I don't know." Mitch shrugged. "Nelson had been with us for years, and even if he'd arranged my shanghaiing, he certainly wouldn't have bothered to steal my clothes."

Jon nodded, disturbed by these new revelations. What did it all mean? "It sounds like someone wanted me to think you were dead."

"But if somebody wanted me dead, why didn't he just kill me?" Mitch, too, found the situation bizarre.

"I don't know," Jon replied. "Maybe we're making too much of this. Maybe Nelson did set you up, and just for the hell of it, he did take your things. Probably somebody rolled him on the coast and that was that." But even as he tried to reason it out, Mitch's question hung between them, unanswered.

"I am eager to know how everything is here," Mitch declared, realizing they could not resolve his question.

"The business is thriving. I've been importing merchandise for Roland Stuart and profits are better than ever," Jon informed him, relieved to be discussing something more pleasant.

Mitch nodded approvingly. "I'm proud of you." He paused. "Jon?"

"Yes?"

"I'm sorry about the way we parted that last day. It bothered me that we didn't have a chance to set things straight between us."

"I felt the same way, Mitch." He paused to draw a deep breath before giving him the news. "I want you to know that I understood your position, but . . ."

"But?"

"Catherine and I were married almost nine months ago. She's made me a very happy man, Mitch," Jon stated. "She stood by me through the entire ordeal of your death."

Mitch's expression didn't change, but he did not like the news. Still, he found Jon's new maturity impressive, and he hoped that Jon had made the right decision. "I'm glad she's made you a good wife. As long as you're happy, you have my blessing."

Relieved, Jon smiled. "Thank you. That means a lot to me."

"I may as well tell you my news," Mitch began cryptically.

"What?"

"I've also married."

Jon was stunned, and it was a moment before a slow grin spread across his handsome features. "You? Married?" He couldn't stop the chuckle. "She must be very special."

"That she is," Mitch answered warmly, his deep affection for his wife reflected in his tone. "Her name is Espri, and I met her on Malika."

"Where is she?" Knowing of Mitch's aversion to matrimony, Jon was instantly curious to meet the woman who'd won Mitch.

"At the house with Mabel," he answered. "I stopped there first after we arrived in port, hoping to catch you at home."

"I can't leave here until Caleb returns, but as soon as he does, I want to go meet your wife." Jon chuckled again as he refilled their glasses, and once more he lifted his tumbler in toast. "To wedded bliss; may we both share equally in its joy."

Chapter 25

As Mabel opened the drapes, sunlight poured into the room. "Mr. Jon never did change these rooms." She gestured toward the heavy masculine furniture that graced the bedroom of Mitch's suite. "Even though Miss Catherine didn't like the furniture in here and was after him constantly for the first few months after they'd married to let her redecorate."

"Jon is married?" Espri glanced at her questioningly, remembering what Mitch had told her about Catherine.

"I suppose I should have mentioned it earlier, but I thought Mr. Jonathan would want to tell you himself," she explained. "He married Miss Catherine several months after Mr. Mitchell was declared dead."

"Oh." Espri paused. "Mabel, you were so shocked when you saw my husband . . . why were you so certain that he was dead?"

"Because Mr. Jonathan identified a body pulled from the bay as Mr. Mitchell. Oh, that was a terrible morning." Mabel sighed, remembering how devastated Jonathan had been after returning from the morgue. "Up until that day, he'd held out hope that Mitch had only been shanghaied, not that that wouldn't have been awful, mind you, but at least there would have been hope."

"But how could he have identified someone as Mitch, when it wasn't him?" Espri was confused.

"It was nigh impossible from his looks," Mabel went on. "The man had been in the water for days. Mr. Jonathan recognized the clothing on the body. We still have it here. Jon brought it home with him. I guess whoever it was who attacked him stole all his money and clothes."

Espri shivered as she imagined that night and Mitch's sense of helpless frustration when he awoke aboard a ship headed for the South Pacific. No wonder he'd wanted to return home so badly. "Mitch certainly has been through a lot during the past year," she said. She was about to say more when a servant boy entered with the trunk containing their belongings.

"Put the trunk here," Mabel directed. "Miss Espri, this is Michael. His mother is our cook, and he helps out about the house. Michael, this is Mr. Mitchell's wife, Miss Espri."

The youth looked up at her, his eyes widening as he took in her dark beauty. He had always thought Miss Catherine pretty, but this lady was much lovelier. "Nice to meet you, ma'am," he stammered self-consciously.

"It's nice to meet you too, Michael. Thank you for bringing up our trunk." She smiled at him warmly.

"Yes, ma'am." He left quickly, anxious to tell all the servants waiting in the kitchen what Mr. Mitchell's wife was like. They were already agog at the news that he'd returned home, and the fact that he was now married, only made things more interesting. They were eagerly anticipating Miss Catherine's reaction upon her return from her outing.

"He's a nice boy." Espri turned back to Mabel.

"Yes, he is. I think you'll approve of the staff here," she remarked.

"I'm sure I will," Espri assured her. She was already impressed with the Williams household.

As Mabel busied herself unpacking the trunk, curiosity

got the better of her. "If you don't mind my asking, Miss Espri, how in the world did you meet Mr. Mitchell?"

"The ship he was on sank during a storm and Mitch was washed up on our island."

"He's doubly lucky to be alive, then, and we're certainly glad to have him back."

"I know he's glad to be back," Espri confided as she went to look out the window. "He missed his home very much."

They fell into a companionable silence then, as Mabel continued to unpack the trunk.

"This is a lovely gown," Mabel commented as she unfolded Espri's rose silk gown.

"Thank you. Mrs. Clark, the captain's wife, and I made it during the voyage."

"You did?" Impressed by the design and workmanship, Mabel looked up at Espri in surprise, her respect for Mitchell's wife growing. "You did a wonderful job."

Espri was pleased by the compliment, for despite Mildred's assurances that she was talented with a needle and thread, she had had her doubts. She smiled. "Thank you, Mabel. I have to admit I was worried about how it would turn out. I'd never even seen dresses like that before we boarded the ship."

Mabel blinked, stunned. "If you didn't wear dresses, what did you wear?"

"On Malika, we wear sarongs. Here, I'll show you." Espri found a sarong at the bottom of the trunk and she unfolded it, holding it up for Mabel's inspection.

"That's all you wore?" The woman looked at her questioningly.

Espri nodded. "It's very hot on Malika, and these are both serviceable and practical."

The maid's eyes were twinkling as she answered. "I know now why Mr. Mitchell fell in love with you. As lovely as you

are in regular clothes, I can imagine how you looked in that."
Mabel eyed the skimpy garment warily. "How do you keep
it up?"

"You wrap it securely about you and tie it. It's very simple.
I'll wear it for you one day and show you."

"I'd like that." The maid was eager to know more about
this delightful woman who'd married into the family. "I'm
sure there will be a big dinner tonight. Would you like me to
have your rose gown pressed so you can wear it?"

"Yes. That would be wonderful."

"I'll also have Sally come up and style your hair for you.
Would you like to bathe?"

"Yes, I would."

"The bathroom is right through here." Mabel directed her
to a smaller room off the side of the bedroom.

Espri stared about in amazement.

"It's wonderful, isn't it?" the maid went on. "Mr. Mitchell
and Mr. Jonathan had the best of everything installed. We
have hot and cold running water . . . the water closet, of
course . . . and a shower." She proudly pointed out the tubing
that rose above the large tub.

"A shower?"

"Here, I'll show you." Deftly, Mabel turned the knobs and
water sprinkled down from the spout above.

Espri laughed happily as Mabel turned the water off.
"That's amazing. I can't wait to try it."

"Why don't you go ahead now? I'm sure it will be at least
another half an hour before Mr. Mitchell returns from his trip
to the office. That should give you plenty of time."

"I think I will," Espri agreed.

"Shall I send one of the girls to help you?"

"No, there's no need."

"I'll be back in just a minute with fresh linens for you,
then, and soap."

"Thank you, Mabel."

"You're more than welcome, Miss Espri," the maid declared as she left the room to get the necessary sundries. Within minutes she was back with a stack of soft, fluffy towels, and a bar of scented soap. "Here you are. I'll bring your gown back as soon as it's been pressed." She picked up the rose silk creation. "If you decide you do need me, just pull that cord behind the bedstead." Mabel pointed out the silken bellpull that would summon her from the kitchen area downstairs.

"I will," Espri assured her, marveling at all the conveniences of her new home. Servants . . . indoor plumbing with hot and cold water . . . gaslights . . . glass in the windows and locks on the doors . . . so many rooms and so much furniture . . . on Malika, you were considered rich if you had a hut with a sturdy roof and a comfortable pandanus mat on which to sleep. She was surprised that Mitch had adapted so well to life on the island, for she was certain that he must have found life there quite primitive.

Smiling at the thought of her husband, she quickly stripped off her clothes and hurried into the bathroom, eager to use the shower. Turning on the water, she watched in delight as the water poured forth. Though the flow was not as stimulating as the waterfall on Malika, it was a wonderful change from her limited baths aboard the *Providence*. Relishing the feel of the warm, silken waters washing over her, Espri stood, enraptured, beneath the shower, her head thrown back, her body arched in sensual enjoyment. It was quite awhile before she roused enough to wash, and then she did so quickly, not wanting to linger too long in the bath for fear of not being ready when Mitch returned. When she'd finished washing her hair, she turned off the water and stepped from the tub, wrapping herself in one of the towels after drying off. Returning to the bedroom, she combed the snarls from her wet hair and was just about to dress when the door opened.

"Espri? Jon's downstairs and—" Mitch broke off in mid-sentence as he caught sight of his wife standing in the middle of the bedroom wearing only a towel. "God, you are so beautiful." Coming into the room, he closed the door behind him and strode purposefully toward her.

Espri smiled as he drew near, and she needed no invitation to go into his arms. "I found your bathing shower to be much like the waterfall at home," she murmured as he bent to kiss her, his mouth slanting possessively across hers.

Mitch's eyes were alight when he broke off the passionate embrace. "You did?"

She nodded, her lips lifting in a suggestive invitation. "You don't suppose . . ."

A flame of excitement flared to life deep within him at the remembrance of making love to her beneath the crystalline cascade on Malika. "Later," he growled, definitely intrigued by the idea but knowing that his brother awaited them downstairs. "Jon's waiting," he told her, capturing her soft, parted lips for one last kiss before releasing her.

Espri's eyes widened nervously at the news. "He's here?"

Mitch nodded. "He's downstairs waiting to meet you, my love."

"Oh." She drew a deep breath.

"There's nothing to be worried about."

"I'll only be a minute." She spurred herself to action, pulling on the various undergarments that Mildred had assured her were necessary to wear beneath her gowns.

"Do you need my help?" Mitch watched in fascination as Espri pulled on her stockings and fastened the garters.

"No, I'll be fine." She donned the only other gown she owned, a simple, long-sleeved shirtwaist of deep blue cotton, then tied back her still-damp hair with a single length of ribbon. Meeting her husband's eyes, she told him, "I think I'm ready."

"You look wonderful," he assured her, and with a guiding hand at her waist, he led her from the room.

Jon was sitting in the parlor when he heard Mitch and Espri on the stairs, and he eagerly went forth to meet them. Having been told of Espri's mixed parentage and of her life on Malika, Jon wasn't sure what to expect when he stepped into the main hall. He knew the woman had to be beautiful, for he was certain that Mitch would settle for nothing less than perfection in the woman he took to wife, but he was not prepared for the vision she made as she descended the steps at Mitch's side. The deep rich color of her gown, plain though it was in style, enhanced her dark loveliness and he stood at the foot of the staircase, gazing up at her in silent admiration. Her long, dark hair was parted down the middle and tied back from her face in a sleek, severe style that set off the classic beauty of her features, and her dark eyes met his in open regard, displaying none of the coy artfulness that women of society were so prone to employ.

"Hello, Jon." Espri spoke first, hating the awkwardness of the moment.

Her accent bedazzled him even more, and he broke into a wide grin as he greeted her in his best French. *"Enchanté, madame."*

Espri smiled. She had taken an immediate liking to this handsome young man who so closely resembled her husband. "It's nice to meet you. I've heard many wonderful things about you."

"And I, you," he replied honestly. "It's a pleasure to welcome you to the family. You are a lovely addition to our ranks."

She flushed with pleasure at his praise. "Thank you."

"Why don't we go sit down?" Mitch suggested. "Do you know when Catherine will return?"

"I would think soon. According to Mabel she's been gone for several hours," Jon remarked as he led the way to the parlor. "I'm sure she'll be thrilled to find that you're alive."

* * *

Catherine stood in Roland's office, adjusting the bodice of her fashionable gown, and she frowned when she discovered that one button was nearly falling off. "Really, darling, we must be more careful with my dresses. What would my husband think if he ever found that buttons had been torn off the bodices?"

Roland regarded her hungrily from where he sat behind his desk. "I'm sorry, love, but it had been so long." He let his gaze roam over her, taking in her passion-flushed cheeks and the wild yet attractive disarray of her hair. "You are always so tempting that it's hard for me to keep my hands off of you."

Catherine's eyes were smoldering with desire as she looked up at him. "I know we can never be married, but isn't there some way we can spend more time together?"

Roland's expression hardened at her suggestion. "You know that's not possible, Cat. We've pushed our luck to the limit as it is. What other husband would be as trusting as young Jonathan?" There was derision in Roland's voice as he thought of all the times he'd bedded Catherine since her marriage to Jon.

"You're right, I suppose, but that doesn't make it easier to suffer through his lovemaking when I'm dreaming of you."

"Just don't call out my name in your passion." Roland leered as he imagined Jon possessing her.

"You needn't worry about that. I rarely feel any desire when I'm in his arms," Catherine replied with distaste. "I 'perform' my wifely duties admirably."

"What a pity that Jon doesn't know what he's missing." Roland chuckled as he stood up and approached her, his eyes fixed on the swell of her breasts against the material of her gown. "I know," he rasped, pulling her close and holding her pinned against him.

"Roland . . . no . . . I've really got to get back. I've been gone for hours," she protested as he thrust his hips against her, letting her feel his hard readiness.

"Are you sure, Cat? It may be days before we can be together again. I don't know if I can wait that long. Can you?" He kissed her deeply as his hand sought the buttons she'd just fastened. Deftly, he opened her bodice and slipped a hand within to fondle the soft fullness of her breast.

Catherine knew she should return home, but the urgency of her lover's caresses wiped all rational thought from her mind. When he bent to kiss her breasts, she swayed weakly against him, and he lifted her in his arms and carried her back to the sofa they'd so recently vacated. Roland didn't bother to remove their clothes this time; he merely unbuttoned his pants and, after brushing aside her skirts, entered her. He relished taking her this way, for it made him feel as if he had some influence over Williams. Jon had refused to sell him the shipping company, but he did have complete control over the younger man's wife.

Catherine, on fire with desire for him, was totally unaware of Roland's thoughts. She only knew that she loved him and wanted him and she met his every movement, avidly. They moved together in a rising crescendo of passion until their excitement burst over them in a shower of throbbing pleasure that left them both sated as it passed.

It was almost an hour later when Catherine's carriage pulled up in front of her home. Mounting the front steps regally, she swept into the house and was about to order Michael to bring in the purchases she'd made that day when she saw Jon emerge from the parlor.

"Catherine . . . darling . . . I'm so glad you've finally returned. I have a surprise," he called, gesturing for her to join them.

"Jon." She recovered nicely from the unpleasant surprise of finding him home early in the day. "Your being home is a surprise in itself. To what do I owe this honor?" She went to him and kissed him dutifully. "Do we have . . ." Her breath caught in her throat as she stared in horrified amazement at Mitch, who had risen to come greet her. "Mitch? Oh my God." She swayed visibly. "I thought . . . we thought you were dead."

"No. I was shanghaied. It's taken me this long just to get back home," he told her.

"Thank heavens, you're all right," she lied, cursing his return with all her being. She looked up at her husband with a worshipful gaze, even though doing so irritated her. "Jon was so upset when he thought you'd been killed. It's a miracle that you've come home to us."

"And I've brought along a wife," Mitch informed her, his tone warm and caressing as he introduced Espri to Catherine. "Catherine, this is Espri, my wife."

"You married?" Astounded, Cat turned her attention to the woman she hadn't noticed before. Eyeing Espri with carefully disguised calculation, she studied the perfection of her beauty and decided immediately that she didn't like her.

"Yes. Espri and I met when I was shipwrecked, and I knew I couldn't leave her behind when I left Malika."

"Malika?" Catherine was still numb from the shock of his return.

"It's a small tropical island in the South Pacific," Espri offered, hoping to be friends with this woman with whom she'd be living.

"Oh. So you're Polynesian?" Catherine asked pointedly.

Aware of her implication, Mitch answered for Espri. "Yes. Her mother was an island princess and her father is French."

"How fascinating." Though she sounded interested, Catherine was thinking that this woman was little better than the Chinese women Roland was importing for sale to the cribs. How crude of Mitch to marry someone who probably wouldn't be accepted in the finer strata of San Francisco society. Cat hoped that her own position as a social leader wouldn't be jeopardized by this "native" newcomer. "So, tell me," she asked with what seemed like genuine interest, "how did you two come to meet? We really must have a party to welcome Mitch home and to introduce you to everyone."

Despite the façade she maintained, Catherine's thoughts were in a whirl. Somehow, she had to let Roland know that Mitch had returned. How could this have happened? Roland had assured her that Mitch had been taken care of. Jon had identified the body. How had he survived? Keeping an outwardly calm demeanor, she carried on a polite conversation, all the while wondering what she would do if Mitch ever found out that Roland had arranged his "shanghaiing" just so she could marry Jon . . .

In disbelief, Roland reread Catherine's brief note. Surely, she couldn't be serious. Mitch Williams was alive and well? Furious, he strode to the door and called for Bill and Joe to come into his office. The men were totally unprepared for the news that greeted them as soon as the office door had been closed.

"I want to know the truth about what happened to Mitch Williams, and I want to know now," he demanded, his tone deadly.

"I don't understand, boss," Bill lied.

"Mitch Williams is back among the living," Roland snarled, turning a fierce, life-threatening gaze on them both. "Now, what happened?"

"It was Bill's idea, Mr. Stuart!" Joe hastened to turn on his accomplice. "He thought we could make extra money by selling Williams to a crimp."

"I see." Stuart's tone was icy. "And?"

"And, since we'd accidentally killed the driver, we just put Williams's clothes on him and threw him in the bay," Joe hurried to explain.

"If he ever finds out who was behind his shanghaiing, you are both dead men. Do you understand me?"

"Yes, sir." Both men were shaken.

"Good. You're just lucky that his disappearance for the past year accomplished the same thing as his death. Now, get out of my sight," Stuart ordered coldly.

"Yes, sir!"

Roland sat back down at his desk, deep in thought. So far, so good. He was grateful that Catherine had sent him the note to warn him of Mitch's return, but he wondered just how safe he really was. Having been unable to convince Jon to sell him any part of Williams Shipping, his fortune was still in the hands of others, and now, with Mitch back in town, it was going to be harder than ever to keep his illegal cargo a secret. Ordering his carriage brought around, Roland knew he had to meet with Alan right away, in order to devise a new and better way to smuggle the girls ashore without being detected.

Clad in the prim nightgown Mildred had given her, Espri nestled close to Mitch as they shared his bed for the first time.

"Happy?" Mitch asked, as he pressed a soft kiss to her brow.

"As long as I'm with you . . . yes," she replied, sighing contentedly.

They had passed the evening in comfortable companionship with Jon and Catherine, enjoying a sumptuous dinner and making plans for the days to come. Catherine was already excited about hosting a "welcome home" celebration for Mitch, and she promised to have a full guest list ready for his approval the next day. Espri already had an appointment the following morning with the best dressmaker in San Francisco. Although Catherine had agreed to accompany her, at

Jon's prodding, Mitch had insisted on going along to help his wife select a complete wardrobe.

"I'm looking forward to our trip to the couturiere," Mitch told her as he drew her above him. "I shall take great pleasure in seeing you dressed properly." There was a hint of a smile in his tone as he regarded her unattractive nightgown critically. "Or should I say, undressed properly?"

"Are you saying you don't approve of my attire?" she teased as his hands worked feverishly to free her from the cotton garment.

"Approval has nothing to do with it . . . I hate the damn thing!" he replied almost vehemently as he struggled to help her slip it off. "That's better," Mitch finally declared as she tossed the plain gown aside and came to lie against him, nude.

"I think so, too," she murmured seductively.

Their world dissolved into erotic bliss, then, as they blended together; each seeking to please the other in the most intimate fashions. Espri needed his closeness this night, and she reveled in the magic he worked on her senses. His sensual caresses had her writhing beneath him, and as his lips trailed paths of fire across her silken flesh, she cried out to him in ecstasy, begging him to take her quickly so they could share the pinnacle of joy. Mitch came to her then, fitting himself to her and savoring the soft, hot confines of her aroused body. Love's need swept them along to its peak, and they shuddered as passion pulsed through them. Later, secure in their love, they fell asleep in each other's arms, unaware of the terror and treachery that would threaten their happiness in the days to come.

Chapter 26

"Good morning, Madame Vigney." Catherine led the way into the seamstress's shop the following day.

"Mrs. Williams, it's good to see you. What can I do for you today?" Felice Vigney took pride in the fact that Catherine Williams dealt exclusively with her, and she always took great care to satisfy the young woman's meticulous tastes, for it was well known that she was a trendsetter among the elite. The couturiere's efforts had been profitably rewarded. During the past year many of society's finest had begun to frequent her shop in the hope of achieving the pinnacle of fashion. "I was surprised to find that you needed another appointment so soon after our last meeting . . ." Felice let the sentence dangle when she saw a gentleman and another young woman follow Catherine into the shop.

"The appointment wasn't for me, Felice, but for my new sister-in-law." Catherine played the gracious matron to the hilt as she made the necessary introductions. "Felice Vigney, this is Espri Williams and my brother-in-law, Mitch."

"Mitch?" The seamstress glanced up at him in amazement. She was well aware of the town gossip, and she remembered distinctly that he'd been declared dead some time ago. "Weren't you supposed to be dead?"

Mitch grinned, knowing that this was the reaction he would be getting from everyone he met for the next several days. "Yes, madame, but it was only an unpleasant rumor that I hope will soon be put to rest."

"I am pleased to find that you are in excellent health." Felice's heart fluttered as he graced her with a charming smile. She had always thought Jonathan Williams attractive, but his brother was even more so.

"Thank you, Madame Vigney. We are here today because my wife is in need of your services. Espri will need a complete wardrobe as quickly as possible," he stated, as he gazed down at his wife, adoringly.

"A complete wardrobe?" Madame Vigney was taken aback. Never before had she received such a lucrative order.

Mitch nodded. "Catherine has assured us that you are the best in all of San Francisco."

"I strive to find the perfect style for each of my customers. Everyone has appealing features, and I try to accent and enhance those qualities," she replied with dignity. "Come, Mrs. Williams. Let me take a good look at you."

Espri had been gazing about the shop with interest, taking in the bolts of colorful fabrics and the various dress forms and sketches that were placed strategically about. At Felice's urging, she came forward to stand before a full-length mirror near the back. The couturiere studied her with a critical eye, and when the woman didn't speak for several minutes, Espri began to grow self-conscious.

"Is something wrong, Madame Vigney?" Espri finally asked, and Felice blinked in surprise when she heard her accent.

"*Vous êtes Française?*" she queried excitedly.

"*Mon père est Français,*" Espri offered.

"*C'est magnifique!*" Felice laughed delightedly as she turned to Mitch and Catherine. "This is wonderful! I am going to create the most fabulous wardrobe for Mrs. Williams.

Her body is perfect and her coloring . . ." She rolled her eyes in appreciation. "Come, I want to show you all the latest sketchings I have and my newest issues of *Godey's* and *Demorest's*."

Ushering them into one of the commodious sitting rooms, she left them to seat themselves on a large, overstuffed sofa while she went to get the pictures.

Catherine seated herself gingerly, concealing her irritation with admirable restraint. *C'est magnifique,* indeed. She was seething. No one was going to outshine her when it came to stylish dressing—no one!

"What do you have in mind, madame?" Mitch asked when the seamstress returned. He was unaware of Catherine's vindictive nature.

"She is tall and slender, so there is much we can do," Felice began as she started flipping through the magazines searching for styles that would best suit Espri's dark beauty. "Her best features . . ." She pursed her lips as she glanced up to study her new client once more. "Pah! All her features are lovely! Madame Williams, you have no flaws that need to be disguised."

Espri flushed under the woman's admiring praise. "Thank you."

"I am not here to pay you compliments, madame, merely to state the truth," Felice insisted. "It is my job to create gowns that will emphasize your beauty, and I think this will be an easy task for me."

During the next hour and a half, Mitch ordered extensively for his wife, sparing no expense in his desire to see her suitably clothed. Espri's measurements were taken and then numerous daygowns were selected from the pictures at hand. The materials to be used were carefully chosen with an eye to color and fashion. Undergarments were ordered, these to be made from the finest silks and satins; corsets, crinolines and all the other trappings that were essential to a modern woman's wardrobe.

"Lastly, Madame Vigney, my wife is in need of a ball gown; something special, I would think," Mitch told the couturiere when the basics had been taken care of.

"Ah, you have an important gathering to attend?"

"Yes, I'm sponsoring a ball in their honor," Catherine replied. "This will be Espri's first outing in society."

"What joy! What excitement!" Felice grew even more enthusiastic. "Monsieur . . . do I have your permission to create something splendid for your wife?"

"Of course, madame." Mitch smiled approvingly. "Money is no object."

Felice's eyes sparkled at the challenge. "I shall take great pleasure in designing a gown that will be unrivaled in style and workmanship."

"Wonderful," Catherine put in, trying to sound pleased by the news. "What is the earliest you could have the gown ready?"

"Have you set the date for your ball?" Felice asked cautiously.

"No. We were waiting to see how soon the gown would be finished," she replied.

"This is Wednesday . . . um . . ." The couturiere paused thoughtfully. "I am certain, if we start right away, that I should have it ready for a fitting by Friday . . . if that is suitable?"

Catherine was pleased. "Good. I shall plan our ball for Saturday evening. Thank you, Madame Vigney; as always you have more than outdone yourself."

"Madame, you are, and always have been, my favorite customer. It pleases me to satisfy you to the fullest." The Frenchwoman smiled her appreciation and then turned to Espri. "I shall look forward to seeing you Friday afternoon, if that will be convenient for you?"

"Of course, madame. We'll be here," Mitch agreed easily as they left the shop.

Their carriage was awaiting them, and Mitch handed Catherine in first before turning to his wife.

"Thank you, darling." Espri was overwhelmed by the amount of clothing he'd just ordered for her.

"You're more than welcome." He smiled down at her as he lifted her into the carriage.

"And thank you, Catherine." She turned to the other woman, who had already taken her seat in the conveyance. "I really appreciate your advice."

"It's a pleasure to help," her sister-in-law responded mechanically, taking care to keep the malice from her voice. Mitch had just spent a small fortune outfitting Espri, and it irked her that Madame Vigney had taken such a liking to the newcomer.

As the carriage rumbled off, Catherine settled back in the seat, wondering if there would be some way she could escape Espri's tedious company that afternoon and sneak off to visit Roland. She was desperate to talk with him for she needed his reassurance that everything would be fine in spite of Mitch's unexpected return.

Mitch excused himself as soon as they arrived at the house, for he had arranged to meet with Jon at the office in order to introduce him to Captain Clark, who, along with Mildred, would be joining them for dinner that night. Catherine and Espri, left to their own devices, had lunch together, after which Catherine pleaded the need for rest and disappeared to her room as quickly as possible without seeming rude. Ringing for Florence, she waited impatiently for her personal maid to come to her.

"Yes, Miss Catherine?" Florence asked when she entered the bedroom to find Catherine dressed and ready to go out.

"As soon as Espri goes to her rooms, I want you to order my carriage brought around."

"But, ma'am . . ." The maid began to protest, knowing that it would no longer be a simple matter to leave undetected.

"Florence, I know what you're going to say and I don't want to hear it. I have to go!"

"What if someone asks me where you've gone?" She was afraid for her mistress.

"Tell them I went shopping," Catherine answered curtly.

"But I just heard you tell Miss Espri that you were going to rest this afternoon."

"Who cares what I told her? Besides, no one is going to ask. Jon will be at the office until late tonight. Now, go on, and call me as soon as she goes to her room."

"Yes, ma'am."

Catherine didn't have long to wait, for Espri was nearly exhausted from her trip to the seamstress's shop and retired shortly after lunch. At Florence's call, Catherine hurried downstairs and quickly climbed into her waiting carriage for the trip to Roland's office.

Espri had been about to lie down when she heard a vehicle pull up in front. Hoping it might be Mitch returning early for some reason, she went to the window and she was surprised to see Catherine leaving. She frowned, puzzled by the other woman's actions. Why had Catherine decided to go out, when just a few minutes earlier she had claimed to be quite tired and in much need of an afternoon's rest? Shrugging off the other woman's strange behavior, she stretched out on the bed to sleep for a while so she would be refreshed for dinner with Mildred and the captain.

"What am I to do?" Catherine demanded of Roland as she stood before his desk.

"Nothing, Cat. Absolutely nothing," he told her candidly.

"Nothing?" Her surprise couldn't have been more complete. "How can I just sit back and do nothing, when at any moment Mitch might discover that I was involved in a plot to murder him?"

"Relax, darling," he drawled. "We've both gotten what we wanted out of the situation. You have your marriage, and I've expanded my business interests in a very profitable direction. Who cares if he's back or not?"

"I suppose you're right, but still . . ."

"Do you have reason to believe that he might be suspicious?" Roland's eyes narrowed as he waited for her reply.

"No. In fact, he seems perfectly satisfied with the explanation that whoever robbed him decided to take his clothes." She paused. "How did that happen, by the way?"

"The men I hired to kill Williams thought to make a few extra dollars on the side by selling him to a crimp. They wanted my money too, so they put his clothes on his driver, whom they'd already killed, and dumped that man's body in the bay."

Catherine smiled wickedly upon hearing this explanation. "Too bad Mitch survived his year at sea."

Roland shrugged. "It doesn't matter one way or the other, now. As long as he doesn't start delving too deeply into my 'imports,' I don't foresee any problem in dealing with him."

Catherine visibly relaxed. "So you don't think we're in any danger of being found out?"

"No, my sweet, our secret is safe." He pushed away from the desk to approach her with lustful intent. "But you will have to take extra care now to ensure that our liaison is not discovered."

A small smile curved her lips as he took her into his arms. "I promise you that I'll be totally discreet, my love."

"That's what I like to hear," he murmured; then his mouth took hers in a kiss of surging desire.

"Captain Clark has decided to sign on with us," Mitch announced happily at the dinner table that evening. "So, I'd like to propose a toast to the *Providence* and her captain. May our partnership be a long and profitable one."

"Hear, hear," Jon seconded, and they all lifted their glasses in salute of the new arrangement. "I think you'll find you've made the right decision."

"I feel I have," the captain responded. "You seem to have a very successful company, your terms are more than fair, and this way, I'm guaranteed a market for my goods."

"We'll do well together, I'm sure," Mitch said. "How soon do you think you can be ready to sail?"

"Easily within two weeks, I would think," he answered.

"Will you be glad to be back at sea, Mildred?" Espri asked her friend.

Mildred was thoughtful and then gave a small shrug. "I enjoy my times in port, but my place is with my husband."

"Don't you grow tired of living aboard a ship?" Catherine was amazed that any woman would want to spend her life that way.

"No. The *Providence* is our home," she said defensively, sensing the slight in the socially prominent woman's meaning.

"Well, I certainly admire your fortitude. I don't think I could do it," Catherine declared.

"To each his own," Mildred responded. "But I find it far more rewarding to be with the captain than to wait behind in some lonely port for his return. How much more exciting to be at his side!"

Catherine shrugged slightly, knowing that, to her, no man was worth such a sacrifice. What kind of life could a lady have under those conditions? Ugh! Plain food, rationed water, crude sailors around one, and endless miles of ocean. She shuddered inwardly, though she kept her polite "company" smile intact. "I'm sure you must find it challenging."

"No more so than any other life, I would imagine," Mildred told her. "One must choose the life that best suits. Only then can true happiness be found."

Her friend's comments made Espri think of Malika. She had been so busy adjusting to "civilized" living the past few days, that she had had little time to miss her home, but now a great sense of loss swept over her. Glancing toward Mitch, she was surprised to find his gaze upon her.

"Someday, Espri and I will sail with you again," he remarked to the captain as his eyes met hers in warm understanding. "I would enjoy nothing more than a return to Malika for an extended visit with my wife's family."

"We will be glad to have you with us." Mildred was pleased by his declaration.

The men's conversation returned to business then, and Catherine listened attentively to their discussion, in the hope of relaying to Roland as much information as possible about this new ship that would be sailing for the Williams line. When the evening drew to a close, she made a point of inviting the Clarks to the ball on Saturday night, thus providing Roland with the opportunity to meet with the captain himself. She knew he dealt with each ship's captain separately and that he would appreciate the chance to negotiate a deal with Captain Clark.

Catherine wanted to send word to Roland right away, but she didn't have an opportunity to do so until late the next morning, after Mitch and Jon had left for the office. Calling her maid to her, she handed her the missive.

"Florence, I want this message delivered to Mr. Stuart right away," she directed in low tones, unaware that Espri had just appeared in the hall.

"Yes, ma'am. Should I wait for an answer?"

"No, that won't be necessary. He'll know what has to be done."

"Yes, ma'am." Florence started out the door just as Espri joined Catherine.

"Who's Mr. Stuart? Will I be meeting him soon?"

Cat was so startled by her unexpected appearance that she wanted to scream at her that she should have made her presence known, but she knew that doing so would make Espri suspicious of her.

"I'm sure you will," she replied smoothly, giving her an easy smile. "In fact, that's what the note is about. Roland Stuart is a business associate of Jon's, and I had forgotten to send him an invitation to the party," she lied, glad now that Espri hadn't been involved in the handling of the invitations. "Since it's so late, I thought it best to send him a personalized note in the hope that he'll still be able to attend Saturday night."

"That's very thoughtful of you," Espri replied, thinking nothing of the matter. "What does he deal in?"

"He's a very successful importer, among other things, and he deals exclusively with Williams Shipping. It wouldn't do to offend him in any way," Catherine added for effect.

"I understand." Espri nodded. "Jon's very lucky to have you to take care of all these arrangements for him, and I certainly appreciate your taking the time to show me all the details that planning this affair entails. I never dreamed it would require so much."

"It is time-consuming to make sure that everything has been arranged, but the results will be worth it, you'll see." Catherine spoke in what she hoped sounded like an encouraging tone. "Very soon, you'll be able to handle it all on your own."

"I hope so," Espri agreed, for she wanted to learn everything she could about life in San Francisco society as quickly as possible in order to make Mitch proud of her. Mildred's advice had helped immeasurably, but she knew she still had a long way to go to achieve Catherine's level of sophistication.

Friday afternoon arrived amidst a bustle of activity as the household prepared for the upcoming event, and Mitch returned from the office early that day so he could escort Espri to the seamstress's shop for her fitting.

Madame Vigney greeted them upon their arrival and quickly directed Espri to a fitting room where an attendant was waiting to help her undress. "Mr. Williams, if you will wait here, I shall have your wife model the gown for you."

"Very well, madame." Mitch leaned idly against a table as he anticipated Espri's return.

Espri stood patiently while Madame Vigney fussed over her. The couturiere had not only completed her ball gown but many of her undergarments too, and she insisted that the younger woman don them now in order to ensure the best fit for the evening gown. Espri found the wispy, silken garments delightfully sensuous, and she felt very feminine as she stood there clad only in the delicate lingerie. Secretly, she wished Mitch could see her, but she knew that would have to wait until later, when they were home alone.

"Voilà!" Felice returned to the fitting room carrying the tissue-wrapped gown she had spent the past two days slaving over in her quest to create the perfect costume to showcase Espri's beauty. "I think you are going to be most pleased." Carefully, the Frenchwoman unwrapped the tissue, and with her assistant's help, they lifted the narrow-skirted gown over Espri's head so she could slip into it easily.

The gown was a low-cut, sleeveless creation of deep turquoise silk. Severe in style, it employed none of the multiple rows of bows and lace that adorned so many fashionable gowns; instead, it relied strictly on the beauty of the woman wearing it to enhance its simple yet magnificent lines. The décolletage was enticingly low, and the fitted lines of the gown hugged Espri's trim figure in a modest, yet revealing, manner. Felice's masterpiece projected glamorous sophistication, and Espri carried it off with a natural grace that left the seamstress smiling.

"I was right. This is perfect for you. You're absolutely breathtaking." She stood back, staring at the younger woman. "Here, turn and see!" she urged, wanting Espri to witness the change in her appearance.

Feeling a bit self-conscious after the woman's generous compliments, Espri faced the mirror a bit hesitantly, and her breath caught in her throat when she stared at herself. She had been impressed by the gown she had made with Mildred, but this one far surpassed anything she'd ever seen before.

"Madame!" she whispered, awestruck. "The gown is lovely!"

"Silly," Felice dismissed. "The gown would be nothing on another woman. It is you who make it so beautiful." Her professional manner returning, she pondered the way the skirt was drawn up in the back to reveal an underskirt of paler blue. "Yes, I think a few changes here and here." She pointed them out to her assistant. "Then it will be ready."

"Yes, ma'am."

"Would you like to have your husband come in, Mrs. Williams?" Felice finally asked when she'd finished planning the final touches that needed to be added.

"Yes, please." Espri was excited and wanted Mitch to share the moment with her.

"I'll send him right in." Madame Vigney went out into the main shop and called to Mitch to join them. "She's right in there," Felice directed. Then she and her assistant left them alone for a moment.

Mitch knocked softly before striding confidently into the dressing room when Espri bade him enter. "Madame Vigney said that you were—" He stopped short when he saw her, his eyes widening in pleasure at the sight of her sensuously cut bodice. "Espri . . . you look wonderful."

"Do you really think so?" she asked eagerly.

He crossed the room to kiss her softly. "Definitely, my love. You'll be the most gorgeous woman at the ball."

She smiled her pleasure at his words. "Thank you. It's a lovely dress."

"That it is. Catherine was certainly correct in her praise of Madame Vigney. The woman is an artist."

"Thank you, Mr. Williams." Felice overheard him as she reentered the room. "I accept your compliment gladly, but I must tell you that not all my creations are worn so well. Your wife's natural beauty was a joy to work with."

"Will a final fitting be necessary?" Mitch asked.

"No. There are only a few minor details that I must correct; then it will be perfect. I shall have it delivered to you early tomorrow afternoon."

"Thank you."

"Most of the lingerie you ordered has been completed, so I will send that along too. Your other dresses should be ready for a first fitting some time late next week. I'll notify you, and then we can set up a time that is convenient."

"We'll be looking forward to it," Mitch assured her; then he left so Espri could change back into her daygown.

Later, as they sat side by side in the carriage, Espri couldn't help but smile as she thought of the delicate undergarments Madame Vigney had insisted she wear home.

"You're looking very contented about something," Mitch remarked, noticing her enigmatic expression.

"I am." She teasingly offered no explanation.

"Oh? Do I have to guess what it is or will you tell me?" He drew her close and kissed her.

Espri sighed when he released her. "I suppose I could tell you, but it would be much more fun to show you."

"Show me?" He was becoming more and more intrigued.

She nodded as she met his lips for another sweet exchange. "When we get home . . ." Her voice was throaty and suggestive.

"Are you sure I have to wait?"

Laughing delightedly, Espri answered, "I hardly think that this would be the place to reveal my secret."

"You'd be surprised at the things that can be 'revealed' in a carriage as private as this one," he told her lustily, his hand sweeping over her in a bold, possessive caress.

"Oh?" She gave him a deliberately innocent look, and he was about to unbutton the bodice of her gown when the carriage drew up in front of the house.

Mitch glanced disgustedly out the window. "Had we not already arrived, my dear, I would instruct him to take us for a nice long drive."

Espri's eyes were alight with desire as she moved slightly away from him when their driver opened the carriage door.

Giving her a heated look, Mitch stepped down from the vehicle and then turned to assist her to alight. He bent to whisper in her ear as he set her before him. "You'll just have to be content to accompany me to our chambers."

"I think I'd like that." Espri leaned slightly against him as they mounted the steps together and entered the house.

Chapter 27

Catherine was the picture of elegance as she swept down the front staircase early Saturday evening. Having spent the better part of the afternoon getting ready for the ball, she knew that she looked her absolute best. Florence had arranged her hair in an upswept style that emphasized the classic beauty of her delicate features and set off the graceful line of her neck and shoulders. Her gown of pale gold-shot silk trimmed in Valenciennes lace showcased her blond loveliness, and there was no doubt in her mind that she would be the center of attention, again, this night.

Jon had gone downstairs earlier to enjoy a moment of quiet before the guests began to arrive, and upon hearing Catherine on the stairs, he moved out into the hall to meet her.

"My darling, as always your beauty astounds me." His gaze was heated as he watched her descend.

She smiled at him appreciatively. "Thank you, Jon. You know I enjoy looking my best for you."

"You certainly seem to have outdone yourself tonight." He kissed her softly, wanting to enjoy a moment of privacy with her before their guests began to arrive.

Catherine sensed his mood, however, and moved quickly away from him to survey the ballroom. "Is everything ready?"

she asked, not wanting to listen to his protestations of undying love right then. Roland would be there soon, and she was anxious for him to see her in her new gown.

"I believe so," Jon answered, following her. Assuming her coolness was due to nervousness over the ball, he smiled patiently, knowing that she would be in his bed when the affair was over.

"Good." Catherine turned back to her husband, regarding him critically for a moment. Dressed in his dark evening clothes, she knew he would be one of the best-looking men in attendance that night, and though she realized she should be thrilled that he was in love with her, she felt nothing. "You look so handsome, darling," she told him with a seductive smile. "I'm sure I'll be the envy of many women tonight."

Jon started to approach her, but the sound of arriving guests prevented him from taking her in his arms. Relieved that she had been spared his embrace, Cat accompanied him into the hall, eager to greet their arriving guests.

Upstairs in Mitch's suite, Mabel parted the heavy velvet drapes and glanced out. "Looks like everyone is starting to arrive," she remarked as she noticed the carriages starting to pull up in front of the house.

"Do we have enough time?" Espri looked worriedly over at the maid.

"Of course," Mabel reassured her. "You won't be going down for at least half an hour."

"I don't know if I like making a grand entrance," Espri said thoughtfully.

"It's quite the correct thing," Mabel confirmed. "This is your debut, so to speak, and it's most appropriate for you to enter when everybody else is already here."

A soft knock at the door drew Mabel from her surveillance, and she hustled across the room to admit Sally. "Hurry now," she bade the younger servant. "Miss Espri will be due downstairs in half an hour, and her hair must be perfect."

"Yes, Mabel," Sally agreed as she moved to the dressing table to lay out the necessary pins and combs. "Miss Espri, if you're ready, I can start on your hair now."

"Of course." Espri sat down at the vanity, watching with interest as the maid painstakingly styled her hair into a cascade of curls.

"Good evening." Elliot Whitney greeted Jon and Catherine as he entered the foyer with his wife Chelsea on his arm.

"Elliot, Chelsea. So glad you could come." Jon shook his hand enthusiastically.

"Where's Mitch? And what's this I hear that he's gotten married?"

"He'll be down in a little while," Catherine put in. "We thought it would be more appropriate if he made a grand entrance with his new bride."

"So it is true, eh?" Elliot smiled broadly. "It was a big enough surprise that he turned up alive after all this time, but to bring a wife back with him . . . what's she like?"

"Espri is delightful," Jon told him. "You'll see."

"Oh, Catherine, isn't it wonderful?" Chelsea sighed as she glanced up the grand staircase, hoping to catch sight of Mitch. "Why, it's just a miracle, pure and simple. To think that we all had thought him dead . . ."

"Yes, it's a miracle." Catherine kept her tone light.

"Now, tell me all about his wife. You know how he made the rounds here and never found a woman to suit him." Chelsea obviously wanted to be the first to hear all the news.

"Espri is lovely." Catherine echoed her husband's sentiments.

"I always suspected Mitch would find a very special

woman," Chelsea remarked sagely as Elliot finally led her off to the ballroom.

"Roland." Jon turned to address his business associate as he came in. "It's good to see you. I'm glad you could make it."

"Thank you." Roland's reply was smooth, but his gaze raked over Catherine in her low-cut gown. "Catherine, my dear, you look marvelous, as always."

"Thank you, Roland. How is Susan doing this evening?" she asked courteously, knowing that the other woman was far too along in her pregnancy to make any social appearances.

"She's fine," he answered, playing along with her charade. "And growing more anxious by the minute for her confinement to be over. She sends her regards."

"Please tell her that we missed her tonight."

"I shall," Roland said politely. "Is Mitch here yet? I'm looking forward to seeing him again and to meeting his bride."

"They'll be down shortly," Jon told him. "Ah, here's Alan, and Laura."

Roland turned to see the other couple arrive. "Good evening, Alan."

"Roland, good to see you. Jon, Catherine, you're looking wonderful." Alan shook hands with the men.

"Has Chelsea arrived yet?" Laura inquired of Catherine when all the greetings had been exchanged.

"Yes, just a moment ago, in fact," she responded. "Your gown is lovely, Laura."

"Thank you. You know you're stunning," she told her. "That color is marvelous on you. I've never seen you looking more radiant. Your handsome husband must keep you so happy."

Cat took Jon's arm and drew him to her, purring, "Of course."

Roland bit back a sarcastic comment as he watched her

performance, and when she glanced casually in his direction, he gave her a quick, knowing look.

"I think just about everyone's arrived now. Shall we join the others?" Jon glanced down at his wife, his love for her obvious.

"Please. We can start the dancing if you like." She gazed up at him adoringly as they went in to instruct the musicians to begin.

The lilting strains of a waltz drifted upstairs as Mabel laid out Espri's new gown.

"Are you almost done there, Sally?" Mabel asked, glancing over to where the young maid was just putting the finishing touches on Espri's hair.

"I'll just be another minute, Mabel," she answered.

"Fine. The music's begun so they'll be expecting them downstairs shortly."

Mitch had finished dressing earlier so the women could have the run of the bedroom, and he now strode back in, eager to join the party below. "Are you about ready?"

"There," Sally said triumphantly as she secured the last curl and stepped back to observe her handiwork. "What do you think?"

"You did a fine job, Sally. My wife looks absolutely ravishing," Mitch complimented as he came to stand behind Espri. His gaze a hungry caress, he stared at her reflection in the mirror, and she felt a shiver of excitement tingle through her.

"You do look lovely, Miss Espri," Mabel agreed. "Come, let's get your gown on you, so you can join the festivities."

Espri took a last quick glance in the mirror, then rose to move away from the dressing table, but Mitch stopped her progress as he drew her near for a breathtaking kiss. "It's a pity we have to go to this party at all," he whispered for her ears only, and Espri smiled at his words.

"If you'd rather not go . . . ." she began teasingly.

"Vixen! Get dressed before I decide to forget all about this ball and spend the evening up here, alone, with you."

"It sounds wonderful, but I think Catherine would be more than a little put out with us." Espri laughed as she hurried to the maids waiting to help her don the dress.

"There is always later, madame," he muttered.

"Indeed there is," she responded brightly as she lifted her arms to slip into the gown Mabel was holding for her.

The sleek garment settled over her slender shape easily, and Mabel quickly fastened the back and adjusted the skirt.

"There now, you look perfect."

"Not quite." Mitch went to his armoire and took out a small package. "I want you to wear this tonight."

"What is it?" Espri looked at him questioningly.

"These belonged to my mother," he said, opening the box to reveal a sapphire necklace and a diamond-encrusted wedding band. Deftly he fastened the jewels about her neck. Then, reaching for her left hand, he slid the ring on her finger. "That's better."

"Oh, Mitch." Espri's eyes were filled with tears as she turned to him after glancing in the mirror. "I've never seen anything so beautiful. I'll treasure them forever."

He lifted her hand to his lips, kissing the ring on her finger. "That's how long I want you to wear this, my love: forever." His fiery gaze locked with hers and their hearts met in silent communication as they stood suspended in time, aware of nothing save each other and the depth of their love.

Mabel and Sally sighed romantically as they let themselves out of the room, their departure unnoticed by Mitch and Espri.

The sound of the closing door broke through their blissful haze and they blinked in surprise at finding themselves alone. Mitch gave her a roguish grin. "You know, my suggestion of earlier does have some merit."

"Mitchell Williams, don't tease!" She laughed. "You know we have to go downstairs and right now."

"I know, but the thought of taking you to bed and making mad passionate love to you is much more appealing." His smile turned to a leer as he pressed a soft kiss to her throat.

"Mitch, don't,'" Espri protested weakly, wanting nothing more than to go into his arms, but knowing if she did she would never be able to repair the damage done to her hair and dress.

Releasing an exaggerated sigh, he relented. "You're a cruel, cold-hearted woman."

"You won't be saying that later." Her eyes twinkled as she started from the room.

Mitch straightened his cuffs and hurried to open the door for her. "Are you nervous?"

Her smile was bright. "Not as long as I'm with you."

He bent to kiss her one last time, then they left the room together.

Mabel had told Catherine that Mitch and Espri would be coming down soon, and when they appeared at the top of the steps, everyone was waiting.

"Ladies and gentlemen, my brother Mitch and his wife, Espri Duchant Williams." Jon made the introduction with a flare, and a smattering of applause greeted their descent, followed by rousing greetings and well-wishing.

Mitch and Espri were delighted by the warmth of their reception, and when the music started again, Mitch led Espri out on the dance floor for a waltz.

"I'm not sure I remember how to do this," she whispered tensely.

"You did say Jacques taught you how, didn't you?"

"Yes, but that was years ago, when I was just a little girl."

"You'll do fine. Just follow my lead, sweetheart, and if you do step on my feet, I promise not to scream too loudly." Mitch gave her an amused look.

She responded with an indignant glare. "My father told me I was extremely light on my feet."

"It's not your feet I'm worried about," Mitch teased as he began to move about the polished ballroom floor.

Concentrating on his movements and the steady rhythm of the music, she was soon dancing gracefully, matching his every move.

"Your father was right," Mitch told her as he whirled her about.

"Thank you."

"You dance as superbly as you make love," he remarked in low tones, tightening his arm about her.

"I could say the same about you," Espri responded, enjoying the feel of being held close to him as they danced.

To their disappointment the music ended all too soon and they were swept into another round of introductions.

"Why, Laura, her dress is so unique, I believe she even out-shines Catherine this evening," Chelsea said as she watched Espri moving about the room with Mitch.

"She certainly is pretty, but her coloring is so unusual. Where did Mitch meet her? She looks almost foreign," Laura replied nastily.

"I haven't heard the whole story yet. I'm sure Catherine will know everything. Let's see if we can find her."

Catherine was with Jon, but when she saw the two ladies coming her way, she excused herself and went to meet them.

"Laura, Chelsea . . . are you having a good time?"

"Absolutely, darling. You know your parties are the best."

"Why, thank you. Have you had the opportunity to meet Espri yet?"

"No, and we were just wondering about her. If Mitch was shanghaied as the rumor goes, however did they manage to meet?"

"It's such a complicated story." Cat grimaced inwardly as

she began to recount, for what seemed the millionth time that evening, Mitch's exploits.

"So Espri is from a tropical island?" Laura was stunned.

"Yes, the island of Malika. I understand, from talking with Mitch, that it's very beautiful there."

"I'm sure. And what of her parentage?"

"My wife is French and Polynesian." Mitch's deep voice broke in before Catherine had a chance to answer. "Espri, I'd like you to meet Laura Harris and Chelsea Whitney. I believe I've already introduced you to their husbands."

Espri smiled openly at the two women. "It's nice to meet you ladies."

They regarded her with interest as they returned the greeting. "Catherine was just telling us that you rescued Mitch from a shipwreck."

Espri looked up at her husband. "He was washed ashore, and I found him on the beach."

"She took excellent care of me, too," Mitch told Laura and Chelsea, confidingly. He looked up just then to see Mildred and the captain arriving. "If you'll excuse us, ladies, there's a couple we haven't spoken with yet."

"Of course."

Laura looked at Chelsea when they'd walked away. "She's as gorgeous close up as she is at a distance."

"It's no wonder he fell in love with her. Her accent is marvelous and her figure . . ."

"I think Mitch has chosen well," Laura remarked.

"Yes, she's perfect for him. They make a magnificent couple," Chelsea agreed, and Catherine breathed a sigh of relief as she realized that Espri's Polynesian heritage would not create a scandal.

"I'm afraid, Catherine, that you may have a rival as a fashion plate," Laura said bitchily. "Not that your dress isn't nice, mind you, it's just that the style Espri has on this evening is sure to start a rage."

"It's all Madame Vigney's doing," Catherine told them, trying to keep a rein on her sudden flare of jealousy. "She designed the gown herself, just for Espri."

"That woman is a marvel, but on anyone else the gown would be wasted. No, it's Espri. She has a natural beauty that's rarely seen," Chelsea commented, and Catherine felt her dislike of Espri grow.

"True," Laura assented.

Grateful when she noticed Jon looking her way, Catherine eagerly excused herself from the other women's presence. "If you ladies will excuse me, I've got to join my husband. I'll see you a little later."

Mildred and Espri were standing together, drinking cups of champagne punch while their husbands discussed business, again.

"Espri, I can't tell you how pleased I am that you've adapted so well," Mildred said happily. "Are you finding that you like it here?"

Espri paused briefly before answering. "It's as you were saying at dinner the other night . . . you can be happy anywhere as long as you're with your husband. I feel the same way."

"But tell me, how are you doing? This can't be easy for you."

Espri smiled. "Actually, it hasn't been as difficult to adjust to living here as I'd thought it would be. Mitch has been wonderful, and though I do miss my life on Malika, the thought of remaining there without him is unimaginable."

"It's good to know you're this happy." Mildred gave her a quick hug. "And I hope you always feel this way."

"I will," Espri assured her.

Catherine was overjoyed when she saw Roland crossing the room in her direction. At last! A chance to talk with him.

"Jon? May I invite your lovely wife to dance?" he asked courteously, and Jon graciously agreed.

"Catherine?" Roland took her arm and led her out onto the ballroom floor. "My darling, I've been waiting for this moment since I walked through the door."

Her eyes were dark with desire as he squired her gracefully about. "I have, too. I must talk with you."

"And I you." His gaze met hers in remembrance of the last time there had been a ball here. "The study?"

A flare of heat surged through her body, leaving her weak with excitement. "Yes, oh yes."

"There is nothing I want more than to hold you in my arms," he murmured erotically, and Catherine was thrilled when the music finally ended so she could discreetly make her way to their rendezvous.

Roland made the rounds of the ballroom, making small talk and greeting his wife's friends with open interest. He knew it wouldn't do for a breath of a scandal to reach Susan, so he attentively paid court to Laura and Chelsea, knowing they would be the first to inform his wife should he transgress in any way. Social amenities seen to, he wandered out into the hall, and when he could enter the study unobserved, he hurried within. Catherine was not there yet, but he didn't have long to wait.

"My love," she whispered huskily. Quickly, she closed the door behind her and went straight into his arms, kissing him fervently. "You don't know how hard it is for me to ignore you out there."

"I feel the same way, darling." His mouth claimed hers as his hand dipped into her gown to fondle her breasts.

Cat swayed weakly against him for a moment, then reluctantly pulled away. "We have to talk."

"I know." He brought his surging desires under control with an effort. "Now, what's this about a new ship joining the Williams line? I got your note the other afternoon . . ."

"Did you see the older man with Mitch?"

"Yes."

"That was Captain Clark. He's master of the *Providence* and he's just signed on to sail for them."

"I see." Roland smiled. "I'll have to make a point of speaking with him tonight."

"I thought you might want to."

Roland was always anxious to enlarge his operation, and the prospect of having another ship dealing in his "goods" was very appealing. So far he had managed to make profitable arrangements with several of the shipping line's captains, and he had no doubt that he could come to a mutually beneficial deal with this one.

"Thank you, Cat. You're a very astute businesswoman."

She was pleased by his compliment. "I'm glad you noticed. Jon thinks I'm merely a pretty decoration."

"I know better," he growled, drawing her into his arms once more. "Kiss me, Cat."

"Oh, Roland, please . . . if we hurry . . ." She met his lips feverishly.

Eagerly, Roland lifted her skirts and brought her full against his hardness. "I want you darling—*now*."

So intent were they upon one another that they didn't hear the door open or see Espri start to enter. She had just finished dancing with Jon and had felt the need for a quiet moment. When she saw Roland and Catherine in a heated embrace and heard his passionate declaration, her heart lurched in painful agony for Jon, and she was exceedingly grateful that he wasn't with her. Backing away, she closed the door discreetly and returned to the ball.

Her mind was racing as she tried to decide what to do. She was well aware of Jon's love for his wife, and she knew she couldn't tell him of Catherine's infidelity for it would be too cruel of a blow. She was tempted to confide in Mitch, but remembering what he'd told her about his friend Andrew, she realized that she would have to keep this to herself until she could figure out the right way to handle it.

"There you are, sweetheart." Mitch joined her as she reentered the ballroom. "I've been looking for you. Let's dance, shall we?"

"I'd love to," she consented, but even as he swept her out onto the floor the memory of Catherine's betrayal stayed with her.

Roland spotted Captain Clark standing near the refreshment table, and he casually approached him. "I understand that you've just signed on with Williams Shipping?"

"Yes, I'm Captain Clark of the *Providence.*"

"I'm glad to meet you, sir. I'm Roland Stuart."

"Mr. Stuart—"

"Roland, please. I'm sure we'll be dealing together in the near future."

"Oh, really?" Clark's interest sharpened.

"Yes. I'm an importer of Chinese goods, and I deal exclusively with Jon and Mitch."

"It'll be a pleasure to work for you, then," Clark told him cordially.

"What type of ship do you have, Captain Clark? A steamer?"

"No, I still rely on the trade winds. Perhaps you'd like to come aboard the *Providence* one day and look around? She's a handsome vessel."

"I'd enjoy that." Roland was more than pleased by the offer.

"Good, good. Just let me know when it's convenient and I'll arrange everything."

"I'll speak with you again, soon." Roland shook the captain's hand as he took his leave.

Then he caught sight of Alan Harris and went to join him. "I've just met the captain of the new ship that will be sailing for the line."

"Ah, yes . . . Captain Clark."

"You've already had the pleasure?"

"Yes. Laura and I were introduced earlier this evening. How did you find him?" Alan was instantly curious.

"I haven't approached him on our 'cargo' yet. He's invited me to his ship, and I thought that would be a more appropriate place to strike our own deal."

"You are a smooth operator, Roland."

Stuart shrugged. "Everyone wants to make money, and I'm sure the illustrious Captain Clark is no exception."

"He and Mitch are close friends, you know."

"Friend or not, every man has his price, Alan."

"That's true enough," Harris observed. "What's yours?"

Roland smiled wolfishly as he walked away. "I don't think any man can meet my price."

Chapter 28

Jon smiled at his wife from where he lay in their bed. "The ball was a huge success, my love."

"Yes, everything did go exceedingly well, didn't it?" Catherine was sitting at her dressing table brushing out her hair, and she smiled at him in the mirror.

"It certainly did. Now, let's make the evening complete," he invited. "I've been waiting for hours to make love to you, darling."

Though Jon was an attractive, virile man, Catherine felt no excitement at the thought of sharing his embrace, and she wished that she could avoid her wifely "duty." But, knowing that there was no way out of it this night, she resigned herself to making love to him. Standing, she slipped out of her gown and approached the bed completely nude.

"You are so lovely," Jon told her hoarsely as he drew her down beside him. "I love you, Catherine."

"And I love you, Jon." She whispered the obligatory response as she gave herself up to his kisses.

He made love to Catherine with abandon, kissing and caressing her until he could no longer restrain himself. Then, pulling her beneath him, he entered her and began to move slowly so she would get a more full enjoyment from their mating, but Cat would have none of it. She just wanted him to finish, and quickly. Urging him on, she used all her knowledge to bring him to completion as hurriedly as possible, and when he finally collapsed atop her, she smiled in satisfaction.

Jon rolled slightly away from her so she wouldn't be burdened by his weight, and then pulled her close to his side, wanting to share this time of intimacy. Cat did not try to move away from him, but she lay quietly in his arms, knowing that he had been satisfied and would make no further demands on her body. Sighing, she closed her eyes and let herself dream of Roland's caresses and of the next time they would meet . . .

Espri solemnly stared out the bedroom window as Mitch began to undress.

"Did you have a good time tonight?" he asked as he shed his shirt.

"Oh, yes. Everything was just wonderful," she managed to respond, though her mind was dwelling on Catherine's infidelity. "Your friends are very nice."

"They liked you, too," Mitch told her confidently.

"I'm glad." In truth, she was, for Mildred had told her that acceptance was everything in polite society.

"You know, something has surprised me greatly since we've been here," he said thoughtfully as he came to take her in his arms and hold her close.

"What?"

"Catherine . . ."

Espri couldn't help but stiffen momentarily. Did he know? "What about her?"

Mitch didn't notice her sudden tenseness, and he continued. "Well, you know what I thought about her before—I was certain that she was only after Jon for his money."

"And you don't think she is now?" Espri prompted.

He shrugged slightly. "I think probably my own prejudices

colored my thinking. Jon loves her, and as long as he's happy, I'll be supportive of their union."

Espri knew then what she must do. Jon did love Catherine very much so she did not want to draw the men into the situation, if she could help it. Catherine had been very kind to her since she'd arrived, and she felt she owed it to her to be discreet, at least for now. She decided at the first opportunity she would speak with Catherine about her tryst with Roland.

"That's good," she said to Mitch. "They seem very content together."

"I think so too."

"By the way"—Espri pulled a little away from him and looked up at him quickly—"who was that woman you introduced me to?"

"Which one?" He frowned, trying to imagine which woman Espri would have noticed.

"I think her name was Lucy."

"Oh, Lucinda Blake." Mitch nodded in acknowledgment.

"What was she to you, Mitch?"

"What do you mean, darling?"

"I think at some time she must have loved you . . ." Espri had observed Lucinda with Mitch and had sensed a certain sadness about her.

Mitch was startled by her perception. "Lucinda and I had a relationship before I was shanghaied."

"A relationship? Were you in love with her?"

"Espri"—he drew her back to him—"you know I've never loved any woman but you, yet I can hardly claim to have been celibate during the years of my manhood. Lucinda and I understood each other. She had been widowed and was independently wealthy, and I wanted to enjoy myself without being tied down. We got on well together, but it was never more than that."

"I see." Espri nodded slowly. "She's very pretty."

"Yes, she is," he agreed. "I'd be lying to you if I told you I didn't think her attractive, but, sweetheart, I have no interest in anyone else. You are my life, Espri. I love you."

Her lips curved into a gentle smile at his words. "I was hoping you'd say that. It's been awhile since you told me."

"It has?" He frowned. "I distinctly remember telling you that I loved you just before we came upstairs."

"Well, it seemed like a long time to me." She looped her arms about his neck and pulled him down for a passionate kiss.

Scooping her up in his arms, Mitch crossed to the bed, and kneeling on its softness, he laid Espri upon the silken sheets. She stretched languidly as he moved away long enough to discard the rest of his clothing.

"I've been wanting you all night." Her voice was husky. "I'm not sure your ways here in 'civilization' are better than ours."

"What do you mean?" he asked as he rejoined her on the bed.

"Well, at any of our festivals, if a couple wants to be together they just leave." She smiled as she ran her hands over the bared expanse of his furred chest. "Here, we had to wait."

"We certainly did. I thought the guests would never leave." He grinned, his body responding quickly to her touch. "But, maybe the heightened anticipation will make our coming together more exciting."

"I don't think our lovemaking can be any more exciting." Espri leaned over him to trail fiery kisses down his throat and chest.

Mitch pulled her up to him and kissed her fiercely. "That's true. You are a very exciting woman, Espri."

"Only for you, my husband." She moved her hips suggestively against him, and he reached down to cup her buttocks, holding her more tightly to him.

"Feel what you do to me with just a kiss and a touch . . ." he rasped as his mouth took hers, deeply . . . passionately.

"Help me take this off," she whispered, eager to feel his

heated flesh against her, and Mitch slipped off the sleek nightgown that Madame Vigney had had delivered with the ballgown that afternoon.

"It's very beautiful," Mitch said as he tossed it carelessly aside. "But I like you better without it."

"So do I." Espri went eagerly into his embrace.

Their fiery passion ignited as she lay full against him, feminine softness pressed to male hardness, and their hands were never still as they sought only to please each other with gentle erotic caresses. Their legs intertwined, they strained hungrily together, wanting that final, most precious embrace.

Desiring to arouse Espri completely, Mitch sought her breasts, pressing heated kisses to their sweet fullness. Thrilled by the hot, moist suction of his mouth, she cried out her plea- sure, wrapping her legs about his hips and inviting him to take her. Needing no guidance to her precious womanly core, he entered her with one smooth stroke. Shuddering as the heat of her body closed around him, he began to move, seek- ing the ultimate rapture of union with her. Moments of pure love followed as they blended together in a frenzy of ecstasy and then reached the pinnacle of joy, their pulsing passion sweeping them away in a haze of sensual bliss.

"I love you." Mitch whispered the ardent pledge as they lay momentarily replete.

"It's good." Espri sighed, contentedly.

"Very good," he responded, his voice a seductive murmur, his arms tightening about her as he felt his desire for her flame to life again.

Espri sensed his arousal and smiled invitingly as he pulled her atop him.

"I don't think I'll ever get enough of you," he growled, his gaze passion darkened.

"I hope you never do, Mitch," she whispered breathlessly as he nibbled at the sensitive cords of her throat.

Gentle kisses soon gave way to heated caresses as he

shifted lower to savor the delicacy of her bosom. His hands worked magic on her lithe form, teasing and arousing her to the heights once more, and his lips followed suit, tracing paths of delight over her satiny flesh until she cried out in ecstasy.

Espri rested, sensually content, for only a moment before the desire to pleasure Mitch urged her on. She moved sinuously against him, her hips pressed rhythmically, tantalizingly to his, letting him know that she was ready, telling him of her excitement. Trailing passionate kisses over his chest and stomach, she smiled when she heard his sharp intake of breath as she touched him most intimately. Then her mouth sought him, loving him, until he pulled her away and guided her above him to straddle him.

Espri took him deep within her body and began to thrust against him slowly, wanting to prolong his enjoyment for as long as possible, but Mitch could no longer wait. She had driven him to the brink, and he needed the satisfaction only she could give. Drawing her down to him so he could kiss her, Mitch took total control, his body claiming hers completely in a driving embrace that left them both spent yet enthralled. Finally, wrapped in each other's arms, savoring the splendor of their love, they drifted off to sleep.

Sunday dawned bright and warm, and though Espri had hoped to speak with Catherine, Mitch's decision to take her on an outing delayed the confrontation. He whisked her away to the Cliff House on the coast, where they enjoyed a late breakfast and then passed the balance of the morning delighting in the magnificent view of the Pacific and the sea lions frolicking there. By midafternoon, however, the temperature began to drop, so they decided to end their sojourn by the sea and return home. Though they had come by way of Geary

Street, Mitch instructed their driver to return by way of Golden Gate Park and Market Street.

"We're going back a different way?" Espri asked as she settled in next to Mitch in the confines of their carriage.

Mitch's expression was enigmatic as he looked down at her. "Yes. It's a slightly longer route."

"Longer?" She glanced at him questioningly. "Why would you want to take the long way home?"

His grin was rakish as he drew her close. "Remember the conversation we had in the carriage the other day?" His hand strayed knowingly to cup her breast.

She remembered distinctly. "As I recall, I was about to reveal something to you."

"I believe that's how it went." He kissed her softly as his fingers worked at the buttons of her bodice.

"But we got back to the house too quickly," Espri continued as he gently pushed her dress from her shoulders and bared her breasts to his ardent caresses.

"This time, love, there will be no interruptions." Drawing her across his lap, he kissed her as his hand strayed beneath her skirts.

Espri found the novelty of making love in the carriage exciting, and she eagerly followed his direction as he positioned her in the most comfortable way to receive him. When he came to her, she was ready and they blended together in a rush of heated joy, the gentle swaying of the carriage enhancing the eroticism of their coupling. Spiraling to the crest together, they abandoned themselves to the fiery force of their desire. Caught in the vortex of their passions, they experienced love's glory, holding tightly to one another as intoxicating waves of pleasure swept through them.

Though the return trip was longer by several miles, Mitch and Espri were too preoccupied to notice. Indeed, they were more than a little disappointed when they found themselves drawing up before the mansion. With haste, they straightened their clothing, and when the driver opened the door for them, they descended with considerable dignity, vowing in loving conspiracy to go on Sunday outings as often as they could.

"Did you enjoy your trip to Cliff House?" Catherine asked as she faced Espri across the breakfast table the following morning after Mitch and Jon had left for the office.

"Yes," Espri confirmed. "The view's beautiful and the food was excellent."

"Jon and I have been there often and we've always enjoyed it," Catherine remarked as she finished her tea. "Have you made any plans for the day?" She was hoping that Espri had somewhere to go that afternoon so she could arrange to visit Roland at his office.

"No. I've decided to stay in today."

"Well, I have a few things to do, so I guess I'd better get started." Irritated, she started to rise from the table.

"Catherine, I need to speak with you for a few moments, if you have the time?" Although Espri was apprehensive about telling her sister-in-law what she'd seen Saturday night, she knew she must. She hoped fervently that there would be no need for this matter to go further than the two of them.

"Of course. What is it?"

"Something happened Saturday night that I feel we must talk about," Espri began.

Catherine was confused. Everything had seemed to go so well at the party; what could have happened to draw this kind of response from Espri? "You sound so worried. Did someone slight you in some way or—"

"No. Nothing like that, Catherine." Espri paused briefly before broaching the subject. "It's just that later in the evening, I was going into the study to rest for a moment, and I walked in on something I wish I'd never seen."

Catherine felt herself grow pale, but she kept her wits about her and asked innocently, "What?"

Espri had been watching the other woman's reaction to her words, and she was amazed at how controlled her response was. "I saw you kissing Roland Stuart."

Panic surged through Catherine. Espri had seen her with Roland! Her mind was racing as she realized the folly of her actions.

"Oh, no." She managed a strangled whisper that she hoped Espri would interpret as desperation. "You won't tell Jon, will you? I could never bear it if he found out . . . but there was no other way."

"What are you talking about?" Espri had expected denials or anger from Catherine but never this sudden fear.

"Roland . . . said he knows something that could ruin Jon's business . . . and that he would use it against him if I didn't agree to sleep with him!" she lied, hoping that Espri was naïve enough to believe her.

"What kind of information could he possibly have?"

"I don't know." Catherine pretended to agonize over the situation. "But I was afraid to cross him. He's a very powerful man, and I know how much Williams Shipping means to Jon."

"How long has this been going on between you?"

"For several months now."

Espri was stunned. "I'll tell Mitch. He'll handle it."

"No!" That thought really alarmed Catherine, for the last person she wanted involved in all this was Mitch. "Please, don't tell anyone. I don't want to risk losing Jon."

"I understand, but if Roland Stuart is doing something to force you to sleep with him, you need someone's help. As soon as Mitch and Jon return, we're going to tell them the truth. It's the only way out of this."

Catherine was alternately furious and frightened, but, faking a resignation she was not feeling, she answered, "I know you're right, but I'm so afraid Jon won't understand."

Espri gave her a sympathetic look. "It will work out. You'll see."

Roland sat across the desk from Clark in the privacy of the captain's cabin. "Thank you for having me aboard. I've enjoyed seeing your ship."

"I was a little surprised to hear from you so quickly." Clark had received Roland's note that morning, and, impressed by his eagerness, he had immediately arranged a tour of the *Providence* for him.

"Time is money," Roland told him. "And I don't believe in wasting either one."

"That's a commendable notion for any good businessman," the captain countered. "Can I get you something to drink?"

"No. No, thank you. But I do have something else to discuss with you."

"Oh?"

"Besides my usual business, I also have very special merchandise shipped from China," Roland began.

"I'm afraid I don't understand." The captain frowned as he tried to grasp Stuart's meaning.

"I'm prepared to offer you a considerable sum to ensure the safe, undetected delivery of my more 'perishable' cargo."

Clark, a very moral man, was immediately suspicious, but he asked, "Just what kind of merchandise is it that you want me to carry?"

Roland's expression was guarded as he contemplated the captain. "If you're a true businessman, you'll appreciate what I'm about to tell you."

"Go on."

"The 'cargo' I bring into the country satisfies a great demand in the city and brings top dollar on the market." He paused for effect. "Your cut would be substantial."

"Yes," Clark said impatiently.

"I supply females for the Chinese crib operators," Stuart finished bluntly.

Clark had a difficult time maintaining a mask of civility. This man was no better than the slave traders who'd flourished in the South before the war.

"Do Jon and Mitch know about this?" Clark's tone betrayed none of his outrage.

"Naturally," Roland lied. "Everyone likes to make an easy dollar. They're not exceptions."

"I see." The captain paused. "I can easily see that your venture would be very profitable, but I'm afraid I do not wish to be involved in it."

Roland was surprised. "There's money to be made—"

"I'm sure, but I'm not interested. I don't believe in trafficking in slaves. It's a filthy business."

Recognizing the finality of Clark's statement, Roland shrugged off his remark and stood up. "Thank you for your time. I'm just sorry we couldn't work something out."

"I'm not, Mr. Stuart." Clark dismissed him coldly as he moved to open the cabin door. "Good day."

Roland strode from the room, seemingly unconcerned by his rejection, and Clark shut the door firmly behind him.

Beside himself with anger, the captain then sat back down behind his desk to think things through. How could he have been so duped? He'd thought he and Mitch had understood each other, but if this was typical of the way Williams Shipping did business, he would have to cease to be involved with that company. He would not sully his ship or his own reputation by carrying human cargo. Wanting to face Mitch and set things straight, he got up and was about to leave when Mildred came in.

"Darling, I just saw Mr. Stuart leaving. How did your visit with him go?" she asked, but when she noticed his thunderous expression, she paused. "What's wrong?"

"I'll tell you later." He started to walk past her, but her hand on his arm stopped his progress.

"You'll tell me, now," Mildred insisted. It was unusual for her husband to be so upset and she was determined to know the cause. "Where are you going?"

"My conversation with Mr. Stuart was very informative," he began tensely. "It seems that the merchandise Williams Shipping is bringing back from China is more than tea and dry goods."

Mildred frowned. "I don't understand."

"They are importing Chinese women to be sold into prostitution," he told her. "And they expect me to deal in the same trade."

Gasping, she considered his statements for a moment before insisting, "I don't believe it."

"It's true. Stuart just told me everything. I'm on my way now to inform Mitch and Jon that I will not be sailing for them. I want no part of their company."

Astounded by the news, Mildred could only nod her agreement. "If it is true, that's the only thing you can do."

"I'll be back."

Clark made the trip to the office of Williams Shipping without delay, and he stood rigidly at the gate while Caleb went to tell Mitch of his unexpected arrival. Surprised by the news that the captain wanted to see him, Mitch quickly went out to greet him.

"It's good to see you again." He offered his hand, but Clark refused to take it.

"I need to speak with you in private, Mitch," the captain told him stonily.

"Of course." Mitch was puzzled by his demeanor, but he directed him to his office. "Come on in and take a seat. How can I help you?"

Clark didn't answer until Mitch had closed the door

behind him and returned to his desk. "I have changed my mind about sailing for your company."

"What?" Mitch was completely taken aback. "But why?"

The captain's eyes narrowed as he regarded the man he'd thought to be his friend. "You know why. I've just had a very enlightening conversation with a business associate of yours, and knowing what I know now, I cannot, in good conscience, deal with you."

"I have no idea what you're talking about," Mitch protested. "Who is this 'business associate' you spoke with?"

"Roland Stuart."

"Roland?" Perplexed, he met Clark's gaze. "You will have to believe me when I tell you I don't know what this is all about."

"Stuart gave me a little insight into exactly what kind of cargo I'll be carrying."

"Yes?"

"Mitch, our conversation is pointless. You, no doubt, are aware of the 'merchandise' your ships carry."

"I'm afraid you've lost me there." Williams was angered by his insinuations. "Why don't you tell me exactly what Stuart told you?"

Clark eyed Mitch askance, but seeing his very real confusion, he suddenly realized that Stuart might have been lying about his involvement. "Stuart offered me a very lucrative deal to insure the 'safe and undetected arrival' of his merchandise."

Mitch grew silent and pensive. "Did he say exactly what this 'merchandise' was?"

"He did. He's importing Chinese women to sell into prostitution."

Clark's words jarred Mitch. After a moment, he said, "If you'll excuse me for a second, I'd like to get Jon."

Clark nodded curtly as Mitch left his office and returned moments later with Jon.

"The captain just had a meeting with Roland Stuart this morning."

"Ah, yes. Roland is a very good customer of ours." Jon spoke approvingly.

"Jon, just how long have you been dealing with Stuart?" Mitch asked.

"For almost a year now. Why?"

"Captain . . ." Mitch urged Clark to answer.

"Earlier this morning, your Mr. Stuart offered to cut me in on a very lucrative business arrangement, a deal he said you had full knowledge of."

"What deal?"

"He's bringing Chinese girls into the country to sell to the crib operators, and he's using your ships to do it."

Jon paled at the news. "The manifests—"

"Manifests can be altered or forged," Mitch said quietly.

"Then you two had no idea that this was going on?"

"None," Jon answered. "And I thank you for coming to us with this information."

Clark nodded, convinced of their innocence. "I didn't want to believe you were involved in anything so corrupt, but Stuart said that he had your approval."

"I think it's time we paid Roland a visit." Mitch was furious. "If you'll excuse us?"

"I'd like to come with you, if you don't mind." Clark said.

"Thank you." Mitch was grateful for his offer.

Roland was working at his desk when he heard a disturbance in the hall outside his office. He'd just started to rise to go investigate it when his office door flew open and Mitch and Jon walked in, followed closely by Captain Clark.

"Good afternoon, gentlemen." He greeted them smoothly and sat back down at his desk, his casual manner hiding the uneasiness that gripped him. "Is there something I can do for you?"

"Captain Clark just paid us a visit," Jon challenged, barely managing to keep a tight rein on his temper. "And the news he brought us was most revealing."

"Oh?"

"You may consider our association at an end," Mitch told Stuart coolly.

"May I ask why?"

"The good captain has told us everything, Stuart," Jon snarled. "Any arrangements we had are canceled."

"You can't do that. I have contracts with you!"

"Those contracts were signed under false pretenses. You're through, Stuart. Give it up."

"You're wrong, Williams! Your brother and I made a deal, and I'm going to see that you hold to it."

Mitch smiled thinly. "I'd like that, Roland. Why don't you go public with this? How do you think your friends would respond when they found out that you're dealing in prostitutes? Face it. It's over. You lost."

Roland's rage was overwhelming, but he was smart enough to know that this was not the time to lose control. He would find another way to get even with them. He still had Catherine, and that would count for something in his dealings with Jon.

"As you say," Roland remarked cryptically, and he watched dispassionately as Mitch, Jon, and the captain left his office without another word.

Cursing himself for ever having approached Clark, Roland got up to pour a drink. Why hadn't that damned fool kept his mouth shut? Pious idiots! That's what they were. Didn't they realize there was a fortune out there, just waiting to be made? Disgusted, but not yet ready to give up, he settled back at his desk, determined to find a way to regain the upper hand in his dealings with them.

Chapter 29

After leaving Espri in the dining room, Catherine returned to her bedroom and began to pace like a caged tigress. Playing the helpless, misguided wife didn't sit well with her, but she had no real choice in the matter for she was determined to try to salvage her marriage. Though she loved Roland, Cat knew she had no future with him. Her future was with Jon . . . she hoped.

The sound of a carriage drew her to the window. Brushing aside the heavy velvet drape, she glanced out, nervously surveying the scene below. Relieved to discover that it was only a passing vehicle and not Mitch or Jon returning early, Catherine sighed and let the drape fall back into place. What was Jon going to do—or say—when he found out? A chilling thought came to her, and she knew she had to speak with Roland immediately. She had to tell him what had happened before Jon found out about him. Her husband might seek to avenge himself.

Calling Florence, Catherine ordered her carriage brought around, and taking great care not to be seen by Espri, she quickly left for Roland's office. Pleased to find that he was in, she swept past the guards, hurrying to him.

"Roland, darling, something terrible has happened," she cried, rushing to him and throwing herself in his arms.

Roland was totally stunned by her appearance, and he assumed that she had heard about his argument with her husband. "Yes, Cat, I know."

"You know!" She blanched. "How did you find out?"

"Jon just left here, not half an hour ago. I suppose he went straight home to tell you the news, eh?" His tone was sardonic.

"News? What news?"

"You mean Jon didn't rush back to tell you that he'd ended our business association?"

"Oh, no." Catherine assumed that Jon had found out about their affair. "How did he find out?"

"From Captain Clark, damn him to hell!" Roland was seething.

"Captain Clark?" Catherine was confused. She wondered how the captain could have found out about their affair. "I don't understand."

"I made a tactical error," Roland admitted angrily. "I confided in the man and offered to cut him in on my dealings with the Chinese girls."

"And?"

"And he went to Jon and Mitch with what I'd told him." Roland raked a hand through his hair.

"Oh, no."

"There's got to be a way out of this. I've got to think of something. Do you have any ideas? Do you think you can influence Jon not to cancel our contracts?"

"A few hours ago, maybe, but now . . . no," she told him bitterly, and when he looked at her inquiringly, she explained. "I didn't come here because I'd heard about your run-in with Jon. I came to tell you that we were seen embracing in the study Saturday night."

He looked at her in dull amazement. "I didn't hear anybody—"

"Neither did I, but Espri saw us and she confronted me about it this morning. Luckily, she hasn't told Jon or Mitch yet."

"Why?" he wondered.

"I think she didn't want Jon to be hurt and she hoped she could warn me off. She's rather naïve about these things, darling."

"Obviously." He sneered. "What excuse did you give her for our 'intimate' moment?"

"I didn't have much time to think." Considering his present mood, Catherine was not anxious to tell Roland the lie she'd invented. "Espri caught me completely off guard."

Roland sensed she was hedging and he pressed. "So? What did you tell her?"

Realizing how totally devastating her fabrication was, she girded herself and answered truthfully. "I told Espri that you'd blackmailed me into being with you, that you had some kind of information that would ruin Jon's business and that you would use it against him if I didn't sleep with you."

His eyes icy with rage, Roland regarded her. "Do you realize what you've done? Of all the stupid, damned lies . . ." He stared at her incredulously, finding it hard to believe that his whole world was crashing down around him. His business dealings were in ruins; his love affair with Catherine was over. "When Jon hears that, he's going to come back here looking for blood—mine! Why the hell did you do it, Cat?"

"It was a matter of survival, darling," Catherine told him calmly, turning away from his vicious glare. "And I am a survivor."

"You seem to forget, my dear, that I am a survivor too." Roland's eyes narrowed as he considered his alternatives. His present position left him little room to maneuver. "There has to be some way I can turn this situation to my advantage," he said thoughtfully, realizing that it was futile to berate Catherine for her tale of blackmail. "I can't just stand by and let them ruin me. I wouldn't be in this position now if Jon had agreed to sell Williams Shipping to me. Damn! If only I had gained control of the company—"

"You said you had enough money to buy them out. Why don't you just start your own line?"

"That could take years." He was disgusted. "The demand must be filled now. I wish to hell Mitch had been killed! If he had, none of this would have happened."

"Well, it's too late to worry about that. At least you've still got your money. Right now, I'm walking a very fine line. If Jon decides not to believe my story, I'm ruined," Catherine pointed out.

Roland regarded her levelly. "Unless we can figure out a way to protect both of us."

"What do you mean?"

"I have an idea." A devious plan was taking shape in his mind. "I must have control of Williams Shipping if I'm to continue my present, very profitable, pursuits."

"Right."

"And you need your husband's acceptance of your story that I blackmailed you, and his subsequent forgiveness—or financial security, should he decide to throw you out. Correct?"

"Callously, but accurately, put," she answered, irritated.

"This is hardly the time to worry about semantics." Roland turned a frosty gaze on her. "The point is that we are both in a difficult situation that demands immediate action. The *Aurora* is due to arrive at any time and she's carrying *my* cargo. I have no intention of backing off and letting Jon and Mitch take charge of it. I want what's mine, and I mean to get it."

"How?"

"I'm going to force them to sell the shipping line to me."

"Force them? How? You know they'll never part with it. It's a family business."

Roland's smile was wolfish as he faced her. "Espri is the answer."

"Espri?"

"Suppose I hold her for ransom—the ransom being the legal sale of the company?"

"That's going to be difficult. Mitch will come after you!"

"Of course he will, but if he wants his wife back, untouched, he'll sell out to me. I'll offer him fair market value. He'll have plenty of money and his wife back, and I'll have the ships I've been wanting for almost a year."

"They can't be aware that I'm involved," Catherine insisted.

"Naturally. Now, tell me, when's a good time to catch Espri alone? Does she go anywhere regularly?"

"No. Although Mildred Clark is a good friend of hers, and she might go out if she received a note from her."

Roland nodded in silent acknowledgment.

"I've got to get back, but I want one thing understood between us."

"Yes?"

"When this is over, I want a share of Williams Shipping."

He considered her demand. "We'll discuss that later."

"We'll discuss it now, or I'll reveal your plan to kidnap Espri."

"You're a hard woman, Cat, but I suppose that's why I love you." He went to her and pulled her roughly into his arms, kissing her passionately. "We're alike, you and I."

"Indeed we are. I want it in writing that I get twenty percent of Williams Shipping, or the cash equivalent, for my part in this."

"Done." He agreed as he went to his desk and wrote out the note she'd demanded. Signing it with a flourish, he handed it to her and said, "I'll deposit the funds in a separate account for you at the bank."

She smiled as she tucked the note into her handbag, pleased by his capitulation. "I really do have to get back now." She grimaced at the thought of the upcoming scene. "This is going to be the most miserable night of my life."

"I can appreciate your sentiments, but remember, you're going to be financially independent when this is all over."

"That thought has merit." Cat looked up at him sadly. "I'm going to miss being with you."

"Perhaps later, when things settle down, we can arrange something." They kissed again and then moved apart.

"I'll be in touch. Don't have the note delivered to Espri until after Jon and Mitch are gone."

"When do they usually leave?"

"I'd say between eight and eight-thirty. Have your man keep watch just to be sure."

After one last desperate embrace, they parted.

Catherine ordered her carriage to let her out in front; then she hurried up the steps and into the house. She had not even considered that Jon might return early from the office, and when she went through the door, she was shocked to hear the sound of his voice raised in anger. It was coming from the sitting room.

"I refuse to believe that!" he declared heatedly, and Catherine's heart sank at his words. Though she didn't want it to be true, she felt certain that Espri had just told him of their discussion that morning.

Usually, Catherine was very confident in her dealings with Jon, but today she was worried. She knew that Jon loved her; however, she didn't know whether his love was strong enough to withstand the humiliation he would feel when she confirmed Espri's painful revelation. Nonetheless, without further hesitation, she walked into the room to face them.

"Catherine!" Espri's surprise was evident, and Catherine

could feel all eyes in the room boring into her. "Where have you been? I thought you'd gone—"

"No. I didn't run away, Espri."

"But where did you go? You told me that you were going to your room."

"Yes, Catherine," Jon put in frigidly, "where *did* you go?"

Cat glanced at Espri before answering him. "I suppose you've told them everything?"

"Yes. I told them of our conversation this morning."

She sighed. "I had hoped to return before you had the chance, but . . ." She took a deep breath before continuing. "I went to see Roland, to tell him that I was no longer afraid of his threats and that it was over between us."

"You what?" Jon looked stricken. "Then it is true that you've been sleeping with him?"

"Yes, but let me explain." Catherine started across the room toward him, but he turned away from her, his movements jerky.

"I don't want to hear a thing you've got to say right now," he told her.

"You must listen to me, Jon! I did it for you," she pleaded.

He turned to her, his expression vicious. "You *whored* for me! Think again!"

"Please, understand. I didn't know what information he had, but he said it was enough to shut Williams Shipping down completely and to disgrace you before society. I still don't know what information could be so damaging, but I realize now that it doesn't matter. All that matters is our love!"

Jon stood rigidly before her, his face an expressionless mask as he listened to her words.

"Jon! Please, say something to me!" she begged, knowing that her situation was far more desperate than she'd originally thought. She had expected some rejection from him, but not this total disdain.

"Catherine . . . I'm sorry." Jon gave her a cold, penetrating look and then walked from the room.

Catherine watched in disbelief as he left. She wanted to run after him, but she knew there was no point in doing so right now. She must wait and hope that he'd come back to her. When she heard the front door open and then slam shut, she rounded angrily on Espri and demanded, "Why didn't you wait until I got back to tell him? Why did you have to ruin everything?"

Espri was so startled by her verbal attack that for a moment she couldn't respond, but Mitch quickly spoke up in her defense.

"Catherine. The truth would have come out anyway, and the results would have been the same."

"But maybe if I'd been the one to break it to Jon, he wouldn't have been so upset," she argued.

"Don't try to fool yourself, Catherine." Mitch was disgusted by the whole situation. "No matter who told him, it would hurt."

"He's got to realize that I did it for him," she protested, turning a tear-filled gaze on her brother-in-law.

"Somehow, I don't think he's going to see it that way." Mitch was brutally frank.

"But he has to! I love him!"

"Espri, if you'll excuse me, I think I'll go after him," Mitch murmured quickly to her as he started from the room. "I don't want him to try anything foolish."

"Of course. I'll be here if you need me," she answered softly.

As soon as Mitch had left the house, Catherine faced Espri. "If Jon doesn't come back to me, I'll see that you pay for this!"

"Catherine, I had nothing to do with what happened here tonight. This was all your own doing. You should have gone to Jon in the very beginning, trusted him to handle Roland Stuart."

"You don't know what you're talking about!" she hissed. "I was protecting Jon! Saving him from ruin! And now you've all turned on me!"

Espri knew Catherine's upset was real, but she could offer few words of comfort or encouragement. The news had been devastating to Jon, and she had no idea how he was going to deal with it. She hoped Mitch would stay with him until he'd had time to think things through.

"I don't understand why you went to Roland's this afternoon," she challenged. "If your relationship with him was forced, as you say, it seems ridiculous that you would want to face him alone. Unless, of course, you wanted to warn him that Jon was about to find out about it." Espri was becoming more distrustful of Catherine. The memory of the "private invitation" her sister-in-law had sent to Roland for the ball came to her mind, as did the secretive trip Catherine had made in the previous week.

"I don't have to listen to your groundless accusations!" Catherine declared. Then she stormed from the room.

As Espri watched her go, she wondered if she'd discovered the truth. It all fit, but why had she done it? Espri frowned. Jon was handsome, intelligent, and rich; and he obviously adored Catherine. Why would she jeopardize her marriage for Roland Stuart? Unless . . . perhaps Catherine had been involved with Stuart before her marriage, and this was just a quickly invented lie to cover up the discovery of their affair.

Remembering Mitch's original misgivings about this woman, Espri felt certain that blackmail had not been involved. Catherine had been caught in a compromising situation. Faced with the knowledge that she'd been discovered, she'd come up with an explanation that she hoped would save her position. Sadness filled Espri as she considered the outcome of Catherine's selfish pursuits, and she wanted to discuss her thoughts with Mitch when he returned.

Jon did not notice the carriage that had pulled up alongside him until Mitch called out to him.

"Jon. Get in."

Numb from the emotional shock he'd just suffered, he did what he'd been told to do.

"Where do you want to go?"

"It doesn't matter, but I could sure use a drink right now."

Mitch ordered the driver to take them to the saloon near their office. After getting a bottle of bourbon and two glasses from the barkeep, they took a table near the back to afford themselves some privacy.

"Do you feel like talking?" Mitch asked sympathetically.

"No." Jon tossed down a full glass of bourbon, then looked at Mitch, his eyes cold and deadly. "I feel like killing Roland."

"There's nothing to be gained by using violence."

"I'll feel better," Jon retorted quickly, refilling his glass.

"You won't if you end up in jail on manslaughter charges."

Jon snorted indifferently. "Do you think I really care what happens to me?"

"Jon." Mitch's voice was deep with concern. "I care."

Pain evident in his eyes, Jon glanced at his brother. "How could Catherine have done it, Mitch? How could she have let him use her that way?"

Knowing that Jon wasn't thinking clearly, Mitch remained silent. He had his suspicions about what had gone on between Catherine and Roland, and he firmly believed that blackmail had had no part in it.

"Damn!" Jon slammed his fist down on the rough-hewn table, drawing curious looks from the other customers. "What the hell am I supposed to do?"

"You've got to think this through carefully," Mitch declared. "There's no point in going off half-cocked. If you want my advice, I'll give it, but only if you ask."

Through the numbing haze of his pain, Jon understood what his brother was saying. Their days as big brother and younger brother were over. They were equals. They were contemporaries. They were family.

"I'm asking," he said stiffly.

Mitch regarded him for a moment as he took a sip of bourbon. Then he asked, "Do you love Catherine, Jon? After all that you've found out today, can you sit there and honestly tell me that you still love her?"

The question seared Jon's soul. It was the same one he'd been asking himself since he'd left the house. Did he love her? "I don't know anymore," he answered truthfully, his mind and heart in a turmoil.

Mitch nodded in understanding. "That's the first and only question you've got to come to grips with."

"But Roland," he protested, "what do you think he knows about the business? What could he use to threaten us?"

"Nothing," Mitch answered succinctly.

"Nothing?" Jon was astonished.

"If he had something he could use against us, he would have used it this morning when we cut him off."

Jon frowned as the pieces began to fall into place. "He had nothing. But why did he threaten Catherine that way?"

Mitch fixed him with a piercing glare. "Think, Jon. Do you really believe he blackmailed her?"

Jon paled. It was true. If Roland had had some damaging evidence against them, he would have used it that morning to ensure that his own business arrangements remained intact. He wouldn't have let them close his operation down without a fight of some kind.

"My God . . . I'll kill them both!" Jon started to get up, but

Mitch reached out and grabbed his arm, forcing him back into his seat.

"Think, Jon. Don't let your emotions rule you. We've already taken care of Roland. There's no way he can hurt us now. We've destroyed him."

Jon nodded as he took a deep drink. His emotions frozen now, he smiled grimly. "Good. And now I'll take care of my wife."

"You've answered the question then?"

Jon met his brother's gaze evenly, and Mitch was startled by the callousness in his expression. "Yes."

They fell silent then, the murderous rage Jon had felt moments ago replaced by an icy resolve to end his marriage to Catherine.

Though it was well past midnight and Catherine was in bed, she could not sleep. Her nerves were stretched taut as she waited for Jon's return, for she knew her future was in his hands. Tossing fitfully, she rolled onto her side and huddled beneath the covers.

"You look very innocent, my dear." Jon's voice cut through the stillness of the night like a knife as he came to stand at the foot of the bed in the darkness.

Catherine gasped and sat clutching the covers to her bosom. "Jon! I didn't hear you come in!"

"As I intended, my wife." His gaze was inscrutable.

"I'm glad you're back. I was worried." Calculatingly, she let the covers drop away to reveal the skimpy lace bodice of her expensive nightdress.

"It's a little late for that, don't you think?" There was no change in his expression as his eyes raked over her partially exposed breasts.

"No, Jon. Please, don't say that! Don't say it's too late!"

She moved to kneel before him, the position she assumed one of humble submission.

Though he had been drinking since he'd left her that afternoon, Jon was not drunk. He knew exactly what he was doing when he reached out and grasped her by the hair, forcing her head back so her eyes met his.

"How lovely you are when you're frightened, Catherine," he said, clearly amused by the fear in her. "Perhaps I should have a taste of this meekness of yours."

Viciously, he crushed her to him, and as his mouth savaged hers, Catherine tasted blood. He'd kissed her with a fury she'd never expected from him.

"Jon," she whimpered, in real terror as his grip tightened on her. "You're hurting me."

"Good," he snarled, grabbing the nightgown by the bodice and ripping it from her in one forceful tear. "That's better. I can see you now—all of you—you deceitful bitch!"

"Don't do this to us," Catherine pleaded, but he ignored her as he pushed her roughly back onto the bed. "This is all Roland's fault. He threatened me. He said he'd ruin you if I didn't sleep with him."

Jon laughed loudly, but it was not an amused laugh, more one of cynical satisfaction. "You can stop lying now, my dear."

"I don't understand. That's the truth, I swear." She groped desperately for some way to convince him.

"Catherine," he drawled as he loomed over her, "I've put it all together. Don't insult my intelligence with any more of your lies."

"But—"

"But nothing! I know the whole truth. You see, Mitch and I had a run-in with Roland earlier today. We discovered that he'd been bringing young Chinese girls into the country to be sold into prostitution, and we put a stop to his operation. Roland did nothing. Now don't you suppose, Catherine, if he had any incriminating evidence against us, he would have used it then, when we canceled his contracts?"

Silence hung heavily in the room.

"Ah, you've no answer for me. I thought not." His grin, as he stared down at her, was almost evil. "You see, Mitch was right when he told me not to marry you. He knew just what kind of woman you were. I was too enamored of you to see it then, but I see it now."

"Jon, you're wrong! I love you!"

"Is that why Florence has been arranging trysts for you with Roland once a week ever since we married?" he demanded, presenting her with the final damning piece of evidence. When she blanched at his words, he knew the whole truth. "The only thing you loved about me was my money." Jon shook his head in wonder at his own stupidity. "What were you going to do if you became pregnant? Would you have known who the father was?"

"I—"

"Shut up! I want you out of here in the morning," he ordered dispassionately. "The servants have been instructed not to allow you to leave with more than one suitcase." He glanced over at her dressing table and seeing her jewel box, he strode to it. "I'll keep these too. I'm sure Roland will provide amply for his mistress. You won't be needing my gifts."

In shock, Catherine watched him stride across the room.

Pausing at the door, Jon turned. "Be gone in the morning, Catherine. First thing. You'll be hearing from my lawyers very soon about a divorce. And if you're expecting a settlement, I'm afraid it's out of the question. You've already been paid in full for your services."

Jon went downstairs, intent on spending the night in the sitting room. He was surprised to find Mabel waiting for him in the hall.

"Yes, Mabel? Is something wrong?"

"No, sir. I just wanted to tell you that I've already sent

Florence packing and that Toby, Miss Catherine's driver, will be gone at first light."

"Thank you, Mabel," he told her sincerely. "Were those the only two servants she brought with her?"

"Yes, sir."

"Good. If you see anything around here that belongs to her, I want you to give it to charity. Do you understand?"

"Yes, Mr. Jonathan, I understand," she answered sadly. "Will that be all for tonight?"

"Yes. I think that's quite enough for one night, don't you?" His smile was sad as he started off down the hall. "Good night, Mabel."

"Good night, Mr. Jonathan. Just call if you need anything."

"I'll be fine. You go on to bed," he said as he disappeared into the sitting room.

Chapter 30

Espri lay quietly by Mitch's side in the privacy of their bedroom. "Then it's over between Jon and Catherine?"

Mitch nodded in the darkness. "Whatever doubt he may have had was completely erased when he questioned her maid."

"Florence?"

"Yes. It seems that Roland and Catherine were lovers even before she married Jon. Her story about being blackmailed was just a lie she'd invented to try to protect her marriage and the social position it gave her." His tone was heavy with resentment.

"I'm sorry."

"Don't be. It's just a shame he didn't find out sooner. Catherine's an opportunist and he'll be well rid of her." Mitch thought fleetingly of Andrew.

"How is he taking it?" Espri remembered Mitch telling her about his friend Andrew, whose wife had left him for a richer man, and she knew he was concerned about his brother.

"Hard . . . very hard. He really loved Catherine. I wish I could be more help to him, but this is something he's got to work through on his own."

"Jon's a strong man." Espri tried to sound encouraging. "I'm sure he'll get through this."

"I hope so, love. I hope so."

Standing with a sheet wrapped about her, Catherine looked up when the bedroom door opened and she was surprised to see Mabel enter instead of Florence. "I wanted Florence!" she snapped angrily. "Where is she?"

"She's been let go, ma'am," Mabel answered sharply.

"Let go! By whom?" Cat demanded, startled.

"By Mr. Jonathan, ma'am. She's already vacated her quarters."

"Damn him!"

"Is there something I can do for you?" The maid's tone was barely respectful.

"No. Nothing."

"Then, if you'll excuse me . . ." Mabel left quickly, glad to be away from Catherine. She was most fond of Mr. Jonathan and she found this woman's infidelity and deceitfulness unforgivable.

Catherine was livid as she watched the servant go. How dare Jon humiliate her this way before the staff! What joy she would feel tomorrow when Roland made his move! She was glad that she'd made an arrangement to get her share of the wealth, for she knew that she was going to need it.

Suddenly anxious to be gone, Catherine threw off the sheet and quickly dressed. Pacing to the window, she stared out across the darkened city as she awaited the first sign of daylight so she could make her exit. She was determined not to slink guiltily off into the night. When she went, she would go with dignity.

As she stood there amidst the splendor of her richly appointed bedroom, she had to admit to herself that she had enjoyed her sojourn as Mrs. Jonathan Williams. As Jon's wife, her standing in the community had been above reproach and her funds had been unlimited. Even so, she found the prospect of independence, in light of the money Roland was providing, most appealing. No longer would she have to pretend to love Jon. No longer would she have to suffer his lovemaking while she dreamed of Roland. Her future looked brighter than ever, she decided, and she was actually eager to go forth into it.

Her single trunk packed to the brim with her best clothing, Catherine was ready to go when the sun finally edged above the eastern horizon. Ringing for a servant, she waited impatiently for someone to come so she could have her belongings carried downstairs and order her carriage brought around. However, when long minutes passed and no one answered her summons, she descended the staircase in search of help. She had just started down the main hall toward the back of the house when she heard someone behind her. Wheeling about, Catherine was startled to find her husband observing her as he leaned negligently against the newel post at the foot of the stairs.

"My, my," he drawled spitefully. "We're certainly up early this morning, aren't we?"

"I've nothing to say to you," Cat replied coolly. "I was just looking for a servant to help me bring my trunk down."

"Please," Jon said sarcastically, "allow me the *pleasure*."

She watched in amazement as he mounted the stairs and returned quickly with her things.

"There you are, Catherine." He set the trunk down heavily. He approached her slowly, his eyes glittering with emotions she couldn't even begin to fathom. "Now, is there anything else I can do to expedite your departure?"

"You're drunk!" Cat charged in disgust as she smelled the

bourbon on his breath. She tried to move away from him, but he grabbed her by the arm and jerked her back.

"Yes, Catherine, I'm drunk." Jon stared down at her critically and then he frowned. Now that he knew of her unfaithfulness, he found little beauty in her. "But not drunk enough to forget your treachery. As I look at you now," Jon went on, "I find it amazing that I ever thought myself in love with you." He caressed her with insulting familiarity as she fought against him.

"Let me go!" she spat out, and Jon did, pushing her roughly away.

Smiling derisively, he told her, "Don't worry, Catherine. I have no designs whatsoever on your body. Roland can have you."

She glared at him, but he only laughed. "You were leaving?" he prodded her.

"Yes, and with great pleasure, I might add." She started toward the back of the house again to order a carriage brought around, but Jon called out.

"There's no point in summoning a carriage. My stables are no longer at your disposal."

Catherine gaped at him as he opened the door and carried her trunk down to the street in front of the house. Returning, he held the portal open for her and gestured for her to go. "I'm sure at this time of day, you'll be able to hire a conveyance to take you wherever it is you want to go."

"You can't be serious," she said haughtily.

"Rest assured, madame, that I am very serious." Jon stood woodenly as she swept past him; then he went back inside, closing the door behind him.

Roland was surprised to find Catherine seated before his desk waiting for him when he arrived at his office that morning, and he chuckled as he eyed her trunk. "Obviously, Jon didn't believe your story," he observed candidly.

"Obviously," she drawled, not amused.

"What do you intend to do?" Roland inquired as he settled in behind his desk and she took the seat opposite him.

"I really hadn't thought much beyond the moment. Did you take care of my money yet?"

"Not yet, but I will as soon as the transaction is complete with Mitch and Jon."

"Good. I'm going to need it to reestablish myself. He's been quite ugly about the whole thing."

"The trunk is all he let you have?"

"Yes. I'm quite penniless at the moment," she told him calmly.

"How much do you need for today, Cat?" Roland took out his wallet.

"I won't be greedy, darling. Whatever you think it will take to settle me comfortably for a few nights."

Roland nonchalantly shoved five one-hundred-dollar bills across the desktop to her. "If you need more, just let me know."

She took the money daintily and placed it in her handbag. Her smile was inviting as she glanced up at him. "I think I may find it quite nice, not to have to worry about Jon all the time."

"I know I shall," he agreed, his gaze lingering on her.

"Have you decided how to keep all these happenings from your wife?" Cat asked with interest. "I'm sure she'll be informed that Jon and I are apart."

"Yes, Chelsea and Emily will waste no time bending Susan's ear with that juicy bit of gossip, but I'm not sure she'll find out the rest. I'm pretty certain that your wonderful husband won't want to spread the word that he's been playing the fool for some time."

Catherine looked thoughtful. "I suppose we could

continue the way we have been. I can just take a room at the Palace for now."

"Fine. And as soon as the deal goes through, we can see about getting you a house of your own."

Her lips curved invitingly. "That sounds wonderful."

"Did Jon say how he was going to handle things?"

"I'm sure he'll be filing for an annulment. I just hope he doesn't go public with it."

Roland nodded. "It won't matter after we pull off our plan. You'll be rich, and I'll have control of the company."

A sudden chill ran down Catherine's spine, and she glanced up quickly. "What if something goes wrong?"

Her question startled Roland. "How can anything go wrong? We'll grab Espri, keep her locked up nice and safe until the papers are signed. I'll have Williams Shipping, and Mitch will have his wife and a lot of money."

"But what if Jon and Mitch go to the police?"

Roland chuckled. "I have a lot of influence there, darling. You needn't worry about that."

She was pleased by that news. "Wonderful."

Glancing at his watch, he was surprised to find that it was near nine. "It's almost time to set our little plan in motion. I'd better—" He was interrupted by a knock at the door. "Yes, what is it?"

The door opened and Bill entered. "We've just received word that the *Aurora*'s been sighted off Point Lobo."

"Perfect!" Roland came to his feet in a single move, and he turned quickly to Catherine. "Go on to the hotel. I'll check in with you later. Bill, find a carriage for Mrs. Williams, please."

The guard nodded and then hastened on his errand.

"But what about our plan?" Catherine didn't want Roland to be distracted from his original purpose.

"Everything will be taken care of right now. I'll send word to you as soon as I know something."

"Fine." Cat had been hoping that they would have some time alone that morning, but she now realized that it was not to be.

"Don't look so worried, darling." Roland came around the desk to kiss her. "When everything has been arranged, I'll come to you."

"What are you going to do about the *Aurora*?"

"I've already arranged with Alan to have my merchandise unloaded before Jon and Mitch are notified of the ship's arrival. There'll be no problem there," he reassured her quickly.

"The carriage is out back, boss."

"Good. I'll see you later then." Roland gave her a quick kiss and then sent her on her way. When the conveyance had driven off, he called Bill and Joe into his office.

"I have an important job for you this morning and I don't want anything—I mean *anything*—to go wrong. Understand?"

"Yes, sir." They knew they had better play straight with him this time.

"This is what I want you to do . . ." Roland quickly outlined his plan for kidnapping Espri, then he handed them the forged note they were to deliver to the house. "As soon as you get her, I want her bound and gagged. You'd better blindfold her too."

"But what if she fights us?"

"Subdue her, but no permanent damage!"

"Yes, sir."

"Once you've got her, meet me at the old, deserted Morrow Warehouse."

"Right."

"Do you have any questions?"

"No, I think we've got it. All we have to do is overpower the driver and take her by surprise, so she can't make a fuss."

"Morrow Warehouse," Roland emphasized.

"We'll be there."

Roland watched as they left the office and he felt good about the plan. It was foolproof, and by tomorrow, with any luck at all, he would have complete control of his destiny. Smiling, he headed from the office, eager to meet Alan and the captain of the *Aurora* at the warehouse and to inspect his newest shipment of "goods."

Since Jon and Mitch had left for the office over an hour before, Espri had been at loose ends, wondering how to spend her day. The quietude of the morning had seemed stifling, and she was more than pleased when a messenger delivered a letter from Mildred, inviting her for a visit aboard the *Providence.* Telling Mabel of her plans, she eagerly ordered a carriage brought around to take her to the dock where the ship was berthed. Not being familiar with Jon's help, she did not notice that the driver was one she'd never met before. She allowed the man to assist her into the conveyance, then sat back comfortably as he drove off.

Bill could hardly believe his luck. Everything was going so smoothly! The stables at the Williams house had been deserted save for one old man, and he had had little trouble overpowering him. After leaving the stablehand bound and gagged, he'd picked up the woman and here he was—just about to rendezvous with Joe. Pulling into the alley where he knew his friend was waiting, he signaled, and Joe quickly jumped into the carriage.

Espri had been surprised when the driver had turned into a dark, dangerous-looking alley, and she'd been about to protest when the door had flown open and a man had climbed in.

"What are you doing!" she demanded, suddenly frightened.

"Shut up, lady, and you won't get hurt."

But Espri was not faint of heart, and she struck out at him as she screamed. Though he hadn't wanted to hit her, Joe had no choice for she was struggling determinedly with him. When he did so, Espri fell back, unconscious, on the seat.

"What the hell is going on?" Bill jumped down from his seat when he heard the woman scream.

"Ah, damn it, she started to fight me. I took care of her, though," Joe replied as he tied Espri's hands behind her and then gagged her as Roland had ordered him to do.

"Don't forget the blindfold," Bill said, and Joe hurriedly complied. "Now, let's go. Roland's waiting."

"Yeah. I'm ready."

Bill closed the door to the carriage and, resuming his seat, started off toward the Morrow Warehouse.

Alan Harris stood in the dark dampness of the large, empty building, two of his men beside him, awaiting delivery of Roland's private merchandise from the *Aurora*. When the ship had first been sighted, he'd sent word to Roland; then he'd dispatched a special messenger to notify the captain of the new point of disembarkation for Roland's special cargo. He hoped that no one would report the ship's arrival to Mitch or Jon before the Chinese women were unloaded.

Glancing out toward the bay, he was relieved to spot a launch heading his way, and he eagerly hurried forth to greet the *Aurora*'s captain.

"Captain Michaels! We're so glad you finally made port! Did everything go smoothly?"

"Yes," Jason Michaels informed him. "We ran into bad weather our first two weeks out of China, and that's what held us up."

"Glad to hear it was nothing serious. Well, how many did you bring us this time?" Alan's eyes glittered with anticipation as he awaited the captain's answer.

Michaels, aware of the agent's lascivious interest in the

females, answered quickly. "We started out with forty-two, but six died on the way and one is very ill right now."

"So that leaves us with thirty-five healthy ones." Alan was pensive. "How long do you think it will take to unload them?"

"Here . . ." Michaels looked around assessingly. "I'd say half an hour. Why the change in plans?"

"Jon and Mitch."

Alan started to explain, but Michaels cut him off.

"Mitch? I thought he'd been killed."

"You couldn't know. He's returned. It seems he was shanghaied instead of murdered, and it took him almost a full year to make his way back."

"Interesting," Michaels remarked thoughtfully.

"Anyway, they found out about Roland's 'imports' and canceled all their contracts with him. That's why Roland and I wanted to make sure we got the women off the boat before they learned that you'd made port."

"I see. Well, let's get at it then. Do you have my money?" Michaels asked pointedly, and when Alan extracted an envelope, thick with greenbacks, from his vest pocket, he smiled. "Thank you. It's been good doing business with you." Striding confidently back to the launch, he ordered his men to return to the *Aurora* and to start bringing the women ashore as quickly as possible.

When he returned Roland had arrived on the scene, and he greeted the captain effusively.

"Jason, it's good to see you. How was your trip?"

"Fine, except for our delay by bad weather."

"Ah, that's what caused the problem. I was worried."

"I can understand why. Harris here was just telling me that Mitch and Jon stumbled onto your scheme. I take it they were less than pleased with the arrangements we'd made?"

"Yes, but I'm hoping to work something out with them," Roland confided. "Have you been taken care of?"

Michaels knew exactly what he meant. "Yes, I have, and if

you arrange something so profitable again, just let me know. I'd be pleased to work for you."

"I'll do that," Roland assured him as he watched the launch return with the first load of Chinese females. "How many do we have?"

"Thirty-five healthy. One ill, six dead at sea."

He nodded approvingly. "Good. I should turn a tidy sum on this shipment."

"No doubt about it. I had trouble keeping my men away from them."

"That's what I like to hear. The more comely they are, the more money I make." Roland called Alan to him. "Have you arranged a showing?"

"Yes, it's all set. The dealers have all been contacted, and they should be here in about three hours."

"Good. You've done well. Take charge here now. See that they're cleaned up, and then put them in the pens until the buyers arrive."

"I'll see to it," he assured Roland.

"And Alan?"

Alan glanced at him questioningly.

"Do whatever you want. Captain Michaels and I will be staying out here." Alan nodded, then hurried off to direct the young women into the secluded privacy of the old building. Roland looked up at the sea captain and shrugged. "It keeps him happy and it keeps him quiet."

"I understand."

Then the sound of a carriage pulling up drew Roland's attention. "I must see to this; excuse me," he said.

"Of course. I'll be returning to the ship now, anyway. I hope you'll be in touch." Michaels shook Roland's hand.

"I'm certain you'll be hearing from me very soon."

"Good, Stuart. I've enjoyed dealing with you."

As Captain Michaels went to join his men on their return trip to the *Aurora,* Roland approached Bill and Joe.

"How did it go?"

"Smooth except for one thing," Joe told him.

"What happened this time?" Roland demanded angrily.

"Nothing serious. She just started screamin' and I had to hit her."

"Not hard!"

"No. Just enough to knock her out for a little while."

"Has she come around yet?"

"Not yet, but we got her trussed real good, just in case she does start stirrin'," Bill assured him.

Roland wasn't pleased to hear that she'd fought so much, and he turned to Joe. "I want you to go back to my office."

"Yes, sir."

"In my desk in the bottom right-hand drawer there's a small bottle. Bring it here. Use my carriage."

"Right. I'll be back."

Roland then said to Bill, "Stay with the carriage and don't take your eyes off of her, not even for a minute. Is she blindfolded?"

"Yes, sir."

"Good. When Joe gets back, send him straight to me."

Leaving Bill to guard Espri, Roland went down to help Alan supervise the unloading of the slaves.

"How is it going?" he asked.

"Fine. One more load and we're done."

Stuart nodded in approval. "The faster the ship gets reported to Jon and Mitch the safer we are. Are they getting the women cleaned up?"

"The two men I brought with me are taking care of that."

"How do they look?" Stuart knew he would get an honest opinion from Alan.

"There are several who're unblemished, and the two young ones should bring a good price. You know how the traders like virgins."

"Just make sure the virginal ones stay that way."

Alan was disappointed, but he understood. "Of course. I'll be very selective."

"Also, as soon as Chun Ki arrives, I'll need to talk with him."

"I'll tell him."

Alan went back inside the warehouse to await the dealers while Roland stayed at the dock to watch the launch make its last trip.

"The captain wants to know if you want the sick one," a burly sailor asked as they started to shove off to pick up the last load of girls.

"How bad is she?"

"Nothing contagious, but she's real weak and sickly."

"How's she look? Is she attractive?"

"Naw," he replied. "She ain't nuthin' but skin and bones."

"I don't want her. Do whatever you want with her," Roland said, uncaringly.

"Captain Michaels said he don't want her aboard," the seaman continued.

"Then dump her overboard! I don't need any sickly women here. I run a clean business."

"Yes, sir," the seaman answered respectfully as he pushed off to pick up the final shipment.

Espri's head was pounding when she regained consciousness, and she couldn't stifle a moan as she tried to move. Her bonds held her immobile, however, so she lay, helpless, on the floor of the carriage, trying to understand what had happened to her. She could remember only a strange, threatening man entering her carriage and their subsequent scuffle.

"Hey, boss! The little lady's stirrin'," Bill called.

Roland was pleased to know Espri had come around and he beckoned for Bill to come to him. "I don't want any names or places mentioned around her. Understand?"

"Got it."

"Good. Let's just keep her in the carriage and out of sight until I'm through with these sailors. When Joe gets back, I'll take care of Mrs. Mitchell Williams personally. You stay with her until then."

Following his orders, Bill returned to his place beside the equipage and waited patiently for his partner's return.

Alan came to join Roland just as the launch arrived.

"I thought I'd told you that I didn't want the sick one!" he snarled as he noticed the thin, young girl clinging desperately to another, more healthy one.

"The captain said you were to do your own dirty work."

Roland looked exasperated as the women started to climb out of the small boat. The stronger girl was trying to help the sick one from the launch, but Roland quickly pushed her aside and motioned for her to go into the warehouse with the others.

"This one's yours, Alan. I don't care what you do with her, but I don't want to see her with the healthy ones. Understood?"

As Alan scooped the weak girl up in his arms and disappeared inside, Roland saw Joe return and he went to get the bottle from him.

"Thanks. Now, go inside and see if you can help Alan," he ordered.

Opening the carriage door, he leaned close to Espri and, keeping his voice disguised, said, "Mrs. Williams, you're going to be my guest for a few days, and I intend you to be an obedient one. I'm going to take your gag off, but if you scream, I will not hesitate to hit you again. Do you understand me?"

Wondering why anyone would want to kidnap her, Espri nodded.

"That's good. Now remember—silence!" Roland quickly

unknotted the rag and pulled it away. "I've got something here I want you to drink."

"Water?" she croaked hoarsely.

"Yes." He grinned evilly as he held the bottle to her lips.

Espri took a deep swallow, choked, and then gasped for breath.

"Mrs. Williams, that wasn't nice. Now, I want you to drink this of your own free will or I'll be forced to *make* you drink it!" Ruthlessly, he pressed the bottle to her lips and poured the potent laudanum into her mouth. He didn't stop until she'd swallowed a substantial amount. "That's better."

"Who are you? Why are you doing this to me?"

"Not to you, my dear. To your husband. Now, be quiet and rest. I'm sure you'll find that sleep will come very easily in the next few minutes."

"No! Please!"

"Gag her!" Roland said quickly when she started to panic, and Bill efficiently tied the dirty cloth back in place. Stepping down from the carriage, Stuart pocketed the bottle and turned to his hireling. "Stay here. I don't want anyone coming near this carriage."

"What are you going to do with her, boss?"

"I plan to have her spend the night in one of Chun Ki's establishments."

Bill looked shaken by that news. "You can't be serious. I doubt she'd live through it!"

"It's not your place to question me!"

"I don't cotton to killin' women."

"Don't worry. I have no intention of having her 'work' tonight. That just seems the safest place to keep her stashed until I make a deal with her husband. There's no need for you to be concerned."

Considerably relieved, Bill watched Roland go back inside the warehouse to check on the Chinese women.

Chapter 31

A workroom at the back of the old storehouse had been cleaned in preparation for the showing of the women, and it was there that Roland waited for the buyers to arrive.

"Chun Ki's carriage has just pulled up," Alan declared as he hastened into the room.

"Good. Do you have the sick girl out of sight?"

"Yes. She's in the cubicle behind the pens. No one will see her there."

"Make sure the buyers don't. I've made my reputation by dealing only in undamaged goods."

"She won't be going anywhere," Alan confirmed smugly.

Roland wondered briefly at his tone, but he let the matter drop. He had, after all, given the girl to Harris.

"In that case, I'd better go meet with Chun Ki before the others show up."

"Can I help you in any way?"

"No. This is personal." Roland went out to greet his Asian friend and business associate.

Chun Ki was a large, shrewd man who possessed great wealth and wielded considerable power in the Chinese community. He was just stepping down from his carriage when he saw Roland approaching. "It is good to see you," he declared cordially.

"And you, my friend," Roland replied before shaking his hand and leading him inside. "Your business is doing well?"

"Excellently." Chun Ki smiled widely. "And you?"

"The *Aurora* has brought us many fine selections this trip." Roland gestured toward the holding pens.

"I'm pleased. The market is very demanding." Chun Ki eyed the naked women with dispassionate interest.

"They are at your disposal. You may inspect them at your leisure."

"The other buyers?"

"Will be here in about half an hour. I wanted you to have first choice." Knowing Chun Ki was his most valuable ally, Roland was catering to him.

"I am flattered by the honor," Chun Ki responded as he went to stand before the cowering women.

"I will leave you now to make your selections. We will settle on a price later."

"That is satisfactory."

"There is a room in the back that has been prepared for the inspections. You may take them there if you like."

"Thank you, Roland. I will meet with you shortly."

Efficiently, Chun Ki selected eighteen of the girls, and after Alan's men took them from the cages, they were led into the room at the back of the warehouse. Approximately twenty minutes later, Chun Ki emerged. He had completed his personal examination of the females, and he was more than satisfied with those he had chosen.

"I will take them all. Everyone seemed sound and fit."

"I am glad that you are pleased."

"As always, in my association with you," the Chinese man said diplomatically. "I have calculated that the eighteen are worth five thousand four hundred dollars. Is that agreeable?"

"Your honesty is gratifying," Roland replied smoothly, though he was overjoyed at the price.

"I pride myself on being an honorable man." Chun Ki counted out the bills and handed them over.

Now that the business part of their meeting was over, Roland said, "Chun Ki, do you have a moment? I have a small problem and I would ask your help."

"Of course, my friend. But first let me arrange to have my slaves removed before the other buyers arrive." After speaking with Alan's men and directing them to deliver his purchases to his establishment, he watched as the women were given white cotton tunics with which to cover themselves and then were herded quickly outside to waiting carriages. Turning back to Roland, he said, "What can I, your most humble servant, do to help you?"

"I have something that I need to put in your safekeeping for a day or two."

Chun Ki looked at Roland quizzically. "It must be a very valuable prize, indeed."

"Suffice it to say, that what I entrust to you will have the power to change my entire future."

"What is it?"

"A woman. The wife of an acquaintance of mine. She must be kept safe until I conclude certain delicate negotiations with her husband."

"Ah," Chun Ki replied sagely. "Extortion?"

Roland smiled. "We understand each other so well."

"Indeed we do. How is she to be treated?"

"I do not want her harmed. It is important that she be returned in perfect condition when I've finished dealing with her husband."

"Do you have a preference as to where I take her?"

"No. I will leave that to your discretion. Just make sure it is someplace where she will not be found. Her husband is a very powerful man and he will not accept this situation without a fight."

"I see. You have her here?"

"Yes. She's in a carriage outside. I have given her a drug, and she is bound and gagged. I do not think she will cause you any trouble."

"Very well. It will be my pleasure to help you in this way. When do you want her back?"

"If all goes well, tomorrow. I will notify you tomorrow."

"And if it doesn't work out as you planned?"

Roland was pensive. "If not, she is yours to do with as you please."

"So these are very serious dealings."

"Very. She is my bargaining chip."

"I will take excellent care of her, you may rest assured. Who is she?"

"The wife of Mitch Williams."

"I have heard of his unexpected return."

"Yes, it is most unfortunate. He has caused me nothing but trouble."

"Then the rumor that they'd canceled your contracts was true?"

"You heard?" Roland was surprised.

"I hear many things." He shrugged. "Your plan will work. His bride is said to be an outstanding beauty of unusual descent."

"She is lovely, and I'm sure many of your more wealthy clients would pay handsomely for the chance to use her."

"Then I will take her with pleasure. Shall we make the transfer?" Chun Ki suggested.

"At once."

Roland led the way to the Williamses' carriage and opened the door to show her to Chun Ki.

"She is not dead?" he asked worriedly, not wanting the death of a successful businessman's wife on his hands.

"No. It's the drug."

Chun Ki nodded. "She would bring a good price. I will take her, and I will anxiously await word from you."

"Thank you, my friend."

As Roland and Chun Ki looked on, Bill quickly carried Espri's limp form to Chun Ki's carriage. Before he'd placed her in it, Alan came out of the warehouse, and his eyes widened in shock as he recognized Espri. Knowing that he couldn't interrupt Roland's conversation, he waited until the other man had gone; then he approached him.

"Roland, wasn't that Espri Williams?"

"You didn't see anything," Stuart ordered succinctly.

"The hell I didn't! What are you trying to do, get us killed?"

"Don't be ridiculous. I'm conducting a simple business deal."

"You can't sell a white woman into sexual slavery and get away with it, not one as prominent as Espri Williams."

"I haven't sold her," Roland declared calmly. "She's merely been placed in Chun Ki's hands for safekeeping."

"Roland"—Alan lowered his voice as his panic became real—"Chun Ki is—"

"Chun Ki is my friend, and he will do whatever I tell him to do. Until he receives word from me, nothing will happen to her. Now, relax. By this time tomorrow, I'll be running this entire operation and Espri will be back in her husband's loving arms."

"I hope you're right."

Alan was still worried, but Roland dismissed his concern as groundless.

"Let's see to our other buyers, shall we? There's a substantial amount of money still to be made today."

* * *

It was late afternoon when Jon finally started back to the house. With the arrival of the *Aurora* that morning, his day had been a busy one, and though he was exhausted, he was glad of that for he had had little time to reflect on the events of the past twenty-four hours. But as Jon entered the foyer, he remembered the scene he and Catherine had played out there that morning and a dull-edged pain knifed through him. He stood still a moment to bring his powerful emotions under control; then, needing relief, he strode purposefully into the study to pour himself a drink.

Unbidden thoughts of Catherine assailed him as he quickly downed a full glass of bourbon. Where had she gone? Was she sorry? Angrily, he threw the empty glass across the room, then watched in furious fascination as it smashed against the wall. He would drive her from his mind! He would force all thoughts of her from his life! She had betrayed him with a lover, and had used him and his business to enrich her lover's coffers.

Jon knew that he must erase every trace of her from his existence, so he decided to move out of the Williams house. He couldn't bear to remain here where memories of Catherine were still so fresh.

"Mabel!" he bellowed as he poured himself another glass of bourbon.

The maid answered his summons quickly. "Yes, sir, Mr. Jonathan."

"Have you carried out the instructions I gave you this morning?"

"Yes, sir. I've removed all of Miss Catherine's things from your suite and have given them to the workers in the missions."

"You're to be commended, Mabel. Thank you." He downed the second tumbler of bourbon just as quickly as the first and then turned to face her. "I want you to pack a few of my things. I'm going to move out of this house. I'm sure Mitch and Espri would enjoy having it to themselves."

"Mr. Jonathan," she protested, "that's not necessary. I'm sure Mr. Mitchell and Miss Espri would want you to stay."

"I have to go," he told her, and for a moment his stoic expression slipped and she saw reflected on his handsome features a flash of the pain that was tormenting him.

"I understand. Do you know where you'll be staying?"

"I think I will stay at the office. There's a room at the back. I can convert it to a sleeping area."

"If you don't mind my making a suggestion, why don't you go to a hotel, sir?"

"The fewer people who know about this, the better."

"Yes, sir. I'll go pack your clothes."

"Mabel . . ."

She looked back at him, her affection for him obvious. "Yes, sir?"

"Thank you."

"You're welcome."

"Is Espri here? I suppose I should tell her what I've decided."

"No, Mr. Jonathan. She left rather early this morning for a visit with Mrs. Clark. I had expected her back by now, but—"

"I guess they're having a good time." Jon wasn't concerned.

"Is Mr. Mitchell due back soon?" she asked.

"He had a meeting on the *Aurora* with Captain Michaels at four-thirty, but I expect he'll be here by six-thirty at the latest."

"Will you be staying for dinner this evening?"

"Yes. I won't leave until Mitch gets back."

"Very good."

Jon refilled his glass and sat down heavily on the sofa. He knew he should be making decisions about his future, but he felt incapable of dealing with more than the rudimentary elements of his life. He was about to take another deep drink when a knock at the front door drew his attention. Thinking it might be Espri, he went to answer it.

A young boy stood nervously before him, clutching a letter in his hand. "I have a note here for a Mr. Mitchell Williams."

"He's not here, but I'll take it for him," Jon offered.

"Who are you?" the youth asked.

"I'm Jonathan Williams, his brother, and I'll make sure he gets it."

"I don't know." The boy hesitated. "I was ordered to give it directly to Mitchell Williams."

Jon was intrigued by the messenger's orders. Taking a silver dollar out of his pocket, he handed it to him. "Here. If anyone asks, I'll tell them you delivered it to my brother. All right?"

"Gee, mister, thanks! Thanks a lot!" The lad handed Jon the letter, then raced down the steps.

Jon watched him until he was out of sight. When he went inside, letter in hand, he started to put the missive aside for Mitch, but something about the boy's nervous manner had made him suspicious. Returning to the study, he closed the door behind him, and ripped the envelope open. He read, in horror, the short, meaningful note Roland had sent.

> *Mitch, as you may or may not be aware, your wife is missing. I can assure you that Espri is safe, but her continued well-being is entirely in your hands.*
>
> *I want control of Williams Shipping, and I am prepared to offer you fair market value for the company. Bring sales contracts with you and meet me at my office at 10 P.M. this evening. Do not contact the authorities or I will not be able to guarantee your wife's safe return.*
>
> *Roland Stuart*

Stunned, Jon reread Roland's letter. Was this man serious? Had he really kidnapped Espri to gain control of the company? He dropped the note as fury possessed him. Not only had Roland used him and destroyed his marriage, he was now threatening to harm Espri! Moving deliberately, Jon went to the desk and unlocked the center drawer. With steady hands, he took the pistol that was kept there, and after checking to make sure it was loaded, he left the room, determined to meet with Roland.

Chun Ki lit a small lamp on the single table in the windowless room and directed his men to lay Espri on the narrow cot that was the only other furnishing.

"Do you need us to do anything else?" his henchmen asked respectfully.

"No. That will be all for tonight."

When Chun Ki was alone with the drugged beauty he turned to look down at her. He considered himself a connoisseur of beautiful women, and he found Espri to be one of the most attractive he'd ever seen. It pleased him that she was still unconscious for it gave him time to look her over carefully without having to worry about frightening her.

Gently, he untied the gag and removed the blindfold. Seeing her features clearly for the first time, Chun Ki smiled to himself. There would be no selling of this one to his customers. Should things not work out for Roland, he would keep her as his own personal servant. The prospect of owning her pleased him, but tempting as he found that idea, Chun Ki knew he could not take measures that would ruin Roland's deal. He was a man of honor, a man of his word. Untying her hands and feet, he went to the door and called to his slaves who waited in the narrow dark hall.

"Yes, Chun Ki?"

"I want her bathed and perfumed. Discard her clothing and dress her in a black tunic and trousers."

"Yes, sir."

"Call me when you've finished."

"Yes, Chun Ki."

The two women worked quickly, stripping away Espri's dress and underthings, and then bathing her with the perfumed soap they knew to be Chun Ki's favorite.

"Who is this woman who has won such favor with Chun Ki?" Ah Linn asked as she combed out the silken length of Espri's dark hair.

"I do not know. She is not white, but she is not Chinese either," Ming Toy responded. "Chun Ki has never shown such interest in one woman before. She must be special. Certainly her body is lovely."

They both regarded Espri's unclad beauty, jealously.

"I fear she will please him greatly," Ah Linn said bitterly. For many months now, Ah Linn had been Chun Ki's lover, and she did not like to think that she would be replaced.

"Maybe not," Ming Toy encouraged. "She is obviously not here of her own free will."

"No, but neither were we at first." Ah Linn remembered the day they had been sold to Chun Ki and the horrors they had suffered in the beginning, when they had tried to fight their fate as his slaves.

"It is not our place to interfere with his plans. We must hurry to prepare her. Do you have the clothing?"

"Yes." Ah Linn handed her the black silk shirt and pants, and watched as the other woman dressed her.

"I will go tell him that she is ready."

"Good, but do so smiling. You would not want him to know of your displeasure. It might anger him."

Ah Linn hurried to Chun Ki's private room, entering when he called out to her to do so. She bowed low.

"She is ready for you, Chun Ki."

"You have done well. Is she awake?"

"No. She did not stir the entire time."

"That is good." He smiled thoughtfully as he followed her from the room. "Bring a tray of food and tea," he instructed, and Ah Linn hurried to do his bidding.

Stepping into the cubicle where Espri lay, Chun Ki stared at her, his expression inscrutable.

"Is there more I can do for you, Chun Ki?" Ming Toy offered.

"Yes. I will need the chains and a small whip. Bring them to me."

"Yes, Chun Ki." She rushed to get the things he'd requested.

Moving to sit beside Espri, he touched her cheek with reverence. Marveling at the softness of her skin, he then trailed his hand down to cup her breast. His taste ran to small-busted women, and he found Espri's breast a bit too large. Still, this time he would gladly make an exception. He looked forward to the next day when he would receive word from Roland on the state of his transaction with Williams.

It was well past seven when Roland finally arrived at the Palace Hotel. He took little notice of its beauty as he hurried to Catherine's room to tell her the news of the day. Cat had been waiting all afternoon for him to come to her, and when he knocked, she anxiously threw open the door and embraced him.

"Darling! I thought you'd never come!" she told him as she kissed him on the mouth.

"It's been a busy day, but a successful one, love." He returned her kiss, crushing her to him.

"You've got Espri?"

"It went perfectly. I've turned her over to Chun Ki for the

time being. He'll keep her for me until I've concluded my business with Mitch and Jon."

"That's wonderful! Come in." She closed the door behind them.

"I can't stay long," Roland explained. "I've arranged a meeting with Mitch, and I want to get there early just in case he decides to pull something."

"I understand. Can you come back here later?" Catherine asked invitingly.

"There's nothing I'd like to do more. As soon as everything has been signed and Espri is returned, I'll come straight here. Susan won't be expecting me until later."

"Good." Cat went into his arms for one last kiss. "I'll be waiting."

Espri opened her eyes, then quickly shut them. Something was wrong . . . terribly wrong. The room was spinning, and she felt too weak to move . . . almost paralyzed. With great effort she lifted a shaking hand to her forehead and, drawing a deep, steadying breath, tried once more to look around. Fighting off nausea and dizziness, she finally managed to focus on her surroundings, and what she saw frightened her. The sparsely furnished room was no more than six by six— and there were no windows.

Levering herself up on an elbow, Espri stared about, trying to recall how she'd gotten there. The last thing she could remember was coming to on the floor of the carriage, tied up and blindfolded, and someone forcing her to take a deep drink of some fiery liquid.

Looking down at herself, she was amazed to find that her clothing had been changed. While she'd been unconscious, someone had stripped her of her regular clothing and had dressed her in a strange-looking outfit of black silk. Swinging her legs to the side of the narrow bed, she managed to sit up slowly and then groaned as she fought not to be sick.

Ming Toy, who had been ordered to stay outside the locked door and to report to Chun Ki when Espri awoke, heard the captive stirring, and she hurried to tell him the news. Pleased that his hostage had come around, he dismissed Ming Toy and went in to see her, alone.

Espri gasped when the door opened unexpectedly, and she stared fearfully at the huge Chinese man who stepped into the cubicle.

"Ah, I see that you have finally awakened." Chun Ki smiled as he closed the door behind him.

"Who are you?" Her voice was barely above a whisper.

"A friend," he answered simply. "And you, my dear Mrs. Williams, are my most-welcome guest."

Espri's confusion was very real as she faced him. "If I'm your guest, then I would like to go home. May I have my clothes back, please?"

Chun Ki chuckled with amusement, and stared down at her. "I'm afraid you're not *that* kind of guest."

"I don't understand." Espri frowned and then tried to stand up, but her legs felt too weak to support her. When she swayed weakly, Chun Ki helped her to lie down. "Who are you? Why am I here?"

"In time you will know, but for now, why don't you just relax? No harm will be done to you. As I have said, you are my guest. There is some food here"—he pointed to the tray on the small table—"and tea. Would you like some? It is hot and strong."

Her thoughts a jumble, her need to get away great, Espri decided to drink some tea in the hope of regaining some of her strength. "Yes. Thank you."

Chun Ki turned his back, and in that instant, Espri, in a burst of energy born of fear, made a dash for the door and what she hoped was freedom. She didn't know where she was or whom she was with. She only knew that she wanted to find Mitch. Chun Ki was surprised by her move. He had thought her too weak to make such an attempt, and he was greatly displeased by it.

"You are not a wise woman, Mrs. Williams," he told Espri as he went after her, catching her just as she would have run out into the narrow, dark hall. "That was a very stupid thing to do." Twisting her arm, he dragged her back into the room and threw her on the bed. "I was hoping you wouldn't fight your situation, but I can see that some restraint will be necessary."

Her eyes widening, Espri rubbed her bruised arm as she watched him reach beneath the bed and bring out a length of chain. "No!" she cried, but her terror only brought a leering smile to his face.

"But yes," he answered coldly. "I do not stand for disobedience from my slaves."

"Slaves?"

"You are not mine yet, but I intend to have you; remember that." Chun Ki's tone was cold and imperious. "Also remember that my women are subservient." Impersonally, he grabbed her left leg and fastened the iron manacle about her slender ankle.

"But why are you doing this to me? Where is my husband?"

"I am guarding you for a friend, and as to where your husband is, I have no idea, nor do I care." His gaze traveled over her dispassionately as she lay, chained and helpless, on the bed. Mechanically, he then handed her a cup of tea. "Drink this."

"I don't want it!"

"Drink it!" It was a command.

Fearfully, Espri took the cup, but her first sip revealed an unnatural bitterness to the tea and she balked. "No! I won't!"

"You will," he told her icily as he reached beneath the bed

to bring out a short, leather whip. Slapping the leather against his thigh, he stood over her menacingly. "Drink all of it! Now."

Terrified, Espri gulped down the hot, drug-laced tea.

"That's much better, Mrs. Williams," he said with satisfaction. He took the cup from her and pressed her down on the bed. Feeling some of the resistance go out of her, he asked, "What is your first name?"

Espri was trying to focus on him, but already her vision was fading. "Espri," she said softly, losing herself in the vortex that was claiming her.

"A pretty name. It suits you."

She heard his voice from far away. Knowing that the drug was beginning to work, Chun Ki took the liberty of intimately caressing her. He enjoyed the sleek feeling the silk gave her shapely form.

"Don't touch me! Let me go!" Espri managed only a strangled whisper as she futilely tried to escape his touch. The opiate was too powerful, and darkness overcame her, sweeping her away from the sordid reality of the situation just as she called out Mitch's name.

Chun Ki drew back and stared down at her hungrily. He wanted very much to bury himself within her sweet body, but his promise to Roland won out. Reluctantly, he left her chamber, locking the door behind him.

Going directly to Ah Linn's room, he entered without knocking.

"You have come to me, Chun Ki?" She was thrilled that he had chosen her this night.

"Do I not, always?"

"I had worried about the new woman."

"She is merely a guest here, nothing more," he told her. "Come. Satisfy me. I find I need you, now."

And Ah Linn went to him gladly, eager to please him in any way she could.

Chapter 32

Mabel was concerned. It was well past sunset, and still there had been no word from Miss Espri as to why she had not returned from her early visit to Mildred Clark's. Glancing at the mantel clock, she was glad to note that it was nearly six-thirty. Mr. Mitchell would be home soon and perhaps he would know where Espri was. The sound of the front door opening drew her from the back of the house, and she hurried forth to greet whoever was returning.

"Good evening, Mabel." Mitch was glad to be home. He was looking forward to spending a quiet evening with Espri.

"Mr. Mitchell," she responded cordially, glancing around. "Miss Espri isn't with you?"

Mitch looked at her, puzzled. "No. Should she be? I haven't seen her since breakfast."

"I don't want to worry you, but she went out for a visit this morning and I haven't heard a word from her since." Mabel twisted her hands nervously.

"A visit? To whom?" He frowned, wondering who would have sent the invitation.

"She received a note from Mrs. Clark, sir, and she left quite early."

"Maybe I'd better take a ride down to the *Providence*. Have a horse brought around for me, will you?"

"Yes, sir." Mabel was relieved that he was going to look for his wife.

"Is Jon here?"

"He's in the study," she declared. When she had finished packing Jon's things earlier, she had come down to tell him, but the door had been shut so she'd hesitated to disturb him.

"Thanks." Mitch entered the room, expecting to find his brother, but it was dark and deserted. Confused, he looked in the parlor and then went upstairs to Jon's suite. "Mabel!" he called loudly as he came down the stairs.

"Yes?"

"Jon's not here."

"Surely, you're mistaken, sir. He told me he would be staying for dinner."

"No, I've looked everywhere. In fact, some of his things are packed."

"Yes, sir. I did that. Mr. Jonathan said he wanted to move out of the house tonight and that I should get some of his belongings together for him."

"He did?" Mitch was surprised.

"Yes. He said that you and Miss Espri might like to have the house to yourselves and that he was going to fix up a sleeping room down at your office, sir."

"I see," he answered, understanding Jon's need to get away. "But where is he now?"

"I don't know. I thought he was in the study all this time."

They walked slowly back into the dark study, and Mitch lit the lamp on the desk. The light it cast revealed that the center drawer was ajar and the gun was missing. "Damn," he muttered.

"Mr. Mitchell?"

"What is it?" He looked up to find her holding a sheet of paper.

"A note, sir, addressed to you. It was lying here on the floor."

Mitch strode quickly to her, and in disbelief, read the letter from Roland. "Oh, my God!"

"Sir?"

"He's kidnapped Espri, and Jon must have gone after him." The missive crumpled in his fist, he ran from the room, a distraught Mabel following him.

"Who?" she asked, but Mitch was already upstairs, heading for his bedroom, where he kept another gun. She waited at the foot of the steps for his return. "Where are you going?"

"I don't have time to explain now," he told her, strapping on his gun belt as he descended the staircase. "Just contact the police and have them meet me at Roland Stuart's office." Then he disappeared into the night, hoping he wasn't too late.

Roland smiled as he entered his office. Everything was working out perfectly. He had a loaded derringer hidden in his pocket, and he'd positioned Bill and Joe in strategic areas outside just in case Mitch or Jon tried something. He was as ready as he would ever be for the confrontation.

Moving to the desk, he lit a lamp and sat down, mentally reviewing the scenario. Mitch would show up, angry but controlled. They would hammer out the deal and then he would be sole owner of Williams Shipping. *Stuart Shipping sounds good*, Roland mused, and he said the name out loud.

"I wouldn't be too sure about that." Jon's voice cracked the stillness of the room as he stepped out from behind the drapes, gun in hand.

"Jon." Though stunned by his unexpected appearance,

Roland disciplined his features into a mask of unconcern. "What are you doing here?"

"It just so happens that I intercepted a note from you addressed to my brother," Jon informed him smoothly as he kept the weapon pointed menacingly at Roland's chest. "There will be no sale of Williams Shipping, and there will be no harm done to Espri. Get her. Right now."

"I'm afraid I can't do that." Roland was stalling in the hope that one of the gunmen had seen Jon's shadow projected on the window and would come to investigate.

"What do you mean, you can't?"

"She's not here. I've left her with a friend for safekeeping."

"Then let's go get her!"

As Jon motioned Roland toward the door, it flew open and Bill barged in, gun blazing. He had seen Jon's shadow, as Roland had hoped he would, and had waited outside in the hall until he was certain he could take him by surprise.

Jon hadn't expected the intrusion, but he did manage to get off two shots in the gunman's direction before a bullet grazed his head. He fell, unconscious, to the floor just as Joe came running into the room with his gun drawn.

"Mr. Stuart, are you all right?" Joe asked, quickly checking on his boss, who had dived behind his desk for safety during the shootout.

"I'm fine. Check on Bill!"

"It's nothing serious," Bill called as he struggled to sit up. One of Jon's shots had winged him, but it was only a flesh wound of the upper arm.

"Good. Both of you, get Williams out of here before his brother shows up!" Roland straightened his clothes and looked disgustedly at Jon.

"Yes, sir," Bill answered as he tied a bandana about his wound to control the bleeding.

Joe bent over Jon. "Is he dead?" Roland asked.

"No, he's still breathin', but we'll take care of him."

"Just make sure you do a better job on him than you did on his brother!" Roland ordered sarcastically. "I can't afford any mistakes this time."

"We'll do it, Mr. Stuart," Joe assured him as they seized Jon's arms and started to drag him from the room.

Mitch had ridden at top speed to Roland's office; as he'd come charging down the back alley, he'd heard shots ring out. Dismounting quickly, he'd drawn his gun and raced up the steps as quietly as possible. He'd just reached the landing outside Roland's office when he heard Roland order Jon's death and then refer to his own shanghaiing. Withdrawing into the shadows, Mitch waited for the two gunmen to emerge with Jon; then he watched as Roland quickly closed the door behind them.

"Hold it right there," he hissed as he leveled his gun at their backs.

"What the . . ." They froze.

"Very quietly, put my brother down," Mitch directed, and as Joe bent low and released Jon, Mitch pistol-whipped him, knocking him unconscious. "Now . . ." he continued, but as he faced Bill, the office door opened again and Roland walked out.

Roland had heard low voices coming from the landing, and he was wondering why the men hadn't already gone. "Why the hell haven't you—Mitch!"

Bill jumped at Mitch then, knocking the gun from his hand just as Roland started to draw his derringer. Throwing off the wounded gunman, Mitch tackled Roland about the legs, driving him back into the office. They wrestled violently, each struggling for possession of the small pistol. Roland sought to point the gun toward Mitch, but each time Mitch managed to force the gun barrel away.

Meanwhile, Bill regained his feet and, gun in hand, staggered toward the office door. He watched the two men grappling for position and was about to shoot Mitch when he felt the pressure of a gun on his back. "Don't move or you're a dead man!" Jon said softly.

Though he was weak and dizzy from loss of blood after he'd regained consciousness, Jon had grabbed Mitch's discarded gun and then gone after Bill. He was greatly relieved when the gunman dropped his weapon in surrender, and as he kicked it aside, the police arrived.

Charging up the stairs, the officers barged into the office and started to separate Mitch and Roland when another gunshot blasted through the room.

"Oh, God . . . Mitch!" Jon roughly shoved Bill out of the way in his desperation to check on Mitch.

Gasping for breath, Mitch pushed Roland's dead weight off him and slowly rose to his feet.

"Quick . . . check that man and see if he's alive," one of the policemen ordered, and while another officer hastened to do his bidding, he turned to Mitch and Jon. "Is one of you Mitchell Williams?"

"I am," Mitch told him. "I'm glad you got here."

"This one's dead," the other policeman declared.

"All right. Now, what's this all about?" the first officer demanded, eyeing Mitch and Jon suspiciously.

"This man"—Mitch indicated Roland—"kidnapped my wife and was trying to blackmail me. Here, read this." He handed him Roland's letter. "He'd ordered his gunmen to kill my brother; I got here just as they were taking Jon out. Roland pulled a gun and we fought. You know the rest."

"I see." The officer frowned and then gestured to Bill and to Joe, who'd just stumbled into the grip of a third policeman. "What about these two?"

"They're Stuart's men and they may be responsible for my wife's disappearance."

"Mr. Stuart ordered us to grab her!" Bill protested. "We were just doin' what we were told!"

Mitch's fists clenched and he started toward him. "Where is she? Tell me or I swear, I'll tear you limb from limb!"

Knowing that with Roland dead there was no hope, the man replied, "I don't know exactly where he's keeping her, but Chun Ki has her."

"Chun Ki?" Mitch and Jon exchanged stunned looks. They had heard of the powerful Asian and were well aware of how the man had made his fortune.

Bill nodded. "Harris at the warehouse can tell you more. He's involved in this too! He's the one who deals with Chun Ki the most!"

"I've got to find Espri before something happens to her!" Mitch was heading out the door with Jon at his heels.

"Mr. Williams! Wait! This is a police matter and we'd better come with you!" The policeman who was in charge instructed two officers to take Bill and Joe on to jail, while he and a companion helped Mitch rescue his wife.

Mitch turned to face the man, his expression stony. "I appreciate your offer, but I won't let anything endanger my wife's welfare. If it looks as though she'd be harmed in a show of force, I want to try to handle things by myself."

The officer understood his contention and agreed, somewhat reluctantly. "We'll hang back, but if you need us, we'll be there. This Chun Ki has a nasty reputation."

"I know."

They headed straight for Alan's house, intent only on finding Espri, and when they arrived, only Mitch went up the steps.

Laura answered the door, and she was surprised to see him. "Mitch! This is an unexpected pleasure. Come in. How's your lovely wife?"

"Fine," he answered curtly as he entered. "Is Alan here? I need to speak with him right away on an important business matter."

"Why, yes. Go on into the parlor and I'll let him know that you're here," she said cordially.

Mitch stood impatiently by the mantel as he waited for the other man to join him, his thoughts filled with visions of Espri. He hoped—no, he prayed—that Chun Ki had kept her safe. If anything had happened to her . . . refusing to think about that possibility, Mitch strode restlessly to the window and stared out into the blackness of the night. Somewhere out there, Espri was alone and, no doubt, frightened. The thought enraged him, and he derived a primitive satisfaction from knowing that Roland was dead.

Alan entered the parlor nervously. He was frightened, and though he didn't know it yet, he had every reason to be. "Good evening, Mitch," he began, keeping his voice as calm as he could.

"It's over, Alan."

"I don't understand. What's over?"

Mitch's expression was murderous, though he spoke softly. "I had always considered you a friend. You've worked for Jon and me for years, and you *chose* to help Roland Stuart undermine our business! You disgust me."

"He forced me into it! He threatened to tell Laura of my taste for . . . exotic women."

"I don't want to hear any excuses, Alan. Roland is dead, and you're through working for us. All I want from you now is my wife! Take me to her immediately or I'll reveal your 'tastes' to Laura before I have the police arrest you for helping arrange a kidnapping!"

"I had nothing to do with it!" he cried. "It was all Roland's idea! He was the one who wanted to gain complete control of your company!"

"Then take me to Espri and I'll leave you in peace." There was a quiet menace in Mitch's voice.

"Of course! She's being held by Chun Ki at his main

parlor house. Let's go." He rushed from the room, almost colliding with his wife, who was coming to offer them refreshments.

"Alan? Is something wrong?" Laura had never seen her husband so upset before.

"No, my dear. We just have a little unexpected business to take care of. I'm going out for a while, but I'll be back," he quickly assured her.

Laura Harris watched in confusion as Mitch walked past her without speaking and followed Alan from the house.

"There is news, Chun Ki." The slave bowed subserviently before his master who was reclining, nude, with Ah Linn on her comfortable bed.

"Yes?" Chun Ki asked with mild interest, refusing to let Ah Linn cover herself in the other slave's presence.

"Roland Stuart is dead."

He nodded solemnly. "A tragic loss, I am sure. How did it happen?"

"In a fair fight with a man named Williams. That is all I've been able to find out so far."

"I see. Your news pleases me, Sing Chee." He was quiet for a moment for he had noticed the slave's open interest in Ah Linn. "Do you find Ah Linn beautiful?"

"Yes, master. Your woman is very beautiful," the slave replied respectfully.

"Then you may have her. I will be needing her no longer." Chun Ki rose from the bed thinking only of the woman in chains in the room down the hall.

"Chun Ki!" Ah Linn started to protest, but a threatening look silenced her and she lay back, resigned to her fate. Drawing on his clothing, Chun Ki left the room.

Unlocking the door to the narrow, windowless room where

Espri was being held, he entered and smiled as he saw her still lying quietly on the bed. A flare of desire surged through him, but he denied it. While it was true that he wanted her and that she was now his, Chun Ki was determined that he would wait until the drug wore off so she would be completely aware of what was happening when he made love to her. Backing silently out of the room, he returned to his own quarters to await her awakening.

Alan had frequented Chun Ki's "parlor house" on numerous occasions, and he was familiar with the people who worked there. Ming Toy recognized him immediately and went to greet him.

"Mr. Harris. It is good to see you. You have brought a friend?" She eyed Mitch admiringly.

"I am not here for enjoyment tonight, Ming Toy. It is important that I speak with Chun Ki immediately."

She noticed his tenseness, and after bringing them both a drink and settling them at a table, she went to tell her master of his request.

"Chun Ki, Alan Harris is here and he says it's important that he talk to you."

"Harris?" Chun Ki found the news interesting. Had Roland's employee come to inform him of his death?

She nodded.

"Send him up."

"He is not alone. There is another white man with him. A very handsome white man."

"Keep him happy while Harris and I meet."

"Yes, Chun Ki."

Ming Toy returned to the main parlor.

"He will meet with you now, Mr. Harris," she said.

"Thank you, Ming Toy." Alan stood up nervously and would have walked away, but Mitch grabbed his arm.

"I'm going with you, Alan. Who's to say you won't sneak out the back door and leave me here?" His tone was so savage that Alan quickly assented.

"I'm sorry." Ming Toy tried to stop Mitch, but he easily moved past her. "You cannot go. Chun Ki said only Mr. Harris!"

Mitch turned toward her, his gun drawn. "I don't want to cause trouble here, but I will if I'm crossed. I only want to talk with Chun Ki—just talk."

Three armed guards appeared around them, knives drawn, but Mitch did not waver.

"Tell them, Alan," Mitch said menacingly.

"There is no problem," Alan said, and the guards backed off a little; but they followed them down the hall to Chun Ki's office.

"Come in, Alan," Chun Ki called out. When the door opened and he saw Mitch, his eyes narrowed dangerously. "I was told that only you wanted to speak with me."

"This is the husband of the woman you are keeping here for Stuart," Alan hurried to explain. "We have come for her."

"Oh?" Chun Ki's expression remained inscrutable.

Mitch's jaw tensed as he sensed the man's reluctance. "Chun Ki. You are a man of power and influence in this city. I would not want it known that you were holding a white woman against her will. It might cause irreparable damage to your reputation and your business."

The Asian pierced Mitch with a deadly gaze. "You must be a very brave man or a very stupid one."

"I am neither. I have had something that I treasure greatly stolen from me, and I want it back," he answered, uncowed by Chun Ki's subtle threat.

"I see." The Chinese man paused. "And if I don't return her?"

"One man is already dead and the police are involved in this now. They have arrested the other men who were involved in my wife's disappearance. We know she's here so it would be wise to return her to me. Otherwise . . ." Mitch let the sentence hang, and the three vicious-looking guards took a threatening step toward him.

Chun Ki held up his hand to stop them. Knowing that the authorities were involved changed the complexion of the situation. "She is a lovely woman, your wife."

"Yes. She is," Mitch answered sharply.

"Would you consider selling her?" Chun Ki asked.

Mitch stiffened. "She is my wife, not my slave!"

Chun Ki shrugged. "There is little difference." Although he found Espri to be a rare jewel, he knew he wouldn't risk his business for her. After all, she was only a woman. Beckoning to his guards, he handed them two keys. "Take them to her."

The men bowed before him and then led Mitch and Alan from the room. Mitch could barely contain his anxiety as he followed them down the dark, narrow hallway, and he waited impatiently while they unlocked the door of her room. One guard finally swung the door open and stepped aside to let him enter.

Mitch's throat tightened as he stared down at Espri, and he quickly went to her, kneeling beside the bed and calling her name softly, desperately. "Espri, darling . . ." When she didn't respond immediately, he became worried and glanced back at Alan questioningly.

"She's been drugged, Mitch." Alan recognized the signs; he'd seen them often.

"I'm getting her out of here." Mitch started to lift Espri, but the clanking of the chain that bound her ankle stopped him and he glared down at it aghast. "My God! Give me that other damn key!"

One of the guards quickly handed it to him, and he unlocked the cuff. "Alan, stay away from me and my family. I don't ever want to see you again," he declared angrily.

Then, swiftly, he shrugged out of his coat and wrapped it

about Espri before sweeping her up in his arms and striding from the building. He met Jon at the entrance. Worried, his brother had just started to go in after Mitch when he'd appeared at the door, holding Espri.

"I was just coming in for you," he told him, relieved that Mitch had effected the rescue. "How is she?"

"The bastards have drugged her. I've got to get her to a doctor."

"Let's take her home. We can have the doctor come there."

"That's a good idea."

Jon held Espri for a moment while Mitch mounted his horse and then carefully handed her up to him. Cradling her against his chest, Mitch rode home as quickly as he could, with Jon and the policemen escorting him.

Chapter 33

After notifying the police to meet Mitch at Roland Stuart's office, Mabel anxiously awaited their return. She paced the parlor, becoming more and more concerned. She had seldom known Mitch to carry a weapon, and she had never seen him leave the house in such a rush. He had told her that Espri had been kidnapped and that Jon had gone to her rescue, but she was desperate for further knowledge. When she heard horses pull up out front she ran from the parlor and threw open the door just as Mitch was coming up the front steps with Espri in his arms.

"Dear God, what's happened to her?" she exclaimed when she saw that the young woman was unconscious.

"It's a long story. Mabel," Mitch said tersely as he entered the foyer and, without stopping, headed up the staircase. "Send for the doctor and tell him it's an emergency!"

"Yes, sir!" As she started from the hall she saw Jon, who had come in. He was covered with dried blood. "Mr. Jonathan!" she cried, "what happened to your head?"

"A bullet grazed me, Mabel. It's not serious. Go ahead and send for the doctor."

"Right away."

Mitch kicked open the door to their bedroom and hurried across the room. Gently, he placed Espri on the bed, and taking his jacket from about her shoulders, he quickly stripped the black silken clothing from her and angrily threw the offensive garments across the room. With gentle hands, he drew a warm blanket over her and then sat down on the bed close beside her to await the doctor's arrival.

"She'll be all right, Mitch." Jon stood in the doorway.

"God, I hope so," he muttered, unable to take his eyes from Espri's pale features.

"Chun Ki wouldn't have risked doing any permanent damage to her. He probably just gave her a heavy sedative of some kind to keep her quiet," his brother said reassuringly.

"I know, but I won't feel better about this until the doctor's examined her."

"Do you want me to stay with you until he arrives?"

"No. Why don't you get cleaned up?" Mitch cast him a quick sidelong glance. "Your head wound may not have been serious, but it certainly was bloody."

In spite of his pounding headache, Jon grinned and gingerly touched the wound at his temple. "Maybe you're right. Mabel was quite upset when she saw me."

After Jon had gone to his own room, Mitch remained at Espri's side. Though her breathing was regular, she did not stir, and he was very worried about her. Taking her hand in his, he lifted it to his lips and pressed a devoted kiss to her palm.

"I love you, Espri," he murmured, his gaze darkening with emotion as he realized how close he'd come to losing her. He shuddered from the forcefulness of his feelings, then he clasped her hand tightly in his as he continued his vigil.

"Mr. Mitchell?" Mabel knocked softly at the open door. "I've sent for Dr. Matlock, and he should be here soon. Is there anything else I can do for you?" She stepped into the room.

"No. Nothing right now, Mabel," he replied without looking up. "Just wait downstairs for the doctor and bring him to me as soon as he gets here."

"Yes, sir."

Though it was only fifteen minutes before the doctor arrived, the wait seemed endless to Mitch, and when he heard footsteps on the stairs he eagerly went into the hall to meet him.

"Dr. Matlock, thank you for coming. It's Espri . . . she's been given a drug and she's unconscious."

"I see. How did this happen?" Matlock followed Mitch to the room.

Mitch quickly explained the circumstances, and the doctor immediately asked, "Do you know what drug it was?"

"No." He shook his head wearily.

"Do you know how long ago it was administered?"

Again he had to admit his helplessness.

"Why don't you wait outside in the hall while I have a look at her," Dr. Matlock suggested. "I'll call you back in as soon as I've completed my examination."

Mitch hesitated, but he knew he had little choice. "I'll be right outside, if you need me."

"Fine, Mr. Williams."

Feeling like an outcast, Mitch was still standing in the hallway when Jon came out of his own suite some time later.

"Mitch? What's happening?"

"Dr. Matlock's examining her," he answered distractedly.

"I'm sure he'll be finished soon," Jon said, intending his words to have a calming effect.

But, as if he had ordained it, the door suddenly opened, and the doctor stepped out to join them.

"Well?" Mitch demanded worriedly. "How is she?"

"She'll be fine, Mr. Williams. If I had a better idea of when she was given this last dosage, I could more accurately predict when she'll be awakening. As it is, I'm almost certain she'll be fully recovered by morning."

Mitch's shoulders slumped in relief. "Thank God." After a moment he asked, "Other than the drug . . . how is she?"

"There's a slight bruise on her jaw, but otherwise she's un-injured."

"May I see her now?"

"Of course. Just let her rest. She'll awake of her own accord when the drug wears off."

"Thank you, Dr. Matlock."

"You're welcome." The doctor smiled as he watched Mitch rush back to his wife. Then, turning to Jon, he said, "I think I'd better take a look at your head."

As Jon led the doctor to his quarters, Mitch entered the room quietly and stood at the foot of the bed, unsure of what to do next. He didn't want to disturb Espri, yet now that he knew she hadn't been injured in any way, the temptation to hold her was overpowering. Stretching out carefully next to her, he took her hand in his once again and held it over his heart. Lovingly, his eyes traced her features, and when he noticed, for the first time, the discoloration on her jaw, anger, hot and dangerous, surged through him. With an effort, he put the emotion from him. Roland would never be able to hurt them again. It was over.

Sighing then, as some of the tension drained out of him, Mitch maintained his vigil, remaining unmoving at her side for the rest of the night until just before dawn, when exhaustion claimed him and he fell asleep.

It was after eight, and Jon sat alone in the dining room, eating sparingly of the breakfast Mabel had had prepared for him. His head wound was much improved this morning. Indeed, despite the bandage the doctor had insisted he wear for at least two days, he was feeling fine. He knew he had much to do, but he did not want to leave the house until he was certain Espri had completely recovered. He was lingering over his third cup of coffee when he heard someone at the front door, and he wondered who would be coming to the house so early in the day.

"He's right in here, Mr. Robinson," Mabel was saying as Jon looked up, surprised to see his attorney entering the dining room.

"Stephen! This is unexpected." Jon rose and went around the table to shake hands with his lawyer.

"Well, when I spoke with you yesterday, you said that you wanted these papers drawn up right away." Robinson handed Jon a portfolio.

"These are the divorce papers?" He was stunned by the other man's efficiency.

"Yes. Of course, the divorce won't be final for some time, but I wanted you to read these over before securing your wife's signature."

"I understand."

"Good. When you've read them, get in touch with me and we'll set up a meeting at which your wife can sign them. I'll handle everything after that."

"I'd like to take care of this today, if you have the time."

"I should be in the office quite late. Just let me know when you need me, and I'll be happy to oblige."

"Thanks, Stephen. Do you have time for a cup of coffee?"

"Thanks, but no. I must be going. I'll expect to hear from you later today."

"Right."

When he'd gone, Jon stared down at the packet in his hand. This was it. The end—the severance of his marriage. Instead of regret, he felt only relief. His marriage to Catherine had been a mistake, a terrible one, and one he would rectify as quickly as the law allowed. Determined to seek out Catherine and set up the meeting with the lawyer, he called Mabel.

"Has there been any word from Catherine since she left?"

"No, sir."

"Damn," he muttered. "Send one of the servants to the Palace Hotel to see if she's registered there. If she's not, have them check the other hotels until they find her. I must see her today."

"Yes, sir."

He returned to the table and began to study the portfolio while he finished his coffee.

Espri awakened slowly, blinking against the brightness that assailed her. Brightness? Where was she? Gasping, she quickly sat up, terrified.

Mitch was startled to wakefulness by her sudden move, and he instinctively grabbed for her, wanting to reassure her. Espri, however, was still in the grip of fear, and she fought blindly against the man lying next to her.

"Let me go! Let me go!" she screamed, and she struggled to free herself from him. Only when Mitch's soft words and gentling hands finally broke through her horror-filled state of mind did she realize who was holding her.

"Espri, darling . . ." His voice was strained as he tried to calm her. "Sweetheart, it's me. I've got you. You're not with Chun Ki anymore. You're home . . . safe."

Shaking uncontrollably, she looked up at him with tear-filled eyes. "Mitch? Oh, thank God! I thought I'd never see you again." She threw her arms around him and clung to him in desperation. "How did you find me?"

"Shhh . . ." He held her, stroking the length of her back as she lay against him. "It doesn't matter. All that matters is that you're here with me now."

"I know . . . I know." She sobbed brokenly. "I was so frightened. That man put a chain on my leg, and he had a whip and—"

"It's over. Don't think of it anymore." Rage tore through

Mitch as he thought of what Chun Ki had planned for her, but he controlled it.

Slowly, her crying diminished until she lay weakly in his arms, grateful for his tenderness. "I'm sorry."

"Don't be. You've been through hell," he told her fiercely. "I'm just thankful that you're not seriously hurt. How do you feel?"

Espri took a deep breath and moved slowly. "I'm a little sore, but other than that, I guess I'm fine."

He pressed her back into the pillows, his eyes meeting hers in perfect understanding, and he bent to kiss her softly. "I love you."

She smiled. "I know. And I love you."

Mitch took her words as encouragement and crushed her to him possessively. The troubles of the past night dissolved in the passion of their kiss, and he was breathing heavily when he released her.

"I was so worried. If Roland had allowed—"

"Roland? What did he have to do with this?"

"He's the one who arranged your kidnapping. He wanted us to sell the company to him, and he said you wouldn't be returned to me unless I agreed to the deal."

"You didn't sell? I know what the company means to you."

"No. Jon and I took care of everything."

"What did you do?"

Mitch wasn't sure whether he should tell her the truth, but he decided that she would hear it soon enough. "Jon got the note Roland had written to me before I did, and he went after him with a gun."

"Jon hasn't been hurt, has he?"

"Not really."

"Good." She breathed a sigh of relief.

"When I found out what was going on, I had Mabel notify the police to meet me at Roland's office. I got there before the police did, though. Roland was just ordering two of his gunmen to kill Jon and to do a better job on him than they did on me!"

"You mean Roland was responsible for your shanghaiing all those months ago?"

"Evidently," he replied. "Anyway, Roland and I got into a fight, and his gun went off. He's dead, Espri."

"Oh, no."

"The police were there. They know everything. They even came along with Jon and me when we went to get you back from Chun Ki."

"Who is he, and where was he keeping me?" she asked, remembering the menacing Chinese man and the windowless room where he'd held her prisoner.

"Chun Ki was a friend of Roland's. He runs houses of prostitution and gambling establishments in Chinatown," Mitch explained delicately. "He was keeping you in the back room of one of his 'parlor houses.'"

"Oh . . ." She swallowed nervously. "Mitch?"

"What?"

"What would have become of me if you hadn't saved me?"

Mitch scowled, but answered honestly. "Chun Ki wanted you for himself. I imagine he would have made you his mistress."

Espri pulled Mitch down to her and held him tightly. "Thank you for rescuing me."

"Sweetheart," he assured her as he kissed her again, "if anything had happened to you, I would have been a madman. You're my life, Espri. I wouldn't want to think about going on without you."

"I feel the same way about you, Mitch."

Their lips blended in a passionate kiss, and Mitch was about to caress her more intimately when there was a knock at the bedroom door.

"Yes? What is it?" he asked gruffly.

"It's Mabel, sir. I was just wondering if there's been any change in Miss Espri's condition."

Giving his wife a knowing glance, Mitch tucked the blanket closely about her and then called out to Mabel. "You can come in. She's awake."

"Oh, thank heavens!" the maid declared happily. She immediately entered the room. "Miss Espri, we were all so worried about you! This is just wonderful. Can I bring you both some breakfast?"

Mitch looked at Espri questioningly, and she nodded. As Mabel started to bustle happily from the room, he asked, "Is Jon up and about yet?"

"Yes, sir. He's been waiting for you in the dining room for some time now."

"I'd better go tell him you've come around." Mitch gave Espri an apologetic smile. "I know he was concerned about you."

"Do that." She kissed him quickly. "And tell him I'll see him later this afternoon."

"I will." Mitch rose and went downstairs.

Jon looked up expectantly when he heard footsteps coming toward the dining room. "Well, good morning. How's Espri?" he asked quickly.

"You'll be glad to know that she's just fine." Mitch went to the sideboard and poured himself a cup of coffee. Then he joined Jon at the table. "She asked me to tell you that she'd see you later today."

"Good. I'm relieved to know she's well."

"So am I," Mitch agreed solemnly, and then, noticing the papers spread out on the table, he asked, "What are those? Contracts?"

"No. My divorce papers. Robinson brought them by earlier. He wants me to read them before I set up a meeting at his office with Catherine, so she can sign them."

Mitch nodded. "Have you given any thought to what kind of settlement you'll be giving her?"

"I don't want her to have a penny of my money!"

"I understand your sentiments, but without a settlement of some kind, she's going to be destitute."

"So?"

"So, if you give her some money, stipulating that she leave town upon receipt of it, you'll be rid of her, but if you divorce her and leave her penniless . . ."

Despite his determination that Catherine would get nothing more from him, Jon knew Mitch was right. It would be far easier to pay her off and get her out of town. Then he wouldn't have to deal with her in the future.

"I see your point," he said slowly. "I'll have Robinson put the terms in writing. She can sign that document along with the others."

"Good."

Catherine stared, unseeing, at the menu in her hand, while she listened closely to the conversation at the next table. What was it she had just heard? There had been a shooting last night and an important businessman had been killed? Roland had not shown up for their assignation last night, and though she had dismissed that as being due to some unavoidable complication, she was starting to worry. It was lunchtime and she still hadn't heard a word from him.

"His name was Stuart," the woman at the next table said to her companion. "Roland Stuart. According to the police, it was self-defense and . . ."

The woman's voice faded into oblivion as Catherine got to her feet, grabbed her things, and raced from the restaurant. Roland was dead! Killed by someone in self-defense. What was she going to do without him? Rushing back to her room, she dumped out the contents of her purse and carefully counted out the money she had left. Three hundred ninety dollars. That was it—every cent she had to her name!

It took a minute for her to realize that someone was knocking at her door. "Yes," she called out abstractly. "Who is it?"

"It's Jon, Catherine. Open up." His voice was cold and demanding.

Pulling herself together, she squared her shoulders and admitted him to the room. "What do you want?" she asked cautiously.

"I've come from my lawyer's office. He has all the paperwork done on our divorce, and if you'd care to come and sign the necessary papers, we can settle the matter now."

"What if I refuse to give you a divorce?" She was recklessly challenging him.

Jon's lips thinned in a semblance of a smile. "I see you've heard about Roland's death." He paused for effect. "If you choose to fight this divorce, my dear, I will smear your name from one end of San Francisco society to another, and I will provide no funds for your day-to-day living. On the other hand, if you come with me now and cooperate in the dissolution of our 'marriage,' I am prepared to settle upon you a sum that will support you comfortably for some time to come."

"You are?" Catherine asked, suspiciously. She well remembered his declaration that she would never get another cent of his money.

"There is one condition." He folded his arms across his chest.

"And that is? . . ."

"That you take the settlement I offer you and leave San Francisco."

"Leave? Where will I go?"

"That's up to you. I just want you out of town, and I think you'll agree that my suggestion merits your agreement."

Catherine pondered his offer only briefly before picking up her handbag. "All right," she told him, thoughts of survival guiding her. "Let's go."

Mitch trailed his hand idly over Espri's silken flesh as they lay together, naked limbs intertwined, sensual appetites temporarily sated. After leaving Jon, Mitch had returned to their suite and had shared the sumptuous breakfast Mabel had served them. When they'd finished the meal, unable to resist any longer, they had made love, passionately and desperately, treasuring this opportunity to hold and caress one another again. Now, completely at peace, they lay in each other's arms, cherishing each sweet touch, each gentle kiss.

"Mitch?" Espri murmured, nestling against his shoulder as she caressed the leanness of his ribs.

"Um?" he murmured.

"I was just remembering the time we made love under the waterfall." She nuzzled sensuously at his neck as her hand trailed lower.

"It was wonderful, wasn't it?" Mitch felt desire stir within him at her erotic touch, and the memory of their passionate exchange beneath the cascading waters stoked its fires.

"Very. Mitch?"

"Yes?" he asked huskily, as he pulled her closer for a kiss.

"We've never enjoyed your own 'private' waterfall." She smiled invitingly, her eyes sparkling with excitement.

Without a word, Mitch got up and disappeared into the bathroom. In a moment, Espri heard the sound of running water and she looked up to see Mitch returning.

"Your waterfall awaits you, madame," he told her teasingly as he scooped her up.

She laughed delightedly and looped her arms around his neck as he carried her straight to the tub and stepped beneath the shower. When he let her wet, sleek body slide down his, they faced each other beneath the soft, warm cascade.

His expression was serious yet filled with tenderness. "I love you, darling, and I promise you that as soon as we can, we'll go back to Malika."

"I'd like that, Mitch. But as long as I'm with you, I've found my paradise." She drew him to her for a rapturous kiss, and Elysian enchantment was theirs once again.